Dead in
the Water

Also by W. J. Chaput:
The Man on the Train

Dead in
the Water

W. J. Chaput

St. Martin's Press | New York

All the characters in this novel have no existence outside the imagination of the author and have no relation whatsoever to anyone bearing the same name or names. They are not even distantly inspired by any individual, known or unknown to the author, and all the incidents are pure invention.

DEAD IN THE WATER. Copyright © 1991 by W. J. Chaput. All rights reserved. Printed in the United States of America. No part of this book may be used or reproduced in any manner whatsoever without written permission except in the case of brief quotations embodied in critical articles or reviews. For information, address St. Martin's Press, 175 Fifth Avenue, New York, N.Y. 10010.

Library of Congress Cataloging-in-Publication Data

Chaput, W. J.
   Dead in the water / W. J. Chaput.
     p.   cm.
   "A Thomas Dunne book."
   ISBN 0-312-06329-6
   I. Title.
  PS3553.H314D43   1991
  813'.54—dc20   91-19051
                                                  CIP

First edition: September 1991

10 9 8 7 6 5 4 3 2 1

87340

for Nana

This novel would not have happened without
Anthony Cave Brown and Thomas C. Wallace.
I owe them more than gratitude, more than
admiration.

W. J. Chaput
March 1991
Vermont

"Wandering between two worlds, one dead,
The other powerless to be born . . ."

—"The Grande Chartreuse"
Matthew Arnold

Dead in
the Water

Are You Lonesome Tonight?

OZZIE Barrett was dead in the water. Fog spat on his wheelhouse windows, as though the muffled gray beast drooled with anticipation. Ozzie punched off the CD player and went out to his rail to listen. He ought to have heard the Atlantic whisper against the islands and the bell buoy that marked the Three Sisters. He rubbed his eyes, took off his yellow fireman's helmet.

He flew a Swedish ensign on the trawler's masthead because his paternal grandmother once conceived an idiot in Sweden; that idiot later grew to full flower in his Uncle Barry, the only free man Ozzie ever knew. Ozzie fished blind off the Massachusetts North Shore, he had a radio he never used, he didn't have radar, and he'd thrown his bottom scanner into a half-mile of water last fall. He fished alone most of the time; his single crewman, Kenny, a Special Olympics freestyle champ, frequently got lost on his way to the dock. The other fishermen went out in tribes of Portuguese sons and cousins, lugging coolers of Miller Lite to lighten the load.

He stepped back in behind the wheel, felt the trawler lurch

with the swells. He cranked over the Cat and brought the bow around, wiping the glass with his sleeve.

Like a wraith through a fur wall, the *Lucia* slid out of the fog and into bright starshine. Ozzie whooped and dieseled through the narrows into Strike's Landing, dropped his catch at MacAvoy's, then nudged the trawler softly alongside Rocket's dock for the night, the harbor lights sprinkling the oily pitch around him with dancing diamonds. He ran to the boat yard to see if F. Ray Nelson had the dory finished.

Then to church, the white Baptist spire near the park on Locust Street. The driveway and parking lot wore new black asphalt. Someone had the spring grass trimmed; the sun had heated the fresh paint to a pungent luminosity of oil and spirits that had congealed in the night air. Ozzie slid silently through a back door and stood with his boots reeking gloriously of fish tummies in the main foyer, as Walter W. Coat called this place. Three doors now, all newly satined with white paint, brass-knobbed and heavy. The one on the left led into the church itself, head of the pews on the right. Door number two opened into the classrooms and kitchens and the church hall and Teen-Scene in the cellar, the coat rooms.

Ozzie walked straight to door number three. He pushed with his fingers, the door whispered over the lime-green carpet. The stairs were a curling white spiral. The walls white. A chandelier hung from the ceiling up there. Ozzie bounced up the runner quickly, his hands sliding on the cool railings. The only door at the top.

Walter W. Coat had got his name done in gilt. Plainly lettered, edged in black. Ozzie turned the knob. Walter W. Coat had his books up here, shelves of books. There was an eight-foot Brazilian-walnut desk in this office that had been winched through the windows. The rug was French vanilla. Walter W. Coat had a lighted globe on a pedestal and a framed map of the Holy Land on the wall; this map was drawn from cartographic hints found only in the Bible as

2

interpreted by a guy in a Mobil station in Goodlettsville, Tennessee. Walter W. Coat's Klan hood from the good days when all things were revealed was tacked to the wall behind his desk. As penance, Coat said.

The Reverend Coat was on the couch by the windows. Long cool drapes of velveteen. Coat was naked, stretched, and had his toes tucked into the pillows. Louise was naked. She was impaled on Coat's manhood in a rather precise degree of carnal knowledge. Ozzie waited until she stopped exercising; she took the hint from the Reverend Coat, who had eyes like barbells.

"What the hell?"

"Oh, jeezus," Louise yelped. "Ozzie!"

"What the hell?" Coat asked again.

Ozzie waved and waited.

Louise leapt off Coat's mainspring and grabbed her shirt from the floor. She wanted to cover her chest. After twenty-two years of marriage, Louise had a rarefied sense of decorum.

"What the hell?"

"I need your car keys, Louise."

"What the hell?"

Louise cried quickly, always cried quickly, and usually enjoyed the salt-pearls in her mouth when she argued. She tossed her bag to Ozzie. The thing hit the floor at his feet.

Ozzie got the keys out—her Land's End key fob that never sank—waved them at Louise, and closed the door as he left.

"What the hell?"

"Shut up!" she screeched at Coat.

Louise could only take so much.

⚓ ⚓ ⚓

Ozzie backed her Volvo into the driveway and left it there, idling, while he went into the house to get rid of his sweater. A soft, favorite denim shirt hung in his closet.

Boots still on, his bomber jacket on the seat because April

3

can be brittle on the coast, Ozzie drove out to Mildred's. There aren't many places like Mildred's. It's a bar, but with a difference: Mildred makes clam chowder that ought to be traded in futures, serves her fish and chips on platters, and stuffs clams and quahogs with mashed potato and cheese. The odd men from Strike's Landing eat their meals at Mildred's when the Brownie Troop is building bird feeders in their living rooms. Mildred always has her chowder ready. The cornbread is hot and heavy, and the Heineken cold. Mildred has windows that frame the harbor's moods nicely; the outside walls are all windows. Ozzie's boat is there across the water, the wharves and boat yards. Strike's Landing is, among other things, a bedroom community for the electronic mirage along Route 128 and for the state college, although an indigenous lowlife of salt fishermen and their hairy Portuguese wives cling to a local paternity.

Wilson Malone sits at the bar with Ozzie. Mildred leaves the steaming bowl of chowder in front of Ozzie. Malone has white hair and a paunch, thinks the Pack will be back, and teaches an education seminar at the college titled "Alternatives and Imperatives in Teaching the Dysfunctional Student."

"My cat died, Ozzie."

"That's a shame."

"I know he pissed on the Persian, but what the hell. Rugs can be bought and sold, right? How's the catch? Why are you so late?"

"Fog, Wilson."

"You always push your luck out there, Oz. Damn cat never cared for me, you know."

"I don't know anyone who does."

"Found him in the clothes dryer. Accidentally gave him a ride when he was a kitty—fluffed and dried his lovely coat. Stupid bastard thought the old Maytag was home. Back to the womb or something. How's your wife?"

"Tickling her womb."

4

"Ya, but you know, cats are smart. That damn cat never ate anything dead. Can you imagine? Never anything dead. Shit, I tried. Used to chuck mice at him out of the garage— he'd look at me like I was crazy. Had a bird fly in my Mercedes once—a common goldfinch—a *Spinus tristis*. Cat took one look at that and puked on my leather seat. Had to sell the damn car. Couldn't get the smell out of it."

"Life's never easy, Wilson. I'm gonna burn down the Baptist church."

"Damn—this chowder's good! Mildred? Hey, Mildred! Damn fine chowder tonight."

Malone wore Daniel Patrick Moynihan's porkpie hat. Years ago, after Hubert Humphrey lost it all in Chicago, Malone and Moynihan accidentally exchanged hats in the University Club in New York. Hat was so big it covered Malone's ears.

"Why the Baptist church? Anything special? How's the cornbread?"

"You want a beer, Malone?" Mildred said as she hobbled by and dropped a beer in front of Malone. Polio-stricken by a 1954 Hartford pediatrician, who had promised Mildred's mother the vaccine was a godsend, Mildred limped, and banged her braces to bits every year or so. Gene Shire, at the boat yard, had welded the woman back to life more than once.

"One in the eye for the crackpots, I guess," Ozzie said.

"Suits me. D'you ever notice those guys got hair like fur? Must be rugs, you think? I can't figure out why they smile so much. Unless, of course, they've got a lock on heaven."

"Or they're holding a second mortgage," Ozzie said.

"Damn, but they make the bucks, don't they? Thumpin' away like that. Randy crowd, I think. Cat bit one of 'em once. Naomi had this fella with a wart in the living room— back when she had her consciousness-raising group. Big wart on his cheek. Cat let him have it in my Uncle Rolf's chair before the guy got his coffee."

"Louise had her *conscience* raised this evening."

"She like it?"

"I didn't ask her. You want more cornbread?"

"Mildred!" Malone shouted. "More cornbread? Here—over here, sweetheart. That's right—cornbread. Good girl."

Wilson Malone suddenly sagged on the bar, his arms around his belly. Ozzie watched him. Beer sometimes gave Malone's peristaltic action fits.

"They just built that church, you know."

"I know," Ozzie said. "A hundred thousand in the land-scaping alone."

"You figure it'll burn like crazy?"

"Don't tip your beer, Wilson."

Malone pushed him away. "Just a twinge."

"Church should burn like hell."

"Let me know when you're gonna do it. Don't do it on a weekend—not this month, anyway. I'm tutoring."

"Are you now? You hate tutoring."

"She's got red hair and hooters like a panda bear. Runs track, you know. Got legs that'll go for miles. Wears little track shoes. Little socks. Damn, that was a twinge."

"Any special night?"

"Nope. Not the weekends. Damn!"

Wilson Malone excused himself and bumped past the patrons to the men's room. Ozzie used this quiet time to search the harbor for Ed Cabral's boat. He thought, suddenly, that Malone was back. Instead, it was the Mobley woman looking for her husband in Malone's chair.

"My husband drinks," she said to Ozzie.

Ozzie said he knew. Hair curled like the ass-end of a duck, her face was shined like a twenty-year-old wingtip. The eyes were obsidian aggies, the hollows dark and puffy. Her nails were plastic and polished a chocolate brown. She sold Mary Kay cosmetics and smoked cigarettes that smelled like burning pencils.

6

"I haven't seen him in weeks," Ozzie said.

"He comes in here, I know he does."

"We all do."

"I'm not supposed to be here, am I?"

"Mildred will give you about three minutes."

"He's not here?"

Ozzie tipped his chowder bowl to get the flecks of pepper in the milk.

"Jenny loves Vassar," the Mobley woman said.

"Try the boat yard. He might be working on his hull."

"I went there. His radio was on, but he wasn't there."

"Over at Arthur's?"

"Arthur's sick again. He thinks he's got Legionnaires' disease."

"Arthur isn't even a veteran," Ozzie said. "He thought he had cholera last November."

Mildred's was smoked knotty pine with a beach shack's high ceiling and rafters, all Tiffany shades and yellow lights, padded captain's chairs hunched around a square bar in the center, and the kitchen was inside the bar.

"Why don't you go home," Ozzie said. "Peter will be along."

"He's worse."

Peter was always worse. Worse than what? Ozzie wondered. This woman's husband did things with silicone chips in his garage that drove oscilloscopes into looping frenzies. He'd rehearsed the lead in the last opera-house performance of *Annie Get Your Gun* until his hair fell out. A month in a Connecticut resort for the ribald had put Peter back on the rails. Now she couldn't find him.

"I don't know why you men don't give him more of your time."

"Peter's a pain in the ass," Ozzie said.

"I know he is, but he's gifted."

"He's been a dime short for years."

7

"But you know him—you were good friends. Until you traded in your Brooks Brothers coat for those horrid boots. You liked Peter once."

"We all did. We liked you, once."

"No wonder they threw you off Wall Street. Louise hasn't forgiven you for that."

Wilson Malone was walking around the bar, searching for his bowl.

"Go home. He'll be along."

"I hope your stinking boat sinks."

"I'll tell Louise you've lost Peter again. She meets him in the morning when she runs. Out near the dump, I think."

"Ah, Virginia!" Malone bellowed. "How nice to see you again."

"It's Madeline, Wilson. You're both very rude."

"I beg your pardon, Virginia. Ozzie here is planning to burn down the Baptist church," Malone said loudly, and then as a conspirator to Ozzie: "I got my hat wet in there."

"You lost?" Mildred said to the Mobley woman, Mildred leaning her wet hand momentarily on her bar.

"Don't hit her," Malone said to Mildred. "She's even tinier than you are."

"I'm looking for my husband," the Mobley woman said. Mildred said, "Not here."

The Mobley woman stomped off and slammed the door behind her. "She's gone crazy since her husband died," Malone said as he got himself seated again. "Mildred? Another bowl, please? I've got to work tonight."

No one at the bar thought this was funny. Malone liked to pose as the good scout. But most of the men at the bar worked for a living. The state college had two types on the faculty; the first bunch, and Malone was preeminently theirs, had old money and fuzzy vision and taught at the ex–normal school to be near their boats; the second group drove the librarians to tears with their badly typed monographs, which survived on the drippings of John Dewey. Most of them

8

were fascists. The women were prone to nervous conditions; many of them were fussy, alone, and belonged to a duck-carving club.

"Why don't we do it now?" Malone asked, bits of corn-bread falling into his beer.

"Women are peculiar," Ozzie offered.

"I mean it. Look," Malone whispered, "we could get something—gas or something—and have that church glowing a cherry red in no time."

"We can use the Vulva."

"Mildred? Never mind the chowder! Gotta run. Ozzie here's gonna burn down the Baptist church."

Malone drove his station wagon and followed Ozzie to the dock, where the gasoline pump was left unlocked for the early fishermen. Ozzie used a gallon jug and had the gasoline running into its pearly throat before Wilson finished pissing off the dock.

"Seems a shame to burn a new one," Malone said. "Take out old St. Mary's—Our Lady of Misery." He pointed across the darkened harbor to the religious hulk near the super-market lights that sparkled in the cold April night.

"Damn thing's brick," Ozzie said.

"You gonna make it look like arson?"

"Think we should?"

"I dunno. What the hell, just douse the bastard. I've got my lighter. Pretty night, isn't it?"

"Good night for mischief."

Ozzie drove the Volvo. Wilson got lost somewhere between the hardware store, where the little jerks always sat on their Suzuki seats, and Mabel Hatchard's on Forest Street. A celestial, silvery light gave the church a solemnity in the dark that its designers should have used behind the pulpit. Ozzie left the car in the lot and walked to the rear door. Tires squealed suddenly. Ozzie stepped back to look toward

9

the street. Malone's station wagon had just come off the lawn and over the flowerbed curbing. Malone didn't have his lights on.

"That open?" Malone yelled as he stopped his car not a foot from the Volvo.

Ozzie raised the jug.

"How about a window?" Malone said, as he hesitated to light his pipe. He had his wool mackinaw drawn up around his ears.

A rocket's red glare blossomed over the trees from the harbor. "Good grief," Malone said, ducking, turning to see. The explosion cracked over the sleeping town like lightning. "Goddam that Rocket Willey—every time he lets one off, he scares the shit outa me."

"What a beauty," Ozzie said, grinning. "Nice red—Rocket's getting his height now—he's using plastic waste pipe, you know."

The two of them tried the windows on the church hall. They got around back. The cellar door was out here, the oil tank, and some kid with a girl in the corner where the chimney cut the starlight.

"Shame on you," Malone whispered. "Shame! Shame! Get the hell home. What's the matter with you two?"

"I'm caught," the kid shouted.

"Damn right. Get the hell home."

"I can't. I'm bleeding."

"Jeezus, see that, Oz? She's on her hands and knees. And he's got his thing out in the cold like that. Makes you wonder what W-W-Two was all about, doesn't it?"

"Mister? Don't go!" the kid pleaded. "I'm caught—it's bad. Real bad."

Malone walked back into the shadow. "Ozzie, come see this." Malone held his lighter over his head.

The girl sat against the wall with her hands in her coat pockets. The kid lay with his legs out in front of him, slumped. His little Nike basketball shoes glowed in the dull starlight. "I'm caught," the kid said to Ozzie as Ozzie put his jug down.

"Serves you right, you little bastard. And how old are you?" Malone asked the girl. "You're one of the Andrews sisters!" he yelled. "Christ, Oz, this is one of Hugh's kids. You aren't old enough, are you?"

"Wilson, this kid has his balls caught in his zipper."

"What are you doin' out so late on a school night?" Malone asked the girl.

Ozzie had kneeled over the kid. "What a mess," he said. "Wilson, get a look at this, will ya?"

"Which one are you?"

The girl put her face on her knees and made not a peep.

"Wilson, this kid's got a problem here."

"I'll say. Her mother will flail the skin off his back."

"He's bleeding," Ozzie said. "Wilson, look at this, will you?"

"Mother will kill her. Imagine being out in the dead of night. This kid with his castanets in his fly. Damn cold, too."

"I can't move it," Ozzie said.

A look of terror had drawn the kid's face into a wide-eyed grin.

"Cut it off!" Malone boomed. "Just cut it off. I've got my knife."

"No! No!" the kid yelled.

Malone brought out his pocket knife and snapped the thing at Ozzie.

"I'm not touching this kid," Ozzie said. "You cut it off, if you want to, but I'm not interested in malpractice."

"What malpractice? You're a Good Samaritan. Jeez, Oz— malpractice?"

"Don't touch me," the kid said. "Put that knife away." His Nikes were shaking. This kid would blow in a minute.

"Well, how the hell you gonna get it out?" Malone yelled.

"Don't touch me. Get that knife out of here!"

The girl jumped to her feet and ran around the corner of the building.

"Let's get him into your station wagon. We'll take him to Bozo's."

"Bozo's a vet," Malone said.

"So what? He's damn good."

"He was always good to the cat. Took a cyst off that cat's tail once. Charged me sixty bucks."

"Please, mister. It hurts bad."

"Shut up, kid," Malone whispered. The night and the stars were working their magic. "We'll get you out of here. He bleeding?"

Ozzie sat in the grass next to his jug of gasoline. "Lots," he said.

"Just don't bleed in my car, kid. Okay? Don't bleed in the car."

"I won't," the kid whined, screwing his eyes into his head. "It hurts like a bitch."

"Shouldn't wonder," Ozzie said. "I think you broke it."

"Imagine that," Malone said. "Sixty bucks to get a cyst off a cat's ass. Thought I'd shit. Don't bleed in the car, kid."

Ozzie and Malone carried the moaning little creep to the station wagon where, in the light of the overhead loading lamp, the kid left droplets of blood everywhere. They drove him to the hospital, where a bleached Valkyrie with size-eleven feet told them to wait in the empty hallway.

Ozzie went to the cafeteria while Malone sat with the kid. Ozzie got two coffees and a raisin Danish and bought a ticket for the rifle raffle from the gray lady at the register. Malone and the kid weren't in the hallway on the orange chairs when he got back, so Ozzie went into the only lighted treatment cubicle. Malone stood by the stretcher with the kid's football jacket over his arm.

"Her father is Vic Loomis's brother," Malone said, pointing to the young woman in the lab coat who was yanking the overhead light down.

Malone took his coffee. Ozzie watched the woman poke at the bloody web of cloth and flesh. The kid had a finger between his teeth.

"Where'd you go to school?" Malone asked.

She didn't answer, and left the cubicle.

Malone and Ozzie waved at the kid and followed the blood spots back out into the parking lot. "Nice night," Malone said, looking up into the stars. "That's Venus, right?"

"It's a star, Wilson."

"I like to think Naomi is one of those stars. I'll never get the blood out of the car. Little bastard bled all over it."

"You drove like an idiot."

"It was an emergency."

"You almost took a left into the drugstore."

"You saw that guy on the moped—he pulled in front of me."

"That was Sheldon Boynton from the bank—on his bicycle."

"Not my fault the bastard didn't signal."

"You were on his side of the road! What'd you want him to do—put his arm out?"

"I hate bicyclists. Where's the gas?"

"Back at the church. I have to get Louise's Vulva anyway."

The church glistened in the starlight, its white walls like a marble escarpment rising out of a midnight Tunisian desert.

Ozzie smashed the jug of gasoline in the parking lot, Malone threw a flaming traffic ticket at the puddle, and the fire department screamed into the lot ten minutes later.

When Ozzie climbed the stairs to his bedroom, the line of light went black beneath his door. He still had his boots on.

"Early day tomorrow, Louise," he said, slamming the

clothes rack on the back of the door into the plaster. "Almost eight hundred dollars at the dock. Little rain last night. Fog most of today." Ozzie dropped his pants and sat on her bedroom bench to kick off his boots. "Wilson's cat died."

"Someone at the hospital called for you," Louise said. Her voice got tight at night, she didn't like to talk after supper.

"I'm going to pick up the dory in the morning—looks great."

"Something about a boy having had an accident. A Dr. Loomis wants you to call her."

"F. Ray Nelson matched the paint."

"And your aunt called. Elspeth. She's selling her Sears shares because they won't fix her dishwasher. And your Uncle Barry is going back to the hospital so that they can get some rest before the wedding. Don't you dare tell your aunts that we'll take your Uncle Barry here."

"I won't go out again until Friday night—engine's not right. I'll have Ruby look at it."

"Who's Ruby?"

"Rocket Willey's daughter."

"What's she know about boat engines?"

"Twenty years in the navy—oughta be long enough."

"I'm starting class again on Friday nights."

"Ed Cabral's boat broke down."

"I'm also working the public-television auction this weekend and next."

"You want some coffee? I've got a pot bubbling."

"I need the car tomorrow."

"Any pie left?"

"Pie was last week. I haven't baked anything."

"Oreos?"

"I think so. Ozzie?" she called as he started down the stairs.

"What?"

She had to speak loudly. "Do you ever feel lonely?"

"Nope."

"Neither do I. Are we lucky?"

"I'm not."

"I'm not either," she said.

A Little Night Music

OZZIE Barrett's Uncle Barry never had enough time. Uncle Barry played Bach as his way of greeting each day, a solo violin every morning in his room. Uncle Barry lived like a spare tire with his two sisters, the twins, Lizbeth and Elspeth, in their childhood home on Bull Run. His sisters lived in the house; Uncle Barry lived in his room at the back of the house, which overlooked the gardens and woods at the bottom of the lawn, lived in the back as a precaution against neighborhood curiosity. Other people opened and closed windows; Uncle Barry used windows. He flew kites from his windows. He pissed out his windows. He nailed a Confederate flag to his windowsill. Uncle Barry fed the lonely pigeons at his window feeders, the finches and sparrows in winter. He hung a block and tackle from the eaves and lowered himself into the rhododendrons whenever his sisters shouted at him and threatened to return his rumpled psyche to the state hospital where no one used the steelmesh windows.

Time was precious, a hoarded reserve, and Uncle Barry maintained a scribbled schedule on his wall calendar with each day's events blocked out in red marker. After the Bach, sometimes a bit of Beethoven, he'd pick grapes or weed.

When it rained, he played chess, alternating between two chairs, frequently trouncing himself. He shoveled, and mowed, and mulched. He kept chickens in the shed behind the garage and washed toads in the bathtub in the afternoons. He kept a loaded twelve-gauge shotgun in the tool shed and his golf clubs in the garage. His passion was leaves; after dark Uncle Barry ran around the neighborhood with his garden cart full of contraband. Everyone's leaves went into his compost pile, a black mound under the trees near the woods. The neighbors left their leaves with the certain knowledge that Uncle Barry would get them up before the snows came. He always did.

Uncle Barry had played nine holes on the Annisquam Lakes public course in 1936. Since then, he'd developed a thirst for driving. He'd take his white canvas golf bag with his unused irons onto the lawn behind the garden and there set six fluorescent red balls in line on tees. Always six. The red spray paint greatly eased his search. After the balls were washed and quiet on their tees, Uncle Barry selected one of his favorite drivers and faced the trees, eighty yards away and a green screen of second-growth maple and red oak at the bottom of the lawn. Uncle Barry swung with precision and rarely hooked a shot. His greatest delight came with the flight, the suspension of belief, as the red balls flew into the blue and hung there like cherry pits. Their plunge was amazingly fast. Uncle Barry remembered where each of his balls entered the green wall because now the afternoon's joy became more than a wish.

Drivers safely back in his bag, Uncle Barry strode the lawn into the woods and passed most of a summer's afternoon in search of the little red spots in the undergrowth. The red paint was a stroke of simple reason. And with the balls in his pockets once more, Uncle Barry would stroll back up to his tees and, if he felt like it and the sun wasn't too hot, he'd blast them back into the woods.

Uncle Barry was proud of his game, knowing that not everyone could return from the woods with a full six in his pocket.

Supper always went off at five sharp. Uncle Barry took almost all his meals in his room from a tray prepared by Elspeth. Lizbeth was about to marry Bud, the bald Bud, a car dealer's accountant, who now ate with the sisters in the dining room below. After seven proposals from seven different men, Lizbeth had finally said yes at the age of sixty-two. Elspeth had never been asked. Lizbeth and Bud would live together in the house after their marriage, with Elspeth as companion. Uncle Barry knew they all wanted him out of the house.

Uncle Barry liked the neighborhood, he liked the dogs and knew them well, and after rain-tossed afternoons sorting screws in the garage, Uncle Barry would grin as he answered Elspeth's call to supper. He would roam tonight. Yes. And later, after a session with the pine model of an English brigantine he was carving, he'd put out his lights early and, certain that the house and sisters were quiet, the block and tackle would squeak and chatter as he lowered himself into the rhododendrons. Time was dear; at seventy-three he'd be dead soon and sleep for centuries.

On this night, a damp-chilled April night when the stars sparkled like cracks in a lampshade, Uncle Barry got through the Richardsons' hedge quickly. Their dog barked once, then scampered into the bushes to meet his friend. Uncle Barry rubbed Tex's ears and spoke to him. The Richardson house was dark; the Wembleys' across Bull Run had a light on in the kitchen and another in the son's room.

Uncle Barry walked across the Richardsons' patio, past the warm charcoal pile in the fireplace, and into the Chenaults' backyard. He swung their garage doors closed for the night, lifted the latch silently to lock in their new Chevrolet.

There was a motorcycle with warm exhausts and a Rhode Island plate near their back door. The house was dark.

The Marlows were next . . . a low yellow house built around an atrium. Uncle Barry thought the Marlows unfriendly, as they did whatever Marlows do within the atrium. The most he ever got was a bit of laughter or a pool splash in summer.

Uncle Barry was at the corner now; Spring Street went west from here behind Strike's Landing's businesses to the fire station and the salt marsh. He didn't know much about the houses on Spring Street. There were cats who used a kid's sandbox, but even the cats seemed to resent his sudden appearance from behind the Russian olives.

He crossed Bull Run and went to the Popowski house to get into the backyards through their gate. A little farther on was the Frost house and some sort of gathering. Two cars in their driveway, the lights on for the front walk. Uncle Barry let himself into their cellar and tiptoed to the stairs. Frost kept shiny paint cans full of grass seed on the first step; Uncle Barry stepped over the cans as he went up to their dining-room door.

The Frosts were at their dining-room table, planning a funeral. Jack Frost acted as referee in their efforts to bury someone named Betty as pleasantly as possible. Uncle Barry didn't know Betty, nor did he care.

The backyard was cool again when he climbed out of the cellar. The trees breathed almost silently with an offshore breeze. Carlyle's house was next; a new family had moved in last fall out of a yellow Mayflower van and three cars. Every kid had a bike.

Uncle Barry went through the trellis, then jumped down onto the grass surrounding Veronica Hammond's pool. He stopped, sniffed the air, realized there was perfume on the night hush, and froze.

Uncle Barry was not alone.

He stepped silently backward into the apple trees. Too early for lilacs, he thought, but I smell lilacs. Veronica Hammond slammed her French door, shut off the light in her living room.

A man was crouched behind the pool shed.

Veronica Hammond was a beautiful widow who always left a jar of cookies on her kitchen counter, usually peanut butter cookies, which Uncle Barry chomped after she went to bed.

The man watched as the Hammond woman turned on her guest-room light. Uncle Barry watched the man. The guy had binoculars, steadying himself against the shed. A small man, much smaller than Uncle Barry's bulk.

The Hammond woman soon switched off her light; the little man at the shed got up, stepped quickly across her grass, passed within four feet of Uncle Barry in the trees, then walked quietly down the Hammond woman's driveway.

Uncle Barry didn't see the man's face.

With the night growing long and most of the neighborhood in its midweek early sleep routine, Uncle Barry drifted across the street, passed his sisters' house and continued on up Bull Run through the grid of side streets and intersections, on up the hill toward the country club and the cemetery where the lone angel stood on the summit as a white marble beacon overlooking Strike's Landing. An ancient cinder drive spiraled out of the graves and around the hill's flank to finally stop at her feet. She was a monument to the Mello girl; fatally drawn thin by tuberculosis, Iris was the only child born to Sonya and Vernon Mello, who once owned the rope factory and sail loft in the harbor. The angel had pointed young breasts, a girdle of windswept linen, and robust feet, and seemed to Uncle Barry a callous marker to the life of a child who never had anything but a willowy chest with sticks for legs. But he liked the world up here, the slender silence of the sleeping partners around him, and he liked the breathless transparency of the lighted streets that bordered this patch of earth. Nuzzling, horrid lives always wheezed in the end as the ether sucked the wind from their feeble lungs. Uncle Barry knew that the bright wind playing at his eyes came from the whirling spirits above.

He sat for a time until he heard the fire equipment, and saw the blast of flame in the Baptist church parking lot.

The 20th Century
Limited

WILSON Malone's office was a gray enamel, cinderblock closet on Trenchant Hall's third floor, a narrow cell of linoleum and leering fluorescence that Malone tried to mitigate with woven tapestries of deer and moose he'd bought in an Esso station one night after his first very heady visit to L. L. Bean in 1967. The old guy at the Esso station kept his pumps armed all night to service the cranks and hunters who felt most comfortable shopping for rubber boots at L. L. Bean's down the road at three in the morning. Malone's largest tapestry hung on drapery hooks—the Pratt woman, who taught "Tests and Measurements," called it a rug—this tapestry had a female moose with one hoof held over a mire of blue silk, her body and ears pricked forever in distrust. Malone thought her attitude about right for this life; but his memories on this score were savagely idiosyncratic, as Malone never considered Ms. Moose without remembering the woman who clobbered a muddled moose on a vacant stretch of Maine secondary road. Malone was alone at the time, his feet in L. L. Bean hunting boots and his arms and hands close to his body for warmth as he leaned the motel lawn chair against the wall of his pink tourist cabin. The woman with those swept and pointed plastic eyeglasses—the rhinestones fell out on her floor mat when her head cleaned out the windshield in the '56 Ford—that woman had yelped as she struggled to stand away from her mangled front end, she'd yelped and Malone watched the moose who, having taken the car broadside, lay feet out and mouth open on the roadway.

A tow truck arrived from some nearby crossroads and winched the destroyed Ford onto its back wheels, and the woman's headlights tinkled on the ground when the operator snapped the tow bar into lock and travel.

The woman sat with Mrs. Mulvey, who seemed to be an official of the motel industry. Mrs. Mulvey wore white socks and carried a pair of Rubbermaid gloves stuffed in her belt; the woman sat with Mrs. Mulvey while waiting for the policeman who had promised to leave some other crossroads straightaway.

Wilson Malone watched the moose.

The woman cried and shook her head as she tried to crunch her lens crystals back into their rhinestone frames. Mrs. Mulvey left her arm across the woman's shoulders as an expression of interest.

Orangy pools of setting sun mottled the swamp across the way; mud-sucking and black, the bog had entertained Malone for some time before the moose crash. And in its midst, this turquoise-and-pink motel with vacancy and a road with a stripe to somewhere. . . . This moose obviously thought so little of men and their needs that it had climbed the shoulder to meet the 20th Century Limited.

A scrawny siren that growled past everyone's patience brought the cop, huge, lumbering, elephantine, with a yellow raincoat stretched over his overall. He wanted to know if Malone was a witness.

"That woman struck the moose," Malone said.

"I see," from the large yellow cop. "Did she brake?"

"Nope," Malone said. "She walked into the road without hesitation."

"You don't understand. We have damage here."

"A reckless moose, I think."

"Not for you to think, mister. Just the facts."

"She," Malone said, pointing over the yellow withers to Mrs. Mulvey and the woman on the lawn, "she hit the moose."

"You saw everything?"

"I'm seeing it now," Malone said.

"You foreign?"

"Born in Indiana."

"You saw the moose—"

Both women reeled from their chairs, hands raised in disbelief, screaming.

The moose was up.

She looked bewildered, as well she might. The Ford had been dragged away. There were two women running toward pink lights and a large yellow thing that moved. But nothing in the moose's experience suggested an explanation for her bewilderment. Still puzzled and probably not a little embarrassed, the moose turned and slid down the shoulder into the swamp and heaved, with tiny careful steps, into the deepening green shadows of twilight and pine.

"We have us a riddle here, ma'am," the cop said. The women were huddled on Malone's cabin porch. Mrs. Mulvey held the woman as though the moose might seek revenge. "Ma'am? Turn this way, please. That's right. Our riddle is this—you've got a car with a stove-in front end, but you didn't hit nothin'."

"She hit the moose!" Mrs. Mulvey screamed.

"What moose?" Malone wondered aloud.

"Exactly," the cop began, his clipboard tapping his knee.

"Your insurance check just walked away. Can't file a report—this here was an accident—I can't file a report without two parties—my form asks for party one and party two. You're party one. Wait a minute—maybe the moose was party one."

"I hit a moose!" the woman screeched.

"What moose?" Malone inquired.

The cop smiled to the understanding Malone. "Look, ma'am. You didn't hit anything."

"I hit that moose!" she screamed.

"Show me the moose," the cop said.

"Exactly," Malone muttered.

"I have a witness—this woman—"

"Mrs. Mulvey," Mrs. Mulvey said. "Deanna Mulvey."

"Thank you. This woman—Mrs. Mulvey saw the entire thing."

"You said you heard a crash," the cop said.

"I did. And a moose," Mrs. Mulvey said.

"What moose?" Malone said.

"Well, this gentleman saw it all," Mrs. Mulvey said, turning to point at the reclining Malone. "I didn't hear the moose—I heard the crash. But I saw the moose."

"I saw a moose myself, ma'am. But you see," said the cop, "there ain't no moose now."

"Exactly," Malone said.

"And there ain't gonna be no moose. You hit nothing, ma'am."

"Can't you write moose? M-O-O-S-E?" the woman asked.

"I did." His clipboard up now, his eyes taking the strain of the dull light from the single bulb over Malone's door. "It says 'moose.' But there ain't no moose."

"Exactly," Malone said.

"And—if you haven't got a moose, you haven't got a case."

"But this gentleman—"

Malone shook his head quickly no: "I'm with the moose," he said.

"You should be!" Mrs. Mulvey screeched. "You men are nuts."

"I may be," said the cop, "but I'm also the reporting officer. And she hit nothing."

The woman began to sob. Mrs. Mulvey offered her a dust cloth and cuddled the wretched being against her side. "You men *are* nuts. Why do you lie?"

Malone flipped his palms over and said: "The moose has a case, I'd say. Good enough to wander off like that. Took a helluva shot."

"You see." Mrs. Mulvey grinned. "You see. He did see it happen. He saw the moose."

Wilson Malone brushed his teeth later in preparation for his midnight ride to L. L. Bean's. Mrs. Mulvey was still screeching at the cop, who by now was rocking in the autumnal chill on her front porch. The woman's husband had come for her in a logging truck. But the cop had stayed, intent as he was that Mrs. Mulvey should understand the finer points of the law. As Malone turned through the gravel driveway past the porch, he beeped his horn. Mrs. Mulvey was whipping the cop in the head with her Rubbermaid gloves.

Then Malone lost his knife in the Esso station.

And truth to tell, the moose on his tapestried wall looked for all the world like that Maine moose of long ago, one hoof delicately poised in indecision above the silken swamp, her gaze beatific and saintly, almost sublime in her febrile gesture of confusion.

Archie Orr was an imported inner-city black basketball player with feet like water skis. He poised his fourteen-and-a-half-foot frame over Malone's desk, scowling. "Coach says I don't play Friday's game if I flunk your course."

Malone looked up at the malignant youth, half expecting to see the large yellow cop. "You dribble?" he asked.

The kid nodded.

"You shoot buckets, right?"

"Baskets." This Archie Orr was sullen.

"Al Michaels calls 'em buckets. Do you know Al Michaels? Television?"

"Who?"

"Al Michaels."

"Never heard a no Al Michaels."

"But you do dribble. Al Michaels loves the Celts."

"I'm a guard," the kid said.

"Are you now?"

"Ya, I play basketball—guard."

"Well, Mr. Orr, I don't play. You are flunking my course—actually, you're the first person I've ever had flunk my course."

"My paper was good."

"Your paper was illiterate."

"You say."

"I did say."

"That paper was good."

"Your paper was bullshit, Mr. Orr. You might be able to dribble but you cannot write."

"Coach says I don't play Friday 'cause a you."

"You don't play Friday because of *you*, Mr. Orr."

"You say."

"No, your coach said that. No memory either."

"Tha's a good paper."

Wilson Malone struck a match on his pants fly. His pipe let off billows of aromatic apple.

"Tain't fair. I'm gettin' mad."

"Wonderful—you're mad, Mr. Orr." Malone let off another cloud of apple-scented Virginian. "You can play basketball in prison, can't you?"

"I ain't goin' to no prison."

"Then learn a trade. You wash cars?"

"You sick, man."

"Damn right." Malone grinned. "I'm sick of slackers like you. Beat it. Go play."

Archie Orr slowly lifted his hand, a long black finger pointed in malice straight at Malone. The kid hefted his books to his hip. He left the door open.

The Boys in the Hospital

Uncle Barry spotted his black hospital satchel by the back door when he sat at the kitchen table to a steaming bowl of Wheatina. This moment was never obvious in itself; there was no prologue. There were always telephone calls, many of them quite private, as either Elspeth or Lizbeth huddled at the hall writing desk speaking to someone, but Uncle Barry could somehow never spot that one phone call that alerted the state hospital to his attendance.

Uncle Barry was always surprised that any day was the day. The hospital day. Time for his "observation period."

He poured cream into his cereal, looking up slowly at Elspeth, who was scraping the porcelain pan at the sink, Elspeth in her housecoat and slippers, her ankles spattered with blue venous destruction after too many days spent on her feet at the library.

Uncle Barry swept his spoon through the Wheatina, twirling the glutinous mixture into maelstroms of anxiety.

He got out to the chickens. Food enough for a while at least. Maybe long enough. He emptied his Maxwell House cans of kerosene and fluffed his paintbrushes before he wrapped them in kraft paper and tape. His bench clear, the nails in their bins, his key boxes locked, he went to his room to clean his violin. He packed his new bow rosin. His rag, the softest flannel patch.

And always the fluttering noise of leaving, as though someone were leaving forever. Elspeth and Lizbeth with their furtive, quick message to callers.

Uncle Barry waited for them in the car. They were always so certain he wouldn't go, they alerted Edna McCue's husband across the way to their departure. Uncle Barry watched the man come out onto his porch and sit heavily into a rocker, the man's hands between his legs, the April drowsy rain on the car's roof. The man would wait for them to leave before he went in.

But Uncle Barry always went quietly. Elspeth and Lizbeth were ignorant of many things. There were busy days ahead for him, days of bars and shiny brass keyholes that had been nicked so often they glistened like airport runway markers along the yellow corridors, days of mashed potatoes and chipped beef on toast, Uncle Barry's favorite. There'd be a new crop of Pakistani doctors, faintly unbalanced themselves, anxious with their alien brown smallness. They combed their hair with Nigel's Creme into black helmets. Their hands shook when they used needles.

Uncle Barry settled in for the ride, so long for his sisters, so short for him. They made their habitual stop at the Dunkin' Donuts in Malden . . . his two creme doughnuts, their lemonade and dry, day-old whole-wheat donuts. They regaled him with a discussion of Mrs. Horton's ruined spleen. Mrs. Horton was the Eagle Forum librarian who razored offensive pages from every book in her collection. After he ate his doughnuts, Lizbeth let him have his box of white milk over the front seat.

The sadness came over him as the car pulled into the hospital grounds, the sadness he never felt at any other time in his life. The hospital was standard antebellum institutional, the buildings corroded brick and stained dark with rust and soot; wide, shade-green, unused verandas faced a central park of live maple and desiccated elms. Lizbeth shut off the motor. Uncle Barry got out of the backseat, his satchel and his violin case in his arms, and went ahead of them into the long corridor with the curved benches to wait while the women made arrangements.

Uncle Barry waited alone for over an hour.

After a day or two in his room, he was released to the general population on the top floor. The bandages on his arms itched. The black janitor, who swore at the "clients," slopped Uncle Barry's legs and slippers with a soaking mop as Uncle Barry passed through the locks and barrier on the top floor. The walls were dirtier than last time. There was the live whiff of fluffy steam heat in the air.

He walked through the solarium and down the short corridor where Ezra lived. Ezra sat at his tiny desk by the window in his room. His books were stacked on the floor, his bed littered with manuscripts, Ezra's wiry gray hair in a bush of light around his head. Uncle Barry stood at Ezra's shoulder and Ezra, of course, only too aware of people behind him, continued to write.

Ezra's tile floor had been newly polished. His walls were still that tangerine, as Ezra called it. Empty and ascetic, the room of a monk with the singular exception of the Chinese screen near his bed. A water crane and reed shafts in tight silk on a black-lacquered frame. Ezra believed that all of what made the Eastern vision probable was available for inspection in the curve of the third reed near the bird's foot.

Francis Sparkman, the floor historian, darted into the room, trailing toilet paper after him. The toilet paper was torn and floor-worn. Francis Sparkman hadn't changed. "It's wonderful, Barry. I knew you'd come back to us. Are you staying?"

Uncle Barry moved his hands a bit and smiled. "My sisters want me at home."

"Ah, I'm sure they do. You're wonderful, Barry." Ezra continued writing. Francis Sparkman went on: "We've missed you, Barry. Good to see your fiddle with you. Ezra has a beef with me just now. I've been interested in Taoists for years. Ezra claims the Taoists are spiritual bigots. He's only a beginner at this, but we won't rub that in."

A shout from down the hall riddled Francis Sparkman's eyes with terror. The man shook suddenly, a pedetic throb in his hands, a rustle of toilet paper. Then he recovered. "You see," he said, backing away from Uncle Barry, "the Taoists were all far too clearheaded to lose their grip like that. Ezra's young yet and inexperienced in these matters. He forces his Western prejudice against what he cannot understand. Rather shameful, but necessary, I think."

Francis Sparkman's nose was a pound of flesh, all knotted and holed. His few hairs were wet with sweat, appearing as if engraved on his glass skull. "Tell Ezra you're here. He'll be pleased. We all missed you, Barry."

Francis Sparkman patted his left ear, his social tic to relay his reluctance to leave anyone. He was short, thick. Francis Sparkman wore slung bags of institutional gray cotton, his hands returning again to their homes in his sleeves. "Tell him," he said as he turned. "You're wonderful, Barry."

"He might have been pleased," Ezra said, lifting his head to his window. "I'm nearly finished, Barry. Francis, change your paper. It's Thursday."

Francis Sparkman winked at Uncle Barry and reached for the door. "I change my paper on Fridays—and he knows it," he said, fluttering the toilet-paper train around his legs. A smile, like a bullet's buzz early in the morning, crossed the old man's eyes and he was gone.

Uncle Barry sat against the wall while Ezra lowered his head prayerfully. The hall noises were distant and agreeable, the flop of a dolly wheel far away. Evelyn Cameroon's soft chuckle from nearby. A door somewhere making its cosmic, institutional clink. Ezra kept his head down, but twisted to see Uncle Barry. "For good this time?"

Uncle Barry smiled.

Ezra nodded, then shook his head as though in sorrowful disbelief. "Your sisters alive—both of them?"

"Lizbeth is going to marry a man named Bud."

"Anything to it?" Ezra asked.

"My chickens are well."

"Anything to that?"

"I've got a hypothermic soul."

"There is something to that."

"My grapes will be good. My wine from last fall is bubbling in the cellar now."

"Anything to that?"

"Is P. D. Sprague around?"

"P. D. Sprague is dead."

Uncle Barry winced and lowered his eyes.

"P. D. Sprague fouled his pants when he collapsed in the hall. Seemed extreme, at the time. But Sprague was a miscreant. His final act was fitting enough—he'd have enjoyed knowing he was a critic to the end." Ezra let out one of his most theatrical sighs. "The land on Cape Breton Island is mine, Barry. I want to live there."

"And Eichmann?"

"That pig!—the manic electrocutioner. Slithers down the hall from time to time."

"Your wife?"

"Nothing to that."

"Letters?"

Ezra shook his head slowly, his eyes like hooded headlights in profile, his eyebrows thick.

"I'm sorry," Uncle Barry said.

Ezra wept.

Uncle Barry hesitated a moment and then started: "We all live such brittle little lives, it's a miracle we want to know

33

ourselves each day. We wear the same dirty shirt, morning after morning. We need a laundry for our selves. You're smudging your work."

"Sparkman was right. We have missed you. And you have your fiddle. Thoughtful of you."

"Some Vivaldi—something somber?"

"Why not." Ezra laughed. "Why not. It's beginning to snow, Barry. And if it were not for me, Vivaldi would be dead. He lives."

"My sister's boyfriend is an officer of the Loyal Order of Moose."

"Anything to that?"

"Haven't asked him."

"The plural of 'moose' is 'mice.' "

"Nothing to that," Uncle Barry said, ticking his violin strings for pitch. He had gently wiped rosin down the bow from the first afternoon here . . . alone in his locked room with bandaged arms and his fiddle. Preparation is everything in this business.

Ezra lowered his head again. "My family has left me the house and land on Cape Breton Island—we're all going soon. Would you like to come with us?"

"Marble Mountain?" Uncle Barry said.

"Marble Mountain it is. Fifty-six acres on the water, eleven bedrooms."

"How will you get there?"

Ezra grimaced. "That's the conundrum, isn't it? P. D. Sprague was going to drive us in his Winnebago."

"My nephew, Ozzie, says he might have to take me in to live with him."

"Anything to that?" Ezra whispered.

Uncle Barry scattered early notes of Vivaldi around the room and down the hall . . . then stopped.

"There's everything to Ozzie," Uncle Barry said proudly. "Well, not everything—he's not happy. Ozzie's a misfit. He married the wrong woman and now she hates him because

34

he left Merrill's Lynch Mob. She hit Oz when he cut up her Saks Fifth Avenue credit card. Ozzie's not a stockbroker. The other fishermen don't like him because he's not Portuguese. When his engine quit in a bad storm before Christmas, those guys left him at sea. Ozzie was blown way up to Maine—and they laughed at him. He wears his yellow fireman's hat I gave him. And he loves me."

Ezra turned his head slowly. "We all do, Barry. Play."

Uncle Barry ripped off the Vivaldi, playing well for nearly an hour, the fiddle's call flapping out into the state-hospital trees like a lost loon.

The Snowstorm

Ozzie Barrett brought the trawler through the worst of the spring snowstorm by nightfall. April twelfth was late for the dreaded slush; the warming sea had even been carrying some of its summer tinge until long southeasterly grunts brought snow after four in the morning, the snow that piled the trawler deck with rime and sleet, the brown sludge of fish-flapping mortification near the hatches. Ozzie kept the wheelhouse doors shut against the howl, his Nescafé mug for around-the-world sailors balanced on his binnacle. He'd finished Bellini's *Norma* an hour ago and hummed snippets of it now. The boat rolled heavily with the snow's weight added to the tons of fish below. The wheelhouse Kero-sun heater baked his rubber boots and toasted Ozzie's sweatshirt.

He tucked up the flaps in his fireman's helmet as he came around Ransom Point in a wild smudge of gray sleet, his reckoning not all that faulty. He and the trawler had made sixty miles since morning. Both man and boat seemed to relax when they picked up the Three Sisters light and came hard to starboard into the wind to miss the Caraway Rocks. For everything Strike's Landing could be, robust and bright on a July evening with the yachts alight, it now came out of the snowy swirl like an abandoned Newfoundland cove. Ozzie took off some way on the flood tide, cranked the wheel

36

to port, the breakwater light off his bow by twenty degrees or so. He shut off the Kero-sun and turned on his bilge blowers. And when he hooked the wheelhouse door against the bulkhead, the wind pattered his face with snow kittens. All the other boats seemed to be in. The harbormaster flashed a welcome from his office window as Ozzie split the harbor buoys, and backed the throttle down, his dyspeptic engine sputtering as it had been for days.

Louise would be at her sister's. . . . Eunice and her forty children, the spawn of the late, nearly great Prince Albert, her husband of no standing whatsoever. Allstate Albert, a man who thrived on disaster, drank eggnog with an extra dash of vanilla, hated tax credits, kept a photograph of his '47 Studebaker in the bathroom, and knew in his heart Nixon had always been the one.

MacAvoy's son waited on the wharf. "We sent the men home!" he shouted, as Ozzie drew alongside the pilings and reached for neutral. The kid knelt in the snow over Ozzie's head. The trawler's way came off slowly with its great weight, and Ozzie's hull made the pilings crack and whimper. Ozzie reversed, listening as the kid told him to keep the fish until morning, they'd unload him early.

Ozzie didn't like the idea at all. His ice was almost gone.

"Well, shit," the kid said, getting to his feet. "Whaddaya want me to do? Ain't no one here. Unless you want to unload yourself. Everybody was in last night, for chrissake."

Ozzie switched on his floodlights, those great arcs overhead that brought the flying snow crystals in fits.

Ozzie tied up, swung the chutes out over his opened hatches and iced his load himself. The MacAvoy kid left for the night, left Ozzie to the darkening wharf. Snow flew into the lights, flat with the wind, Ozzie's hands cold, and his wrists raw where the wind got in with the wet. The harbor was quiet, some of the other boats at moorings where they lay into the tide like marzipan dwarfs asleep on a fold of gray Jell-O.

Rocket Willey, the deputy sheriff with a difference, a fire-works enthusiast, owned a maritime junkyard of rusting Ev-inrudes; two or three trucks welded up to look like tanks; an assortment of rusted hulls on cradles; strange lonely deckhouses, like a row of French heads after the guillotine; and the only reliable crane in Strike's Landing. Rocket's crane could winch fifty tons straight into the air, props drip-ping bilge ooze and plankton, and deposit any trusty craft on his rails with little fuss. Rocket Willey was the Charles Ives of rockets, his fingers stained by the chemical prepa-rations he mixed to fuel his hopes for the perfect fireworks display.

Rocket was there in the snow, his pole lights gasps of white wool over the water, waiting on his wharf for Ozzie. Ozzie cut the engine to let the trawler just kiss Rocket's wharf. Ozzie's hatches and gear were tight. So was Rocket.

"Where the hell have you been, boy?"

Ozzie tossed a line at the old man.

Rocket didn't flinch as the line went past his face: "I called the Coast Guard, you damn fool."

"What for?" Ozzie said, stepping through the snow toward the stern.

"Why don't you turn on your goddam radio? I've been callin' you since yesterday."

"I was way out."

"Goddam fool—you been out for years—out like a fuckin' light!"

"What's the matter?"

"Oh, so innocent—what's the matter? You're missing!"

"I'm right here," Ozzie said, leaping onto the wharf with a stern line.

"Now you are—goddam it!"

"I've got some cod for you."

Rocket ran back and forth, scooping snow, pelting Ozzie with snowballs as Ozzie got the *Lucia* snug for the night, her lights off, her engine still.

Rocket's dock was a long remnant collection of derelict warehouses, dolphins, broad wharfs, and sliding doors, all of it gray, weathered, crooked, and snow-laden.

"I don't want your goddam fish! I found the valve, Oz," Rocket said. The old man leaned back for another tug on his pint.

What valve? Ozzie wondered. Rocket announced his victories. "Where'd you find it?"

"Back in the old Owens. What do you care?" Rocket said, walking toward his lighted shop.

"How's your dog?"

"Damn worms could kill a shark—ever seen one o' them tapey things? Twenty foot long—all growin' inside the poor bugger. No wonder he's more listless than usual."

Ozzie grabbed for the old man's coat but missed, as Rocket slid back down his office ramp, eyes wide, past Ozzie in a slalom, and landed on his knees. "Some April this is," Rocket said, getting up.

"I can't go out again until I look at the engine."

"Fuck your engine. You can call the Coast Guard yourself, tell 'em you ain't lost at sea, you damn fool—jus' lost. Take your hands off me!"

Ozzie got the old man into his overheated shop, or YARD OFFICE, as the sign read over the desk. Rocket owned most of the harbor waterfront, leased whole chunks of it to the yogurt shops and the tony summer boutiques that sold painted umbrellas and cheap silver sea gulls, and on any given day Rocket produced from his green pants a wad that easily had three thousand dollars under its elastic band. Owl, Rocket's Labrador, raised his head out of whatever was eating him and yawned.

Wilson Malone skidded through the door, his head wrapped in a scarf. "I lost my hat, Oz."

Owl growled and closed his eyes, shuffling his limbs on the braided rug.

"Rocket just fell down again," Ozzie said.

"Been a drunk for years, Oz. I saw you at MacAvoy's—where the hell you been? Mildred's got cranberry muffins tonight."

"Get away from me," Rocket said as he swiped at Malone's outstretched hand. Rocket clicked his teeth, reached for his pint, and sat back next to the stove in his office chair, a Stratolounger that owed its integrity to duct tape.

"Had my hat this afternoon," Malone said, rolling his eyes. "In the dean's office. I've got permission, Oz." Malone giggled. "Shit, fifty-two years old and I still need permission to piss. Got my new course, Oz. Wanna hear the title?" Malone spread his arms, inviting a sacred vision. " 'The Identification and Ramifications of Identification of Culturally Disadvantaged, Underachieving, At-Risk, Gifted Minors'—like it? Title's a little long—but I'll get years out of this one."

Ozzie had just realized Ruby had come into the back room, where Rocket stored cases of motor oil. Her bright blond, almost white hair had flashed in the light when she opened the door from their living quarters.

"I can start in the fall. No kidding. I used pink typing paper this time and that half-assed dean bought it. Is he dead?"

Ozzie looked down at Rocket, who was slumped in his chair.

"He's cold, Wilson."

"So am I—this scarf of Mildred's is angora and far too fragile for this business," Malone said, swinging his arms over his head as though waving off Corsairs aboard the *Wasp* in the Solomons.

"Let's go," Ozzie said. "You're stepping on the dog, Wilson."

Ozzie had moved for the door and then held his hand over the latch, waiting. And Ruby came out of the dark back room into the office, wearing jeans and a black Gold's Gym T-shirt lettered in pink. She looked at Rocket, took in Malone and Ozzie.

"He was worried about you," she said to Ozzie.

She crossed her arms over her breasts, her wide pink braces like ribbons on her shoulders.

40

"I'm okay," Ozzie said. "All safe."

Ruby was the most beautiful woman Ozzie had ever seen.

"You gotta keep your radio on," she said softly. "Either that or tell this old man you don't want anything more to do with him. He can't do this."

"He's always done this," Malone said. "He was passed out the first time I ever met him."

"Hear me?" Ruby said to Ozzie.

Ozzie nodded.

Ruby did not entertain fools gladly. Her lipstick was a sparkling pink. "And take Chuckles with you," she said.

Malone was embarrassed.

"You've known Wilson for years," Ozzie said. "Don't do that to him."

"Go!" she said.

Ozzie stood at the door. He watched Malone wrap the scarf around his ears. Then turned to Ruby. Ozzie said nothing; he studied her eyes for acceptance and didn't find any.

"I think I left my hat in the dean's office," Malone said. "Foolish thing to do. Never mind, Oz. Let's go."

Ozzie leaned off the door and reached for Malone's arm, Ozzie's eyes on Ruby and that hair like spun silver.

" 'Night, Rocket," Malone said.

She let her hand rest on her father's shoulder, her hard eyes on Ozzie.

"I've been your father's friend for a long time," Ozzie said softly. "I was taking care of him when he didn't even know where you were—which is most of the past twenty years."

"Do you want to fight about it?" she said.

Malone said, "I don't."

"Not now," Ozzie said. "Later."

Malone's car was layered with snow, a large pillow of the stuff fuzzing its headlights. Ozzie hesitated in the penetrating stillness on land, so unlike anything he and the *Lucia* had known for days.

"Helluva course title, ain't it?" Malone said across his roof, opening his door. "Came to me on a wave of frustration while I was waiting for an oil change at Dave's."

Ozzie got into the roasted, darkened interior of Malone's car. The radio doing Lionel Hampton. Malone backed through Rocket's gate and into the harbor road without so much as moving his eyes, let alone turning his head to look for traffic.

"Louise is at her sister's. I'll go home, I think. I'm tired."

"Cranberry muffins, Oz."

"Home, Wilson. My legs are killing me. I've got to get up early and unload."

Malone plowed through the Grand Union parking lot, bashing a half-dozen snow-sculpted grocery carts into scrap metal, and dipped into Spring Street for the gentle run up the hill past so many sleeping windows in this quiet town.

When Ozzie got the kitchen lights on, there was a Louise note on the counter near the spice rack. The house was cold. Malone was stuck in the driveway, his tires whining. Ozzie read the thing without touching it.

> At Eunice's. I shall be there for a while.
> I need to think. Tortiere in the oven.
> L.

Fair enough, Ozzie thought. Fair enough. Spice rack and all. Malone hit something, but was at last on his way, his horn bleeping farewell.

Fair enough, thought Ozzie. So this is how the world ends. At Eunice's . . . an abode of deep thought, a Pampers palace where the diapers lay about like wet cats in the living room and Allstate Albert polished his riding boots in the cellar while listening to his Cleveland radio station.

Fair enough.

Ozzie got the pie into the microwave for a ten-minute jolt. His dill spears in the fridge. His Molson's. And ice cream. "What more could I want?" he muttered. "What more did I ever want? I've got the *Lucia,* my boots. Louise has the Vulva. Snowing on the crocuses. House is cold and dark. Bird feeder is empty. Place is clean beyond reason. Malone must be home by now—Malone?" Ozzie shouted. "Malone! Listen to me! I'm alone. That's right, alone. You heard me. More alone than midnight on the Rub' al Khali without a Perrier. 'Gifted Minors.' " He winced as he poured the Molson's. "There are no gifted minors. Gifted majors, surely. Probably a gifted captain or two—this captain is gifted. But no one can be gifted and be minor. Negligible gifts for minor minors. But no gifted minors."

The telephone rang in the front hall. His boots tracked the rug with wet. Louise would scream. The big clock near the stairs had stopped. Uncle Barry was going to be held indefinitely. "They have found considerable deterioration in his condition."

"There's been some deterioration in my own condition, Aunt Elspeth."

"But, honey." Her voice smiled. "Lizbeth thinks he's never coming home again."

"You mean she hopes he never comes home again. How's the wedding coming?"

"He's difficult to handle, Oz."

"Get Uncle Barry out of there."

"There's a chance he might be dangerous—that's what they said."

"The state-hospital quacks?"

"They mean well, Oz."

"Don't be silly. Uncle Barry is too shrewd for suicide."

"Dangerous to others, Oz! Good heavens—he doesn't know his own strength. You've forgotten a lot. But then you can, because he doesn't live with you."

"Just get him out of there."

"It's out of our hands. Lizbeth is very concerned."

"Lizbeth is a neurasthenic spinster. Just get him out of there."

"That's not fair, Oz—we raised you, we gave you everything we could when your parents could not. We loved you as if you were our own. He's not right."

"Who is, Aunt Elspeth? You surely are not."

"Ozzie! Stop that! You have no call to say these things."

"You can't lock him up in a jail just because he's inconvenient. My pork pie is just about zapped. Thanks so much for calling. We all love you."

"But his doctors—"

"Just get him out. Better yet, have Bud trade places with him."

"Is Louise there?"

"No."

"Are you drunk?"

"Not yet."

"I thought so."

"Just get him out."

"Never. He's ill."

"Get him out of there."

"The state—"

"The state is some diseased psychotherapist with nicotine fingers and a vicious twitch."

"Where is Louise?"

"Just get him out, Aunt Elspeth."

"I knew you wouldn't understand."

"You knew I *would* understand—save your potshots for Bud. And get him out of there."

Ozzie slopped the Molson's over the desk blotter as he ripped the telephone jack off the wall.

Who's Sorry Now?

"**H**E doesn't like the bars on his windows," Ozzie said.

Elspeth straightened her tea doily on the tray. The silver pot had cooled too quickly and she didn't want to reheat this conversation. "I sometimes think he does, Ozzie. He has his friends. His meals."

"No," Ozzie said.

"We've planned this wedding for months. We didn't anticipate Barry's illness. Lizbeth does have a right to her happiness, you know."

"What illness?"

"Ozzie! You have your father's sourness!"

Ozzie Barrett got a few of the lemon-cake crumbs off his pants and finished his tea.

"You have no cause to accuse me of anything untoward. I have cared for Barry for years," she said.

"You took care of him, but you never cared for him."

"You know that's not true. And don't roll your eyes at me, either. I have never complained about raising you. Your father was *my* brother, after all—Robert was our pride and joy. Before the war Barry was a different man—you do know that. Something dreadful in the war changed him. He was always so determined in high school to be a success at something. Bud and Lizbeth will be married on May third. They plan to honeymoon nearby."

"You hope they honeymoon nearby."

"Bud's work, Oz. He's never taken a sick day."

"Gosh," Ozzie said. "Bud's never sick?"

"I think this marriage upsets you as much as it upsets your uncle. Has Louise come home yet?"

"Don't pretend this marriage doesn't upset *you,*" he said. "What will you do? Will they let you keep your part-time job at the library, or will you have too much to do here with Bud in the house? The Maid of Honor becomes the old maid of honor."

"Who took you in when your mother ran off as an army nurse to look for your poor father?" Aunt Elspeth had stroked her ace gong with Ozzie.

Ozzie fiddled with his teaspoon, a kid waiting for the sermon to end.

"And when neither of them came home, did I complain?"

Ozzie recited the litany: "No, Aunt Elspeth, you just took care of me."

"That's right. Just like I take care of Barry. That's what I do—I take care of people. Everybody has a cross to bear. You've never wanted to face the fact that Barry isn't normal. People used to call it soft in the head. I don't know what it is. I certainly don't know where it came from—Robert excelled in everything and Lizbeth and I have managed in this world. But Barry's always been a daydreamer who couldn't adjust. He's more like a child, really—full of wild ideas. And you're becoming more and more like him."

Ozzie groaned.

"It's the army's fault—they should never have made him a medic," she said. "I don't even known exactly what did happen to Barry over there—he's never talked about it."

Ozzie said, "He has to me."

"Those were only bedtime stories, Ozzie. Barry's always confused the real world with his imaginary world. We knew when he came home that he'd never be right. All he wanted was to live upstairs in his room and be taken care of so he could cut glass and make keys at the hardware store. And putter around with you. You were only a little boy, and we never for a moment made you feel like an orphan. Lizbeth and I did our very best for you."

The enveloping Victorian sitting room was overdone in browns and yellows. A thready, tattered rug ran under the hard chairs. The long clock with the mercury-filled pendulous vials gently bobbed the passing time like a great counterweight of doom. A fireplace throat with a brass peacock screen. Hundreds of curios . . . transparent glass geese on mirrored side tables. The lamps were dim with age. And Aunt Elspeth, something of a Victorian curio herself, sat opposite Ozzie in her afternoon chair, as she called it. As a child Ozzie was allowed into this room only for the holidays.

"I don't think Louise is coming home," Ozzie said slowly, placing his teacup on the saucer.

"Her mother was a Cunningham."

"We know all about the Cunninghams, Aunt Elspeth. I called the hospital. Uncle Barry will be ready in the morning. Your request for a committal hearing was refused—but I expect you know that."

His aunt shook her head quickly, as though a chill had just run across her back. "Lizbeth did that. We cannot take him back this time," she said.

"But you will take Bud—and you will always do as Aunt Lizbeth says. I'll go and get him," Ozzie said.

"You will, will you? Will you take care of him? Will you be responsible for him? Will you do that too, Ozzie?"

"He'll be all right with me."

"Don't be silly. What will he do when you're at sea?"

"He likes to fish."

47

"You have no idea what you're doing. He's lived in this house all his life. He needs rules. His things are here. He'll drown."

"I'll move his things. He hasn't got much. He can have the back bedroom with the balcony."

"And if you lose the house in the divorce?"

"What divorce?" Ozzie stopped. Aunt Elspeth had so often known more than she said as she sputtered through her household chores. As a child, Ozzie had expected to be trapped in every lie, every caper.

His aunt pursed her lips, ever so knowingly. "And if he becomes violent?"

"He's never been violent."

"A dormant volcano."

"Bull—he's got his medication."

"He doesn't take it—he only pretends. I crush his pills into his Wheatina. Have for years."

Ozzie stared at the photograph of his parents on the piano. His father looked lost, unsmiling, his mother with a frightened expectancy but somehow willing to press on with her life, as though she suspected the worst. This was Ozzie's only likeness of his parents, his father a marine missing in action in the Pacific—Ozzie had no memory of him at all—his mother a soft woman with white, thick thighs in his memory as she sat on a toilet somewhere with her tiny son standing in front of her. She had become an army nurse, left her son with her husband's sisters, and gone off to find her missing man. She was killed by an unexploded American artillery shell in the Philippines two months before the war ended. Uncle Barry came home from Europe as a discharged army medic who talked only about snow, mules, meals, tents, and French mud. Ozzie loved his Uncle Barry from the first ecstatic moment the man leapt off the Boston train. Uncle Barry would say, "Did I ever tell you I've been to France?" as his permanent signal that he was about to sit and talk to the boy.

"I'll go and get him," he said. He looked away from the woman. He felt twelve years old.

⚓ ⚓ ⚓

Uncle Barry rode silently in Rocket's battered tow truck, his violin case on his lap, his satchel on the holed floorboard, with Route 128 flashing by beneath them. Ozzie felt better as they turned off the highway for the sea. He'd found his uncle in the hospital corridor, waiting on a bench, the old man's eyes like a bird's, as though no connection were possible between the species.

Uncle Barry finally let his hands droop in his lap. "I don't know why I can't go home."

"You're staying with me for a few days—maybe longer."

"I'd like to, Oz. But I can't stay with you."

Ozzie downshifted the truck for the intersection, waiting for the traffic light.

Uncle Barry said, "I haven't hurt your feelings, have I?"

Ozzie shook his head no.

"My chickens, Oz. My grapes—I have stuff to do."

"You can't go home, Uncle Barry. You have two choices— I can take you back to the hospital or I can take you home with me."

"Why not home, Oz?"

"Because Lizbeth and Elspeth have the wedding."

Ozzie got the truck moving again, rattling up through its gears, chasing some panicked professional mom with a BABY-ON-BOARD sign in her van's rear window. Rocket's tow truck hadn't seen a muffler since the original one fell off decades ago. Uncle Barry was crying.

Ozzie drove for miles without saying a word.

⚓ ⚓ ⚓

Bud was at the door, waving his arm for Ozzie to come into the kitchen. The women were at the table, their sandwiches half eaten. Lizbeth stared at her plate.

"How is he?" Elspeth asked.

Ozzie said he was fine.

"Is he outside?" Bud asked.

"He wants a few of his things."

"Go to it!" Bud said. And then, expansively, as Ozzie bounded up the back stairs to Uncle Barry's room: "Yell if you need any help!"

Ozzie grabbed some of the old man's clothes, his garden hat and gloves, his chess set and homemade board. He looked out the window to be certain Uncle Barry was still in the truck. Then downstairs again. Lizbeth was gone from the table, Elspeth sipping tea, her library dress on for her afternoon duties, Bud at the sink. "If he gives you any trouble, call me," Bud said.

Ozzie kicked the door open with his boot. "You're the last person I'd call for anything, Bud."

"What's that supposed to mean?" the accountant said.

"Why didn't you ever take him to the country club with you?" Ozzie asked. "The old guy loves golf. Just once."

"I haven't played since last fall."

"Don't, Oz," Elspeth said. She turned in her chair, one of her hair combs hanging, her eyes red.

Ozzie let the door bang as he trotted down the stairs and tossed the things into the back of the truck.

Uncle Barry was gone.

Bud was out on the porch. "I don't care for your tone. You don't have to like me, but I'm here to stay. Where the hell'd you get this piece of junk?" he said, pointing to Rocket's truck.

Ozzie went for the chicken house, then the garage. And found Uncle Barry among his grapes in the bright April sun. "Not now," Ozzie said.

His uncle twisted in the dirt, shielding his eyes to see Ozzie. "When?"

"I don't know—we'll come back over."

"When?"

"Goddam it, I don't know when. Get into the goddam truck!"

Uncle Barry moved slowly, his sturdy black steel-toed machinist's shoes picking up clods of wet earth as they walked out of the garden. Ozzie spotted Lizbeth at her bedroom window as he slammed the truck door.

"We haven't had lunch," Uncle Barry said as Ozzie backed the truck into the street.

"We'll eat."

"When? It's late for lunch."

"When we get home."

"When we get to your home, you mean. Not my home. This isn't fair, Oz."

"Goddam it, Uncle Barry, since when is *anything* fuckin' fair?"

"I've always been fair to you."

"You son of a bitch."

"Don't swear at me," Uncle Barry said.

"This isn't easy."

"I think you made the choice, Oz."

Ozzie just caught third gear, ran the light on Spring Street and headed up the hill.

"Will Louise be there?"

Ozzie said Louise was gone.

"What will we do, then?"

"About what?"

"Food? Clothes?"

"We're a couple o' bachelors—we'll do for ourselves," Ozzie said, bouncing into his driveway.

"We can't do for ourselves, Oz."

Ozzie stared at the Century 21 FOR SALE sign on his lawn.

Uncle Barry was out, swinging his violin case up the back stairs, his satchel. His garden hat scrunched on his head. Waiting. "Where'd you get that, Oz?" he said, puzzled at the sign Ozzie carried up the stairs.

51

Ozzie couldn't get his key to work, dropped the sign, and bent to check the door lock. "I'll be damned," he said.

"Try it again," Uncle Barry said. "It's a Yale lock—the tumblers sometimes get stuck when they've taken weather."

Ozzie told him the lock was new.

"Try one of my keys," Uncle Barry reached for his key chain.

Too late. Ozzie kicked the door in, the glass shattering against the refrigerator. Ozzie bent to retrieve the FOR SALE sign, and gestured for Uncle Barry to enter. "My home is your home."

"I don't think you have a home anymore, Oz," Uncle Barry said, as he stepped carefully over the glass shards.

"How could she do this?" Ozzie said. "Louise? You here?"

Uncle Barry waited patiently, his arms filled with violin and satchel, his hat off. "I don't think she's here, Ozzie."

"The goddam woman's going to sell the house out from under me! How the hell can she do that?"

"Isn't fair," Uncle Barry said, chuckling.

"Not now, old man—this isn't funny." Ozzie whacked the splintered door against its jamb.

"You've got to admit, Ozzie, this is peculiar—now we don't have a home."

"We are not going back to your place."

"Not my place—that's Bud's place. What'll we do?"

"Put your stuff upstairs in your room."

"Not my room, Ozzie."

Ozzie raised his eyes, drawing in his breath.

Uncle Barry, enjoying himself, said, "Right—upstairs."

Ozzie listened to him climb the stairs. He wondered what cogs in what escapement must be turning even now to grind his days into dust. The FOR SALE sign slid away from the counter, crashing onto the sparkling glassy floor.

Don't Look Now

ON THIS night, a night of penetrating dark, as dark as a snake's dream, Veronica Hammond opened her front door after eleven to greet the clearing spring air. The man with her slid quickly past her silken flank, adjusted his tennis hat, and with a wave scampered off across her lawn. Her carriage lights were off; the swatch of light from her doorway seemed too bright on her shrubs. He never wanted to be seen with her and maddened her by shutting off her house lights every time he came. Veronica stepped back inside the house, mumbling to herself: "You got what you wanted, you son of a bitch," she said, sliding the bolt home. "I barely got started."

Veronica Hammond was a beautiful widow climbing the stairway to her bedroom, the room with the sweaty-sweet sheets, his cologne on her pillows. She got the light at the top of the stairs.

Veronica Hammond had been left with over eight hundred thousand dollars by her husband, Martin, who believed his own insurance drivel and expired on the pool patio watching the Sox lose another one in last summer's heat. Veronica was the personal secretary to the president of the First Seaman's Bank, the woman in the good clothes who sat just inside the oak railing in the bank's lobby, guarding the president's vast desk behind her.

On Bull Run, Veronica Hammond's house was a few doors down from Uncle Barry's garden and grapes, her cream house with the screened porch and hip roof, its last light blinking off in the darkness, her wine-red Riviera basking in the cool starlight.

She lay thinking, her mind awash with physical jolts that told her he'd cheated her once more. Her brown hair, with its gray streaks and luster, bothered her cheek. She swept it away, then got up, dropped her nightgown on the carpet, and headed for the shower.

He was already inside her house.

The hot water blasted her skin clean, the Crabtree & Evelyn peach froth washed his salty drops into her drain spiral. She let the spray brush her breasts, her back; neck down and heavy, she tried to lower her shoulders, her knees aching because he always took her on her knees. Martin was long gone . . . more than months away by now.

She let the towel scratch her back, rubbing hard to get the last of him gone. "It hasn't been fun," she said, smiling, determined that his twice-weekly jogging trysts would end.

She hit the light, wandering down the hallway to the guest bed, brushing her damp hair behind her ears. Tonight was his customary pizza-in-a-box night and tomorrow the bank would stay open until six to let the fishermen cash their fishy checks.

He was already on the stairs.

The sheets in here smelled of cool softener, her neutral ground, as she crawled under her mother's goose-down quilt, her head aching slightly. She breathed slowly, drifting, her breasts cushioned against the pillows. The Richardsons' dog yapped quickly, then stopped. In the beginning she'd said yes by not saying no to him; but after only four months, she felt she'd violated her best instincts. This summer would be different, the days long enough.

He was already in her bedroom, standing over her night-gown. He wore a clear plastic rainsuit he'd picked up in a K mart camping aisle, his hands in pale rubber medical gloves.

She took one last long breath, moved her aching right knee slightly. The long summer days on the beach . . . her lotion-scented legs covered in powdery sand.

He was already in her bathroom, sniffing her peach-heavy nearness, the water dreamily tapping the shower tiles, his plastic K mart rainsuit rustling as he turned for her hallway.

⚓ ⚓ ⚓

The chickens were very happy to see their mentor and feed finder, even if he didn't stay long. Uncle Barry locked them in carefully, then, irritated and impatient with the ignorant Bud, who obviously didn't know a thing about fowl, he left thirty-two eggs on the back stairs for his sisters to find. He had six in his pocket for his breakfast. Ozzie didn't like eggs. Tex, the Richardsons' Doberman, was happy to see him, and whacked Uncle Barry's legs with his tail as they made their way back through the hedge together.

There was a light at the Carlyles', a strangely forlorn bulb in their attic window. Uncle Barry went through the fence and across the lawn. Uncle Barry was glad to be out again, glad for the night, and pleased with himself.

He heard the splash and stopped.

Where? he wondered.

Uncle Barry scratched his face, his nose.

Somewhere ahead in the dark. The Hammond pool? Too cold for a dip; most of the pools were covered and hadn't been cleaned yet.

He went behind the garage, along the wire-mesh fence where the oblivious Carlyles lost every raspberry that ever grew there to the one man left awake. He halted near the hedge, listened.

Nothing, and then something.

Uncle Barry held his breath. Why would she be out on a night like this? The neighborhood kids were in their houses hours ago. She was a good woman who made the best peanut-butter cookies.

He leaned through her hedge, carefully. Tex pranced across the grass to her pool and stopped, head down, curious. Her house was dark, a French door open onto the patio.

Something was not right. He could feel it. He whistled softly through four bars of Vivaldi. Scratched his head. And walked out of the hedge, straight for her pool.

And there she was. Floating facedown. Bathing suit on. Not moving but the pool water glistening with stars.

He heard himself say, "Oh, no!" He reached for her, too far. He jumped into the water so cold to his waist, pulled her warm arm toward him, readied his legs to take her weight, and then picked her up quickly, sloshing toward the steps, his knees pushing water.

He kept saying "Oh, no! Oh, no!" as he eased her body down on the cement, turning her over, her eyes open. He stuck his fingers into her warm mouth, felt for her tongue, touched her neck for a pulse. Nothing. Uncle Barry arranged her flat, found her ribs over her heart . . . three hard breaths into her mouth, her eyes staring back at him . . . then he started counting out loud, whining to himself as Veronica Hammond's body took his weight under his hands, her hips rolling when he pushed.

The Richardsons' dog kept coming back to him, nosing the woman's legs, dashing back across the lawn, and finally ran off around the house barking.

Uncle Barry stayed with her for a long time, working and weeping, then shouted into the night and ran for her house and its open door. He felt so alone, so helpless.

He crashed through her dark living room, upending tables and chairs, kicking shoes on her carpet, to get to the telephone. He dialed for the operator and waited, spinning a softball bat.

"Come on—come on!" The line clicked . . . a voice was there. He said he needed an ambulance. "Bull Run," he said. "Eighty-two Bull Run!"

"What city, please?"

"What?" he said.

"What city, please?"

"Here!" he shouted. "Here!"

"I'm sorry, sir—but I need to know the name of the city you're calling from."

"It's a town," he said.

"The name of the town, please."

He told her, then the street again. "An ambulance, please—she's not breathing—no pulse at all!" he screeched.

Then he threw the phone down and ran back through the living room and out to the pool.

"Oh, no," he said when he realized she was still there, that this wasn't one of his awful dreams when the ants with the sharp sticks poked his eyes out. "Oh, no," he moaned, studying Veronica Hammond. She was so beautiful. So soft. She steamed in the cold night air, the thin vapor coming off her arms and legs like smoke, her life leaving her.

Uncle Barry started again, the slow counts, the hard breaths, listening for her to say anything, to wake up and tell him to get home . . . anything.

But she didn't.

He finally heard the siren, a faraway whooping out on Route 1, out near the mall and the Sears store. But as he was breathing hard into her chest, he saw headlights spray her driveway, sweep over her grass, and light her face under him.

The police were here.

Uncle Barry looked up at a young cop with no hat on, black hair. "She's not breathing," he said to the cop.

Uncle Barry caught his breath, then blew two more heavy breaths into the woman.

She did not move.

The cop pushed him aside . . . he heard the cruiser's radio scratch and claw at the night air . . . garbled voices . . . another cop suddenly beside him with an aluminum respirator case . . . more police arriving, and the ambulance backing up her driveway and over her grass to the pool's edge. And all he could do was kneel there and cry while they worked on Veronica Hammond.

They took him into the house, into her living room where he sat on one of her wooden chairs instead of where they pointed because he didn't want to get her couch wet with his clothes.

They had her lamps on. There were cops in the house, upstairs, in and out to the pool where the woman lay cold in the night and a man with a camera flashed signals of misery to Uncle Barry.

Another cop held a videotape camera to his shoulder, going from room to room.

"My name is Tagliano," a man said to him. "I'm the state's attorney. Tell me who you are and what happened."

Uncle Barry whisked his hands across his eyes. "I told the other man," he said softly.

"Tell me," Tagliano said. He wore a red sweater and faded jeans, sneakers. He gripped Uncle Barry by the arm and led him out the French door to the cement patio.

Uncle Barry simply waved his hands, trying to make himself vanish into nothing.

"Do you know this woman?"

Her eyes were open but frozen.

Uncle Barry looked up at Tagliano. The man needed a shave, a cigarette behind his ear. "Yes, I know her," he heard himself say. "My name is Barry Barrett."

"Barry Barrett?" the man said with rampant disbelief. "Does she live here?"

"Well, of course she lives here—this is her house. She's dead, isn't she?"

Tagliano sat Uncle Barry into a metal chair on the patio. Tagliano sat on the brick wall. "And you were walking around out here and found her in the pool?" he said.

Uncle Barry said that he'd heard the splash first.

"What were you doing out here?"

"Going home."

"You go home through people's yards, do you?"

Uncle Barry said he did. He brushed his soaked pants smooth.

"What splash?" Tagliano asked suddenly.

"The splash when she fell in," Uncle Barry said.

Tagliano spat between his legs.

"Did you hit her hard or just give her a tap?"

Uncle Barry knew when he heard this that a gate had just crashed shut over his days and nights, that no day would ever be the same again, that all would change in his life, and that all he loved would be taken from him. "I need to find Ozzie."

"Your nephew, right?"

Uncle Barry nodded.

"We sent a car for him."

Uncle Barry started to cry again. He didn't want to. But how could anyone not cry, sitting ten feet from a dead woman who was being zipped into a dark green plastic bag.

Tagliano stood up, sighing, as though he had better things to do.

Uncle Barry thought, Maybe they'll forget about me. He kept his eyes closed, thinking he'd never open them again, never.

His six eggs had somehow been crushed in his jacket. And Uncle Barry slowly circled his fingertip through the greasy yolk drool on his wet pants.

Ozzie leaned over him and whispered, "Are you okay?"

Uncle Barry kept his head down.

Phones rang all over the police station.

"Listen very carefully to me," Ozzie said. "Are you listening?"

Uncle Barry nodded.

Ozzie raised Uncle Barry's face, his hand gentle under the old man's chin. "Open your eyes," he whispered.

Uncle Barry opened his eyes . . . the same white room like a doctor's stark examining room without the intestinal flowcharts, gray chairs, bright ceiling lights. "Oh, Ozzie," he said. "This is awful."

"You'll be okay," Ozzie whispered. "Are you listening to me?"

"Yes."

"Don't think of anything else for a minute—just listen to me."

"I am, Oz."

"Listening?"

"I'm listening."

"Do not talk to anyone unless I tell you to. Do you understand me?"

"I talk to no man."

"Don't talk to women, either."

"I won't, Oz."

"Say nothing to anyone."

"Why?"

"I have a lawyer for you—she's coming as fast as she can. I'll introduce you to her—you'll like her. She's on our side, and doesn't like cops."

"How do you know, Oz?"

Ozzie smoothed the old man's hair across his bald spot. "I know, Uncle Barry."

"You know a lot, Oz. She was steaming, do you know that?"

"You didn't do anything wrong."

"Well, I didn't bring her back, did I? I don't think I did Red Cross CPR right. I couldn't remember the numbers."

"I don't think she needed CPR," Ozzie whispered. "There's something strange going on with these guys. They think she may have tripped and hit her head before she went into the pool."

"Poor Mrs. Hammond. What an awful night, Oz. She shouldn't have been swimming on a night like this. I remember GIs used to steam like that—but only when we opened their coats in the snow, Oz."

"I'm going to find some coffee," Ozzie said. "I'll try to find you some hot chocolate."

"I'm cold, Oz."

"I know you are. Wilson Malone has gone over to our house to get you dry clothes. Wait here."

"You won't leave me here, will you?"

"Never," Ozzie said. "Tell me what you're supposed to do?"

"I'm not talking."

"Good man," Ozzie said, leaving.

⚓ ⚓ ⚓

The lawyer's name was Lily. She sat with Uncle Barry and Ozzie in an office. A cop sat across the desk.

Lily spoke first to Uncle Barry, trying to be precise and on her toes at four in the morning. "They are going to charge you with first-degree murder—this is an *untimely death;* you'll be arraigned in the morning before a magistrate. They're asking for a psychiatric evaluation, which means you'll have to go the state hospital—those doctors know you. Otherwise, they'd keep you here in the county jail and have the shrinks visit you. The state hospital is better for us."

Uncle Barry looked straight ahead, his eyes on the black window, the harbor lights twinkling in the distance. "Not better for me," he whispered.

Ozzie looked at the woman as though she were a cartoon. "We'll hear what they have to say in the morning," she said, understanding that nothing she said made sense to these men. "You'll have to stay here until morning."

"Will they lock me up?" Uncle Barry said quietly.

"Yes," she said. "Until morning."

"But Ozzie and I can come over after breakfast."

She looked to Ozzie for help. Got none.

Uncle Barry lowered his head.

"Does he understand?" she asked Ozzie.

Wilson Malone, porkpie hat in place, was out in the main office arguing with two cops about something, gesturing, pointing at them.

"Better than we do," Ozzie said to her, realizing Malone would be in here next.

"Take a hike," she said to the cop. "I need a half hour with my client."

"Up to you," the cop said, getting out of his chair.

When the door was opened, Ozzie heard Malone shouting about police states and the Third Reich.

In the stillness of that office, the lawyer tried for twenty minutes to soften their plight. But Uncle Barry grew only more subdued, more withdrawn, more defeated the longer she went on. Ozzie felt like a man in an anaconda's grip, the Amazon closing repeatedly over his face, as some dread collision of events threatened to squeeze the life out of him.

He left Uncle Barry sitting there tall and proud in the gray chair beside Lily, the old man's eyes on the harbor lights.

"I've called the judge, Oz," Malone boomed from the row of chairs in the corridor.

Ozzie pulled on his bomber jacket and walked for the door, a crushed man. "What judge?"

"My lawyer—Magnuson—he's a federal judge in Boston. He'll tear their pricks off. You okay, Oz?" he said, galloping after his friend.

Ozzie stood on the steps. Dawn was just seeping into the eastern sky, miles out at sea where the fish dawdled through their lives waiting for his net. "I've never seen him look like this, Wilson."

"They threatened me in there, Oz—said they'd find a charge for me, if they had to. Old Magnuson will eat 'em alive, he drinks martoonies that taste like napalm."

Ozzie turned to Malone. "I've just never seen him look like this." Ozzie braced himself. "Something's happened to him."

Malone threw his arm across Ozzie's leather shoulders and walked him down to the street.

The Morning After

THE silent harbor was a wash of grays and blues, the black water like oil and dimpled when Ozzie jumped down onto the *Lucia*'s deck at dawn. He balanced his "COME-BACK-FOR-COFFEE" mug from Eldridge's drugstore on the winch housing. The sky was high and lightly flared with mackerel clouds, the sun a bleary brightness that would grow hot.

A loud crash banged across the harbor, over near Mildred's.

The engine fired once, ran for four seconds, and shut down. Ozzie hit the button again. Nothing.

Hatches up, the *Lucia* smelled of oil and bilge water, and of exhaust down in under the deck, where Ozzie examined the fuel filters on the Cat diesel. He felt tired, his muscles buzzing with the overload, the police-station rites of passage for that old man hot on his mind. Uncle Barry had said, "You won't leave me here?" And even as Ozzie had answered, he knew that much of what would happen to Uncle Barry was not something for any man to control, let alone a man who couldn't start his engine, couldn't start his wife, and didn't much care that he couldn't.

Ozzie pushed the ignition switch on the engine-room bulkhead.

The Cat started and ran smooth.

"I'll be damned," he said, hurrying up the ladder to the wheelhouse.

Another crash from across the harbor. Ozzie turned as he heaved in line, leaping for Rocket's dock, his fishing boots skidding on the wet wood. Someone was banging hell out of something across the harbor.

The *Lucia* took on way slowly, rolling slightly as Ozzie jammed the transmission ahead. He spun the wheel, the engine stuttered.

Ozzie backed off the throttle, making for the channel, the *Lucia*'s wake a foamy green.

But nothing was right. Ozzie shifted into neutral and the trawler's stern took the gentle rise of his wake. Not a chance, he thought. This engine is a cripple.

He reversed, spun the wheel, and headed for Ruby's across the harbor, weaving through the moorings like a whale among dolphins.

She was lifting weights on her decking, wearing a powder-blue outfit, a white sweatband around her silvery hair. Ruby let the weights crash to the deck. She shook herself, then worked her arms.

Ozzie sipped his coffee, watching her.

The weights went up again to her hips, then to her chest, then all the way up over her head, and down again with a great crash onto the deck.

Ozzie let the *Lucia* drift slowly, with enough way on to bring her bow to starboard. Ruby was easily the most bewildering being Strike's Landing had produced in the past quarter century: she'd abandoned an undergraduate career after two months at Tufts to join the navy. Rocket had spoken of his lost daughter wistfully for over twenty years, even though the woman had returned home to her father, the fireworks enthusiast, every year or so for long visits. Ruby was the finest mechanic in the harbor, with her light, powder-blue soul, and not easily understood by men. When they whistled, Ruby whistled back. When they offered themselves in jest, as she lugged a heavy diesel's cylinder past their beer-stained guts, Ruby described their offerings with a tongue dipped in acid, as though she'd seen things in her travels these men could never imagine . . . and had no hope of living up to. Ruby had her parrot, Larry, who never talked but lived with her and flew over the moored Chris Crafts and Bertrams to land in the rigging above the working Ruby. Larry perched on radar antennae for as long as Ruby sweated in engine rooms, a clear distaste for humans festering in the bird. Twenty years in the navy does things to women. And to parrots.

With Rocket more than a little shaky in every way that matters, Ruby Willey had herself discharged in Norfolk, Virginia, and flew home to be his daughter once more. She made all the difference to Rocket. Men in suits wanted his land, his wharfs and junkyard, his empty warehouses that sagged on pilings around the harbor. They wanted to build condoms, as Rocket called them—condos and restaurants with nets and brass mirrors, new touristy shopping malls, like the two Strike's Landing had now, that looked like miniature Dutch villages.

Ruby had other ideas.

She let these men date her; Lizbeth and the women at the bank clucked their tongues and said they knew Ruby got off to Boston for weekends with men. Ruby looked ripe in golden silks when the men took her up to the country club or to the glitzy Switzer's out on Route 1 in their cream Lincolns. Ruby was the perfect confection of every man's most tangy dreams, but Ruby had other ideas.

She never budged. She had decided her father would finish his days in this harbor as he had lived them, no matter what.

Ozzie let the trawler drift up to her pilings, just touching reverse to hold his hull away from the wooden poles.

She crashed the weights onto the decking, looked at Ozzie, then threw her shoulders back. "What?" she shouted.

"Engine's sick," he said from the wheelhouse door.

"Now?"

"I'll wait," he said.

"Not easily, you won't. Wanna fight?"

"Later."

"Always later with you, isn't it?" she said.

Ruby's powder-blue outfit looked like cool chrome on her legs. Ozzie watched as she pulled on a sweatshirt, and climbed down the ladder to leap from a middle rung onto his deck.

"Crank it," she said squeezing past him into the wheelhouse. "Nice dentist's chair," she said, startled by the old white, armless contraption Ozzie used as a comfortable helm chair.

She concentrated as Ozzie started the engine, her head cocked to one side, her hair falling out of her sweatband.

"Enough—enough!" she said, and dropped down the engine-room ladder in the cabin.

Ozzie waited, washed in the lively spicy odor of this woman.

She shouted from below and Ozzie pushed the starter button again. The engine started, skipped, then smoothed out.

She wanted to know about fuel filters and when he'd cleaned them last. He watched as she came up the ladder.

"Shut if off," she said, winding her hair into a knot on her head. "When do you want it?"

"Any time," he said, realizing he was living in quicksand.

She glanced at him, confused.

"I've got a mess with my uncle—I don't know when I'll go out again," he said.

"When's the last time that engine was torn out?"

He said two years ago.

"Can you leave it here?"

He turned off the key and, resting his coffee on the binnacle, went out on deck to make the trawler fast to her dock.

She climbed up to wrap his lines and neatly snubbed him in. "I won't let anything happen to her," she said. "Weights make me horny as hell—you?"

He gripped the ladder. "I don't do weights."

"You should," she said. She had a smile that could crack glass.

"My uncle's been arrested."

"They finally caught him?"

He told her about Veronica Hammond and the pool. Uncle Barry was being arraigned this morning . . . he wanted to be there.

"I'm sorry, Oz," she said, rolling her weights toward the warehouse wall.

"I thought you lived with Rocket?" he said, turning to look across the harbor.

She grinned, the sweat over her eyes running down her cheeks. "Could you live with Rocket? This is much better for both of us. I live in this half—my shop's in the other half. Just to be safe he's got his telescope in his bedroom window."

Four open glass doors had been fitted into the warehouse wall, the curled cedar shakes cut brightly new around the door edges. She'd painted the interior white: white beams and floor, white walls.

Ozzie looked back at her to where she was hanging weights on hooks under the eaves of the single-story shack. "He used to keep motors in here, didn't he?" he said, feeling exhausted.

"Just one big room—you wanna see it?"

Ozzie said he didn't, couldn't.

"What made your uncle do it?" she said. She stood in the sun.

Ozzie said his uncle hadn't done anything.

Ruby smiled quickly. "Oz, he was running around this town at night when I was young and frilly. He was bound to get into trouble—you know how people are."

"Would your father kill someone?"

"He might, I'm afraid," she said. "Only god knows all the things he's done. Right place, right time, and he could do anything. Is it true your wife left you and is selling the house out from under you?"

"I don't know," Ozzie said. He felt badgered.

"Mildred says Louise is gone for good and good riddance."

Ozzie wanted to get away from this woman.

"It'll get straightened out," she said. "Who was she?"

"Worked at the bank with my aunt. A widow. Do you remember her husband, Martin—owned the boat that caught fire off the beach?"

"Nope," she said. "What happened to her?"

"Fell in her pool, I guess—fell on the cement—I don't know."

"Last night?"

"I don't know."

"You don't know much, do you?"

"Much more than I'd like to know," he said.

There was a familiarity about Ruby he didn't understand. He had watched her eating at Mildred's with the fishermen, but Ozzie had never spent so long as ten minutes with her alone, and knew her only as Rocket's distant daughter returned to the nest. But she seemed to know him.

Ozzie had the spine-tugging jingle that nothing ever again was going to be all right.

⚓ ⚓ ⚓

Bernadette DeSilva had yogurt and fruit in bed with her on a silver tray, the morning paper on her lap. She swept her hair behind her ears, short frosted hair, shaved in the back so that when it began to grow in, her neck had a five-o'clock shadow. Babs DeSilva, the only living Maguire daughter, controlled her own affairs with immensely liquid assets, owned this house, was the linchpin on the school board, and flew off to Elizabeth Arden's in New York every month for mud packs and derring-do in Bonwit Teller's, with an additional three weeks each winter in Germany for sheep-cell injections. She'd had everything tucked and sucked, stapled and rebuilt, though she did worry about the imperfect job done on her ears.

"I'll be damned," she said, opening the paper.

Richie DeSilva looked at her in the mirror as he finished dressing. "Market down?" he said.

"Nothing to do with *your* first love—though maybe it does."

Her father had given her high school sports star a job in the Maguire bank, but had never liked the boy, as he so frequently told his daughter.

"Your pretty secretary is dead."

Richie DeSilva left his hands in his coat pocket—seeing all with a flash.

"They found your Veronica in her swimming pool last night," she said, looking up at him to see if his wind vane was swinging round. "Police are calling it an untimely death—Barrett will be arraigned this morning. Which Barrett?"

DeSilva stood still, his eyes fluttering. He strode to the bed, snatched at the paper. Babs held onto the thing, then let it go, the paper tearing as he searched the front page.

"Oh, shit," he said.

Babs steadied her tray, dipping for another yogurt drop and kiwi slice, ever so civil in these bouts with him. The woman watched him shrivel as he read.

Richie glanced at her, saw her ready suspicion mixed with smugness. "They think this guy killed her," he said. "She worked yesterday—she typed all afternoon. That old retard—that son of a bitch."

"Won't this set the town on its ass—lonely, sexy widow murdered in her pool at night. Bank president touched by his loss, has no idea what he'll do without her."

70

"For chrissake, shut up, Babs. You are so spoiled—so fucking perfect, aren't you?"

"Do tell," she said, letting herself go. "Then why don't we have children, Richard? We all know what a potent Portagee stud you are. Your Veronica—"

"—was a real woman. You bet your ass! Satisfied?" Richie threw the paper at her, knocking her coffee into her lap.

And the band played on . . . all over Strike's Landing this morning. From kitchen to kitchen, from boat to boat, the local radio station, WSEA, broadcast the news to the vigilant town, from firehouse to courthouse, from the garbage trucks to the post office. Elspeth, Lizbeth, and Bud were shattered at their kitchen table, as the radio announcer filled them in: "—a secretary at the First Seaman's Bank, declared dead last night at 11:33 by the state's medical examiner . . . cause of death not immediately known. Barrett, seventy-three, will be arraigned this morning. Police obviously suspect foul play but have released no details, nor will they confirm rumors that Barrett, who has no prior convictions and is a lifelong resident of Strike's Landing, was recently a patient at the Medford State Hospital. We'll keep you posted, folks."

Uncle Barry sat alone in the old courtroom, in handcuffs.

Ozzie walked the twenty feet down the aisle and through the gate to the tables before the bench.

"Oh, Oz," Uncle Barry said when he saw his nephew. "This is a terrible thing. They locked me up, you know."

Ozzie sat with him, listened as best he could while people passed in and out of the room.

"These people swear something awful, Oz."

Lily dropped her briefcase on the table and patted Uncle Barry's arm.

Elspeth and Lizbeth walked in with Bud and sat near the back.

7 1

Lily said, "Well, I'm not sure how to tell you two this, but the state's attorney believes he has this locked up." She took Uncle Barry's hand. "They're going to arraign you in a minute—first-degree murder. They're sending you to the state hospital for an evaluation—sixty days, exactly as we thought. Tagliano thinks you did it; he thinks all sorts of rubbish, but basically he believes you killed the Hammond woman. He hasn't got everything straight yet, but he does have sixty days to get all his ducks in a row. The police say they know you."

"I don't know them," Uncle Barry said.

"They say they've had calls about you before. That true?"

Uncle Barry said he didn't know.

"Have they ever brought you in before for anything?"

"No."

"Are you sure it wasn't just an accident?" she asked softly.

"It was an accident," Uncle Barry said.

"Oh, shit," Lily said, sucking in her breath. "Let's hear it."

"She had an accident and I found her in the pool."

"Not what I meant," she said quickly to Ozzie. "You'll be okay," she said to Uncle Barry. "I'll be back. I have got to have a cigarette. You're not supposed to be sitting with him," she said to Ozzie.

She went off without her briefcase, was stopped by Bud in the back of the room, then left.

Ozzie felt Uncle Barry take his hand. He knew the old man was crying again. The magistrate eventually showed up on the bench, a bailiff sat behind Uncle Barry, and Lily came back and spoke with force and diligence against the wishes of the state, those wishes being proposed by an officious young woman in a tweed suit, with bobbed hair and no makeup, who almost sneered when she referred to Uncle Barry as the defendant.

Ozzie gripped the old man's hand and tried to listen.

"Who are you?" the bailiff leaned over and asked Ozzie.

"I'm with him," Ozzie said, pointing to his uncle.

It was all over in a flash. Uncle Barry was taken away by the bailiff, Lily had to dash off for her office, and his aunts left the room without speaking to him.

Ozzie sat there alone, breathing carefully, aware that he was more responsible for this legal tableau than anyone else. Ozzie felt older than his forty-seven years, older and sick to his stomach.

What He
Doesn't Know
Won't Hurt Him

Ozzie stopped at Eldridge's for coffee, easing the drugstore's screen door closed, feeling like the guilty party, the half dozen folks at the marble counter instantly aware that he was among them, their conversations growing louder as he made his way to a stool and ordered a sweet roll from Helen, the scattered harpy in the pink waitress's uniform who kept all the tabs in her head because she could never find her receipt pad. The brass prescription wicket was camouflaged in the back by medications and leg braces, tall wooden shelves of aspirin and witch hazel, an EYE-CARE PRODUCTS sign, hanging crutches, and a Whitman's Sampler display next to the magazine rack. Eldridge's was a vintage, Rockwellian drug emporium with nearly black woodwork and suspended glass globes with "Rexall" emblazoned in red, its floor of shiny, infinitely small white tiles. There was a wooden telephone booth, and Eldridge's still served cherry Cokes.

"Eat this, love," Helen said to him, pushing his sweet roll

at him. "You're staring into space this morning, aren't you?"

Ozzie glanced back at the woman.

"Looking a little peaky, Oz," she said and patted his hand. "Drink your coffee. You could use some of old Helen's mattress therapy, you could."

Ozzie wondered why he bothered to live in Strike's Landing, what it was about the place that brought him back from New York, back from Boston, to live out his days here as a trawlerman. Who was he trying to kid? People here regarded him as more than a slight social aberration: as a man who had cut his own throat. Strike's Landing had its strict layering: people who worked for people doing dirty jobs wore green or blue clothes, or had their first names embroidered on their Kelvinator shirts. People who worked for people doing clean work, wore suits and ties and had their last names on office doors, signs, or granite chunks on their desks. Doctors wore white, nurses wore white, Old Man Eldridge himself wore a white tunic stuffed with pens but violated the dress code with a shock of Einsteinian hair. Anxious Rotarians, all free-market imams, girdled themselves in Anderson Little vests and solid black shoes. People who worked for themselves wore whatever they felt like wearing, the easy crowd, like the women in jeans and long skirts who ran the White Shop on the main wharf near MacAvoy's.

The Hill people, most of them hopelessly anxious, raised kids with serious expectations and facial tics, and lived north of the harbor, north of the park and its library and elementary school, on a landscaped elevated grid of Victorian trees, porches, flags, cast-iron street lamps, all the way up to the pinnacle of the Hill people, the country club up near the cemetery, up where the extravagant homes were sequestered behind bushy screens on streets with names like Brightthorpe Terrace. Their version of Saab-burbia.

The salt marsh divided the town south of the Strike's Landing business quarter, south of the two new Dutch village malls, Eldridge's, the bank, the insurance offices with geraniums in windowboxes, the marsh's salt flood licking the very yards of the huddled and dark Portuguese in their boxy houses with all their fluttering lawn ornaments. St. Mary's Catholic Church belonged to the Portuguese and closet papists, while the miniature Gothic stone piles to the north, encircling the park, belonged to the better crowd, the car dealers and lawyers.

The Portuguese worked on the sea; the Hill people played on the sea; and while the harbor was the winter refuge for the *Portageez*, as they were called, the Hill people reclaimed their water rights each summer, stuffing the harbor with catamarans and seventy-foot white fiberglass tubs, sailboats and roaring Thunderbirds that prowled out of the harbor at full throttle. And the harbormaster, who owed his livelihood to these fine folks, said nothing but fumed behind his windows as the Solomon of moorings.

The road along the northern harbor cusp wound out past Rocket Willey's derelict enterprise, out past the yacht club to The Breakers, this town's version of a Chautauqua inn, out to flat Fontana Beach, where the Hill people children baked themselves through the hot summer afternoons.

The Portuguese were confined to the southern cusp, the road out past Mildred's and Ruby's, past Phil's boat yard and the fuel-oil tanks, to that night stalker's delight, the teetering boardwalk across a quarter mile of salt marsh to the very lonely, the very evil Reeve's Beach, where the undertow was sufficiently strong to weed out the darker population. Reeve's Beach had crabs, rocks, and jellyfish. Fontana Beach had lifeguards named Duncan in white trunks and pith helmets who drove stripey-pink Jeeps with Syracuse stickers on the bumpers.

Originally populated by lawless misanthropes and privateers as a fishing outpost on the Massachusetts north shore, a tantalizing remove from colonial courts, Strike's Landing was invited into the real world of capital investments with the erection of the foundry by the Maguire family in 1857, just in the nick of time: the Maguires pirated millions in Civil War cannon and built the first big houses on the Hill, one of which Louise had decorated and Ozzie had tolerated as home.

Ozzie left his sweet roll on Eldridge's counter to walk down to the First Seaman's bank, a building originally constructed as a synagogue until the Maguires put their collective feet down, manhandled the Jews out of town through land manipulations, and decided the cavernous brick building would make a fine repository for Maguire money. Ozzie walked past the shops, the warm snuff of bagels when he passed a new mall, only tiny shops with thatched roofing, a video store, and bakery, the bookstore and the art gallery, Ozzie feeling every bit the stranger in a strange land. He swept into the bank, beneath its vaulted ceiling and its high, round Star-of-David window, across its soft green carpeting, and waited at the counter. Lizbeth's desk was unoccupied. Veronica Hammond's desk had been cleared, her chair tight against her typing table. Some of the bank officers watched Ozzie from their desks under the balcony, and the bank president, one Richie DeSilva, jabbered away on his telephone. The teller said his aunt wasn't expected until tomorrow.

Ozzie knew these people would hold him righteously accountable for their loss.

He crossed the street to MacAvoy's to get his check, the fish plant office loud and shot full of laughter and wide grins, Ozzie waiting again at another counter while the Hendricks woman thumbed through her envelope stacks for his name. "Must be hard on your sisters," she said to him, as she pushed his check across the Formica.

"Must be," he said, not knowing what was hard or why anything was hard for them alone.

Ozzie walked home, desperate for his bed, up the sidewalks past the park and into the Victorian grid.

There was a police cruiser in his driveway.

"Trouble with your door?" the cop said, getting out of his car.

Ozzie said, "What door?"

Manny the cop, a sergeant now on the Strike's Landing nine-man constabulary, a vicious little man with an enormous black firearm on his hip, leaned on his fender. "Your kitchen door, Rob."

Ozzie said his name was Ozzie. Manny kept his confusion hidden nicely.

"We need some information about your uncle—we were hopin' you could help us. Mind if I come in? You should fix that door."

Ozzie said he did mind.

Manny was confused again. "Well," he started, "I understand your uncle was staying with you. I'd like to see his room, his effects, if you don't mind."

"I do mind," Ozzie said.

"I can get a search warrant."

"That's fine," Ozzie said. "Get one."

"Makin' it tough on yourself." Manny crossed his arms. His eyes had a peculiar cast, one somehow lower on his face than the other.

Ozzie walked up his driveway.

"State's attorney's office isn't going to like this!" Manny shouted after Ozzie.

Ozzie climbed his back stairs.

He slept for hours, waking in a drizzling dark. He was hungry, still tired, as he tumbled down to the cold kitchen, its window running with an afternoon's weight of gloom.

Ozzie heard the footsteps on the back porch, heard the clumsy scrapes on the house, and Malone's whistle. The porkpie hat.

"Hey, Oz," Malone said.

"Hey yourself, Wilson."

78

"I rang and rang. Were you taking a meeting—you been sleeping?"

"I haven't got a phone."

"Sure you do—you don't?"

"I killed the phone, Wilson."

Mildred's chowder was hotter than anything Ozzie had ever put in his mouth; chunks of halibut, scallops, and potatoes like rocks.

Malone said he'd called the judge; the judge would drive up from Boston soon. "I had to take Gurney's seminar this afternoon, Oz. Gurney's play theory."

"That where you got the bat?"

"Gurney believes play should be integrated into our lives—should be part of every school curriculum. Can you imagine? He's got this miracle three-D slide show for superintendents and school boards—those creepy people. Guy's got the play market in his pocket—gives these bats to school administrators"—Malone fetched a red sponge bat off the floor and whapped the bar like a rifle shot—"they must take time out from screwing our kids to bash each other in school hallways. Gurney's making a bundle."

A man's voice on the other side of the bar yelled, "Goddam it, Malone, don't do that again!"

Ozzie looked for Ruby.

Malone said, "Oz, you gotta do something. Ya can't keep on like this. What the hell's happened to ya?"

Ozzie pushed his hands through his graying hair, settled into his chair. "I'm whipped."

"I didn't touch you, Oz." Malone rolled the bat on the bar and cut into his fish, separating the stuffing from the flaky flounder.

"Listen to me." Ozzie stopped looking for Ruby. "My uncle's locked up—I'm the guy that pulled him out of the state hospital so he could find a dead woman. I've got cops in my yard. My wife is about to sell my house."

"She can't sell your house, Oz."

"That sign didn't say BED AND BREAKFAST, did it? I think I'm getting a divorce. My boat's sick."

Malone took a long pull on his beer.

Mildred came to lean on her bar near them, sipping her constant iced tea, resting.

Ozzie said, "Uncle Barry didn't kill that woman. The poor bastard was just lucky enough to find her. And everybody thinks he did it because he's a nut. It's like I'm strapped to one of Rocket's rockets."

"That's bullshit, Oz. I don't think he did it. She had an accident and he happened to be there at the wrong time. Simple."

"Not simple—her skull was crushed. The police don't think anything was an accident."

Malone reached for the tartar sauce. "The judge will straighten this all out."

"I don't think so," Ozzie said softly. "It's like I lit the fuse—boom. Being locked away will kill the old guy. It'll kill me."

"You didn't do anything."

"Damn right. I sat here in this bar while he dragged her out of the pool, Wilson. I'm responsible for him."

Mildred poured another beer and dropped it in front of Malone. She hesitated before leaving them, then stopped in front of Ozzie. "This town will hang your uncle," she said, "because they need to think a nut killed her—and he is a nut, Oz." Mildred leaned over, her face not three inches form Ozzie's face. "How about an intruder?"

Ozzie shook his head. "I don't know."

"That's the point, isn't it? You don't know."

"The police know," Ozzie said.

"Ya, well the police around here just fell out of high school," Mildred said.

"Damn fine fish, Mildred," Malone offered.

"Just eat it, Wilson," she said. "Oz, if you think you got the old guy into trouble, then you get him clear."

Ozzie said, "Skulk through bushes looking for clues?"

She tossed her hair. "I don't know shit about clues, Oz, but I do know you're a smart guy who needs some answers, and there isn't anyone going to find them but you. The cops have their man and he's your uncle. They won't help you. No one in this town will help you."

"I will," Malone said, chewing his fish, tipping his beer, his eyes above the rim huge like a trout with glasses.

Mildred glanced at Malone and giggled. "You are a fool, Wilson."

"I know I am," Malone said, grinning. "That's where I get my strength—I know just what I am, no complaints, I'm a satisfied customer, you wicked little cripple. Love the fish tonight."

She reached for Ozzie's hands, taking them in hers. "You can either let them beat hell out of you, Oz, or you can beat hell out of them. You won't like any of this—your heart's too soft. You tell me what you need, I'll do all I can to help you. I promise," she said, kissing his cheek.

Ozzie felt suddenly paralyzed with sensations: he envied this woman's dark reserves he knew nothing about. He lowered his eyes away from hers, leaving his hand in her soft paws.

Malone tapped her arm. "Right here, Mildred," he said, pinching his cheek, tartar sauce on his lip.

Mildred kissed Malone.

⚓ ⚓ ⚓

"I don't want to, Ozzie," Uncle Barry said, "I don't ever want to think about that night again. They ask me about it all the time—everyone does."

Ozzie sat back in the broken wicker chair.

"I'm happy to see you, Oz."

"And I'm happy to see you, Uncle Barry."

The old man turned his head away from his nephew in the bright state-hospital solarium. The attendant had gone to stand against the farther white wall after Ozzie had asked him to leave, a sluggard in white pants and lab coat.

"This is awful, Oz."

"I know it is," Ozzie said. "We're going to get you out of here. But we have to work together—and we do work together well, don't we?"

"Always have."

"Then tell me."

"What?"

"Tell me where you were when you first saw her."

"The dog saw her first."

"What dog?"

"The Richardsons' dog."

"Was he with you, the Doberman?"

"Tex wanted to help. He ran all around while I did my CPR."

"Tex found the woman in the pool?"

"He's a smart dog."

"What did you do?"

"When?"

"When you found her in her pool."

"I pulled her out."

"Did you see anyone else?"

"Just Tex."

Ozzie let his chin settle in his palm, watching a blue dump truck circle through the grounds.

"Where did you call the ambulance from?"

"Inside her house."

Was the door open?"

"Yup."

"How did you know where the telephone was?"

"She has three, Oz. One in her kitchen, one in her living room, and I think she has one upstairs."

"Oh, god," Ozzie said. "How do you know that?"

"I've been in her house, Oz."

"She let you in?"

"Well, no—but I went in to get the cookies."

"Damn. How the hell could you do that?"

"Don't yell at me, Oz. She didn't mind—she left cookies on her counter all the time. Peanut-butter cookies in a jar. And on Wednesday nights she left pizza for me."

"Think, Uncle Barry: What lights were on when you went in?"

"No lights at all. I crashed all over the place, I'm afraid—the police asked me if she and I scuffled in the living room. I don't scuffle, Oz."

"No lights? What was she doing outside in a bathing suit in the dark? Maybe she was coming home from somewhere. But that doesn't make any sense—you don't think she went swimming somewhere?"

"I doubt it, Oz. The ocean's too cold and they don't clean the country-club pool until May."

"Someone's private pool, like the Stearns' pool—inside."

"Maybe."

Ozzie scratched his cheek, took a deep breath. None of this made any sense. "If someone's going for a dip in their pool—"

"Not in her pool, Oz. Her pool wasn't clean yet—well, a little bit. The pool guys couldn't finish because the pump motor burned out."

"How do you know that?"

"They left a note for her last month. They said they would come back to finish. That pool isn't very clean, Oz."

"So why was she out there? And why were the lights off in her house? How did you see to use the telephone?"

"Little green light on the dial."

"Was the room already messed up when you came in to telephone?"

"No. I did that. I tripped over a chair first. Some shoes on the rug, then banged into a glass table, which hurt my leg something awful. Look at this."

Uncle Barry rolled up his pants to expose his bruised calf.

"What shoes?"

"Shoes, Oz. Shoes!"

"Boots?"

"No, Oz—shoes."

"Big shoes? Little shoes?"

"Shoes!"

"Little fussy slippers?"

"Shoes, Oz!"

"Dammit!" Ozzie said. Uncle Barry was losing his grip as if his radio signal were being blown off in a solar flare. "Would you like a hot chocolate or something? They might be able to get us a drink."

"No, Oz. I think we should stop."

"She took off her shoes and walked out to her pool barefoot on a cold April night—she couldn't have done that because she wanted to. Did she hear you outside and come out to meet you?"

"That's enough, Oz. You act like a policeman. I don't know why she went outside—I don't know why she had to fall and hurt herself like that. This is awful."

"Quit saying everything's awful. We'll get out of this somehow."

"I don't think so, Oz." Uncle Barry tugged at his nephew's sweater and blinked his eyes. "Oz, they were rubbers!"

"She had rubbers near her door? Garden rubbers?"

"Black rubbers. One of them smacked when I kicked it against the wall. I remember how soft it was, not like the table."

"Near the telephone—the front door?"

"Inside on the rug—the pool door."

"But she was barefoot when you found her."

"And those rubbers weren't there when I went back in with the policemen."

"You kicked them."

"Only one. The other one went under the table or something. Just flew."

"Did the police pick them up?"

"That awful man told them not to touch anything—they have their chain of evidence, you know."

"Tagliano? Did you tell the police about the rubbers?"

"No. Hey, Oz? There was a man in her yard one night two weeks ago or so. He had rubbers on."

Ozzie didn't move a muscle. "What man?"

"A little man behind her shed—he was hiding there, watching her house."

"Did he speak to you?"

"He didn't see me. I saw him."

"Who was he?"

"I don't know. I couldn't see well enough in the dark."

"Was she home?"

"Yup."

"Did he come out of the house?"

"Nope—but he walked down her driveway. I think he was a Peeping Tom, Oz."

"Oh, brother," Ozzie said, taking a huge breath. "And he wore rubbers?"

"Yup. He was only there for a moment. Not long. He watched her and left."

"Describe him."

"Little guy—wore perfume—sort of scrunched up when he walked. He had on a jacket or something—regular pants."

"And rubbers."

"The grass was wet. He snuffed a lot—he shouldn't have been out in the wet like that."

"Was he there the night you found her in the pool?"

"I didn't see him. Can we stop now, Oz?"

"Show me how tall he was on you."

Uncle Barry stood up and placed his hand in the center of his chest. "A little guy, Oz."

"Did she have lots of people visit her?"

"Not lots."

"Men?"

"There's the man who jogs all the time."

"Not the Peeping Tom?"

"Could have been, Oz. They're both little guys."

"Any other men?"

"The florist—he comes all the time."

"Flowers?"

"Lots of flowers."

"Did you have the dog with you the night you saw the Peeping Tom?"

"No. But I smelled lilacs—it's too early for lilacs, Oz."

"Did the dog bark at all the night you found her?"

"Just when he and I got excited. He wanted to help. Well, not then but later, when I was trying to remember my CPR numbers. He barked then."

"Does Tex bark at you?"

"Sometimes."

"Did he bark at the police?"

"He wasn't there then—he left."

"When did he leave?"

"When I was doing my CPR, Oz. You don't listen very well, you know. He barked and ran away."

"But he stayed with you most nights?"

"He's my dog."

"He's the Richardsons' dog, you borrow him! He didn't stay with you that night—where did he run?"

"I don't know, Oz. He ran. He ran around the house."

"Out front?"

"I don't know."

"You were doing CPR and the dog ran away before the police came."

"He barked first, Oz—before he ran away. *He* thinks he's my dog."

"She was still warm in the pool," Ozzie said with restraint, but the pressure was building in his chest. "You pulled her out. Tex was with you, barked, and ran around the house. Does that dog bite?"

"Yup, but he wouldn't bite me."

"Did you hear anyone scream or yell as though they'd been bitten?"

"No, Oz. Tex barked. That's all. Dogs bark, Oz."

"And you kicked rubbers when you went in to call the ambulance—rubbers that you didn't see when the cops took you into the living room later. And the little guy you saw behind the shed wore rubbers. Are you with me?"

"I'm always with you, Oz. You think Mr. Killer was in the house while I was there—someone who put his rubbers on and left before the police came. You think Tex went after him."

"You're very smart," Ozzie said.

"I know I am."

"Damn, but I think we've got us a clue. Was her front door open?"

"How should I know?"

"Did you see one of the policemen unlock the door?"

"Nope."

"Think. You're sitting in the living room and the police are there with you—they've got the lights on. Who touched the front door?"

"No one. They used her pool door. I'm very tired, Oz. Can we stop?"

"Where's her kitchen door?"

"Stop, Oz."

Ozzie gripped his uncle's arm, loving him more than he ever had.

"I'd like to go to Marble Mountain with Ezra," Uncle Barry said. "He's invited me, again. He says we can build a golf course there."

"Cape Breton Island is far, far away," Ozzie said.

Uncle Barry's eyes squinted tight. "Lilacs in a dead land, Oz."

On the Outside

OZZIE bounced over the foundry railroad tracks into Strike's Landing, pleasantly exposed to the evening in Rocket's jeep, an olive-drab prize with its windshield flat on its hood that Rocket had eagerly taken in trade for work. The jeep was the real thing, and had nothing above the level of its seats: no doors, no roof, no canvas curtains. Rocket's sunroof.

He drove to Ruby's and left the jeep ticking cool beside Ruby's shop doors to walk across her catwalk to her door.

"Not yet," she said when she answered. She kept the door close to her side, as though to keep Ozzie outside, a champagne flute and tiny cigar in one hand. "You've got a burned piston," she said, tossing her hair.

Ozzie knew he was carrying more than a bad engine. Ruby had salt-blue eyes. The liquid in her glass let off bubble chains.

"How long?" he asked.

"Few days. I think the other pistons are solid—I have to check. One of your filters was full of water, bub. Don't you ever think about water in your fuel?"

Ozzie heard himself say, "All the time." And knew he didn't.

"Well, you've scorched a hole clean through one piston. Call me Saturday."

Ozzie could see past her shoulder, could see the man's khakis, his tennis sneakers quivering on her rug. Ozzie tried to keep the news to himself. He stepped back, foolishly touching his forelock as a menial, meaning to salute her, he supposed. He didn't know what he was doing. He said, "I'll call," and realized he'd very likely never call her.

"Are you okay?"

"Better than ever," he said, starting off across her catwalk. He didn't look back, but stumbled along the boards over the black water.

Ruby turned off her porch light.

"Who was that?" Richie DeSilva said to Ruby. He patted the cushions on the floor next to him for her to sit.

"Ozzie Barrett," she said. She came across the rug, the leopard cushioning her intentions with grace.

"What's *he* doing here? He's a jerk. His retard uncle should have been locked up a long time ago. Whole family's crazy. They let that old creep run around until he killed someone. Veronica Hammond was the best secretary I ever had. God, I can't believe she's dead."

Ruby let herself down beside Richie, crossing her legs. "That's his trawler tied up outside. Engine needs work. Forget him. Tell me about the taxes."

"Your old man's in deeper than I thought he was. Helluva mess. IRS thought your old man was dead. He hasn't paid his real-estate taxes in seven years. Christ, he's sitting on millions in waterfront. Did you know he owns that woods behind the mall?"

"He's old," she said, as though being old were an explanation for anything.

"He's senile," Richie said. He reached to rub her knee.

90

Ruby tossed down the champagne. "I worry about him so much—he's all I've got. I'm afraid he'll get sick on me." She licked a champagne drop from her chin.

Richie DeSilva drew his fingertip along the seam of her jeans; her thigh was hard under the denim. "Tough for you, but with a little balls, a few phone calls to people I know, I think we might be able to save some of it."

She heard the tide thump her dory against the pilings beneath them.

"He's never been to a doctor in his life," she said.

He let his finger push a bit harder. "I'll help, if you want me to. It'll take hard work and brains, but we can help him."

"You haven't changed much in twenty years," she said. She watched his finger. "You still go for the soft parts first."

"I know what I want—I get what I want."

"Are you getting what you want now?"

"Not yet."

"Do we have to sell everything?"

"Too early to tell. That land behind the mall might be worth some cash. Some guys want to build a theater complex around here. Hard to tell."

"I don't want him to know," she said, crushing her cigar in the ashtray beside her.

Richie held up his hands. "Hey, bank presidents have so many secrets in a town this small we can't sleep at night."

"Sure you don't mind taking the time?"

"When did I ever mind anything you asked me to do?"

"I never asked you to do anything I knew you didn't want to do."

"Do you remember when we used to sneak kisses on the stage in the auditorium—in the dark?"

Not only had he not changed, Richie DeSilva was still the adolescent he'd always been, still the football, hockey, basketball star in a town gone mad for a hero, even if the hero had to be Portuguese. Twenty years hadn't done a thing for him. "I remember the morning you hung my bra off your car antenna. Nothing embarrassing in that for me, was there?"

"We were crazy about each other."

"We were?" she said.

Ruby's was a resurrected eighteenth-century fish wharf and cartage-loft. In the boom years after the Great War, these single-story sheds had been machine shops. Ruby had stripped out the walls and stanchions, the cast-iron lathe pedestals and floor plates, leaving an open span of triple flooring and notched beams that she'd sparsely furnished with wicker, her white bed suspended on four hawsers like a giant porch swing. There was a small kitchen area, and the bathroom barely large enough for her shower and its ceiling tank with its brass chain pull. With Joe Cocker from the speakers in the beams and champagne flutes on the rug, her home had a cleanness about it, as though Ruby had chased away all the crawly things that like to hang off walls in webs.

Larry the parrot didn't care where Ruby lived so long as he was with her, so long as she covered his cage with his tarp near sundown, so long as she fed him honey-glazed cashews, fruit salad, and his cheeseburgers, which for some reason the yellow-naped Amazon bird regarded as sustenance. After flitting through aircraft carriers and guided-missile cruisers wallowing in Norfolk's harbor, Larry found the harbor at Strike's Landing constraining, but livable because he never had trouble locating his mistress.

Ruby seemed comfortable. Too comfortable for Richie DeSilva, who disliked human satisfaction, believing as he did that this world was a fruit picker's paradise: he was the orchardist growing cash trees, toiling against the parasites and vermin who would, if they could, destroy his trees, rot his chances, gobble his wealth. Richie liked his women pliantly, obediently blind to the orchardist's fanaticism, agreeably willing to accept his every word as the gospel according to a mover and shaker of great limbs, including theirs.

Richie DeSilva never had caught on to the woman.

And truth to tell, Richie DeSilva didn't much care for Ruby.

♲ ♲ ♲

Ozzie couldn't help himself. He stood on her wharf, her gauzy glass doors alight, and he knew he should move, knew he shouldn't care. But he did. He'd been down into the *Lucia* for no reason other than to secure himself to something he understood, his hands on her dead wheel, and now found himself staring at Ruby's windows. They were on the rug. Ozzie couldn't make out who the man was through the curtains, but Ozzie could see her pink shirt and her silvery hair catch the pink light in there.

He knew he should leave.

But he couldn't. He watched them on the rug until the thought occurred to him, like a weather bulletin: Like uncle, like nephew.

He had stayed far beyond simple curiosity.

93

Blood and Roses

"**O**z, look at this," Malone said, gathering a length of yellow police crime-scene tape into a ball.

"Where'd you find that?"Ozzie said.

"Over near the garage—guys aren't very neat, are they? I think you should hurry up, Oz."

As Ozzie tried another key, the rain pelted his back, the night a swamp of wet and wind.

"Your uncle have a key for every door in town?"

"I think so."

Ozzie tried another key in Veronica Hammond's kitchen-door lock.

Malone said, "I haven't heard Rocket come around again, have you?"

"This one, I think," Ozzie said, easing the key against the tumblers, the door giving just enough to encourage him.

"Smart to not leave my car out front on a night like this, Oz. I love my MityLite you got me. You've thought of everything. I had no idea you were a criminal. That Rocket?" Malone tried to see around the house, tried to see the ever-circling Rocket Willey in his jeep, as Rocket randomly shifted through the sleeping streets, a cabbie with a mission on this night.

Ozzie held the door, then pushed it open.

The kitchen smelled musty, like opening a cottage in April.

"Save the lights," Ozzie whispered.

"Oz, I think someone's here."

"Then you talk to them. Living room first, Wilson."

The darkened house was layered with gloomy shadows; the two streetlights on Bull Run were rain-dull. Ozzie and Malone went through a dining room into a hallway. Ozzie stepped into the long living room. No one had been near enough to this woman, in many ways, to clean the place up. Everything seemed to have the spookiness of crime about it, that pestilent breath after evil events that lingers over abandoned bloody cars in roadside rest areas.

Ozzie realized he was alone. "Wilson!"

Not a sound.

Ozzie hurried back into the hallway, his heart thudding.

Malone's light was suddenly bright, then off. "Oz, this painting's a real Grant Wood—that's not a print. I can feel the brushwork."

"Don't touch anything," Ozzie said.

"I'm wearing my sinister black gloves."

"Then how'd you feel the brushwork, Wilson?"

"Quit worrying."

Ozzie returned to the living room, searching for the rubbers, his flashlight darting under couches and chairs, along the walls. Malone stayed near the front door and hallway.

There were no rubbers here. No shoes of any kind. All life in this room had been suspended.

"Do you see anything?" Ozzie whispered.

Malone was at one of the front windows. "I haven't heard Rocket; have you?"

Ozzie was going for the stairs when he saw that the den door was cracked slightly. He whistled Malone into the hallway, and then into a den lined with dark bookshelves, a writing desk near the window shutters, two leather couches and a table. A large television in the corner. Ozzie opened the desk drawer.

Ozzie sat down.

He found a pen, emptied one of the envelopes, and copied down as much of Veronica Hammond's life as he could: her doctors, the bill of sale for her car, her dead husband's checkbook, her dues receipt for the Business and Professional Women's Club, the Hammonds' used check registers, receipts for clothes from Fanny's out at the mall, a work order for her dishwasher pump from Strike's Landing Electric, two Boston parking tickets with the street location and meter number for each and the cops' badge numbers, green matchboxes from Switzer's and The Breakers, and a napkin from the Joy Street Kitchen on Boston's Beacon Hill.

"They liked Stephen King," Malone said from the bookshelf. "Lots of travel books—*London by Blimp* must be a ripper—lots of sports stuff, Frank Gifford and the great Yaz. A very pretty Oxford English Dictionary, Oz."

Ozzie took his time, using five newly vacant envelopes to record the figures of her life. There was a note from a company called Pretty Pools: "Cannot clean pool—pump burned out—will call."

When they climbed her stairs, Malone whispered, "There's someone up here, Oz."

The beds were empty. A master bedroom with a dressing room, the bathroom all mirrors, a spider plant hanging over the shower under a skylight.

"I thought cops went crazy? This house hasn't been touched," Malone said from the bedroom. Ozzie had the medicine bottles out, copying down prescriptions.

Malone opened the bed, lifted its sheets.

Ozzie heard Rocket pass the house.

"There must be an easier way," Malone said. "I don't even know what I'm looking for—who'd wear rubbers to bed?"

Ozzie searched under the sink in the cabinet among the hair dryers and broken hand mirrors.

Malone was in the doorway. "Hairs of two colors, Oz. Light short hairs and black short hairs—both in the same bed. Whaddaya think?"

"She could have fallen in the pool. She could have met some creep in the living room. She may have had company. Who knows?" Ozzie said, leading Malone to the hall runner. "Martin and Veronica had a daughter—she live here now?"

"I hope not. Peace Corps—digging ditches in the jungle."

Malone had pushed into the guest room, standing there on the Persian, his MityLite against his leg. Ozzie saw the carnations and roses, wilted and brown on the desk. Malone looked under the bed, heaved off the quilt, examined its sheets, the pillows, and found Veronica Hammond's towel stuffed between the mattress and the headboard.

"This towel's damp," Malone said. "Stinks."

Ozzie scattered the desk-drawer contents, and murmured to himself when he found greeting cards, all signed by someone who called himself "A Secret Admirer," and a collection of florist envelopes . . . she'd had dozens of deliveries. And as he picked out each tiny card, Ozzie found the same initial written in different hands: "R."

"Uh-oh," Malone said softly.

"Hang on a second, Wilson—I've got something here."

"There's blood on this thing"—Malone's voice cracked—"there's a lot of blood."

Most of the towel had been drenched in dark blood. Malone held the thing away from himself. "Some on the sheet under the pillow—some on the wall. Oh jeez, Oz."

"Put it back," Ozzie said, poking the towel with his flashlight. "Just as you found it."

"This isn't at all attractive," Malone said, doing as he was told.

"Some guy named 'R' sent her a lot of flowers," Ozzie said.

Malone thrust a sheet of paper at Ozzie. "He also sent her a letter."

"Bank stationery, Wilson. Veronica worked there."

"Read it, for pity's sake—I know she worked there."

"Where was it?"

"Under the quilt—I thought the police searched dead people's houses?"

"This is stupid," Ozzie said, reading.

"Get to the end."

" 'I can't let you do this to me. Their after me. If I can't have you, no one can. I won't let you ruin me. You can't threaten me like you do. I am a passionate man. Richie.' " Ozzie shook his head. "Wilson, this is terrible."

"Guy's illiterate."

"Five days ago. Someone named Richie is illiterate—Wilson, she was Richie DeSilva's secretary at the bank."

"She did more than type, Oz."

"Richie DeSilva's a jogging fool. Wilson, my Uncle Barry said a jogger came to visit her often. And the guy hiding in her yard only stood as high as Uncle Barry's chest—Richie DeSilva is a little guy."

"Must've worn his rubbers with Veronica, don't you think?" Malone said, taking the letter and folding it into his raincoat. "Oz, I think this is where it happened."

"And these?" Ozzie said.

Malone took the greeting cards.

"Veronica Hammond had a secret admirer, Wilson."

"My, my, my."

⚓ ⚓ ⚓

"Give me your flashlight."

"Oz, for Pete's sake, this is brand-new!"

"I'll buy you another one."

"You'll get sick and die. Look at all the crap down there. Thing could be full of AIDS." Malone was leaning over the

98

pool's edge. "This is dumb. Every disease known to the Surgeon General must be in here."

"Wilson! Give me the light!"

"The cops must have searched the pool."

Ozzie looked up at Malone, the water around Ozzie's waist. He held out his hand.

"Oz, you can't see shit in this rain. Let's try again tomorrow."

Ozzie didn't move his hand.

They had searched her house, poked through her laundry-chute pile of clothes in the cellar, found pizza growing new life forms in the kitchen. Ozzie had copied out names and numbers from her address book. And they'd searched the Riviera that someone had left in the garage with her keys on its dashboard.

They hadn't heard Rocket pass for over an hour.

"Give me the light, Wilson."

Ozzie went under gingerly, gasping with the rush of green water around his chest and face. Malone watched, muttered, "Flipper!" Ozzie went along the bottom, keeping the MityLite near the cement, searching through the winter's detritus of leaves and muck, trying so hard to keep his vision long so that he might see anything dropped in here, thrown in here. He surfaced many times, each time looking for the exhausted Malone, who stood in the rain, a puzzled man.

Ozzie came up out of the pool, pressing his treasure against his chest.

"Dumb, huh?" he said to Malone, holding his hand up.

"A paintbrush, Oz." Malone had his pipe billowing clouds.

"Strange?" Ozzie said.

"Oh, very strange—it's a sash brush."

"How does a paintbrush get into a pool?"

"Not the brush, Oz. The strange part is you think you've found something unusual. That's a paintbrush! I can think of a zillion ways to get a brush into a pool—I'll show you one way right now."

"Not so fast!"

"I'm going to flag down Rocket, Oz. You've got the bends or something. Hold this."

Malone headed across her patio, down the driveway. Ozzie opened his hand and held the ring under the MityLite, a class ring: CLASS OF 1972 NORWICH UNIVERSITY.

"Malone!" he yelled.

But Malone was gone, the night bathed in wet, the air a soaked curtain of desolation.

Rocket was asleep in his jeep in Veronica Hammond's driveway, drenched and cranky when they woke him. "He's DWI again," Malone said. They hoisted Rocket onto the rope piles in the back of the jeep.

"Wanna tell me about this?" Ozzie said, holding up the ring as he started the jeep.

"I don't think so," Malone said.

Waking Up

OZZIE had been home for a long time before he saw his Uncle Barry's hat on the floor in the old man's room. Uncle Barry's satchel was open on the bed. The violin case had been left unlocked, the rosin block loose within. Someone had been in this house.

His own bedroom had been rummaged through. The telephone in the downstairs hall had been returned to the desk; someone had absently picked the thing up and as absently wrapped its cord around its neck.

I'll be damned, he thought, twisting through his rooms, now seeing the signs that someone had been in every room, opening cabinets, leaving books not sitting square in their dustless rectangles, his cigar box opened, and his pistol with its magazine left beside it in the kitchen broom closet, as though someone were teaching him proper gun handling.

Ozzie felt hunted. He looked quickly at the cellar door, couldn't resist, and went down amid the cracked canoe paddles, his racks of moth-cratered Wall Street suits and neckties, and the boxes of junk, all of them moved, opened, and bearing signs that they'd been searched.

Not good, he thought. Not good at all. Why would the police, if it was the police . . . why would they paw through everything he owned?

"I'll tell you what," Mildred said as she leaned over his sandwich. She had just clicked the lock shut on Ozzie's goatskin briefcase, the briefcase Louise had given him for their last New York Christmas. "If you take all this stuff you found in her house to the cops, they'll arrest you. Goin' into someone's house is a crime, Oz. Your family doesn't think so—but the rest of us do."

"They might. But Uncle Barry is the wrong man. These things would at least give them another name to think about. They just didn't look."

"They'd like to hear that, honey. They love being told they've screwed up again—you'd think they'd get used to it by now."

"But they couldn't have looked at all, Mildred. The letter was under a pillow. The ring was in the ashtray on her picnic table. The florist cards were in her guest-room desk."

"Oz—lots of people get flowers."

"From 'R'?"

"From 'Qs' and 'Ps' and 'Ds,' for chrissake. And people do get cards in the mail." Mildred was exasperated. At this late hour, her business had subsided to the few straggling men needing that last double-pull of whiskey for the night and the odd, sometimes very odd, mismatched couples who sat rubbing each other furtively. "Go to Tagliano, if you want, but I think you're slitting your own throat."

"Mail copies to him anonymously?"

"Sure—but if they found out it was you licking the stamps, they'd be on you like a blanket. You want your Uncle Barry out. They want him in. Drink your coffee, honey. I've got to close down the kitchen."

"But why would they search my house?"

"Your uncle was living there. Seems natural to me."

"Maybe," he said.

"Everything in this bag says ol' Veronica had an active

life. Nothing in here says your Uncle Barry didn't kill her. Oz, they found the guy with her body."

"They did,"he said. "And never looked back."

"You don't even know how she died."

"Lily says Veronica was hit by an aluminum softball bat."

"Have you seen it?"

"No."

"There must be a coroner's report—fingerprints? Oz, you're on the outside lookin' in."

"In more ways than one," he said. Ruby's curtains, he thought. Life with Louise had been a parched trek across marriageland. Ozzie had concentrated on business, then concentrated on the *Lucia*. At no point had he concentrated on Louise. Didn't want to, after a few years. But now, like some goofy teenager, he'd been smitten by a powder-blue mechanic. All from a distance, all safe, but smitten nonetheless.

"Drink your coffee and go home," Mildred said. "It's getting late."

It is, he thought. Forty-seven is late for a lot of things, including powder-blue mechanics. Late for a man to decide he'd never had much he cared about, never had much to lose. More frozen than free.

⚓ ⚓ ⚓

O'Donnell's Funeral Home, owned by a churlish Irish family, was a painfully frail remonstrance to grief. Somewhere in the transplanted Celtic mind an arrogance of style and composure had bubbled up in the O'Donnells that forbade any emotional expression other than the means they'd blearily fastened onto somehow, so that they insisted their patrons follow the O'Donnell Standard Course in dealing with the remains of a life. The O'Donnells claimed to be certified Grief Counselors and discouraged wailing. Their white house was empty of any warmth, its shrubs and green awning an invitation to sterility, the O'Donnells themselves

hulking presentiments of mortality wherein all deathly matters were handled with calculated dourness. Corpses, flowers, shattered spouses, bemused children, the coffins . . . all
were interchangeable. O'Donnell's Funeral Home was a lug-
gage carousel of constantly conveyed lives.

The parking lot was jammed as Ozzie walked between the
cars with Malone. "I want to see her, Wilson. And I want to
see who's here. It's that simple. Wait in the car, if you like."

"We've all seen her, Oz. She sat in that bank like the queen
of finance. Damn rude, she was, too. What if it's a closed
casket?"

Ozzie stopped, looked at Malone.

"Okay," Malone said. "I hate funerals and wakes. Keep
seeing myself asleep on silken pillows. Where'd you get that
suit?"

"Like it?"

"Hate it."

"Stay out here."

"You're lawyer's right, Oz. You're gonna get yourself into
big trouble."

"I'm not kiddin', Wilson."

"Tasteless, I think, for the bad guy's nephew to drop in
for the wake, don't you?"

They went into O'Donnell's, in beyond the coat racks and
the framed landscape of an Emerald Isle crofter's cottage,
to the loitering O'Donnell son who pointed for them to turn
left into a babble of mourners. Ozzie tugged at his necktie
as he moved along the chapel wall, excusing himself through
knots of women, waiting finally behind three men standing
in front of her open casket. Everyone was subdued, uneasy,
chatting softly. Ozzie and Louise saw each other across the
room. Louise's face registered nothing, not a single synaptic
jolt of remembrance or concern.

Women are peculiar, he thought, stepping up to the casket. Veronica Hammond was bathed in a pink light, her

attitude composed, cheeks pale and powdered, lips too evenly drawn with rose lipstick, her eyelids brushed with purple. Veronica Hammond had been a beautiful woman. But now she was missing a harried urgency Ozzie had seen so often. Ozzie knelt as if in prayer, the better to see the base of her skull.

Ozzie wished he could reverse everything, let the woman live. He'd like to see what she saw last. There was one person on this earth who was the last to see this woman alive. Who was it?

Malone had stopped at the doors, looking a bit now as though he'd been crushed by death himself, grinning at people, clutching his hat.

A couple waiting behind Ozzie with their weeping teenage daughter became frightened that this man had leaned into the casket near enough to kiss the deceased.

The husband said, "That's enough of that."

Ozzie flinched when the man's hand gripped his shoulder, he jerked backwards, neatly crushing the child's sneakered instep. The daughter screamed.

"Sorry—sorry," Ozzie mumbled as he fled.

A woman sitting in the chairs wailed suddenly as Ozzie passed her row. A short, stocky being, like a black rolled sleeping bag, had collapsed in grief on her husband's shoulder, clutching her hanky and purse to her face. Ozzie recognized the man as Sheldon Boynton from the bank.

Poor thing, he thought, stepping around the mourners at the back until Richie DeSilva grabbed Ozzie's lapel.

DeSilva nodded angrily toward the doors and pushed Ozzie.

Ozzie turned to the man, tripping into the Beamans and their two freakily tall sons, who had small heads like gourds.

Ozzie swatted DeSilva's hand away. The bank president greeted the Beamans, momentarily regaining his Rotarian balance in the face of old, old money.

The Beamans went on.

DeSilva looked into Ozzie's eyes. "You haven't got the brains of a maggot." DeSilva's jaw was gripped tight.

Ozzie started to say something, but knew any discussion with this reptile would only lead to nastiness.

"How could you show up here? You and your retard uncle are completely stupid!"

Ozzie tried to move around DeSilva, who bobbed after him like a Lakers guard. Ozzie said, "I came to see her, Richie. I knew her."

"Came to apologize to her brother for what your uncle did to her?"

What brother? Ozzie wondered, and then said, "My uncle didn't do anything to her—other than try to save her."

DeSilva gripped Ozzie's coat and tugged Ozzie, bumped into coat racks, and then Ozzie let himself be hurled outside. O'Donnell's awning took the rain like a drumhead. Ozzie could barely hear the infuriated DeSilva.

The bank president may have been a slight man, but he'd learned early how to intimidate people by arching his shoulders and neck, standing up on his toes to shout into faces he didn't like. And he didn't like most faces.

Mourners went in and mourners came out. All curious, all displaying their distaste for what they were witnessing.

"I didn't know she had a brother," Ozzie said. He turned away.

"I'm calling in your loans, Barrett!"

Ozzie turned back to him. "Unlike everyone else around here, I don't have loans with you."

DeSilva's face reddened. "You won't ever get 'em, either."

"I wouldn't ask," Ozzie said.

DeSilva pursued Ozzie out into the rain, leaping to stop him. "That retard killed her and you have the gall to show up at her wake!"

"Leave it alone," Ozzie said.

"I never could stand you—you and your half-assed fishing boat. You're a loser, Barrett!"

Ozzie tried to step around him.

DeSilva shouted, "I'll get you—I'll get your house—I'll get your boat! Your wife at least had the brains to leave you."

"Skip it," Ozzie said, his hand on DeSilva's wrist, holding the man away from him. He was certain DeSilva would take a swing at him.

"Your ass is grass and I'm the lawn mower!" DeSilva screamed.

"What?" Ozzie said.

Malone's hand closed over DeSilva's arm like a terrible medieval omen. Slowly, and with deliberate strength, Malone brought the man's arm up, DeSilva's hand releasing Ozzie's coat, stretched DeSilva's rain-soaked suit up, until the towering Malone held DeSilva up on the points of his bank president's tasseled loafers.

DeSilva couldn't figure it all out. He searched Malone's face for recognition, comfort, anything. "We're talking," he said to Malone. "We're talking, pal."

"Don't talk to him anymore," Malone said.

"I'm talking with this guy—I know who you are! At the college!"

"Then talk to me," Malone said.

Ozzie said, "Leave him alone, Wilson."

Malone inched DeSilva up one more notch. "Where'd you go to college?" Malone said. "Let's talk."

"You're crazy—you're all nuts! I'll have you arrested."

"Put him down, Wilson," Ozzie said.

"What college?" Malone said softly. "I'm an educator— I'm interested."

"Are you with him?" DeSilva said, jabbing his head toward Ozzie.

"Name the school," Malone said.

Ozzie saw men watching from beneath O'Donnell's awning. Louise stood behind the men.

"Norwich," DeSilva said.

"Class of what?" Malone said. "Seventy? Seventy-four?"

"Seventy-two."

Two men were moving toward them. Ozzie tapped his friend. "Drop him, Wilson—the Irish drunks are here."

Malone turned himself and DeSilva to face the approaching figures, one of them an O'Donnell son, the other from the bank. Malone spoke up, his eyes intent: "Richie here wants you boys to know about Veronica Hammond," he said. He hiked DeSilva up another notch. "He left his class ring at her house. He sent her tons of flowers. Wrote her letters. Sent her cards—did everything he could to make a widow happy. Isn't that right, Richie?"

"Put him down," the O'Donnell kid said.

"He is down—check his feet," Malone said. "You're not wearing your rubbers, Richie. Shame on you." And to the men: "Obviously grief-stricken over his honey's death, our Mr. DeSilva here is having a tough time with all this."

DeSilva shouted, pointed to Ozzie: "This bum's uncle is the guy who killed Veronica! There!" he said strangely.

"There what?" Malone inquired.

"Put him down, Wilson," Ozzie said. "That's enough."

Malone handed the bank president to the two men, saying, "Take him inside—take him home. Do something with him."

As soon as DeSilva felt Malone relax, the bank president threw a punch and missed. The O'Donnell kid pulled DeSilva away.

Malone said, "You should carry a ladder with you, Richie. Take care of the little fella," he said gently to the men holding DeSilva. "He's quite lost without her."

Past-Due Accounts

"**H**E didn't say how large," Ozzie said to the Rockport florist. "He said you'd know what to do. Creams, pinks—daisies, if you have them."

"I do," the woman said, jotting down details on a filthy pad. "I have to add our standard extra delivery charge for distance—but he knows that, doesn't he?"

"Whatever you usually do is fine," Ozzie said.

The woman was stocky, her purple pants stretched across her bottom. She seemed to take him in stride. "This afternoon—late? That suit Mr. DeSilva?"

"Fine," Ozzie said.

"Do you work for Mr. DeSilva?"

"No, I don't," he said. "I drove over for engine parts."

"Awfully good of you to stop for him. He always telephones. He likes my arrangements. Such a kind man. My boy is in college, so I'll have him deliver this after he gets home from classes. Eighty-two Bull Run?"

"Same address," Ozzie said. He raised his eyebrows. "Mr. DeSilva hoped you could charge it?"

"On his bill. Did Miss Hammond enjoy the carnations, do you know?"

"Very much," he said, remembering the floral tribute withering in that bloody guest room.

"D'you know if Mr. DeSilva bought the hotel in Marble-head?" she said.

What hotel? he thought. "Which one?" he said.

She seemed surprised; she stopped writing. "Well, the new Hyatt," she said, pausing. "Does he have more than one?"

"Four in all," Ozzie said. He had no idea what the woman was talking about.

"Goodness. Mr. DeSilva had in mind to lease me space for my new shop in his Hyatt. Four hotels? The man is a wheeler-dealer, isn't he? I'd love to be in his new shopping esplanade at the Hyatt. Have you seen the architect's paintings?"

"Something, aren't they?" Ozzie said.

"I'll say. I'd give anything to be next to the Banana Republic. Mr. DeSilva said he thought I was a natural. This isn't much," she said, raising her eyes to a bloated frog planter suspended on wires.

"I think you'd make a bundle in the Hyatt."

She beamed and spanked her order pad. "I do, too."

Her shop was one of the dirtiest he'd been in. Tacky ribbons, tacky ceramic duck families, tacky raccoon planters, and machine-perfect herbal wreaths, all shrouded in a delicate scent of burned margarine.

Ozzie left feeling tacky himself. He had managed to get through his life without fraud, without the greedful glad-handing that brokers based their commissions on. He hadn't traded inside tips for a new pool, and was in many ways the misfit in the steel-and-glass corporation that perpetuated the American business modus vivendi of chicanery and stealth by allowing its traders their heads in exchange for deniability, as they openly called it.

Certainly not a mission for Ozzie Barrett, but having an ethical compass at all had cast him into the corporate depths of the marginally unattractive and not with the spitfires in their red braces and tortoise-shell visions of big money, big seats at the Patriots games in Foxboro with big names doing big deals. Benson Benson MacGregor & Ayers were relieved to see him finally leave. Not hungry enough, his office partner from Wharton had said.

But now, even the simple task of hoodwinking a florist by tweaking her greed button gave him the creeps. Richie DeSilva must operate in quite another way, Ozzie thought. And his own revulsion for that man was exceeded only by the remembrance of a quaking old man in a state-hospital solarium.

The *Lucia* was clean. Impossible to lie. The boat either brought back fish or it didn't. Fog was fog. Fishing was straightforward. The solitary man adrift over Georges Bank was not the investment world's notion of anything close to a sure bet.

If Richie DeSilva were sending flowers to his secretary only to help her accommodate her husband's death, he very likely would not use a florist eighteen miles distant and far enough away so that the florist hadn't known Veronica was now dead.

$$\text{\textit{\textperthousand}} \quad \text{\textit{\textperthousand}} \quad \text{\textit{\textperthousand}}$$

He drove back to Strike's Landing sipping on a vanilla frappe in Rocket's jeep, the salt musk in the marshes as he sped over them a reminder that his money wouldn't last much longer. He needed to fish.

Lily was late back from court, late pounding into her office and dropping bags, books, foolscap pads, and shoes in a heap on her rug. "Ah, Mr. Congeniality—don't get up," she said to him. He was slumped in her couch, nearly asleep, having been left in her office by a receptionist who typed in unison to reggae in her headphones. "Want a cigarette?" Lily said, offering Ozzie a Pall Mall. "God, I hate this job," she said. "I just had a client lie about everything but his name. Not a word he said was true. The judge will destroy him." She pushed at her hair.

Ozzie lighted her smoke before his own.

She flopped into the couch next to him, placing an ashtray between them. "My kids are killing me," she said. The lawyer put her feet up on her table. "I'm going to South Carolina for a legal institute in plea bargaining—I'm not coming back! Tagliano's not happy with you. What's the deal with the bank president—what's his name?"

Ozzie told her.

"The slimy guy with the blown-dry brains? Yes?"

Ozzie said yes.

"His wife is the blond bitch on the school board?"

Ozzie nodded.

"They deserve each other. Well—you've got a state's attorney truly pissed at you." Lily glanced his way, got nothing, and went on: "He says you assaulted the bank president— says you're out of bounds. How did you know about the ring?"

"I found it at Veronica Hammond's."

"Isn't that cozy? You aren't supposed to be at Veronica Hammond's. Notice how I never ask for details. DeSilva says you stole the ring."

"That's drivel."

"Oh, you'll laugh, my boy. Tagliano will eat you for breakfast. The police may be cretins, but they don't like civilians doing their job for them. In fact, if I thought you might listen to me, I'd tell you to cut it out. DeSilva's yapping about some letters."

"I found one letter—some cards."

"I'll bet. I'll say this only once: You mess with these piranhas and you'll spend some time in court, Ozzie. But— you don't listen to counsel. Tagliano could charge you with being an accessory to murder. At the least, he could arrange for you to pay me mucho bucks in fees. He could grand-jury you, he could have you arrested. The man can make your miserable life even more hideous. Got it?"

"I'll talk to him," Ozzie said.

"No, you won't talk to him."

"What about my house?"

"Ah," she said, letting her head sink against the couch. "Problem number thirty-six on your agenda. Louise wants half the house—you either pay her off or sell the house and she takes half. She's filed the divorce papers."

"How soon?"

"Not soon enough for her. The house has to be appraised first. We'll do an agreement, then we'll fight it out—you take the forks, she takes the piano."

"How long for the divorce?"

"A year, probably. But you'll be in jail by then."

"DeSilva and Veronica Hammond were sweeties."

"Were they?"

"He stopped at her house when he went out jogging. His letter to Veronica sounds as though she was going to dump him. Letter sounds nuts, actually. Frantic. His ring was there. He sent her flowers from Rockport where no one knew her—cards. And the bathing suit doesn't make sense—her pool is filthy. She wouldn't swim in it. And there's nowhere else she'd be swimming at this time of the year at night."

"The state college has a pool," she said.

"Where was the softball bat?"

"In the house," Lily said. "The state labs found her tissue, her hair and blood on its sweet spot."

"Where in the house?"

"Not sure," she said. "Near the front door, I think."

"And the rubbers?"

"Man's a pig to leave used rubbers around."

"No—feet! Uncle Barry says he kicked rubbers when he went into her house to call the ambulance. The rubbers were gone when the police took him inside later."

"So?"

"So, someone got rid of the rubbers. And Uncle Barry knows there was a Peeping Tom in her yard who wore rubbers."

"Did that guy have his wonker hangin' out?"

113

"She was thumped in her upstairs bedroom."

"How do you know that?"

"Blood."

Lily took a deep pull on her Pall Mall and said with forbearance, "You *are* going to jail."

"There's a blood-soaked towel, but there's no blood on her stairs. He wrapped her head upstairs, then carried her out to the pool and dumped her. Maybe we were supposed to think she accidentally fell and hit her head. He probably didn't know the pool guys didn't finish cleaning her pool. He chucked her into a dirty pool anyway—went back in to freshen up. What could he do?"

"I just know you'll tell me."

"She was going to dump DeSilva—crime of passion," he said. "DeSilva's a land mine."

"Oh, god," she said. "What do you read? All crimes are crimes of passion—the law's only a net we throw over the sods who can't control themselves. So, what's she doing in her bathing suit?"

"He stuffed her into the thing after he killed her," he said.

"And his softball bat?"

"He's held together with kite string—he blew. Uncle Barry surprised him. DeSilva was in the house; he saw Uncle Barry out at the pool with her, he was still there, somewhere, when Uncle Barry tripped over his rubbers."

"Joggers wear rubbers a lot, do they, Oz?"

"But there were five or ten minutes between Uncle Barry's telephone call and when the police arrived. DeSilva could have collected his rubbers and left Uncle Barry there as a happy accident. DeSilva's an opportunist. He didn't plan it this way—he couldn't shoo Uncle Barry away. He left the softball bat, forgot it. He couldn't come back for it—he heard Uncle Barry call the ambulance. Tex chased him when he ran."

"Who's Tex?"

"He's a Doberman—Uncle Barry's buddy."

"Oh, shit," she said, wiping her eyes.

"Jogging shoes leave distinctive tread marks—DeSilva wore rubbers over his jogging shoes so he'd leave a flat print. Maybe he wasn't wearing jogging shoes that night—the rubbers would quiet his penny loafers in her house."

Lily shrugged. "You have got to drop this—a rubber's treadmark is distinctive all by itself. I'll talk to Tagliano—we'll see. I want you to be a very good boy. Just drop it. No shenanigans, no finding letters and rings. And stay away from Richie DeSilva."

"He killed her," Ozzie said.

"Don't sink your boat. You're gonna need it for bail."

Ozzie swung through the bank's drive-up window to retrieve the last of his checking account. The gum-chomping teller said his account was closed and that he should see a bank officer.

Ozzie left the jeep at MacAvoy's and hurried across the street to the bank. The upright sleeping bag from Veronica Hammond's wake was standing inside the bank doors, two wretched children with her, one on a leash; the other one, in her arms, picked its nose.

Ozzie glanced quickly at DeSilva's empty desk and crossed to the only man sitting under the balcony, his green lightshade snapping dark as Ozzie got to him.

"We're closing," he said to Ozzie.

Ozzie said, "The kid at the drive-in wouldn't cash my check."

"Are you Mr. O. Barrett?"

"You know I am, Sheldon."

Sheldon Boynton hunched his trench coat over his banker's suit, busy with leaving. "The bank does not care to have you as one of its customers, Mr. Barrett."

"And my money?"

"Your account was overdrawn again. You owe us thirty-

115

eight dollars and twenty-one cents, including overdraft charges."

"How do you know the numbers? I wasn't overdrawn."

"You always are, Mr. Barrett. The bank would like to sever its business relationship with you."

The sleeping bag had come up beside Ozzie with her coughing tadpoles. Smiling, she nodded to Ozzie, obviously there to assist her husband.

Boynton said, "We'd like cash, Mr. Barrett."

Ozzie took out two twenties and handed them to the balding Boynton.

"I can't, not now," Boynton said. "Our drawers are closed."

"Not the drive-up window," Ozzie said. "I was there ten seconds ago. I'll wait."

"Bring it in tomorrow, Mr. Barrett. The drive-up window is a separate system."

"Now or never, Sheldon," Ozzie said.

The woman spun the leashed child around in his sneakers by twisting his blond head. Ah, the perils of having a banker husband.

"You look divine, Darla," Ozzie said to her. He remembered the bloated frog in the flower shop.

Boynton had stalked off for Ozzie's change.

She sniffed, bounced the other drooling child on her hip, and looked away from him for her husband.

"Love the leash," he said.

"He's hyperkinetic," she said. The woman was as ugly as ugly gets without trying: a rush of mustache on her upper lip, her chest as though she carried yet another child in there with her, and snugly curly hair. A thick odor of rotting lilacs about her. "We're on our way to a parent-teacher conference for Shellie."

"Are we?" Ozzie asked.

"He's gifted," she said, spinning the tyke once more for

116

emphasis. "We have reports that he's making his letters backwards—don't we, young man?"

"I wouldn't worry about it," Ozzie said. "First grade should fix that."

"Second grade! And I'm not worried about it at all. Shellie must be developing in unusual ways we don't understand and his teacher needs guidance at this point in time. We'll talk."

"I wish I could be there," Ozzie said. "He looks gifted."

She brought out two crayon drawings for Ozzie to see, but Boynton returned too quickly, left Ozzie's change on the receptionist's desk near the front door, and came over the carpet, the proud but indignant pop reclaiming his family.

"We're late, Sheldon," she said.

And off they went, the leash suspended between the two adults as Boynton carried his active son. Ozzie watched them go, riveted on the tiny moon face in the lace hat over the woman's shoulder, a yellow Happy Face without a mouth, a nonchalant vacancy already in place.

Ruby came around Mildred's bar like a pre-Raphaelite princess in a motorcycle jacket dotted with sequins, and turquoise and silver rivets.

"If you sit with me, I'll buy you supper," Ozzie said.

"Lucky you," she said, pausing at his shoulder. No one else was sitting on this side of the bar. "Your engine's all set, but I need to go out with you for a little while. The transmission oil smells roasted but looks fine. D'you ever have trouble shifting?"

Ozzie patted the captain's-chair pad.

The woman smelled like juniper berries and beach plums. She sat down next to him. "I need food," she said. "Big slab of swordfish will do. You don't look so hot."

"I'm not," he said.

"Rocket said you can keep the jeep. Said he never expects to see it back, anyway. The police searched your boat this morning while I was torqueing down the head. They had a warrant. They didn't take anything. I tried to call you—you're disconnected."

"I've gotta fish tomorrow. I'm broke," he said, feeling the weight drop on his shoulders.

"Not until we check the transmission. I listened to your opera while I worked on her. You like that stuff—those fat ladies stabbing themselves?"

"Can't live without it," he said.

"Opera's kinda screwy. Could you ever fall in love with a four-hundred-pound porker with horns on her head?"

"A leap of faith," he said. "It's not what you see."

Mildred nearly fell off her braces when she passed them and overheard Ruby say, "When's the last time you fell in love?"

Ozzie dove for his chowdery clam-clumps. "Long time," he said.

"I'll bet never."

Mildred waited, then nodded when Ruby ordered swordfish and salad.

Ozzie said, "You're wrong."

"I doubt it," Ruby said.

"Select one of the last nine times you fell in love—let's hear about that one," he said.

"Cruelty will get you everywhere," she said. "Hard to pick one. Last nine times?" She shook off her jacket, rolled up her sleeves. She wore cotton long underwear beneath a denim work shirt. "There was this navy pilot in Long Beach—used to take me to smokers in the officers' club. He had a sweet touch on the throttles, sweet touch."

Mildred dropped Ruby's beer and clomped around her bar.

"I love your muscles," he said.

"But he started flying cocaine out of Honduras in navy planes. Hell, I thought he was the Lone Ranger until I saw the stuff. I heard later he was taking money on the side from a nasty bunch of cheated Texans who'd bought phony Van Goghs from a German in Mexico who had an assembly line of Mexican spray-painters in a bakery. They wanted my pilot to find the guy. He did. Texans lost their shirts. Ever notice how people who've had money spilled into their laps are scared shitless someone's gonna take it away? They don't do a thing to earn the bucks, and can't imagine how they'd earn it if they lost it. People are awful scared, don't you think?"

"They have reason to be. What happened to the pilot?"

Ruby lowered her beer. "I dunno. Did you love your wife?"

"I thought I did," he said, squirming. "In the beginning. I just made it up as I went along."

"Love bites."

"Does it?"

"I'll show you my scars sometime."

Ruby's fingernails were shiny pink and perfectly shaped, her small hands quick and lightly dark with the sun. He wondered how she could tear diesels apart and yet have hands that said she did nothing of the kind. Ozzie found himself studying her cheek, the light fuzz in front of her ear. Her earrings were silvery wafers on chains.

Mildred brought the swordfish; Ozzie went after more cornbread and chowder, helping himself in the kitchen, and walked back to Ruby, balancing his eats, feeling as though he'd just surfaced after kicking out the windows in a submerged car.

She turned to him when he sat down, and said, swordfish in her mouth, "Rocket says your uncle will never get out. That true?"

Ozzie stacked his cornbread cubes. The chowder steamed into his face. "Could be," he said. "He didn't kill the woman, but that doesn't mean anything." As soon as he said it, Ozzie felt himself slide under the ripples again. He spooned a bit of chowder, then stopped.

"Was her head crushed?" Ruby said, chewing.

Ozzie nodded. The harbor was dark and Mildred's was all there was of this world. "I guess so."

"Poor thing," she said. "Husband's dead, and she dies alone with some asshole bashing her over the head—in her own house. Creepy, isn't it? Who did it?"

"I don't know," he said. "It's getting creepier." The water was sliding cold for miles over his head, his lungs pulling for air.

"Where'd you go with my father the other night?"

"Bowling," he said.

She paused, her fork held in midair. "What happened to you—I mean just now?"

"That old man in his nuthouse room."

"Eat," she said. "We've both got our old guys." She looked away to call Mildred for another beer. But the polio queen had long been on the prowl and rested now, one hand on her quasi-paralytic hip, as she watched them from her cash register, surrounded by hundreds of shiny liquor bottles. "Hold it, babe," Ruby said to her.

Mildred stalked along the bar.

Ozzie raised his eyes, once more surprised that women did these things without warning.

"Don't you hurt one hair—not one hair—on this man's head!"

"I wouldn't," Ruby said. "Christ, Mildred."

"Yes, you would."

"Is he yours?" Ruby said. She put her fork down.

"He's not yours. Where's Malone?" she said to Ozzie.

"Tutoring," he said.

What Iceberg?

Ozzie cast off his lines just before midnight. Ruby had the *Lucia* reversed against its rudder, swinging the bow out as Ozzie leapt off the wharf ladder onto his deck.

"You're sort of a mess, aren't you?" she said when he came into the wheelhouse. She snapped the toggles for his running lights, threw the wheel hard over, and buried the throttle. Ozzie felt the trawler dig in under him and come hard to port. Ruby clicked off the wheelhouse lights.

"A little peaky, lately," he said. He smelled rain on the breeze, the harbor a fallow pool of spangled, ricocheting lights from the waterfront as she pushed the *Lucia* into the channel and signaled the harbormaster they were leaving. Ruby switched on Ozzie's radio, dialing for the emergency Channel Sixteen, then turned down the volume to a hush.

"Why don't you ever use your radio?" she said.

"Don't need it."

"How do you find the fish? Let them come to you—like everything else?"

"They love opera."

"Doesn't anyone ever need to get you when you're out?"

"I'm disconnected," he said.

"You are that." She let the *Lucia* clear the harbor, then

brought the bow over and pushed the trawler out of the narrows into a beam sea.

Ozzie let *Norma* take them away from shore, the music plucking them away from confused old men and dead women in pools, far away from the mud-sucking madness to the black solvency of the sea. Ruby handled the boat better than he did; she was less compulsive, less anxious than he, more willing to allow the beast to swim on its own.

She took them far out, then went below after shutting down the engine. The trawler humped along on the swells.

"Start it!" she yelled up to him.

Ozzie was eager to please.

"Now—take it up a bit, then shift into neutral, reverse, back to neutral, then forward."

He did.

"Stop!" She came up the ladder, wiping her hands on one of his shirts. "I think you're okay, but you've got a clunky reverse."

"Always been there," he said. He shut off the engine. "I need to fish tomorrow."

She took his bottle of Lux dish soap aft, where she tossed his water bucket over the stern and pulled it dripping onto the deck. Ozzie waited for her, sitting on his winch housing, the night heavy with impending weather.

"Pretty night," she said, washing her hands.

When she passed him, Ozzie reached out for her shirt. He reeled her in, she let herself be moved without any fuss, and he kissed her . . . once for luck and possibly never again, but harder when she leaned into him with her face up to his. Ruby didn't feel like Louise, not a sinew felt the same. Smaller hips. A waist. And calm. She felt solid in his arms.

She pulled away, thought better of it, and returned to him, offering him her neck. "You're hungry," she said.

Ozzie guessed they'd come out forty-five nautical miles, give or take a few miles on a beam sea with five-foot waves. He toggled on his masthead fishing lights, his green over white. With the engine shut down, the *Lucia* dipped gently, a silent tub drifting over seamy depths where goggle-eyed beings chomped and flew at each other. Ruby stayed on the port rail near the wheelhouse, searching the blackness for other fishermen's lights.

"Does the dark ever bother you when you're out here?" she said.

He was in the wheelhouse doorway. There were no shipping lanes nearby, but April was itself near enough to summer for the yachts to be streaming back up the coast from the tropics. And they might be out here like white sharks with the sea in their teeth. "Wind's coming up," he said. "Dark side of the moon, isn't it?"

"Radar would help," she said.

Ozzie shrugged.

"It's always the one you don't see that gets you."

"Is it?" he said. The Bellini had started again. Ozzie slid the canvas bag off the wheelhouse. He carried the bag forward to the hatch cover, with Ruby chattering as he found the bag's release assembly. The raft hissed with compressed air, tearing at its Velcro closures, exploding on the hatch cover, its roof filling more slowly, crackling round like a giant balloon.

Ruby laughed out loud, hiding her face from him, as he dashed into the wheelhouse for his coats and the blanket. Ozzie lashed the raft to the hatch cover, tossed its fly out of the way, and dove in, Ruby standing behind him expectantly, Bellini being swept off by the wind.

"Care to explain what you're doing?" she said, as he reached out of the raft for his coats.

Ozzie got the emergency light on inside the survival raft, his coats soft under his knees.

He got out. "After you," he said.

She came over to him, resting her hip into him as she bent to see inside the raft. "It's like a huge magic pumpkin," she said.

He slowly turned, making certain there were no other lights around them, holding her near, as she watched with him.

"No one here but us," she said, with a trace of uneasiness in her voice. "You're a very thoughtful man," she said. She pushed again on the raft's roof.

"Not exactly first class," he said, as he checked his masthead again. "This is a fishy boat."

The raft was a sheltered cocoon away from the wind, warm with its sides taut and snug. He began with her shirt buttons, her hair in his mouth as he kissed each button loose, using his teeth to nibble open her zippered jeans.

She said, "I've been watching you."

"And I you."

"Did you know I was?" She heard the waves slosh against the hull, the Bellini far away.

"Sometimes," he said. "Did you know I was watching you?"

"I wanted you to," she said, arching her back when he kissed her tummy. "Love-bites," she said.

"Does it?"

She murmured something, but then stopped as he lifted her cotton shirt up over her breasts. She kissed his hands, his shoulder and hair, as Ozzie tasted her skin, his tongue flicking her nipples hard.

She lay before him in the red light, her skin like cool stone, her breath flavored with the small cigars she smoked. He told her she smelled good, kissing the backs of her legs and knees, finding her breasts with his fingertips.

She didn't realize he'd stopped. And then: "What's the matter?" she said, curling around to see him kneeling there, reaching her hand for his leg. "What are you doing?"

"Memorizing you."

"Are you?" she said, rolling onto her back, her left hand

brushing against the raft wall lazily. "Aw, shucks," she whispered, offering him her breasts as she lay there, her feet pushing into the coats.

Ozzie watched her.

Ruby opened her legs slowly, sliding her hands up her thighs to open her dark-golden fur, waiting for him.

Ozzie knew he could stay here forever inside this bright orange pumpkin adrift on the sea. Never so wondrous as she, never so languid, so strong in her hips, never so open, so invitingly enveloping as he lay into her. She took him completely in his first push as though she could hold all that he was. She raised her legs over his hips, squeezing him into her.

The *Lucia* rocked them gently, soft in the curl of the sea, her tiny two lights like lost twin stars tucked into a far corner of the universe where no one cared that two people might find each other, no one watched while two people grew warm in each other's joy, no one gave a damn where the bright pumpkin took them.

As the boat drifted out of sight, Ruby laughed suddenly, suddenly burst into giggles and whoops.

The night and the sea were left to their own hideous silences.

Bankers' Hours

RICHIE DeSilva was on his best behavior when the First Seaman's Bank opened this morning. His desk faced the lobby. No walls, no glass, nothing to inhibit his hands-on approach as he sat there with *fire in his belly*. Richie DeSilva was enraptured with his fire in his belly and said so often when he got off to the bankers' confabs in Boston, last year with the unpopular Babs to Puerto Rico . . . Babs had stroked across the pool to the French bartender under the straw kiosk on the first day and remained with him, topless until the end, her personality tinged by gallons of planter's punch. DeSilva liked to wave to customers while they stood at tellers' windows, more casually nodding his head to his favorites, stunningly ignoring the deadbeats and people he couldn't use.

His coffee this morning was in a Styrofoam cup because Veronica Hammond was not here before him to brew his Nigerian mocha in the staff coatroom. He'd chatted in the bagel shop until ten and then wandered down to the bank in time to see Ed Zalinsky waiting for him in one of the four chairs DeSilva rearranged around his desk every business day.

Zalinsky was a dentist gone foul of the law. Badly foul. Zalinsky was dangerous and illegally over his enormous head in insurance fraud, phony holding companies, stock and land manipulations, and marketing prescription drugs to his favorite patients, none of whom had Zalinsky work in their mouths because Zalinsky was a rank sadist. Zalinsky had been investigated and exonerated four times by the state dental board for improper billing procedures, and, in three separate instances, for unprofessional conduct with gassed teenage girls. Zalinsky frightened Richie DeSilva, but not enough to discourage a man with fire in his belly. Besides, DeSilva and Zalinsky and another dentist from Lynn owned between them seven miles of North Shore seashore. Zalinsky knew how to make money. Richie DeSilva knew how to launder money.

Within minutes of the bank president's arrival, Sheldon Boynton felt the adrenaline flush into his gut when he got the famous DeSilva finger; the bank president, there for all the world to admire in his hushed domain, would simply give any loan officer, teller, janitor, or customer the well-known, come-hither wiggle of his index finger. His crooked finger of fate, as his bookkeepers called it.

Sheldon Boynton left his desk to cross the carpet, buttoning his blue suitcoat. "Yes, Mr. DeSilva?"

"Sheldon, when did I ask you to reconcile our special accounts? Week ago, wasn't it?"

Boynton knew he was not late. "I gave you my preliminary work yesterday," he said.

Zalinsky sat there like the puff adder he was.

DeSilva waved a sheet at the flustered Boynton. "You call this shit a reconciliation?"

"No," Boynton said. "I don't. I gave you that overview just to let you know where we're going."

"Not good enough, Sheldon." DeSilva glanced once at the infidel dentist and braced himself for a good time. "I want that work on my desk before you go home tonight. I want it done right. I want it complete. Understand?"

"You said two weeks, Mr. DeSilva."

"Either get it on my desk by tonight or don't bother showing up tomorrow morning. That straight?"

Boynton said, "Very straight."

Boynton knew their special accounts held money these two made for short-term gains before they moved it elsewhere, and Boynton was the only man, aside from the three thieves, who knew the bank never reported any of these hidden accounts to the IRS, each account holding bags of cash in excess of tax-statute reporting levels.

"Do it!" DeSilva said.

Boynton avoided Zalinsky's lipless smile. He dropped his head, and made his way back across the carpet, excusing himself through the customers at the windows. The man had said two weeks.

There was a kid sitting at his desk.

"Help you?" Boynton said to the kid.

"I need money for a bike," the kid said.

Boynton didn't know the kid, but the olive skin and dark eyes gave him everything he needed. "How much?" he said, sliding his chair up to his desk, patting his blotter. Darla would be annihilated if she ever knew how her *sweet* Richard DeSilva treated her husband. But what could Boynton do? They had him snagged, bound in with them as an able and conscientious conspirator for over two years in a rigged game. Any hope he had of ever pleasing Darla, and pleasing Darla was a full-time job, rested solely on Richie DeSilva's choice for the next vice-president; only then might the woman be satisfied when her husband, who was, she said, "at the bank," finally flew her to her first banking hootenanny in some distantly exotic spot like Seattle.

"What kind of bike?" Boynton said to the kid.

How the man loathed the greasy-locked little bastards, their crooked teeth and first finger joints tattooed with KILL or RAGE or FUCK.

"Eighty-four Kawasaki—I wanna buy off my friend."

Boynton thought the kid had meant bicycle, not one of those things. "How old are you?" he said.

"Seventeen," the kid said. "October, I'll be seventeen."

"Not old enough," Boynton said. He opened, then slammed his drawer to punctuate his resolve. Always helped. "Gotta be eighteen."

"My old lady'll sign for me."

"No, she won't. Where do you work?"

"Lost my job."

"Doing what?"

"Sorting bottles—Marty's Subs."

"How'd you lose your job?"

"Guy was an asshole, man."

"Wanted you to work?"

"I get my money or not?" the kid said.

"You don't."

"Hey!" the kid said. He sat up, actually rigid in the chair. "This buddy I know—he got a loan here for his truck. His old man signed."

"We cannot loan money for a used motorcycle to someone who is sixteen and unemployed."

"My buddy's sixteen!" The kid was irate now. "Don't stiff me, man."

"We cannot loan you money."

"Hey!" the kid said, his palms threateningly on Boynton's shiny desktop next to Boynton's Citibank Full-Auto Desktop Telephone Directory Darla had given him a month before his birthday because her anticipation was killing her.

"This sucks!" the kid said. He stood up and looked at the customers to be sure his voice had carried. He shook his curls.

Boynton saw DeSilva look up from his paperwork. Zalinsky hadn't moved. A customer who did not matter in any way always proved a juicy sacrifice for advancement. The more insistent they were, the better. Let those in line see

129

just how fortunate they were that the First Seaman's Bank liked them, allowed them to deposit their paychecks.

Boynton stood up. Frightened. He knew that all eyes were now on him for the inevitable plunge into animosity.

"Don't fuck with me, man," the kid yelled. "I don't need this shit!"

"Then why did you come in here?" Boynton asked.

"Hey—fuck you! This sucks!"

Boynton leaned over his desk, pleasantly, his voice securely in a whisper: "You suck, punk. You swing at me and cops will be here before you can pick your ass up off the floor."

"This sucks!" the kid yelled, backing away.

DeSilva had pushed his chair back, watching, wondering if Boynton needed help.

"Go away," Boynton said to the kid.

"This fuckin' sucks, man!"

"Go away."

And the kid did. They always did.

At the Helm

OZZIE hauled nets before dawn with his fireman's helmet on, while Ruby stayed at the *Lucia*'s wheel, responding to his whistles, leaving a straight wake behind them. She was good. She never asked questions, but used slight moments of watchfulness that Ozzie at first took for indecision; then he realized she learned very quickly. She forgot nothing. As the sea took on the steel-gray cast of morning, the *Lucia* wallowing in deeper troughs, Ruby anticipated his every direction. Ozzie stopped whistling to her when she whistled for him to swing out the boom after she idled the engine to hoist the net.

The rain came cold against the wheelhouse glass in the afternoon. Ozzie had made them salami sandwiches and coffee in the only cabin the *Lucia* had, a nest behind the wheelhouse where he kept his marker buoys, lines, refrigerator, and the survival raft, crunched now into the narrow berth. Ruby had them on a quartering course for home, the diesel pulsing like a heart.

She took from her jacket a small black box that had an antenna string, then placed the box on the binnacle. Rocket's homing device. They sipped coffee, Ruby downing the last of her sandwich, steering with her feet from Ozzie's armless dentist's chair. "I don't mind," she said, after Ozzie had shrugged off Rocket's signaling box as a needless intrusion. "He needs to know where I am—we've both got old men."

Ozzie had thought the black box was a tape recorder.

"The Coast Guard had fits when he first made the thing," she said. "He jammed their survival beacons."

Ozzie thought quickly that Uncle Barry had no idea where Ozzie was. Simply knew Ozzie was not with him in those stark rooms.

"Rocket keeps the radio in his office—the old Philco boat radio," she said. "I can't let him suffer. Not anymore."

"When did you?"

"I hated that man. He's a junk dealer—a lunatic who launches homemade fireworks off his gas dock. He showed up at my high-school prom—I was sitting there with Richie—the prom queen, no less—in walks Rocket. Had on his only suit, that ghastly green suit he bought during the Depression when he thought the Marconi company was going to hire him. Know that story?"

"Only too well," he said. His coffee was hot. The wind had suddenly come round out of the northeast. The *Lucia's* bow plowed into green foam.

"A prom queen, can you imagine?" she said. "We had dance cards and Richie signed his name for every dance. Where were you then?"

"I have no idea," Ozzie said. He wondered, but the years had gone to cracked celluloid fragments by now, scenes in another man's life, all black-and-white and stiff. "New York, I think. I can't remember."

"I was sitting at our cutesy table. My dress was even more gorgeous than I was, my hair was glued with cans of hairspray. Jimi Hendrix was my hero—and Janis. That Cabral boy with the harelip had just been killed in Vietnam. In walked Rocket, wearing the necktie I'd made for him when I was a kid—had Santa on it. I was so embarrassed. Furious with him for being there. He just wanted to watch for a few minutes, stood over by the bleachers in the dark—alone. I never went near him."

She anticipated the boat's motion, unconsciously precise and effortless on the wheel. "What a shit I was," she said. "Couldn't wait to get away from him. He came to Tufts once when I was there for my one-semester undergraduate career—his old beat-up Ford truck—said he wanted to see where I lived. God, how I hated that man."

The *Lucia* took water over her bow. Ozzie saw Ruby look up, then neatly bring the bow over to slice into the next wave.

Softly she said: "All he did was raise me by himself. My mother gave me to him when I was a baby—said I was his. I wasn't. My mother's family didn't want me. I went to see them in Florida, when I had my first leave in the navy. One of my mother's sisters—the stupid woman said my mother's baby had died when my mother died. How d'you like that?"

The rain came across the stern now, sheets of wet swirled with white foam and fish parts on the deck. The *Lucia* was heavy but waltzing with the Atlantic. Ozzie kept listening for the diesel to falter. Nearly in, he thought. North of Strike's Landing by miles, probably.

Ruby was silent for minutes, then said: "Now the old goat makes me wear a radio beacon like a tagged porpoise—the thing eats batteries and probably gives off gamma rays." She turned to see him. "I didn't have it on last night, though. He'll be out in this rain with his directional antenna. He'll know you're out, but he won't put the two of us together—we won't make sense to him."

"We don't make sense to me," he said.

The woman withdrew into silence. Ozzie fired up the Kero-sun to warm the wheelhouse, took the helm after they spotted the Newburyport water tower, and heaved the *Lucia* south into the weather.

Ruby stripped off her jeans, her red silk undies, and hung

133

them over the stove to dry. Ozzie sat in his dentist's chair, surprised that she was unzipping his pants, and more surprised when Ruby straddled his legs, kissing his face, allowing the *Lucia*'s lurch and fall to slowly ease him inside herself. "We're doing the bad thing again, aren't we?" she said, nuzzling his neck, resting her head on his shoulder. She sat on him for miles, hugging him, moaning from time to time as the *Lucia* brought them home.

"When are you going to give me back my jeep?"

"I'll buy it," Ozzie said. Rocket's wharf felt suspiciously solid under his feet. Standing on land after riding wild over the ocean gray always brought that thickening numbness to his legs, like palpable dread. Ozzie distrusted the land, and took its dirt permanence as a premonition of sliding sand closing over a man's head.

"You haven't got a plugged nickel. And I won't take fish, neither."

Ruby climbed up onto the wharf, the harbor lights a mush of rain and wind.

Rocket didn't move, intent on his daughter.

"I'm here," she said and tossed her jacket over her father's soaked shirt.

"I know you are. Now, I know you are," Rocket said.

She waggled her black box beeper at him.

"I heard you," he said. "What're you doing out with him?"

Rocket had all the heft of her bar weights, his shrunken shoulders narrower than her own, his neck scrawny, hair white. Ruby hugged him.

Rocket said, "You must've been miles out—I didn't get your signal until this afternoon."

Ozzie kicked his last line tight on the piling, the *Lucia* exhaused below him. "We got in a good load," Ozzie said. "I asked her to go out with me."

134

"Did you now?" Rocket said. And waving his arms over his head: "This look like a fuckin' spring shower to you?"

Ruby walked the old man ahead of Ozzie down the wharf, her arm across her father's shoulders. "Did you eat?" she said to him.

"How could I eat?" Ozzie heard the old man shout.

On Thin Ice

TAGLIANO swiveled his office chair and opened a desk drawer to rest his feet. "I told you there were no rubbers—Mr. Barrett, you don't seem to understand how this works."

Ozzie heard the morning rain splatter against the curved window behind him. Tagliano's office was at the top of a courthouse turret. "Someone was there that night with a videocamera—a news cameraman?" Ozzie said.

"We tape everything."

"Maybe you weren't looking for rubbers?"

"Mr. Barrett, I'll let you see the tape sometime."

"What about DeSilva's wife?"

"What about her?"

"Did you think of her?" Ozzie said. His back ached, his head ached.

"You don't get it at all, do you? You don't present the evidence—I do."

"Did she know her husband was having an affair with Veronica Hammond?"

"Goddamit, I'm not stupid. Mrs. DeSilva is clear, Mr. Barrett. Clear—got it?"

Ozzie nodded.

"Mr. DeSilva himself is clear," Tagliano said. "No forced entry. And she didn't fall and kill herself accidentally."

"Where was DeSilva?"

"In the country-club sauna."

"The blood on the towel in her guestroom—that clear, too?"

Tagliano studied Ozzie, then sighed. "What blood?"

"I understand there was blood."

"How do you understand that?"

"Sergeant Cabral. And the softball bat belongs to Richie DeSilva."

Tagliano dropped his feet to the floor and stood up. "I'm tired of you, Barrett. I can't change the fact that your uncle killed her."

"He didn't kill her," Ozzie said, standing up.

"We know all about Mr. DeSilva—he and the woman were having a relationship, Mr. Barrett. Happens too much these days—our country lacks moral direction. Some of his things were in her house."

Whose moral direction? Ozzie thought. "Where are they now? Where's the bat?"

Tagliano headed for the door. "The bat with your uncle's thumbprint?"

"Where are DeSilva's other things?"

Tagliano opened his door into the corridor. "I haven't decided what to do with you. You were at Mildred's that night—we checked."

"Did she drown?"

"Stay out of this, Barrett."

"You searched my house and boat. What are you looking for?"

"If you keep it up I'll have *you* in front of a jury."

"I'd be happy to talk to a jury."

"You don't know shit, friend."

"I know DeSilva's bat was used to kill the woman."

"Sergeant Cabral again?"

"Just heard it. I know she was going to dump DeSilva. Richie DeSilva does not get dumped by anyone. Richie dumps. I know his wife can't stand him and might have gone to Veronica's to have it out with Veronica. Richie DeSilva is the high priest of the big buck around here—I know you'd lock up an old man nobody respects before you'd believe the worst of the worst."

"You finished, Barrett?"

"I'd like to see the videotape."

"Take a hike."

"I've got time," Ozzie said.

"I want DeSilva's ring and correspondence in this office by tomorrow morning, or I'll have a warrant issued for your arrest. Do you understand me? Leave Richard DeSilva alone. Got it?"

With any luck, Ozzie thought as he walked for the stairs, Sergeant Cabral will hit the fan inside the hour. He also thought that he hadn't done well with Tagliano. The state's attorney was no amateur and Ozzie was.

Through a Glass
Darkly

"**B**UT you hate this place, Oz," Malone said as he fell out of Rocket's jeep. An April drizzle bathed the country club in mist.

"I could grow to love it."

"You've got to get a car with a roof," Malone said. He entered the cool country-club foyer, its stone floor polished and hushed. "They've never seen fishing boots in here," he said as he guided Ozzie to the bar. "Let's have lunch first."

Ozzie instantly saw Babs DeSilva, her exceedingly short bob with other women at a table near the windows, the golf course beyond in the rain, the tennis compound, a line of white golf carts under the trees.

Malone ordered their beers, greeting the bartender with an arcane and elaborate shadow-boxing ritual like a Masonic greeting, that seemed to please them both. When Malone turned for Ozzie, he saw that his friend was halfway across the room, heading for Babs.

"I'm sorry for the intrusion," Ozzie said to her as he bent

to speak into her imperfect ear. "How long have you known about your husband and Veronica Hammond?"

Babs excused herself from the lunchtime gaggle and said, "Who are you?"

Ozzie introduced himself, offering his hand. "My uncle's been arrested for her murder."

She said, "I don't know you." She looked for the waiter.

"You must know they were lovers."

"Michael?" Babs called to the waiter.

She returned to her aerobic-togged lunch gang.

"Pardon me," Ozzie said to the other women.

"Michael, call the police," said the woman sitting on the other side of the pine-cone centerpiece, this woman in purple with red stripes crosscrossed on her chest, her hair wrapped in a scarf, the yacht-club burgee on her sweater.

"This'll only take a minute," Ozzie said to them. "When did you find out they were lovers?" he said to Babs.

"Michael?" she cried. "Michael, right now, please!"

Ozzie saw her fingers shake as she lowered her fork.

"It's that dreadful man from the college," another woman said as Malone stepped up behind Ozzie, taking Ozzie's sleeve. "Ladies," Malone said, "don't pay any attention to him—he's a little gaga. This way, Oz," he said. And to the waiter: "Ah, Michael—perfect timing. I'll have the grilled Reuben and my guest will have your sirloin tips."

Ozzie couldn't wrench his sight from Babs DeSilva's tight face. "Good god, you've had your eyes done?" he said to her. Ozzie pulled the corners of his own eyes, peering at her through slits.

"What starch, Oz?" Malone said.

"Starch?" Ozzie said, releasing his eyes. "Have you got french fries?" he asked the waiter, and to Babs: "Looks painful—is it?"

"Michael!" she shouted.

Malone put his hand on the waiter's chest. "This gentleman will have his tips on a linguini bed, Michael. Ladies—

always a pleasure. Whole damn family's crackers." And gesturing for Ozzie: "This way, Oz."

Ozzie allowed Malone to lead him between tables to the bar, where Ozzie downed most of his beer in one throw.

"You're a little frayed around the edges," Malone said, hunching his shoulders as he settled on his stool.

Michael stayed at the table, the women hurriedly gathering their bags and purses, flipping sweaters off chair backs. One woman suddenly swung her bag at Michael. The waiter watched them go, rubbing his chest, a helpless thing in his white jacket with the club crest on its pocket.

Malone waved to them as they left. "Pleasant in here sometimes," he said. "Afternoons are usually quiet." He ordered more beer, then led Ozzie below into the locker rooms, down into the rancid chlorinated breath of swimming pool and hot showers, down to the sauna.

Ozzie opened its door. Went in to stand in his boots on its cedar floor.

"Almost never used," Malone said.

Ozzie stepped back out and nodded toward a door along the wall. "What's in there?"

Malone said, "Outside—tennis courts, I think."

Ozzie pushed the release and opened the door wide.

"Wait a minute—where are we?" Malone said, sticking his head out "Ah—the ninth hole. Pretty, isn't it?"

"I see why Louise likes it here."

"This is the men's locker area, Oz. Louise can't—"

A skinny naked man dripped along the rubber mat toward them, greeted them. Malone said hello and then asked Ozzie who the man was.

"Richardson—our new mayor."

"You think our boy Richie went out this door to Veronica's that night, don't you?"

"Then jogged back for a sauna. I wonder who was here with him?"

"I'll ask Boomer, the bartender. He'll know."

"Dreary, isn't it?" Ozzie said as he held the door open to the rain.

"Dreary is as dreary does, Oz."

Ruby heard the footsteps on the deck above her, heard the steps cross the salon, then a scrambling on the ladder that led down to the passageway she faced from inside the engine room.

The yacht was an eighty-foot Trumpy with twin diesels, four double cabins for ardent cruising couples, crew quarters forward, and a Cobalt runabout on davits. Ruby had been alone on this boat, alone and wiping her hands between the engines belowdecks.

Although her companion, Larry, the yellow-naped mute, was silently perched on the Trumpy's mast, Larry was not a watchparrot. Never so much as a squawk. She didn't know why, but she felt trapped down here, had been strangely uncomfortable for an hour or so. A hatch thudded somewhere forward. She was kneeling.

Then she relaxed and said, "What are you doing here?" as he came along the passageway toward her.

"Wanted to see how things are."

She stood up.

This engine room was crammed with water-purifying equipment, generators, air-conditioning units, and the diesels that hunched on their mounts like yellow sarcophagi. She was surrounded by ductwork and wrapped piping. All white, all clean. "I can't find anything wrong with either of them," she said. She patted the port cylinder head. "Tell me again what he said."

DeSilva wore his boating gear, his rain slicker and deckshoes. "Captain Brownie said he came up the Intracoastal Waterway with no trouble—had no trouble all winter on the charters. But off New Jersey, he couldn't get full power. I told you he went in, had them checked out. Arrived here day before yesterday."

Ruby said, "I ran them up for twenty minutes. I can't find anything wrong with them."

"That's what he said. 'Course he's half in the bag by the time he reaches New Jersey on that trip. Could've been nothin' but booze talking."

She tossed wrenches into an open toolbox. "Larry still up there?"

"Didn't see him," he said, bending to pick up a coffee can. "This shouldn't be here," he said.

Ruby gathered her tools off the deck.

DeSilva sniffed the can, swished its contents. "Brownie's been washing parts."

When she bent to retrieve her screwdrivers and ratchet, Richie DeSilva lost his grip; the can dropped to Ruby's back, drenching her in diesel fuel.

She jumped away, swore, then let her arms dangle as the liquid seeped through her clothes and around her waist. "Dammit!" she said. She raised her head, exhaling slowly, arching her back to get the cloth off her skin.

Richie went to pieces, yelling, "I'm sorry! I'm sorry!" He ran for towels, and came back quickly, patting her coveralls.

"Leave it!" she said, throwing tools into toolboxes. "How could you?" she said.

"I'm sorry," he said. "I'll buy you new everything—new— it slipped."

"I'm allergic to the stuff—my skin," she said. "Dammit, Richie."

She quickly left the engine room, her toolboxes dead weights as she hurried up the ladder to the salon, where she dropped one of the boxes and took the other one out to the stern and her dinghy.

Larry was poised in the rigging, his parrot feathers dripping with rain.

143

Ruby went back for the box in the salon. She could hear Richie yelling somewhere in the boat; he was forward, she thought, as she lifted the heavy steel case off the peach rug. Richie's decor was ridiculously done up for a doge, its glass tables and furniture with Venetian clawed feet: what Miami takes for elegance.

"Wait!" he yelled as he strode into the salon. His arms were filled with clean work clothes, more towels. "Wait! I feel terrible about this," he said. Then he grinned. "It'll take you twenty minutes to row over to your place. Jump in the shower here—Brownie left the hot water on. Get that shit off your skin." He offered her the clothes.

Ruby shook her head and ran for the stern.

"Please!" he called after her. "My fault! My fault!"

She balanced the toolbox on the transom, ready to spring for the swim platform . . . then hesitated. Her skin felt as though there were fluttering blue flames licking at her back and breasts, her waist.

She reached for the box, shut her eyes. The flames fluttered even hotter. Her skin would flare and itch for days. She leapt back up onto the deck, sucking in her breath as the flames reached her nipples.

"I'll show you," he said. "I'm so sorry. Come on!"

No choice. Another second was too long for her.

Ruby ran after him as he dodged down the ladder and ran along the passageway to the end, kicking into the master suite.

"His or Hers?" he said, motioning to the heads. She chose Hers and hurried through its dressing room into the head, slamming the door. Her coveralls came off her shoulders sopping and greasy; she fought the zipper, slapped her coveralls against the bulkhead, her shirt and jeans, her underwear.

"I'm sorry!" Richie yelled from outside. "My fault! My fault!"

Ruby spun the dial, the spray flourished, and in she went,

squeezing gobs of bath gel down her back, rubbing her back against the shower tiles, then under the spray, over and over. She realized she was crying. The pain would stay in her skin for at least a week . . . the itching . . . and the worst ever had come for her once in Italy on a blazing Mediterranean afternoon when she'd been trapped beneath a dripping fuel tank for over an hour before they found her. She tried to quiet herself, waiting while the water and gel slowly doused the flames, leaning hands to the tiles with the cold rush down her back, turning slowly to rinse her chest.

She'd got it in time; she'd be as pink as a Brooklyn file clerk on Aruba in March. No rubbing, nothing coarse on her skin. The navy doctors had used cortisone shots. She'd have to get her cream.

She had no idea how long she'd been in the shower when she stepped out to grab a towel off the deck. "I'm all right!" she yelled to him.

He didn't answer.

She scrubbed out her hair, the yacht unheated and frigid. She went into the dressing room, in under the heating lamps between the mirrored cabinet doors. Ruby held her breasts up to get the air on her skin, her chest mottled with faint itchings, warm like a sunburn. Twenty minutes rowing home would have been twenty minutes too long, she thought.

Ruby stood there, hands clasped on her head, allowing the musty spring air to do all it could. No rubbing, she thought. Don't touch it.

The mirror she faced had a peculiar yellow depth she recognized. She turned to face the other mirror, that one more clearly mirrorlike, hard silver. She looked again at the yellowy glass. She stepped up to it, arms up, hands on her head.

Then deliberately appearing unconcerned, she bent for the towel and eased out the side door and into the passageway, into the next cabin with its ship's office and garish lamps. She clenched her jaw as she opened the closet in here: She saw into her dressing room through the closet's glass panel. Richie DeSilva whirled, the dressing-room glow on his face. He had watched her.

"You still like 'em?" she said, lifting her arms over her head, swinging her breasts. "You used to call 'em melons." She turned to show him her bottom. "Still look good to you, Richie?"

"Sorry," he said. He pointed at the mirror as he stepped out of the closet. "I think you're beautiful, Ruby."

"I am," she said. She shook her breasts at him.

He came for her, hands out as though he were blindfolded.

"You touch me, Richie DeSilva, and I'll burn this fuckin' tub to the waterline."

He opened his eyes. "I still love you." He had his best basketball-hero's crease on his face, that cherubic coyness he wore when he told the photographers he couldn't have won the state championship in the Boston Garden without the team.

"Right to the waterline—hear me?"

"I'm sorry," he said. "I said I was sorry."

"Being sorry doesn't cut it, Richie. Sorry is all you ever offered—you haven't learned a fucking thing in twenty years of being an asshole."

"I love you," he said. He waggled his head, wiggled his come-hither finger at her.

When he reached for her breasts, she hit him so hard he collapsed over his knees first, his legs eventually giving way until he sprawled on the carpet.

"Oh, my god!" he whined. "My god—you've broken a tooth!"

He tried to stand but fell backward into the closet.

"Right to the fucking waterline!" she yelled and slammed the door into his head.

But when she arrived in the salon, dressed in mechanic's clothes nineteen sizes too big for her, Richie was holding his head in his hands. He rose to face her when she came up the ladder. "I shink I got a broken chaw," he said. He was confused.

"Go look in the mirror, Richie."

Ruby cast off in the dinghy and rowed herself across the harbor in a cold rain that felt good on her skin. Larry flew over her, his wings beating for home, undoubtedly as choleric as a parrot could get.

$$\text{⚓ ⚓ ⚓}$$

"I'm glad you're here," she said after he kissed her. She wore a white cotton gown; she'd bound her hair in black ribbon.

Ozzie slipped into Ruby's home and knew as he did that all had changed between them. She went ahead of him, Ozzie gingerly following as she crossed her white room, her bed swaying slightly. Her few books, furniture all in white, the exposed roof and beams as though they'd been painted with cream.

Larry was perched on her rocking chair by a glass door, his head moving to see Ozzie. The bird was pure malevolence.

"I need you to do something for me," she said, coming from the bathroom. "I dumped diesel fuel on my back today." She came over to him. "I'm allergic to the stuff—would you spread cream on my back?"

"I thought we might walk down to Mildred's."

"I had soup."

She held up the tube of cream and went to her bed. She eased onto the bed, tugging the gown off her shoulders.

Ozzie pulled the gown's hem up over her legs, off her bottom, to find her back red with blotches that looked like early blistery poison ivy.

"Don't rub too hard," she said. She dropped her face into a pillow, patted his leg. "I was on DeSilva's boat."

"The fiberglass tub."

147

"He's worried about his engines—can't stand the idea that something he owns might not work right."

Ozzie dabbed cream on her skin, barely brushing his fingers over her back. "How can you work around engines and be allergic to fuel?"

"I don't know," she said. She sounded hoarse, tired. "I try to be so careful—this was an accident."

"Hurt?"

"Yup. Cream helps, though."

"I think DeSilva killed the Hammond woman."

She opened her eyes. "Don't be silly."

"I'm not."

"Richie DeSilva's many things," she said. "But he's a sheep in wolf's clothing. He couldn't kill anyone."

"They were lovers. She was killed with his softball bat. She was dumping him."

"Anyone see him there?"

"My Uncle Barry saw a Peeping Tom who could have been DeSilva."

Ruby thought of the mirror, DeSilva huddled in his closet. "Maybe," she said.

"DeSilva's sixteen waiting for the next basketball game," Ozzie said. "Always the local hero—he's hanging by a thread. Funny how so many of these jocks play with balls, isn't it? I mean, why balls? Why not tree bark or chinchillas?"

"How well do you know him?"

"I know he's dangerous."

"He's helping me with Rocket."

"Is he? What's wrong with Rocket?"

"Money. Rocket's too old to remember everything. He's used to getting by with a roll of bills in his pocket. He's over his head. Richie DeSilva's helping me straighten his money out."

Ozzie stopped spreading cream. "DeSilva will rob you both blind. He'll take everything Rocket owns, and Rocket owns almost the entire harbor. Richie and his aardvarks want

Strike's Landing to be a yacht basin—chuck out the stinking fishermen, build restaurants that specialize in asparagus quiche, all mollusk shells and nets strung on their walls, aggrieved waiters who insist that people know their names. Richie and his pin-striped pals hide behind real-estate holding companies. He tried to buy out Mildred—even had the town threaten to widen the road out here, hack seven feet off her bar, if she didn't sell. She went to a zoning meeting and told a Harvard MBA to get his ass back to Nashua and think again. But she knows they're not finished."

"More cream," she said.

He asked her to turn over.

"He says Rocket owes the IRS a bundle," she said, rolling for him.

"How does DeSilva know that?"

"I didn't ask. I thought bankers knew those things."

"Only the crooked ones."

"Why would he lie?"

"He couldn't spot the truth if he stepped in it. He'd make Rocket appear incompetent to convince you that only Richie DeSilva can save you. Would you rather deal with the IRS or your old heartthrob Richie?"

"I've slept with him," she said.

He said too quickly, "Since you've been home?"

"God, I knew you'd hate this, but I can't lie to you."

"Then don't tell me," he said. "I'll keep the fantasy."

"I'm not a fantasy."

Ozzie capped the cream.

"I haven't been to bed with him since I've been home. He's tried. He always tries. Women are like trophies for him. I didn't know that about him until it was too late when I was a kid. I thought he loved me. But he was lifting every skirt he could lay his hands on. And I'll tell you something else about him."

Ruby tossed her gown over her legs, irritated that she had allowed this time with Ozzie to fizzle into recrimination and frustration. "He always said we were lucky, but I think he's infertile."

"He's infertile, all right."

"No, listen to me. We never used anything—no rubbers, no pills, nothing. I was too stupid—I probably wanted to get pregnant. He always said it was because he knew what he was doing. He didn't. And every other female I ever talked to about him said he laid them left, right, and backwards—not one of them got pregnant by Richie DeSilva."

"Maybe he did know the ropes."

"Trust me," she said. "He didn't. He never did anything but flop on a girl and leave his little love gift to womanhood. I used to get sick worrying about being pregnant."

Ozzie said, "He's still screwing everybody he meets."

"He's an infertile swine. I'd bet the ranch on it."

"So, the ice queen, ol' Babs, who's congenitally bitter, very likely can't have chilluns because Richie's missing a few links in his DNA chain."

"How do you know she's bitter?"

"Look at her. Women don't become bantamweight brawlers because they're happy. My wife knows her—Louise is attracted to bitterness. The ice queen has had all the tests to figure out why she can't Xerox herself. Richie doesn't do tests. But Louise and her tennis zealots know about a Cliffie Richie got pregnant when he was a college boy."

"I'll bet it's not true. Where is Louise?"

"At her sister's, I think."

"Is the divorce for real?"

"Lily's charging me money—must be real."

Larry flew into his cage, sidestepping on his perch, head dipping. Ozzie went over to him. "Ozzie's here," he said.

Ruby was up, wrapping her hair again. "He doesn't talk. He's a mute."

"Mutant," Ozzie said. He stuck out his tongue at the bird, rolled his eyes.

"He wants his cover. He can't sleep without it."

Ozzie dropped the cloth over the cage. "Ozzie's here," he said, drumming his fingers on the metal cage bottom.

Something in the shape of the bars, the latticework of confinement, caused Ozzie to touch the cage with his fingers. Something there is that doesn't love a wall, he thought, that wants it down. "Why doesn't he talk?"

"He's foul-tempered," she said. "Too stubborn. If he thinks you want him to eat, he won't eat. He was passed from ship to ship because he bites. I worked in a maintenance section in Norfolk—Larry flew in every morning from a fleet tender he roosted on at night. Nobody owned him. Eventually he stayed with me. I couldn't leave him. And now he loves me."

"How do you know?"

"Because he never leaves me."

"Is that the test? Maybe he can't leave—he's in parrot prison. Trapped inside himself."

Ruby had gone to her stove. "I'm making tea."

"Love to," Ozzie said. "A parrot psychopath." He lifted the cloth, Larry's round eye was in there . . . blinked. Ozzie put his hand inside Larry's cage, his fingertips touching the bird's breast.

Larry bit him. And the second time, gripped Ozzie's finger painfully. Ozzie raised his hand, raised the psychopathic Larry onto his parrot toes. The bird would not let go. Still higher until Ozzie saw the parrot's little feet straining to grip the perch. Ozzie went a bit higher, the bird's feet losing their purchase, the great yellow beak slipping. Ozzie's finger started to bleed. One tough bird, he thought, lowering his hand, the bird instantly relaxing, its eye on Ozzie. The bird released him. Ozzie removed his finger from its beak and rubbed the parrot's head.

"Don't tease him" she said, beside him.

"Larry and I are talking about walls," he said. And to Larry: "You're only a bird."

"Which one?" she said, offering Ozzie choices in tea. "He won't sleep if you don't cover him."

"How do you know he sleeps when you do cover him?"

"He snores."

"Never talks?"

"Never."

"Maybe he needs a violin." Ozzie reached into the cage to slowly rub the seam in the bird's beak. Larry tilted his head. "Ozzie's here," Ozzie whispered.

Needles

OZZIE sat at his kitchen table later that night, a single piece of reversed Christmas wrapping paper taped to the table. He got out Magic Markers and pens, a ruler, a French curve, and began to construct a blueprint of Veronica Hammond's life, with squares and circles, connecting lines and question marks. As DeSilva had come clear for Ozzie when Uncle Barry was removed from the murder equation, now Ozzie was trying to remove DeSilva from the equation, to move that one step beyond the obvious. Ozzie drew a circle around the addresses of Veronica Hammond's two Boston parking tickets. Somewhere in the last few months there was a name that knew how Veronica Hammond died . . . something Ozzie hadn't seen, some connection to explain why she was dressed only in a bathing suit, floating dead in her pool.

He flipped slowly through the couple's check registers from the den drawer. Martin had led a dull life—either that, or a secret life, because his check notations provided only the litany of a public man in golf togs who watched his money and kept a thousand-dollar cushion in his checking account. He had written monthly checks to a Lacey Beal for one hundred and fifty dollars, a single check to her, on December sixteenth two years ago, for three hundred dollars. The country club, the marina and yacht club, professional dues . . . not much, Ozzie thought. Where are you, Martin?

Veronica Hammond had a prescription for Valium from a Dr. Zalinsky and two prescriptions from a Dr. Peterson, one for an antibiotic, the other for Septra. Ozzie checked his notes from his midnight foray into the Hammond woman's bathroom cabinets, remembering the name Peterson. Dr. Peterson had also prescribed Veronica Hammond's new diaphragm in October of last year. Checks had been made out to Peterson, but none to Zalinsky.

She'd paid cash for the Riviera . . . had the car serviced on time. She went to Puff's in Marblehead for haircuts. Two checks made out to the Haymarket Hotel in Boston, each for one hundred dollars. She bought her groceries at the Fernandez Supermarket in the mall. Clothes, Eldridge's drug store, and the Drug Mart in the mall for her diaphragm. She had the Boston *Globe* delivered, watched cable TV, had enormous phone bills to Zaire some months, and sent Greenpeace five hundred dollars in February.

Ozzie got out the phone book, checking addresses. Peterson's gynecological practice he knew; however, there was no Dr. Zalinsky in the book. He'd have to ask Bozo.

Ozzie got it all down; the wrapping paper became a map of Veronica Hammond's life. Something there is that doesn't love a wall, he thought. Uncle Barry would be lost for eternity unless Ozzie connected the dots.

He knew he had no choice.

"I can't talk anymore, Oz."

"What's happened to you?"

Uncle Barry had the appearance of a lost dog, his shoulders bent forward as though sheltering his soul, a tremor in his limbs that vibrated with lost bearings. He was dirty and smelled. "You know I hate needles."

"What needles?"

"Needles!"

"Why don't you visit Ezra and the boys upstairs?"

"I'm not good company, Oz."

"They think you are."

"They're generous."

"It's hard for them to have you this close and not see you."

"No, Oz."

Uncle and nephew sat together on the bed, the room a cell, the nephew feeling helpless. Ozzie said, "You know I love you, don't you?"

"Love isn't enough, is it?"

The old man's eyes were red-rimmed and glazed. He squeezed his fingers again and again in rhythm to some internal dirge.

"I'll get you out of here," Ozzie said softly, touching his uncle's arm.

"It's okay, Oz—you don't have to come anymore. The needles drain me—I don't feel sad, I don't feel lonely. Sometimes it's not so bad to feel nothing. Anything wrong with that?"

"You're killing yourself."

"No, I'm not. Mrs. Hammond is killing me."

Ozzie spotted the violin case under a blanket on the cell floor. "How often do they let you out of this room?" he said.

"I have to pee in a bedpan at night. Isn't that awful?"

"It is when you usually pee out your window."

"Quite a change, isn't it?"

"I need you to help me," Ozzie said. "Why did you touch the softball bat?"

"Don't, Oz. I don't want to talk."

"Tell me where it was, please?"

"Then what—more questions?"

"Only a few."

Uncle Barry breathed in a full chest of air and allowed it to whistle through his teeth slowly. "I told you," he said.

"I don't remember," Ozzie said.

"By the front door."

155

"Why did you touch the bat?"

"I don't know—I touched it."

"Do you have a key for the bank?"

"Of course I do."

Ozzie felt the hair bristle on his neck. "Where is it?"

"Second cabinet on the right in the garage. There are two identical keys under the tag that says BANK."

"You miss the hardware store, don't you?" Ozzie said.

"I miss everything," Uncle Barry said. "I miss you. Can you come tomorrow?"

"No," Ozzie said. "I can't. But soon again—what should I bring you?"

"Don't bring anything, Oz. What I need you can't carry."

"What do you need?"

"Oh, Ozzie, don't—" Uncle Barry wept, the tears running over his cheeks, his eyes open and turning for the window. A silent Ozzie sat with him for a long time. A paint flake drifted off the wall.

"I need to get into Richie DeSilva's desk."

"Take the entire third row of keys—all bank keys. Be careful, Oz. You'll wind up in here with me."

"Was Richie DeSilva at Mrs. Hammond's that night?"

"I didn't see him, Oz."

"Did he go into her house a lot?"

"You've got only thirty seconds to shut off the bank alarm after you turn the key in the front door. There's a green metal box on the left wall behind the lamp. It's got a thermostat dial on it, but it's not a thermostat. Just unlatch its cover with your thumb and open it. There's a keypad inside. Press nine, zero, zero, nine, three to cancel the alarm system. But you can't fool around the way you do, Oz. And lock the door while you're inside. There's a new policeman who walks the sidewalk at night. He rattles doors."

"Who is Lacey Beal?"

Uncle Barry didn't speak. His hands were tight, his gaze distant and unconcerned. And then: "Only thirty seconds,

Oz. Reset the alarm when you leave by pushing the same numbers. Why don't you go in through the cellar? There's no alarm—the tunnel comes right in there from under the library. The library bulkhead is always open so Hector can get in on weekends and stoke the furnace."

"The bank sits there wide open?"

"Sure—but you'll have to crouch in the tunnel and there's rainwater in there sometimes. The tunnel comes out in the bank's boiler room. The old coalbin has hinges on its bottom three planks—easy."

"A tunnel?"

"A good tunnel. Lacey Beal is that poor girl who lives out by the marsh with her father. Lacey Beal was Mrs. Hammond's cleaning girl. She's smart, Oz. She's also very sad. She sometimes sleeps at Mrs. Hammond's."

"And the courthouse—do you have a key?"

"In the cupboard over the garage window."

"Which courthouse door?"

"One key works 'em all."

"Alarms?"

"Nope—who'd break into a courthouse, Oz? That's like having a fire station burn down. Put my keys back, please."

Ozzie said he would. "I'm sorry you couldn't talk."

"Me, too," Uncle Barry said. "But I can't help it, Oz."

"Maybe you'll be able to talk when I come again?"

"I don't think so. I don't have anything to say."

"Do you love me?"

"I've always loved you, Oz."

"That's all you need to say."

"That's easy," Uncle Barry said.

⚓ ⚓ ⚓

Ezra and the boys, about a dozen of them, were in an upstairs screened porch. Ozzie waved to them; they didn't wave back. He got into Rocket's jeep and drove the wrong way around the driveway loop to stop beneath them. "Are you guys all right?" he shouted up to them. They were motionless, as unmoving and forlorn as Wrigley Field bleacher bums watching the Cubs blow another season in the ninth inning.

Francis Sparkman waved slightly, then stopped. Their silence was as accusatory as anything Ozzie had felt in his life. He remembered being here, visiting his Uncle Barry with his aunts in Lizbeth's green '53 Chevy. Some of the men were here even then. "What do you want me to do, goddam it?" he yelled up to them. Aunt Elspeth had stitched him plaid shirts all the way through grade school. They ate rice pudding. Ozzie did his chores, and when he was sick, Lizbeth had fumed at her sister's attentions to the boy. "You'll spoil the child," Lizbeth said behind her hand. And when Elspeth brought Ozzie the newest, spine-snapping books from the library, Lizbeth would inspect each one for Christian content. Lizbeth wore her hair in a bun in those days. She had suitors, but tired of them quickly. Until Bud came along. Lizbeth and Bud had a seven-year engagement—ought to be enough time to gauge marital prospects, Ozzie thought.

"Are you guys all right?" he shouted.

The men didn't move.

"Answer my question!" he shouted.

They didn't.

"At least I haven't given up like you nuts, have I?"

They watched the jeep drive away.

Withdrawals

Ruby fastened his coat pocket and smiled. "It's the first one he made. But it works. This way I can find you."

"An electric leash," Ozzie said. He scratched his nose. "What if I forget to turn it on?"

"You won't do that."

Ozzie took off his coat. Larry was awake.

"I went into your house," she said.

"Ozzie's here," he said to the parrot as he smoothed its feathered head.

"Such a big house," she said. Her hair was wet from her shower, her robe a velvety maroon. "Are you going to sell it?"

"Louise wants her money right away. It's a funny thing," he said, as he looked up at her, his hand extended for the parrot to step onto his fingers. Ruby rubbed cream on her face. "I never liked that house until now," he said. The bird made not a move toward his hand, but did gaze at him with its head cocked. "Beginning to feel like home," he said.

"I hope you can stay there."

"I'd like to," he heard himself say. He knew otherwise.

"Where have you been?"

Ozzie told her about the hospital, about Uncle Barry. "He'll die in there," he said.

"You'll get him out."

He left Larry inspecting the harbor from the bird's rocking-chair perch. He asked about her skin, her back. She said she was better, almost told him about DeSilva and the coffee can. She didn't want to get him started; he seemed quiet. Instead, Ruby went to her bed and flipped the quilt into a chair.

"Now?" he said.

"You've got something better to do?"

He knew he didn't, not truthfully better. But he also knew time was working on him, crushing his choices into obsession. "I can't stay long," he said.

"Will you let me sleep with you all night in your house—this week?"

"What day is it?" he said.

"Tuesday."

How could this be Tuesday? he wondered. His days had become time-lapse events. "A sleep-over?" he said.

"Larry and I will bring our jammies."

"I'd love it," he said. He opened her robe.

"No, you first," she said. "Start with your boots."

Ruby sat on her bed, creaming her face and neck, watching Ozzie unzip and unbutton until he stood before her. "Turn around," she said. "You've got shoulders like a trawlerman."

Ozzie turned, saw Larry watching. "Ozzie's here," he said to the bird.

"Ozzie's here all right," she said, bouncing herself onto her back. "Let's see what you can do with that thing."

After Ozzie threw his shirt over the perched parrot, the shirt bobbed in parrot fury. When Ozzie came dripping out of the shower, Larry was gone and the cage was covered.

Her bed swayed like a tree in a storm. He tried to be careful, gentle with her skin. Ruby didn't seem to care and swung with him as he stayed deep inside her for what seemed like hours. When Ozzie woke up, the bed had only a Richter-

160

like suggestion of love. Ruby was asleep, her head on Ozzie's shoulder, her breathing soft and scented with her juices, whispering against his skin.

Never like this, he thought. Never.

⚓ ⚓ ⚓

"We aren't making a withdrawal, are we?"

Ozzie felt the lock click neatly in three distinct metallic pings. He ducked in quickly, found the box with his light, opened its cover, and dialed relief. He shut the cover.

"What are we waiting for?" Malone said.

"Turn the lock on the door, Wilson."

"I did."

Ozzie said, "Thirty seconds. Listen."

There wasn't a sound as the bank slept peacefully, digesting its cash in a strangely empty darkness.

"Try not to use your light, Wilson," Ozzie whispered. "The police drive by all night."

"The hell they do. They eat jelly rolls out at the Dirty Doughnut all night. I don't hear anything. Silent alarm?"

"We won't know until it's too late," Ozzie said.

Malone crossed the carpet through a Star of David shadowed by moonlight high in the round window overhead, Malone fishing DeSilva's letter to Veronica Hammond out of his mackinaw. He went from typewriter to typewriter tapping out the same sentence on each machine onto the back of the letter: *I am a passionate man.*

Ozzie had DeSilva's desk open with the fourth key. He looked up for the front door and windows, expecting flashing blue bubbles. All was still.

DeSilva had Celtics tickets, a lot of Celtics tickets, in an envelope. Blank mortgage forms, accounting slips in files. An unused diary in his top drawer, assorted pens and paperclips. Rubber stamps. Ozzie inked one of the stamps and stamped DeSilva's signature on the man's blotter.

File folders in the bottom drawer. Ozzie opened each one

161

quickly, his nimble fingers hurrying through bank business and venal correspondence.

"Nothin' yet," Malone said, as he let the gate to the tellers' cage clunk back and forth on its springs. "Hard to type with gloves on, Oz."

"Wilson? Whoever wrote the letter doesn't know the difference between 'their,' 'they're,' and 'there.' Right?"

"Pitiful, isn't it?" Malone said, poised to head across the bank. "So what?"

"Well," Ozzie said, taking out a file, "our boy Richie does know the difference."

"Or Veronica did," Malone said. "And corrected all his stuff."

"Possible," Ozzie said. "Did you get her typewriter?"

"Not yet," Malone said. But then he whispered: "—Oz?"

"What?" Ozzie wedged the file back into the drawer.

"Is your light out?"

"It is now. Why?"

"Because there's a cop peeking in the front window."

Ozzie didn't want to look, didn't want to see that all was revealed, all lost, nothing forgiven. There was a policeman, hands on either side of his face, peering into the bank.

"It *is* a silent alarm," Malone said softly, calmly.

"Don't move."

"I couldn't move if I wanted to. Did you dial the wrong number?" Malone said.

"No," Ozzie said. "Maybe they changed the number."

The cop at the window drifted sideways to the door, which suddenly clattered, the lock holding.

"Oz?"

"What?"

"My entire sordid life is passing before my eyes—things I don't even remember doing."

The cop came back to the window, hands up again. And then went away.

Ozzie scampered behind desks along this side of the bank,

keeping to the balcony's shadow. He got to the window edge, behind a couch, expecting the cop's face again not six inches from his own head.

Ozzie stayed low to see through the gilt letters. There was a police cruiser over in MacAvoy's parking lot, the cop sitting in it with his dome light on, his feet out onto the asphalt. "He's using his radio," Ozzie said to Malone. "I see only one cop."

"One's enough," he heard Malone say from the blackness in the back.

Something moved outside and to Ozzie's right . . . a shadow on the carpet.

"Here's another one," he heard Malone say.

Ozzie pressed his back against the wall, heard this cop try the door, and then watched the shadow move toward him to vanish at his feet.

"Wait!" he heard Malone say.

Ozzie took a very deep breath, exhaled. Another breath, trying to quiet his heart.

He peeked through the letters. The police cruiser's brake lights sparked, then the car eased out of MacAvoy's, its headlights flooding the bank's interior. "Are you there?" Ozzie said.

"Where?" Malone answered.

"They're leaving—I think." But the cruiser's directional light began flashing just before it passed out of Ozzie's line of sight. He wasn't certain.

"You think they'd mind we're in here?" Malone said.

Ozzie dashed back to DeSilva's desk, slid the bottom drawer shut and opened the credenza behind the bank president's leather chair.

Malone was clacking on typewriters again.

In a wooden box, Ozzie found credit-card receipts for the Haymarket Hotel. Restaurant receipts. "Thank you, thank you, thank you," he whispered.

In flat folders in an inside drawer, Ozzie found sheaves

163

of paper, stapled and identified only by numbers at their tops. But then he realized he was looking at business accounts, investment records, and in the bottom folder, handwritten buy orders and commodity margins going back three or four years. Boston and New York telephone numbers, bank transfer codes. The First Seaman's Bank mother lode.

Malone was sitting at Veronica Hammond's desk, typing his now-famous sentence. . . . Malone was a passionate man.

Ozzie glanced again at the front window before hurrying behind the counter. The copy machine clanked and purred when he turned it on, its tiny green lights blinking madly.

"Oh, bingo!" he heard Malone say. "Veronica had the best typewriter in here—and guess which one matches the letter's typeface?"

"She wrote herself that letter?"

"Makes sense that Richie would use her machine if he needed to, though, doesn't it?"

The copier was flashing for more paper. "Damn!" Ozzie said.

Ozzie went through a door into a rear office, the bookkeeping office. Many desks. All's well so far, he thought, as he skipped to see out the back windows . . . nothing. The lawn behind the bank was empty and dark, the moon having etched the grass with tree branches. The library in the distance.

Ozzie found paper in a coatroom closet off the bookkeeping office. And in the fifth wooden locker he opened, Ozzie found a pair of rubbers, size eight. "Well, well, well," he said, using his light to study the treads, searching for anything to indicate he should know what he was holding. There was a thermos on the locker bottom. Nothing in it but the noxious whiff of mold and ooze. "I'll be damned," he smiled, examining the masking tape label and name before clicking off his light. "Sheldon didn't eat his beef stew."

Malone was clacking away somewhere in the balcony's shadow.

Ozzie copied as many sheets as he could, as many cryptic codes and telephone numbers as he dared until he couldn't stand to see the copy machine flash its green signal on the ceiling one more time. "I must be nuts," he said to himself, as he shut the thing off and hurried back to DeSilva's desk. "Positively nuts," he muttered, swinging the credenza doors closed.

He located the computer disks, booted DeSilva's IBM, and turned down the screen's brightness to a dim blue haze. He glanced again at the windows. Malone was whistling "The Washington Post" in the dark distance.

Ozzie couldn't remember. He tried to enter the computer, but realized he was instantly stymied.

Malone stood at his shoulder. Malone had his pipe going.

"It's been too long, Wilson."

"What are you looking for?"

"I'm trying to get into the bank's records—I haven't any idea how to do this. There must be a mainframe somewhere in this bank. I don't have the access codes."

"I got all the typewriters I can find, Oz."

"And the cops?"

"Right," Malone said, chugging toward the front windows.

Ozzie shut everything down, made certain the desk was tidy, tapped DeSilva's stamped signature on the man's blotter, and went to find Malone.

When they got into Rocket's jeep a few minutes later, Malone said, "You sure you punched the right numbers to reset the alarm?"

"What difference does it make?" Ozzie said. He started the jeep.

"Some of my money's in there, Oz."

"There's also a pair of rubbers in a coatroom locker in there, Wilson."

"I'm not kiddin', Oz. You didn't even ask me if I wanted to break into a bank tonight."

Ozzie backed the jeep out of Mildred's parking lot, Strike's

Landing hushed at three in the morning. "Not that again," he said, turning into the road. "I apologized, Wilson. Next time I'll ask."

They drove past the bank.

"You assume I'll follow you anywhere, my captain," Malone said, miffed. "You should ask me."

"You never say no," Ozzie said as they belted past Eldridge's and the dozing docks.

"Doesn't mean you shouldn't ask," Malone said.

"I've hurt your feelings."

"Damn straight you have."

"Next time, I'll ask."

"Thank you," Malone said, pulling his hat down to master the breeze over the jeep's hood.

Up to No Good

"CAN we do it?" Ozzie said, sitting down beside Malone.

Malone looked up out of his fish and chips, hat on. "You have got to get a phone," Malone said.

"I don't want a phone."

Mildred said, "Whose bed did you just crawl out of?"

Ozzie said he'd slept until two this afternoon. He was starved.

Mildred grunted and listened to his order. "Ruby Willey stopped by. She says she has to work late tonight on that Nova Scotia dragger over at MacAvoy's. D'you know the Coast Guard might arrest him for fishing in our waters?"

"We fish in theirs," Ozzie said.

Mildred clattered off to the kitchen.

"What's goin' on?" Wilson said, chewing his chips.

"Can we do it tonight?"

"We can," he said. "I mean the woman."

"I'm not sure," Ozzie said.

"I don't believe you," Malone said. "You and I have been hanging around together for years."

"You jealous?"

"I am. I'll bet you don't take her to banks."

"She and I are friends—that's all."

"That's never all. Isn't that right, Mildred?"

167

Mildred slid Ozzie's beer down the bar, her cigarette holder dangling from her lips. "She's a close friend," Mildred said. "You be careful, Oz. You're not exactly the Aqua Velva man."

"I know what I'm doing," Ozzie said.

"Don't believe a word he says, Malone," Mildred said as she left them.

"I don't," Malone called after her. And then to Ozzie: "Sophistry, my lad. Pure sophistry. You're deranged. Hand me the vinegar, please. And the salt. And tartar sauce?"

While Malone ate, he listened to Ozzie's tale of the courthouse that morning.

"You didn't ask me to go?" Malone said.

Two uniformed state troopers walked into Mildred's, took off their caps, edged along the bar toward Ozzie and Malone.

"You said you were tired," Ozzie said.

The troopers, both of them like gray-blue sequoias, hung their caps on coathooks, walked behind Ozzie and Malone and sat down next to Malone.

"Afternoon." The trooper nearest Malone smiled to them. Malone said, "Hi."

"How's the fish here?" the other trooper said.

Ozzie said, "You haven't had fish until you've had Mildred's haddock."

Malone had gone pale, chewing, his eyes like pinballs signaling Ozzie.

Mildred was in front of the troopers almost before they were comfortable. She nodded to Ozzie that she'd take the helm, glanced only once at the rattled educationist, and began chatting as though she were sensing the troopers with her tongue.

"I went in while I had time," Ozzie said to Malone. "Found the tape and watched it. No rubbers."

"I see," said Malone. "And"—in his loudest voice—"what else drew your attention at the conference?"

Ozzie started to speak.

Malone's eyes leapt like slot-machine lemons. "Not now, Oz!" he whispered.

"I found a copy of her will," Ozzie said. He handed the first trooper the sugar bowl over Malone's plate. "She left the house and some stock to her daughter."

"Ozzie!" Malone looked like he'd detonate.

"And she left fifty thousand dollars to Lacey Beal."

Malone swiveled to grin at the troopers, trying to chew his fish.

"I found a lot of stuff," Ozzie said. "Did you talk to Bozo?"

"What?" Malone said. He was veering out of control.

"Bozo," Ozzie said, sipping his beer.

Malone jerked another terrified glance at the troopers, who seemed like easygoing guys, rather glad to be here. "Yes, I talked to Bozo!" Malone shouted. "Bozo says the doctor in question is a dentist in Lynn. Bozo's my vet!" Malone offered to the trooper beside him.

Mildred delivered cornbread to the troopers, asked Malone if he'd like another beer, then took the troopers' orders for fish and chips. "Onion rings?" she asked them. "Eat your fish, Wilson," she said to Malone, who was careening over the guardrails now.

Ozzie wondered why Veronica Hammond would go all the way to Lynn for a Valium prescription. Maybe she collected Valium prescriptions. "What about dog bites?" he said to Malone.

"Dog bites!" Malone boomed. "No dog bites—Bozo said he checked. No dog bites!" And then, as an afterthought to Ozzie: "How's the fishing, Ralph?"

Ozzie said, "Fishing's fine, Norton."

"No trouble this morning?"

Ozzie shook his head. "In and out like a judge," he said. "Copied her entire file."

"Good, Ralph!" Malone said. "Fine! That's just grand, Ralph."

Malone was recovering, returning to his plate. Salt and

pepper dredgers to the troopers who, when the moment arrived, chuckled like kids as Mildred let them see their meals.

"You were right," the second trooper said across his partner's plate to Ozzie. "Looks great."

"It eats better than it looks," Ozzie said.

"Malone!" Mildred said. "Drink your beer."

Ozzie turned to look out the windows at MacAvoy's lights, the Canadian dragger tied up against the pilings.

"You're up to no good," Rocket said. The old coot had his feet up on a shotgun can next to Owl. He closed his eyes again, levering his Stratolounger back against the wall.

Ozzie fiddled with the old man's 1962 desk calendar, leafing through one or two notes while he waited for Boynton to answer his telephone. Rocket's office reeked of kerosene. "How's the plastic pipe working?" Ozzie said softly.

"Dandy," Rocket said. "I've mixed a new batch o' powder that'll smack the clouds. When do you wanna see it go?"

"Whenever you're ready."

"I'm soakin' fuse now—might be the best beauty yet," Rocket said as he squirmed, the better to see Ozzie.

Sheldon Boynton came on the line: "How may I help you?"

"Federal Reserve in Philadelphia," Ozzie said. "Is this Sheldon Boynton?"

"Yes."

"My name is Sproston—my COIN number is forty-five nineteen."

Boynton was awfully quick: "Who?" he said.

"Philadelphia—I have very little time, friend. I spoke to your president. He's passed me on to you for access code verification."

Boynton looked up. DeSilva had the *Wall Street Journal*

open on his presidential desk. "I don't understand," Boynton said, almost whispering.

"Well," Ozzie said, "we've got a problem. Actually we've got two problems—one with a fax transfer in January and the other with a waybill passage for three hundred thousand on February fourteenth—that was Valentine's Day, wasn't it?"

"Yes, it was," Boynton said, remembering his Valentine's cake that Darla had refused to eat because he'd made it with butter. Darla and her infamous cholesterol number . . . "Do you want these children to grow up and die?" she'd yelled at him.

Boynton had no idea what a fax transfer was, nor did he know what a waybill passage was. "What'd you say your name was?"

"Sproston," Ozzie said.

Rocket opened his eyes to see Ozzie. Ozzie waved him off.

"The First Seaman's Bank sent the January fax transfer to a Dayton, Ohio, rolling-mill credit union. Are you aware of that?"

"No," Boynton said. "But I don't handle these things."

"Well, your president—what's his name, Silver?"

"De—Silva," Boynton said.

"He said you would be able to assist us. If you can't," Ozzie said, "would you kindly transfer me to someone who can?"

"Tell me what you need," Boynton said. DeSilva folded the *Journal* and checked his watch against the bank clock over the front door. You bastard, Boynton thought.

"I need to verify the access codes, please."

"What access codes?"

"Boynton, is it?"

"Yes."

"Please transfer me back to your president."

"Tell me what codes, please."

"Your president, please."

"What codes?"

"Your computer in—where are you?—Strike's Landing? Is that a town or what?"

"It's a swell town," Boynton said. "We're on the ocean. Are you in Rotary?"

"Federal Reserve funds did not download off your on-line storage. Obviously, we have to find out why that happened. Is your computer up and running now?"

"I think so," Boynton said. "Sure it is—we're open. Must be."

"I'll give you the seven-digit access codes as we have them here for verification. Are you ready?"

Boynton copied down numbers that meant nothing to him.

Ozzie said, "Now—can we validate the first two, please?"

"I'll check," Boynton said. He excused himself, dropped the phone, ran to Noel Flagler, who was writing the mortgage for his brother's apartment house. "I don't understand," Flagler said to him. Boynton tried the Jerrold woman, but she sent him away with a wave of her pointy nails and returned to a phone conversation of her own. Boynton was cornered; he went over to DeSilva and said, "Federal Reserve in Philadelphia needs to verify our computer access codes."

DeSilva lifted his blotter and handed Boynton a sheaf of paper. "Return it to me, please."

"Yes, sir," Boynton said, hopping across the carpet to his desk.

Rocket had his eyes closed. "They're gonna throw away the key when they get you, boy."

"I'm here," Ozzie said into the telephone. "Speak, please."

"I have numbers," Boynton said. "But they don't look anything like the numbers you gave me."

"Are your codes current?"

"I don't think I should provide this information over the phone."

"Please buzz me back to your president—Silver, is it?" Ozzie said.

Boynton read Ozzie a flock of numbers, none of which made sense to Ozzie.

"They're gonna throw away the key," Rocket said from his chair.

"Okay," Ozzie said. "We agree on the waybill passage number except for two digits. But I'm afraid the others do not check out. These aren't current numbers." Ozzie thought he recognized an IRS code in the flock. "Thank you, Boynton. I'll have to get back to you. If you don't mind, I'll leave a note on your down-line log for today and confirm our codes there. Is that satisfactory?"

Boynton agreed and hung up the phone.

"Everything all right?" DeSilva said when Boynton walked the papers over to him.

"They'll confirm on today's log," Boynton said.

Rocket said, "Do you have any idea what you're doing?"

Ozzie said he didn't as he folded July 4, 1962, into his coat pocket.

"They'll have your ass, boy."

Later in the afternoon, DeSilva passed Boynton's desk and said, "Who wanted those codes?"

"Federal Reserve," Boynton said. He slid his arm into his raincoat.

"Over the telephone?"

"I've got his COIN number."

"His what?"

"COIN number."

"What the hell's a COIN number, Sheldon?" DeSilva sat down.

Al Wasserman scratched his chin. His screen was a puzzle. "Give me the next one," he said.

Ozzie read the next number. Malone stood at the computer lab's glass wall, the one room in the school that connected every department to every other department, and the state college to the cosmos.

"That's no good, either," Wasserman said. The man had hair like a 1928 brilliantine lothario at a Monaco chemin-de-fer table. A mustache like a line of ink over his lip.

"Oz, I told you Al was good," Malone said from the window. "Ever tutored before, Al?"

"Nope," Wasserman said, intent on his screen.

"Tutoring's been the single contribution of higher education to my life," Malone said. "Naomi's been dead for seven years—always think about her in the spring."

"One more," Wasserman said to Ozzie. Wasserman tapped his keys, prompting the monster of the midway around them to belch in binary codes. The lab was one massive computer, buff-colored cabinets and spinning tapes, countless bleeping lights bringing the good news from Ghent.

Malone said, "I sure do miss her," and shoved his hands into his pockets.

Wasserman said, "Wait a minute—that's a bank! That's our bank!"

He glared at Ozzie.

Ozzie said, "In like a worm, Wilson."

"They want our ID," Wasserman said, as his screen filled with blinking text.

Ozzie read him the ID code for Benson Benson MacGregor & Ayers.

"Getting late, Oz," Malone said. Malone was ruminating.

"Hold on," Wasserman said. "You guys can't zing a bank— we can go to jail for this."

"It can't be this simple," Ozzie said. Ozzie shoved Wasserman off the chair and sat down at the monitor. "I'll do it," he said, as he typed his old investment firm's access code. The monster gulped, the screen went blank, then sat expectantly available. "How can that be?" he said. Ozzie used DeSilva's handwritten sheets, dashing through his copied mother lode of bank info to find—"Son of a bitch," he said—checking accounts, savings accounts, bad debts, debits and credits for this month, this year to date. "Printer on?" he asked Wasserman.

"Hey look—I can't do this!"

Ozzie got up, checked the printer, then downloaded the entire First Seaman's Bank into a cardboard box on the state-college computer lab's floor. "You want a few bucks in your checking account, Wilson?"

"Very thoughtful, Oz," Malone said, turning from the window to wink at Wasserman. "Can you get the Bank of Boston?" Malone explained again to Wasserman that he and Ozzie believed the First Seaman's was crooked—"Criminal intent!" he yelled—that Wasserman would not be implicated: Malone would answer anyone's questions about the lab's involvement.

"But you don't know anything," Wasserman said to him.

"I put the lights on when we arrived—you saw me do that. Besides, you'll be a hero—"60 Minutes" will show up—Ed Bradley—the works."

Al Wasserman was not convinced: "We're gonna lose our tenure."

Sleeping Over

Ozzie dropped Malone at the country club, where Malone was to chair the greens committee for a two-hour bash on turf management. Ozzie got to the mall late, ran in for his pork lo mein, fried rice, and Mongolian beef, then hurried to Ruby's, where she was waiting with an overnight bag.

"I think I could love you," she said, getting in beside him as Ozzie fired up the jeep.

He stopped in the road. "You do?" he said.

"Do you know what's happening?" she said.

"Funny you should ask," he said. "I thought I was the only one."

"You're not."

"I'll be damned. How did that happen?"

"I think it's your dentist's chair," she said. "Put on your lights."

He drove quickly past Mildred's, past the bank, the dark shops, past the courthouse, up the hill and into the residential maze of Victoriana and forsythia. They bounced into his driveway, snagged a quick smooch for the umpteenth time and toddled up his back stairs into his kitchen.

Malone's moose tapestry was rolled up on Ozzie's kitchen floor. A housewarming gift, Malone had called it, intending that Ozzie should make the house a home with genuine north-woods aplomb. Ozzie put down their Chinese meal on the kitchen table.

He stopped.

"What's the matter?" Ruby said, lifting champagne from her bag.

"I hung that moose up a week ago—in the living room over the fireplace," he said, as he walked into the hall, then into the living room.

Ruby heard him swear as she passed his ruined telephone. When she heard the faint scuff on the stairs, Ruby looked up and met Louise for the first time.

Louise was in a yellow nightgown. "Who are you?" Louise said to Ruby.

Ozzie bounded out of the living room, skidding on the hall rugs.

Louise fluffed her shower-wet hair as she descended the stairs: "Ozzie, who is this woman?"

"What are you doing here?" he yelled.

"I'm home," Louise said.

"Home?" Ozzie said. "You aren't home, dammit!"

"I think we should try again," Louise said. "Dr. Belsen—he's my new therapist—he thinks we should give it another go. And I've got a new church. And this is new," she said, pirouetting to let him see her nightgown. "I'm home, Ozzie."

Ozzie gaped at Ruby and, as soon as he did, Ruby stepped backward, shaking her head. "Don't go," he said to Ruby. "Please? Wait?"

"Who is she, Ozzie?" Louise said, smiling off the stairs as though she were being presented at the yacht-club June cotillion.

"Ruby!" he yelled.

But Ozzie was far too late, far too scattered, and far too slow.

Ruby was out the door with her case and into the jeep. "Take your hands off me!" she said. She wrenched her arm loose. Started the jeep.

Ozzie reached for the key and missed, as Ruby almost took off his foot when she reversed down the driveway and into the road. Ruby paused out there, safely distant from him. Stared at Ozzie. Then she hit first gear.

"Who was she, Ozzie?" Louise called from the back porch.

"What?"

"Who was she?"

"No one you know, you old cow."

"Are you at all pleased to see me?"

"I'm not, Louise. You can have the house—Louise. Have the furniture. Have the clocks—have my Old Town canoe!" he said, digging up the porch stairs past her. "But you can't have the Chinese food, Louise. And you don't get the fucking moose!"

She closed the kitchen door behind her. He got up off his knees, moose tapestry in one arm, Chinese food in the other.

Louise said, "I'm glad to see you."

Ozzie thought his heart would seize on the spot.

"How could you?" he said.

"How could I what? This is my home."

"You can't just walk in here like this."

"I can, Ozzie Barrett. Now, when you're more able to discuss our rift, when you resolve some of the things eating at you and understand I still love you, we can share our feelings without hurting each other. Are you surprised?"

Ozzie believed that his body would seep a green slime at his joints first and then burst to cover these kitchen walls. They'd be scraping his green goo off the cabinets with putty knives.

"No, I'm not surprised, Louise. I should have known. You don't get the Chinese food, Louise! The Mongolian beef is mine!" he said, going for the door.

"Think before you leap, Ozzie."

He crashed the door into the refrigerator. Glass shattered. "If I thought about it, Louise, I would jump!" He went out

178

onto the porch. "It's all yours, Louise!" he yelled. "All yours!"
"You'll be back," she said. "You always come back, and so
have I. And when you do come back—do you hear me?—
when you do, I'll be here. I'll leave the light on for you."

Ozzie hit the driveway on the run, ran through the tulips
and down the sidewalk. He kept on running. Ran for hours.
Hard on a guy who's forty-seven.

⚓ ⚓ ⚓

With Veronica Hammond's demise came Richie DeSilva's
momentary disquiet at the prospect of his discovery as a Don
Juan. But the police had been helpful, had given him his
things from her house with a wink and a nod that let him
know he had friends in low places. But they kept his softball
bat. Babs knew what he and the woman were up to. She
never said she did. But DeSilva and Babs had been darting
each other for years; she took his need to conquer women
and real estate as an embodiment of his genetic weakness;
he took her purposeful blindness to his shortcomings as
proof of her innate sense of quality, her acceptance that only
little people resorted to displaying their liabilities. Maguires,
on the other hand, had nothing to prove.

His name was Kurt. He was an Argentine ocean racer
stranded in Massachusetts when his boat went south as a
wedding gift for a Miami lawyer. Kurt's owner had sold the
wheel right out of Kurt's hands over an October weekend
and given Kurt a few thousand to get lost. Kurt was on the
run, so to speak, as American immigration goons thought
they heard the strains of the Argentine national anthem
calling Kurt home. But the deliciously powerful Kurt, his
legs like horse's necks, his arms veined with wire and
muscle—the Argentine was asleep beside Babs DeSilva in
her king-size bed, a blue platform the size of a Montana
backyard.

Richie had driven off for Logan Airport this very evening,
his cream Cadillac with its sparkling wire wheels dipping

hard into Wayland Terrace when he left without saying good-bye, heading off for a Las Vegas bankers' meeting without her. Within the hour, Babs had cruised out of their garage and down their drive in her Mercedes. She'd headed south to Marblehead where the delicious Kurt lived alone over a sports shop he managed.

It never took Babs long to return, seemingly alone in her Mercedes, Kurt a crouched bundle of testosterone next to her, as she drove into her garage and dropped the door against the watchful others who could somehow never ignore Babs DeSilva.

Babs loved having Kurt in Richie's bed.

Kurt did things to Babs she'd never dreamed would be hers, wicked sexual things more deviant than she'd ever hoped for. There were women in Bangkok who smoked nine cigarettes at once . . . Babs knew about that. Some Caribbean women took three men simultaneously . . . Babs knew about that, too. And Richie DeSilva? Well, she'd sigh, and think to herself, Richie never got outside Richie and, in their early days, she'd only squeaked once or twice while Richie climbed all over her.

Oh, but Kurt! There were no hoops on this man's expectations. All of Babs was fair game to him, every nook she owned had been kissed, caressed, nurtured, and splayed. Kurt was indefatigably powerful enough to bounce her over his head, catching her before she hit the bed, strong enough, hot enough to work our Babs over so completely that she frequently lost consciousness, regaining herself in time to feel Kurt playing somewhere inside her body. She'd go out again, lost on a liquid blush of K-Y Jelly. She repeatedly awoke, crawled out of her exhausted bog to find him snoozing at her shoulder, his delicious Argentine hair like black feathers.

Babs began buying canned Argentine corned beef and usually drove to Marblehead, but had recently taken Kurt into her bed, relishing her discovery that Richie DeSilva

180

made the perfect cuckold. All heroes who insist on their heroism have been cuckolded by hubris to begin with . . . Babs knew that.

But on this night Babs awoke once, the powerful arm covering her tiny teacup breasts. Kurt slept like a man, his flaccid thong pulsing against her leg, not like a child. Kurt didn't move, breathed stealthily.

He was already in her house, rustling through her unlocked laundry-room door in his plastic K mart rainsuit.

Babs listened to Kurt, listened to herself, her hair still cool with sweat. Richie DeSilva probably couldn't wait to roll off one or two Las Vegas bimbos, ever the tiny Portuguese bank president with aspirations to arrogance. Babs closed her eyes again. Her bottom felt stretched, her hips flicking love notes to her.

He was already in their den, opening Richie DeSilva's gun cabinet, selecting Richie's 9mm Colt automatic, its stainless-steel barrel like ice in his rubber glove. He dropped its magazine, chuckled deep in his gut when he saw the cartridges, and slid the magazine home again.

Babs knew no woman in Strike's Landing could take on the delicious Kurt. Frightened little people, she thought. They talk and titter, give their docile hubbies a dutiful weekly grunt just to keep their men in check. She'd like to videotape one of *her* performances with the mighty Kurt, surprise them all at the club some rainy Thursday afternoon, let them sit in their own moistness.

He was already on her stairs, already climbing tread over tread, his surgeon's gloves smooth along the polished railing, his rubbers silent.

Babs felt Kurt's hand noodle her left arm. She was reassured and at peace, the house still. All dreams liquid.

He was already outside her bedroom door, already pressing the brass latch, already here. He came into her bedroom, more a shiny specter than a shadow, crossed to the bed, cocked the hammer, and fired.

Mildred kept Ozzie in the kitchen, replacing his mug of coffee every time the old one got cold. Ruby's house had been dark. She didn't answer her door, her phone rang and rang and rang. He'd gone around to her doors on the wharf, but she wasn't there. Not a sight, not a sound, not a glimmer of love left for this man.

Ozzie knew it was late. Malone's moose tapestry was propped against Mildred's cooler. The Chinese food was feeding the harbor crabs by now.

Mildred banged into her kitchen. Her help had gone home hours before. "Ozzie?" she called. She held the door with her hip.

"I'm sorry," he said, getting to his feet off the milk crate.

"Nothing to be sorry about," she said. "Malone's out here—he's looking for you."

"What time is it?"

"After three," she said. "I've got to go home."

"I'm sorry," Ozzie said.

"Don't cry anymore," she said. "Makes me want to cry, too."

"I'm going. Thanks."

Malone stood in the darkened bar, his hat in his hand, pipe billowing. "Hey, Oz," he said.

"Hey, Wilson."

"You okay?"

"No."

Malone reached for Ozzie's briefcase. "I stopped at your house—talked to Louise," Malone said. "Where are you going to sleep tonight?"

"I don't know," Ozzie said. He gripped the moose tapestry with his arm. "I think I'd like to see my Uncle Barry."

Mildred hugged Ozzie in her sticklike arms, her head to his chest.

Malone said, "I'm glad I found you, Oz."

Mildred rubbed Ozzie's back as a mother might.

"Whole town's coming apart at the seams tonight," Malone said. "I was real worried about you."

"I'm okay," Ozzie said to Mildred.

Malone said, "Babs DeSilva shot a man tonight."

"I don't care, Wilson," Ozzie said.

"You will. The guy was in her bed when she shot him."

"DeSilva?" Ozzie said. The harbor cast winking pings of light through the darkened bar.

"No," Malone said. "Some Chicano guy, I guess. Somethin', huh?"

"Sound and fury," Ozzie said. "Sound and fury."

Nowhere to Run,
Nowhere to Hide

OZZIE woke up in the *Lucia*'s berth slightly before noon the next morning. He'd slept on Malone's moose tapestry as a mattress. From the wheelhouse, Ozzie saw that the sun was bright, MacAvoy's was busy, people jostled in and out of the First Seaman's Bank and the supermarket, a tour bus roared through town. There were new boats in the harbor, new moorings clenched to the harbor bottom for the season. DeSilva's white yacht was one of seven other yachts out for the summer.

Strike's Landing was going about its business, he thought, while he felt more muddled, more frightened than he'd ever felt. What the hell is wrong with Louise? he wondered. The woman is mentally ill. Unbalanced. Ruby had backed away from him with her hands raised to ward him off as though he were green slime incarnate. She'd been strong in the jeep when he tried to stop her.

Ozzie remembered standing in London's St. Paul's once with its peculiarly ascetic clear-glass windows, most of its stained glass having been blasted by the Blitz. Blitz is right, he thought, as he tried to regain his balance, sitting in his dentist's chair, his Nescafé sailor's mug perched on his knee. No matter how resolute his actions, no matter that he thought as clearly as he could, no matter what he did, the bombs kept coming through his windows, carrying away his glass. His life as a trawlerman escaped from a fiduciary asylum was being blasted into bits of stained glass, his entire life becoming a night in the Blitz . . . whole chunks of masonry, mullions, and tracery thudding onto his heart's stone floor.

Ozzie cranked over the diesel to let it warm up, then climbed up onto the wharf and walked slowly to Rocket's office.

"I knew you was here," Rocket said.

"Where is she?"

"She's over workin' on that Canadian dragger—guy's got a fearful mess, he has. We had a cutter in here this morning. They gonna arrest him, ya think?"

Ozzie asked him if Ruby had slept here last night.

Rocket said, "She did." Rocket's eyebrows fluttered. "You two havin' a spat?"

"I don't know what we're having," Ozzie said, leaning against the office door with the sun on his back.

"Girl took the truck over to her place this morning early."

Ozzie backed out onto the ramp to see across the harbor. The Canadian dragger had a rusted hull and flew the Maple Leaf. "She say anything?"

"Nope," Rocket said. "Said she didn't wanna dance with you."

"Anything else?"

"Nope. She said she might have to pull the Canadian guy's engine—I'll have to tow him over here to get that one out with my crane."

"Anything else?"

"Nope. But I need you to drive me to Boston soon."

"Why not Ruby?"

"Fannydancers, Oz. Think we could?"

185

"Up to you."

"Don't say a word about this to the girl. I got some business in Boston. Not for her to know everything, is it? Can you take me?"

"Always have, haven't I?"

"Yup, you have. Can we buy some licky and do those fannydancers in that hotel?"

"Why not?" Ozzie said. "Been a while for a randy old bastard like you."

"Has, hasn't it?" Rocket said, adjusting his cloth cap.

Ozzie said he might go out tonight and stay out for a full load.

Ozzie eased the *Lucia* alongside the Canadian boat, heaved his line to a young crewman in waders and hard hat. Larry was perched up on the radar. Ozzie whistled at the bird and said, "Ozzie's here."

She was below in a dank engine room with two men, one of them the Canadian captain.

Ozzie held onto a bulkhead until she saw him from beneath the engine, her hands black with grease, face grimy.

She patted the deckplate for a wrench, then leaned back and under where her light was.

Ozzie waited for her. The captain had a cracked rod. "I didn't plan on this," he said to Ozzie. Ozzie knew the man's heart had to be in his throat, badly broken down in an alien harbor, Coast Guard cutters nosing around, the repair costs astronomical, the man feeling as if he might never get home.

Ozzie introduced himself to the man.

And waited uncomfortably until Ruby slid out from beneath the engine and reached for a rag. "It's coming out," she said to the Canadians. "Can't touch it. We've got a crane here that can lift it out in nothing flat. Have it back in as soon as we find a rod."

Ozzie wanted to smile at her, but she ignored him until she told them what needed to be done.

"I haven't got cash enough," the captain said to her.

Ruby looked back at the man and said, "Send it to me when you get home."

"You sure?" the captain said.

"Why not?" she said, rubbing her hands with a filthy rag.

"Yards usually do cash," the captain said, worried.

"This yard doesn't. How the hell else you gonna get home?"

The Canadian captain tipped his cap at Ruby, genuinely relieved, smiling at his crewman.

She turned to Ozzie, then stepped into a companionway and up the ladder.

"I'm sorry," he said, when they stood at the rail next to MacAvoy's pilings. Ozzie listened for *Lucia*'s exhaust.

"So am I," she said. "So am I."

"I didn't know she was there."

"Obviously."

"I apologize," he said.

Her hands were creased with oil. "You've got enough to do," she said. "Get your Uncle Barry straightened out. Get your divorce straightened out. If you're not going to live with Louise, you need to find yourself a place."

"I'm not living with Louise!"

"She thought you were last night."

"*She* did—she wouldn't know sanity if it bit her. The divorce papers are already filed."

"Well," Ruby said, watching a man struggling with a winch motor; "you get your divorce straightened out—get yourself free."

"Then what?"

"I don't know," she said. "I've done husbands before—it's not worth it. You have to go through your divorce, I don't want to."

"I'm hating every second of this. We're finished?"

"I don't know that we ever really got started," she said. "When you're not worried sick about your uncle, your wife is cascading down your front stairs in a new nightgown. Ugly thing, she is, too."

He wanted to open his jacket, fold her against his chest, never release her.

She said, "I've gotta get this engine out."

"Would you have supper with me—tonight?"

"Over at Mildred's with all your cronies? I don't think so. You go home," she said, stepping toward the hatch. "Go home and straighten out your life first."

"Don't stick around for the hard stuff, do you?" he heard himself say.

Ruby froze, her eyes narrowing.

"You better skip on home and see if Louise has your lunch ready."

⚓ ⚓ ⚓

Ozzie cleared the harbor, passed a white fiberglass tub in the narrows, and drove the *Lucia* into the clean blue Atlantic, the sun striping shadows across his deck as a stiff breeze blew through his wheelhouse. With only enough fuel for a hundred miles or so, he was not about to fish. Ozzie punched his CD player for Bellini and kept the trawler on a straight course.

Much later, after he found himself steering wide circles, Ozzie shut down the engine and went back into the cabin. He opened the aft door that hadn't been cracked since he bought the boat, swept the cabin clean, chucked the mold-fuzzy refrigerator contents over the rail, hauled in buckets of seawater to bathe the cabin deck with soap, then hosed the whole thing out. He nailed Malone's moose over the berth. He stowed his gear forward in the bow, opened his cabin portholes, and made himself coffee on his clean pro-pane stove.

"Fine," he said aloud. "Fine."

He felt like he was chewing glass.

Malone's moose gave the cabin a mysterious touch, but he could throw some paint in here . . . lighten it up.

Ozzie went on deck and washed everything he could, his broom scraping fish scales and fins out of the scuppers, his hose hard to blast everything foul off this boat.

He washed out the wheelhouse, cleaned its windows, oiled all the hinges and doors, the porthole hinges and his windshield wiper. He polished his running lights and went up the swaying mast with a roll of paper towels to dissolve the salt on his masthead lights. From aloft, he thought the *Lucia* was dazzling, her decks drying in the sun, the sea around him empty and brilliantly speckled with sunshot waves.

Ozzie hung up there for a while, his bleached Swedish ensign snapping, listening to the wind scatter Bellini all the way to Spain.

When he got back into the wheelhouse, Ozzie went into his locker for his sweatshirt and fatigue pants, then out to the stern, where he tossed a line over the side, stripped off his clothes, doused himself in Murphy's Oil Soap and dove into the Atlantic, the sea with an icy clench at his lungs as he pulled as deep as he could. He let his own buoyancy lift him to the surface, the brine bubbles fluttering under his chin, his legs treading slowly, his weathered hands like dark mitts, arms winter white.

The French Don't
Live Like This

"You know Wendell—he's custodian at the courthouse. Christ, Oz, your mind's nothin' compared to mine." Rocket rapped his pipe empty on the wharf. "I just welded up a set of swings for his grandkids—you took 'em over with me last fall—that early snow?"

Ozzie remembered a withered woman had invited them in for coffee, into her basement, where her husband had a stove carton filled with thousands of yellow tennis balls because the husband refused to play with used balls. Remembering anything now invoked his St. Paul's afternoon. Ozzie recalled the stained-plastic lamp on the guy's wet bar. Rocket and he were served their coffee in that basement, the place reeking of formaldehyde, a plump nude in a barnboard frame over the guy's tennis trophies.

Rocket had gone on without him: "They arrested her this afternoon, took her right to Judge Mahoney, who still owes me two hundred and fifty bucks. Old Mahoney give her bail. She musta paid that herself with one of her New York City checks. They think she shot him, Oz."

"Shot who?" Ozzie tried to sit solidly quiet in the rocking chair, the harbor before them asleep.

"Jeezus, Oz! The Mexican!"

"You said he was Argentine."

"Same thing," Rocket said, and filled his pipe. "Shot him in her bed. Musta had a lovers' squabble or somethin'—she shot the son of a bitch right through his rump."

"What was DeSilva doing in Las Vegas?"

"I dunno," Rocket said. He used a kitchen match to light his pipe. "Wendell says they had to call the poor bastard— tell him his wife just shot her loverboy. I mean, we did damn stupid things, Oz, but I never shot anyone. Well, once. But that son of a bitch was beggin' to be shot."

"Did you kill him?"

"He jumped, doncha know. I thought he was mine."

"Where is Babs DeSilva now?" Ozzie asked. The lights had flicked on at Ruby's place.

"I dunno. DeSilva had to fly home today from Las Vegas. Are you ready?"

"Not yet," Ozzie said. "What else did Wendell say?"

"Nothin'," Rocket said, a smoke plume around his head. "He said the DeSilva woman's pregnant."

"How does Wendell know that?"

"Same way he knows everything, Oz. He reads. Wendell always was a good reader. Says she's a few months along— probably have one of them chico kids. When are you gonna be ready?"

"Almost," Ozzie said.

"I'm gettin' anxious."

"I thought you had to dry the fuse?"

"I did. Good sun today. Dried jus' fine."

"What else did Wendell say?"

"Call 'im, Oz! Christ, call Wendell up and ask 'im yourself. He didn't say nothin' else. But the cops have the pistol she used. It's DeSilva's pistol, too. She musta gone on down to his den, got this big dandy pistol and plugged the son of a bitch while he was dreamin' o' Jeannie or somethin'. Hard to figure, isn't it? Nice woman like that. Pushy but nice when she paid you. Didn't bark once."

Ozzie's mind was a snakepit of possibilities, but more than anything else, he saw now there was hope for Uncle Barry. Strike's Landing hadn't had a murder in forty-four years. And now one murder and one attempt only weeks apart, and both touched by DeSilva. "Wendell say how big the guy was?"

Rocket spat into the harbor. "Nope. Jus' said he was a Mexican fella."

"Argentine."

"You ready?"

"I am," Ozzie said. "Where do you want me?"

"There's good." The old man came out of his chair, gathered what equilibrium he could, then hobbled up his ramp into his office.

Ruby's windows were pinky soft through the *Lucia*'s mast and rigging.

Rocket shouted for help.

Ozzie found him in his laboratory, cradling a four-foot plastic wastepipe with a blunt nose fashioned from a Ra-Pid-Gro plant-food container. The pipe had fins on its base.

"This your biggest yet?" Ozzie asked.

"Nope," Rocket said. "You take the rocket, but try not to bang it any. Mixture's a touch tender—I had to use dynamite."

Ozzie lifted the rocket in his arms. "You can't use dynamite."

"Well, no, you can't—not as dynamite, you can't. But I have a special blend in there that should punch a hole right through God's back porch."

Rocket carried his mortar, and together they made their rickety way down the wharf, passing empty shacks and patched windows, the wharf creaking with their steps.

"I called Ruby—she's gonna watch," Rocket said, as he opened the supports on his mortar and leveled its mouth straight up.

Ozzie had looked toward Ruby's, but now slowly slid the rocket down into its firing tube. Rocket was on his knees, working fuse through the hatch at the mortar's base. "Don't bother with her," Rocket said. "She ain't out there yet."

"I'll bet DeSilva didn't go to Las Vegas at all," Ozzie said.

"You gotta think about somethin' else, boy. Hold this fuse."

Rocket worked for a few minutes, Ozzie watching for Ruby from time to time. Ozzie said, "I'll bet that son of a bitch shot the Mexican himself—made it look like his wife did it."

"I hope Barry's watching tonight. He'll see this one from Medford. You said her loverboy was a chico."

"Not chico, for chrissake—chicano! And he was Argentine."

"Then why'd you say he was Mexican?"

"Let's light this."

"Not yet," Rocket said, standing. "Go sit in your chair—I'll be along pronto."

"Richie DeSilva's on a rampage of death and destruction," Ozzie said.

Ruby was standing on her wharf, a silhouette against her doors.

"Go sit down, boy. This is going to be a beauty."

Ozzie walked back along the wharf, the *Lucia* ahead of him, their chairs. And Ruby across the harbor. Another clink of stained glass smashed on his heart's stone floor.

Rocket came along in a few minutes, his face bright with a new pipeful of cherry, eyes alive.

"Did you light it?" Ozzie said.

"You're gonna wet your pants."

Ozzie looked for Ruby quickly, but then he caught a burst of orange spark far down the wharf. Another burst. Silence.

The thing went up like a French Exocet, a blurred streak of smoke hanging in the night air after it, like a photo negative of a lightning stroke.

"Where'd it go?" Ozzie said.

"Hush, boy."

There wasn't a sound in this harbor. Until directly overhead bloomed a gargantuan chrysanthemum of blue followed by pink followed by a silver shower that lasted for five seconds or more. The thundering blast rocked the harbor, echoing and repeating for miles.

Another silver shower, then blue, and a phosphorescent white flare dangled high over Strike's Landing.

Then another boom.

"You've never had one that high," Ozzie said, watching the flare drift over the waking town.

"What a beauty!" Rocket yelled. "A beauty, Oz! Son of a bitch! I'll bet that was a mile up. Wasn't that jus' the most beautiful thing you've ever imagined?"

"A beauty," Ozzie said.

"Was a beauty, wasn't it?"

Rocket watched until the flare disappeared over the cemetery hill.

Ruby had gone in.

Get the Gaff

OZZIE found Lacey Beal's house in the morning, one of many shacks with dimpled tin roofs, refrigerators and freezers oxidizing in the surrounding woods, the Beal shack hidden with others at the end of a dirt road that wound an uncertain way beside a salt marsh. Ozzie left the jeep and went through a fence to knock on a paint-flaked door. Old toys, empty Gulf gas cans, red STP bottles had been permanently dropped to the dirt long enough ago so that spikes of witch grass grew around each one.

Lacey Beal opened the door. Ozzie said who he was, that his uncle had been mistakenly charged with Veronica Hammond's murder, that he wanted to talk to her, if he could.

She said she didn't know anything, couldn't help him, her arms white and thin. She might have been pretty in another life not squandered in poverty. Early twenties . . . a dark age of untenable compulsions all shoved into one human frame had already flexed her skin into worry-webs around her mouth, her eye sockets moodily brushed with madness.

"Did you clean her house after she died?" he asked.

"I don't dare go back."

"Do you know that Veronica Hammond left you a thousand dollars in her will?"

Lacey Beal tilted her head, picked at her thumbnail. "Not a thousand," she said.

"You do know!"

"Me and her talked about it. She wanted me to finish high school. I'm gonna go to secretarial college. It's fifty thousand—that's my college money. She give it to me. She was very good to me—she give me clothes. Coats, boots, stuff like that."

"My uncle didn't kill her."

"I know who your uncle is," she said, head down suddenly as though she couldn't stand for Ozzie to look at her. She had long, wispy blond hair in unwashed hanks. She wore dirty tennis sneakers. "I used to stay over her house a lot." Her mind seemed to drift for a beat, then she said, "But I can't now. She had a bad time when her husband died—she let me live with her, sometimes."

"Did you sleep in her guest room?"

"That's my room," she said. "She called it my room."

"She was good to you."

"She was." She lifted her face, but looked past Ozzie. "Your uncle used to come around sometimes—he brought me grapes last fall after I told him I'm partial to grapes. I think it's terrible he killed her."

"He didn't."

"How do you know about her will, mister?"

"The police know about it. They talked to me about Veronica Hammond—about you, and the men who used to visit her."

"So?"

There was a man walking down the road from the marsh, a stooped figure in the woods. Ozzie had seen her eyes flicker a silent alarm. The man carried two five-gallon plastic buckets.

"When did she think she and Richard DeSilva would be married?"

Shocked, she said, "You're crazy. She wasn't about to marry any man. She hated men."

"Did she hate Richard DeSilva?"

Lacey Beal glanced again at the approaching figure on the road. "What is it you want, mister? I don't have to talk to you."

He said she didn't. He also said it was up to him to convince the police his uncle didn't kill Veronica Hammond.

"They wouldn't lock him up if he was innocent," she said. She couldn't take her eyes off the man on the road.

"Did she date other men?"

"She didn't date any men."

"But Richard DeSilva came to her house often," he said.

"No, he didn't."

"He sent flowers."

"Nope—nothin' like that."

The man with the buckets slowed to inspect the jeep, turned hesitantly to take in the girl and Ozzie at the shack's door.

"That's my pop," she said. "You better go. I can't tell you nothin'."

The wobbly old drunk, skin brown and creased by weather, lurched through the fence. His buckets were covered with cloth tied with clothesline. "Who's this?" he said to his daughter, avoiding Ozzie.

Ozzie said who he was, said why he was standing in the man's yard.

"She don't know nothin'," the old man said. "She weren't even invited to the burial."

"Nobody sends out invitations to a burial," Ozzie said.

" 'Course they do!" her father said. "Get 'em all the time. She didn't get nothin'."

"Where do you set your lobster pots?"

"They ain't lobsters!" the old man said, pushing past his daughter. "They's fish."

197

Ozzie could smell the lobsters. And there was little likelihood this man had a license for lobster traps. The old drunk had been out raiding pots. Fishing boots, his oarlocks tied at the waist of his plastic rainsuit, his hat stained with salt.

Lacey Beal leaned off the shack and went inside. The door smacked the loose jamb hard.

Two kids, who should have been in school, were fighting in front of another shack nearer the marsh, one of them beating the kid on the ground with a naked doll.

Ozzie had never been down here, or possibly here hadn't been here when he was kid. He remembered the salt marsh; he'd gone crabbing in the marsh with fish heads and a bushel basket. But no one lived down here then, no shacks and trash, no road at all.

Lacey Beal knew about money and wills, and very likely a good deal more. And Lacey Beal lied.

Ozzie stopped at his house. There was a Louise note on the counter: She had her therapy this morning, marketing, Tagliano had telephoned for him. Supper at five.

Not very likely, he thought, passing the repaired telephone in the hall as he bounced up the stairs into their bedroom. Her cosmetics were back on her grandmother's oak dressing table. He found his clothes washed, ironed, and hanging in his closet.

He collected the things he'd need into two duffel bags. Grabbed sheets and his army-surplus blanket, his shaving gear and toothbrush. Up into the attic for his rain poncho that had held him in its muggy grip in Vietnam, his machete and Marine Corps footlocker. Quickly downstairs and out to the jeep. Ozzie went back in for his pistol, into the hall table for his wallet. He found his faded soft cap from Parris Island in the cellar, grabbed his toolbox and ship's clock. Everything into Rocket's jeep.

Back upstairs for the mattress off one of the single guest beds, the mattress too big by miles for the *Lucia*'s berth.

Ozzie stood in his living room, mattress balanced on his head. He was leaving here most of what he ever owned. He took his CDs from the bookshelf. He'd leave all the books, except for the Matthew Arnold.

He consciously said good-bye to the place, almost room by room. The baby was two years old and her photograph, that child of two in a white nightgown, film-frozen before she went up to bed so long ago, that curious lilt in her face she always wore when she sat with him in the evenings, as though she were somehow surprised to be alive . . . she was there on the wall. He frequently couldn't remember her name, now. Rarely did he ever think of her, each remembrance with a sting, as he inevitably finished these recollections with a vision of the last memory: that tiny child, her hands gone soft like sleep, cold, his Molly dead with traitorous blood after two sudden years of life.

Ozzie took her photograph off the wall.

His Mayfly Molly.

He'd keep this one. . . . Louise can howl for as long as she likes, he thought.

When he backed the jeep into the street, Ozzie pleased himself because he realized he'd never return to this house as an occupant. "Address correction requested," he said, as he headed up the hill.

⚓ ⚓ ⚓

But before he could swing away from Strike's Landing and drive the ten miles out to the state college, Ozzie sped through the lights at Forest Street and wound the jeep up through the lawns of the insurance moguls and money managers, the parasitic physicians, the Legion of Decency guy who owned the fuel-oil business, past their tree-laden lots on curiously curved roads that had to present these residents with a drunken gymkhana after country-club dances, up onto the crest of the hill, high in Rotarian heaven, Rocket's jeep idling nicely. Richie DeSilva's cream Cadillac was in the drive, a yellow crime-scene tape from tree to tree out here near the road.

One of those windows, Ozzie thought, held visions too frightening to think about. But think about them he would.

Ozzie was surprised by the police cruiser that pulled up behind him. Sergeant Cabral. "Can I help you?" the cop said.

"Just looking," Ozzie said.

"Looking at what?"

"She really shoot a guy?"

"Somebody did," Cabral said, finishing his inspection of the battered jeep crammed with Ozzie's life's savings. "You aren't allowed to park up here."

"I'm not parked—I'm sitting. Parked is when the driver leaves the vehicle unattended."

"Crime scene—state law."

"State law, my ass," Ozzie said.

"Care to have me read you your rights?" Cabral stuck his fingers in his gunbelt. The guy was loaded with cop paraphernalia and carried a radio.

"You can't read, Cabral," Ozzie said.

"Now, hold on here, Barrett." Cabral didn't quite know what to do with his feet, so he gripped Ozzie's seatback and the jeep's windshield.

He'd like to yank me out by the neck, Ozzie thought. "How could you not remember that you and I sat next to each other in Miss Varney's geometry class?" Ozzie said. "Cabral, I don't understand you. I gave you every right answer you ever got in her room. She had big tits and you always got excited when she drew circles on the board—don't you remember? Her big wooden compass? How the hell can you forget that I saved your geometric ass?"

"Don't remember," Cabral said.

"You should. I made that year easy for you—you passed. And you never said thanks, you son of a bitch."

"Don't remember."

"Try."

Ozzie had the state-college computer lab to himself, the computer on line and ready to please. The afternoon had clouded over and rain licked the glass walls, Ozzie fascinated with drops fleeing down the glass. He thought two years was not long to live, but full enough in its way and as full a life as most lives, were it not for the disquieting fact that we expect more. Mayflies don't wring their wings in consternation that the fly-fishing Art Hibbing, up to his waist in pond water, has already lived thousands of times longer than they ever will. Maybe Mayfly Molly did have a good life.

Ozzie opened his briefcase, the copies of Richie DeSilva's credenza notes from the bank. He opened the box of computer-generated bank records, these huge pages cumbersome as he spread them on the floor. He'd never worked in a bank's belly, but by cross-referencing some of DeSilva's handwritten notes and codes, Ozzie started leafing through massive spreadsheet presentations, searching for the man's methods.

Ozzie was alone for over an hour until a spindly woman in a raincoat, carrying a giant canvas bag, flew through the lab to drop a red folder in front of him. Ozzie looked up at her, startled.

"Where is Dr. Traynor?"

Ozzie said he didn't know, checking to see where she might have come from.

"I went to his office—I can't wait! Have this ready by four," she said. "I'm due in Dr. Lott's office in five minutes."

Ozzie looked for a clock: quarter of three.

"Where did Dr. Traynor say he was going?" she said. The

woman was like a rampant sandhill crane, a towering thin woman with graying hair and giant blue balls as a necklace around her neck.

"He didn't," Ozzie said.

"Where is he?"

"I don't know," Ozzie said. Whoever Traynor was, Ozzie knew the guy had the right idea in not being here.

"You're all incompetent," she said. "I can't wait any longer. I need that by four—I've made corrections. See that you deliver it to me in my office. My presentation is tonight. The council will not tolerate errors!"

The woman pelted from the room, Ozzie abandoned in a puzzled state, sitting the lone sentinel over ranks of computer hardware.

He went back to work until Malone joined him after five o'clock. "Pure chance," he said to the incredulous Malone. "Somehow the access code from my old company in Boston has been retained in the bank's program as a live entry— unless the bank still does business with the Boston bandits. That could be. I used to play with the buttons at work— jump into the bank for fun, transfer funds from my checking account at the First Seaman's into my slush account at work."

"I think you're a whiz," Malone said. "What's all that?" he said, gesturing to the screen that Ozzie had filled with numbers. Malone was stuffing his pipe with the purest Virginian tobacco.

"Account numbers that match cash-transfer numbers I found when you and I made our withdrawal the other night. DeSilva had these accounts in that cabinet thing behind his desk, handwritten. I searched the records and found huge bucks in these accounts, and very peculiar activity. Someone's been shifting cash in and out of this bank—four hundred thousand in, and two weeks later two hundred thousand out, then drain the account a week after that. Some of these accounts are empty for months—but then they'll suddenly have balances of hundreds of thousands. I can't figure it out."

"How do you know all this? You never tell me anything."

"I don't know shit," Ozzie said. "Shots in the dark with a little help from an old life. But now watch, Wilson—watch this name."

Ozzie typed whole sequences, the state-college lab seemed not the least responsive, but the screen flipped.

"Zalinsky, Oz! You son of a gun," Malone said, pulling up a chair beside his friend. "That's the same name we gave Bozo—the guy who wrote Veronica Hammond's Valium prescriptions."

"Curiouser and curiouser," Ozzie said.

"These crumbs are diddling the bank, Oz." Pleased with his insight, Malone tipped back in the chair, touching his pipe with flame.

"These accounts are not with the bank's daily business. Sometimes these accounts vanish, then reappear as though they were new, but with parts of their old numbers in their new numbers. It's like some sort of self-generating code that can be run backward to get to an original account number."

"Peculiar?"

"Damn peculiar, Wilson. And, as far as I can tell, one Bernadette DeSilva, a.k.a. Babs Maguire, hasn't got a nickel in her daddy's bank. Can't find a thing with her name on it."

"Registers a certain lack of confidence in her hubby, wouldn't you say? Why are those numbers changing, Oz?"

"The bank's using its computer."

"You mean both you and the bank are mucking around together in this machine?"

"At the bank, Wilson." Ozzie checked the clock. "They're closing."

"But you are talking directly to the bank's computer?"

"We've been chums all afternoon. I've also talked to a few other people, Wilson. I called every telephone number I could find. The best answers came from the Bahamas—Zalinsky owns a plane—and one at the Chicago Board of Trade, where someone named Preston wanted to sell me piggies at a curb rate. Curb rates are illegal."

"Did you buy any?"

"I didn't, but DeSilva did. And when I told Preston I was Zalinsky, Preston said he'd never dealt directly with me before but he sure was glad to know things were looking up again."

"Oz, these guys are going to be pissed when they find out." A thick layer of pipe smoke hung in the air.

"We can only hope," Ozzie said. "There's a woman in Panama who knows Richie by the sound of his voice. Said I wasn't Richie and hung up."

"Where'd you call from?"

"Right here," Ozzie said, pointing to the white phone on the counter.

"Son of a bitch," Malone said. "The dean will shit when he gets these bills."

"I charged them all to Richie's AT&T Calling Card."

"Ozzie, they're gonna have your ass."

"There are three of them, Wilson—and possibly someone else at the bank. I don't know how they've done it, but there's enough here for the Securities and Exchange Commission. These guys are crooks, Wilson. I called the IRS in Boston and said I was Dr. Zalinsky—gave them a false Social Security number and said my banker was up to some funny shit with my money—hadn't reported my accounts that held more than ten thousand dollars to the IRS and I was worried the IRS would come back on me. They're going to visit me at my office tomorrow afternoon."

"Oz, I think you should leave this alone. Someone's gonna get you for this."

"Not if we get them first. When is your judge coming?"

Malone shook his head. "I'll call him again," he said. "Oz, you're going too fast."

"I found Lacey Beal this morning—she lives out near the salt marsh in a hooch. The girl knew exactly how much money Veronica Hammond was leaving her."

"So?" Malone was transfixed by the scrolling numbers on the monitor.

"A man was there. She said it was her father—an old drunk."

"Ya?" Malone said, fascinated now.

"If you were dirt poor and you knew your daughter had been willed fifty thousand dollars by a woman she cleaned house for, d'you think you might wish that woman ill?"

"Can't say—I've never been poor, Oz. What are these things?" Malone said, tracing the screen with his fingertip.

Ozzie shrugged.

They left the lab, shut off the lights, but followed Al Wasserman's instructions and left the computer powered up and busy. On their way down the corridor to the kitchen loading dock, where Ozzie had stashed the jeep out of the rain, Ozzie dropped the sandhill crane's red folder into a custodian's hamper.

Love Among the Ruins

DARLA had gone to Baltimore for two nights and left Sheldon Boynton alone with her children, which meant that he'd slept the last two nights at his mother-in-law's, the children slumbering in nests in their grandmother's room. Darla didn't trust her husband alone with her little ones. Her bilious harangue to all and sundry was that Boynton couldn't boil water, couldn't make it to the sitter's on time from the bank, couldn't keep track of either kid. Boynton raised carrier pigeons, adored his cooing feathered buddies, and too often became so engrossed in plotting routes from Syracuse and cleaning cages that his own gifted nestlings wandered down the driveway to play in the storm drains. Darla had never been away overnight before; she'd called her mother both nights to get the straight poop.

Darla had been elevated to assistant principal for her elementary school this year. The Baltimore conference, a blistering affair for school administrators, was titled "Co-operative Learning: The Cutting Edge Methodology in the Mastery Learning Environment." In plain language, two men with dandruff in Ohio had discovered after three years of research that kids taught kids well.

It was all grist for Darla's peppery mill, as was the news this morning for Boynton when Richie DeSilva poured through the bank's doors, went immediately to the telephone, and took calls for an hour. The perky Chastman girl had become DeSilva's Veronica in more ways than one, Boynton suspected.

Boynton appeared busy at his desk. But he wasn't. He was sucked into a flume of incongruities with DeSilva's brusque presence this morning. What went wrong? Boynton wondered. Boynton chose a pen for the day . . . never the Cross ballpoint Darla had given him for his promotion to loan officer.

No way in hell should Flagler be VP of anything. Noel Flagler was a smartass Bentley graduate who had played high school hockey in this town only six years ago. Flagler was a kid, hadn't actually done a thing in his Flagler life but smack pucks around. But that was more than enough, Boynton thought, more than enough to land Flagler the long corner desk by the window, the yellow floor lamp from the director's room. Flagler and his car-dealer friends, who constantly funneled customers and cash into each other's pockets.

Flagler with his Toyota Supra on permanent loan from his brother, Flagler who dated flouncy women with hair like a palomino's tail, women who were tanned in February, persistent in December as they dove into the bank to fix a smack on the gleeful Flagler who, despite his peccadillos in the corner, despite his outrageous suits and toffee Italian boots, nevertheless seemed to tickle DeSilva no end. DeSilva had just made the egregious Flagler his new VP. DeSilva went down to Flagler's desk, down and back so often Boynton wondered why the rug hadn't collapsed its shag on the path or why Flagler didn't simply move his desk on top of DeSilva's desk.

Boynton watched these two this morning, as they huddled on the leather couch behind Flagler's desk near the bank's name on the window. Bastards, Boynton thought, as he made an Agway shopping list of grains and pellets for his carrier buddies. Bastards. They sit there telling secrets. Not even looking his way. Coffee cups on their knees. Beers down at Trilby's after work. They skate together, smash each other silly every week in a men's hockey league. Pricks, Boynton thought; he couldn't skate but his best pigeon, Conqueror, was a master of the skies, having flown from Cleveland last fall through hail-infested thunderstorms over New York State. Conqueror was good.

Darla was due home this afternoon; with her principal behind the wheel, back-seat-driving Darla would hand-signal insistent jabs about traffic all the way from Logan, which beer truck hadn't signaled, what color the traffic lights were. Darla announced school zones in a car as though she were a British Rail conductor on a commuter crush through Surbiton.

Boynton sat there, just sat. His Agway list was complete. He needed a haircut before Darla got home; she'd left instructions. Maybe he'd do that now. Step down to the barber shop, have a coffee at Eldridge's, buy a *Popular Mechanics* as though he were an independent person.

When he got his raincoat on, Boynton realized he wasn't wearing socks; another chink in his lead-lined life. He left the bank without so much as a whisper to anyone as to where he was going and especially not even a nod to DeSilva and that bum on the couch. DeSilva and his board of directors had passed over the wrong man this time.

⚓ ⚓ ⚓

Ruby came up out of the dragger's engine hatch, up past Larry on the mast, her foot neatly in the crane's hook, one hand to the cable, the other peeling her sweatband out of her hair. She shook her hair loose as her father swung her high over the Canadian deckhands, over the sailboat with its broken chock and the woman in the stadium coat who stood on its deck and watched Ruby dip through the air forty feet up, Ruby's left leg serenely free in the wind. Rocket lowered his daughter to the wharf, directly in front of Ozzie.

"Not again," she said to Ozzie, stepping off the hook and motioning to Rocket, who sat like a gnome in the rusted black crane cab. "Your Aunt Elspeth is looking for you," she said.

The crane's engine staggered, the cables clacked, and Rocket wound the hook up to the boom as he shuttled the crane backward on its ways into the junkyard.

"I don't want to fight with you," Ozzie said.

"Are you going out?"

"I hadn't thought about it," he said.

"You've got tons of money, have you? Don't have to worry about bills?"

"I've got money at MacAvoy's from last month—that's all."

She watched her father for a moment. "I thought if you were going out, I'd pull the dragger in where the *Lucia* is. I guess I don't need to, now. Engine's back in. He'll be out of here on the tide. I wasn't asking about your money."

The woman on the sailboat had called up to Ruby, and Ozzie had seen Ruby deliberately slight the woman.

"I know you and my father gab like two old hens. Please don't say anything to him about his money, about my trying to work things out. He's in deep. Confused. Forgetful. Owes people a bundle. His tax bill is huge."

"I said I wouldn't—I won't."

"Let's not start."

"Richie DeSilva got it all sorted out, has he?"

The woman on the sailboat shouted again. Ruby scowled at Ozzie, then went to the wharf edge. "Hold on!" she said to the woman, who seemed jittery as she hunched her shoulders. "Your husband said he'd be right back."

"I know," the woman said. "I don't need to be stuck here, that's all."

"You're lucky you *are* stuck here," Ruby said to her. "Only take a few minutes to bolt the new chock in. He'll be right back." She faced Ozzie. "No more cracks about DeSilva."

"You sleeping with him?"

"I'm not telling you!" she said.

"You are sleeping with him!" Ozzie howled. He swung around and kicked at a bollard. "How do you do that?" he yelled. "Jeezus, you do scamper from bed to bed like a bunny!"

"You don't own me," she said.

"I don't want to own you, for chrissake. I want to love you!" Ozzie wanted to run, snatch the woman, lean off his Arabian prancer and scoop Ruby up onto his pommel. But he wasn't a prince, she wasn't anything even close to a damsel, never mind being in distress, and this wharf and his boots were not heather and hoof.

The Canadian crewmen were interested: they'd had time enough with Ruby on their boat. Ozzie knew they hadn't seen a Ruby in any Nova Scotia fishing shanty. The sailboat woman was troubled, calling again.

"Well, you can't love me! I won't let you!" Ruby screamed. "What the hell's the matter with you?"

"Listen to me," Ozzie said. "Having you out with me on that trawler meant everything to me. I understand it could have been just another lay for you. But not for me!"

"Another lay? I am not some flat-assed whore!"

"Then what are you? Now you're screwing that reptile DeSilva."

"I never said I was. Are you deaf?"

"Then what are you doing?" Ozzie shouted; he took two steps backward.

"He's helping me save my father!" she yelled.

"He's stealing this wharf out from under you!"

"I'll be lucky to save this wharf!"

"I'll say you will! Why can't you see it? For crying out loud, how can you crawl between the sheets with a sleaze?"

"I won't have any choice, will I?"

"Excuse me?" the sailboat woman called.

"Shut the fuck up, lady!" Ruby yelled. "Your boat's not broken—your husband's coming back—you're safe, lady!"

"You won't let yourself be loved—that's it!" Ozzie shouted.

"Not by you, I won't!"

"You *are* a fraud!"

"And you're nuts!" she shouted. She swung her sweatband at him. "You're crazy!"

Ozzie felt the sweatband lash his face. He knew he was shaking.

Ruby came for him again.

Ozzie raised his arm in time to take the sweatband. But she whipped him instantly the other way. Ozzie stumbled back, pulling off his jacket, and went at her, twisting the bomber jacket around her shoulders.

He tried to hold her. But Ruby drove him into the shack's wall, his jacket over her head, Ozzie like a matador missing the big one. He couldn't breathe.

Ruby got her head free, her shoulders and arms. She whipped his jacket across his face.

"I give!" he said.

She hit him again, the zipper this time raking his eyes.

"Enough!" he yelled. "Enough!"

Ruby held the jacket up. And stopped.

"I won't bother you again," he said. He stood away from the wall, watching her, raising his hands. "Enough," he said. "You're on your own."

"You need help!" she said.

He reached for his bloody cheek, his lacerated nose.

"Not for that!" she yelled. "For what's left of your mind!"

Ozzie felt blood run warm into his mouth. "My mind is okay," he said. "It's here!" he shouted, as he pointed to his chest.

"That's heartburn!"

"You've got it all figured out," Ozzie said. "But you've got it figured out wrong."

"I don't think so," she said.

"Enough," he said. "I'm not up for tag-team love pats with you."

"You're not up for much."

"And this isn't some Hong Kong bar."

Rocket came onto the wharf, whistled. Then waited, taking everything in. The woman on the sailboat was irritated again, the Canadians laughing as they left the dragger's rail.

Ruby threw his coat to him. Ozzie caught the sleeve, then walked past Rocket and around the shack's edge toward the jeep.

⚓ ⚓ ⚓

The attendants asked Ozzie to wait while they went to fetch his Uncle Barry. Ozzie sat in the third-floor solarium, alone until Ezra showed up with Francis Sparkman in tow. The men sat down on the couch in front of Ozzie. The hospital had its disinfectant musk, as though the state were trying to cleanse itself of these men who had no homes and were too old and too far gone for threading bolts and weaving potholders in a "residential setting."

"We have to do something," Ezra said to Ozzie. "He's dying."

Ozzie watched as another man in a bathrobe limped into the solarium to sit on the couch next to Francis Sparkman. "Where is he?" Ozzie asked Ezra.

"He won't come out of his room. He won't eat. He won't talk to us."

Ozzie had a greenhouse tray of tomato plants on his lap. Another man with an empty eye socket scuffed across the room in paper slippers to sit next to Ezra on the couch arm.

"He's not gonna make it," the one-eyed man said.

Francis Sparkman was weeping.

"How old are you?' Ozzie asked Ezra.

"Seventy-four last week. Why?"

"How many years in these dumps?"

"Who counts?" Ezra said.

"All your life?"

"Certainly not."

"Why do you stay here?"

"You want to take us home with you?" the one-eyed man said.

"It's not disagreeable," Ezra said. "Monastic, surely. Our needs are not many."

"What needs? This is a dog pound!" Ozzie leaned forward. "There's an entire world out there," he said.

"Is there?" Sparkman said, wiping his eyes with toilet paper. "Is there a world out there any better than this?"

"Freedom," Ozzie said.

"Are you free?" Ezra asked him.

Ozzie thought for a moment, watching another man decide to join them. "Reasonably so, I think."

The new man sat next to Ozzie and brushed the tomato leaves with his fingers after he scrunched himself into the couch.

"Then you haven't considered all the points," Ezra said. "My family has left me an island, Ozzie—a mere dot on the most refined map of Cape Breton Island. We call it Marble Mountain."

"We're going there someday!" the one-eyed man said.

"The hell you are," Ozzie said.

"Oh, we are!" the tomato lover beside him said to Ozzie. "Aren't we? Yes, we are. Ezra has his money. And the house has a bedroom for each of us—it's a grand house, isn't it, Ezra?"

"It will do," Ezra said. And to Ozzie: "I might be free there. But, you see, the island does not exist for me—I've

213

never seen it. This does," Ezra said, slapping the couch. "My world here is as filled with possibilities as your world out there."

"That's bullshit," Ozzie said. "Where will you swim—China Beach?"

"Are you a doctor?" the tomato man said to Ozzie.

"He's not a doctor," Francis Sparkman said. "Look at his hands."

The tomato man said, "I ask, you see, because I'm afraid of you."

Ozzie turned to consider this ersatz human being.

"I can play the ocarina," the tomato man said, as he brushed the leaves again. "My name is Evelyn Cameroon."

"Don't insult us," Ezra said. "We live without insult here."

"The hell you do!" Ozzie said to them all. "These bars are bad enough—but you insult yourselves by believing you belong in here."

Uncle Barry was wheeled into the solarium in a white wicker chair, the attendant rolling him into the group around Ozzie. "I'll be down the hall—you call me," the attendant said to Ozzie.

The men stared at Uncle Barry as they might stare at a dead man.

Ozzie got up to kneel in front of the old man, rolling his Uncle Barry toward him, touching those old knees. Ozzie glanced at Ezra for help, then back to his Uncle Barry. "Hey, pardner," he said.

Nothing.

"What happened to him?" Ozzie said to the men.

"He's medicated," Francis Sparkman said.

"So are you," Ozzie said.

"No, we're not," Francis Sparkman said. "Nobody in his right mind would swallow poison, Ozzie."

Uncle Barry's eyes were portholes into nothingness.

"I brought you some tomatoes," Ozzie said as he held up the greenhouse tray. "For your garden this summer." And as he said that, Ozzie knew there was no garden, no summer, and all days had become the same for this old man.

✠ ✠ ✠

Shaw, the hospital administrator, peered at Ozzie over Uncle Barry's file. "I can give you three minutes."

"I want the needles stopped," Ozzie said.

"Not your decision, sir. This is legal. Besides, you're not listed as the responsible party, not even as next of kin."

"Who is?" Ozzie said.

Shaw's office had a high ceiling, a nineteenth-century gas-light fixture, gray walls and floor, massive ornate radiators, and closed windows. The desk was metal and scratched.

"Lizbeth and Elspeth Barrett—and Edward Bunting."

"Bud," Ozzie said.

"Even if you were responsible, I'm afraid the hospital has rather strict guidelines governing family input in severe cases. The treatment we've prescribed," the man said, letting pages fall in the file, "is the standard treatment for acute depression. Your uncle—he is your uncle?"

"He is," Ozzie said.

"Your uncle is a very sick man. He has been for a good part of his life. Don't you know that?"

"I know everyone says he is."

"He was extremely difficult to handle when he first came to us—"

"He's been coming here for years!"

"Be that as it may," said the red-haired Shaw, a weedy man barely tall enough to see over his desk, a collapsed chest. "I can't say—I'm recently appointed, if you know what I mean?"

"Uncle Barry is a puppy."

"On the contrary, sir. He's quite violent."

"You do know he's been charged with murder?"

"Of course." Shaw tapped the file with a pencil.

"Would you be difficult to handle, Mr. Shaw, if you were

215

charged with murder, hauled in here for observation—and you didn't and couldn't kill anyone?"

"Actually, it's Dr. Shaw. I'm not the subject of this discussion, sir. Your question is irrelevant. My people, Mr. Barrett, you will be relieved to know, are medical professionals excellently trained and highly qualified. This institution takes great pride in the dedication—"

"Why does he smell?" Ozzie said softly.

"I'm sorry?"

"He smells."

"Many family members are not aware that incontinence is common with the emotionally disturbed. Our staff—"

"Are you a recording? Half your staff has had too much sun, wears a turban, and eats curry for breakfast. I want the needles stopped."

"Mr. Barrett, I know you're concerned, but really we are following common protocols for your uncle's illness."

"He's not ill."

"Oh, but he is, Mr. Barrett. He most assuredly is."

"He's never been sick a day in his life. His mind is not like my mind, and certainly not like your mind—he understands things differently—but he wouldn't be sick now if your common protocols weren't killing him."

Shaw shut the file. "I appreciate your concern. We've nearly completed our evaluation."

"And?"

Shaw shook his head. "Really, Mr. Barrett, this is a legal matter before the courts. We have three choices—he was insane at the act but competent to stand trial now, insane at the act and incompetent to stand trial, or perfectly sane and competent in both instances."

"Those aren't choices," Ozzie said. "The man is innocent."

"Not for you to say, sir. Are you a qualified observer?" Shaw bent to see why Ozzie was leaning over. "What are you looking at?"

"I'm trying to see if your feet touch the floor," Ozzie said, raising his head. "I'm at least as qualified as you are. What is it with you, Shaw? Your *cojones* all shriveled up into raisins? You don't give two shits about these men."

Shaw pushed a button on his telephone.

Ozzie stood up. "You can shake your rattles and beads all you want, but the fact is you're gutless. You hide behind common protocols because you haven't got any treatment that isn't lethal. All smoke and mirrors, Shaw. Stop giving him those shots. Let the poor son of a bitch take a breath. Leave him alone—he'll be more okay than you are."

Ozzie had heard the door open, knew there were men behind him. "Take your fucking hands off me!" he said when they carefully took his arms. "I'm not one of your inmates."

Ozzie looked at both men, waited. They were earnest attendants, hands on his arms. "Take your hands off me," he said softly.

They did.

"Common protocols?" Ozzie asked Shaw, gesturing to the two men.

"I'm sorry you don't agree with our treatment," Shaw said. "Maybe you should talk with your uncle's sisters. I have my appointment now, sir. I did make time for you."

Ozzie said, "I'm intensely grateful for this audience with Your Holiness."

"Let's go," the man on his left said to Ozzie.

"Touch me," Ozzie said to the attendants, holding up his hands, "and you and I will tango." And to Shaw: "Any time you'd like to do a little deep-sea fishing, you let me know."

"Let's go," the attendant said.

⚓ ⚓ ⚓

Ozzie let the jeep roll onto the grass before he left the hospital grounds, his head slowly down on the steering wheel, hands tight. His face throbbed under the gauze patches he'd taped over the gash on his nose.

He wondered why it was that a man could get up every morning, expect to work hard and be honest, volunteer to be shot at by kids wearing black pajamas in a rainy, stinking country that wasn't worth a shit to start with because raising his hand at the time and saying "I do" seemed right when he did it, later bail out of crookedness to buy a boat, and all the while never ask a great deal of anyone, including himself . . . why was it, he wondered, that events are balanced by a celestial clockworks wherein all the great wandering galaxies can slip that last cog to reveal a man's half-second of destruction? And destruction it was. No mistaking it.

Marble Mountain did exist . . . but in Da Nang. His dreams always delicately reproduced the soft whuff of idling rotor blades at the I Corps marine base at Marble Mountain, where the dust ground his teeth as he unloaded body bags with his men, the scolding stares from intelligence guys when Ozzie was incoming after four days of being pinned down by snakes, swamp, North Vietnamese Regulars, and hot lead. Even the saffron mists from the sea a mile away couldn't bathe the bits of his men off his helmet, the bits of human meat off his arms. More than dreams were born at Marble Mountain. All the bad began at Marble Mountain.

A marriage finished, house gone, no money, no car, no Ruby, no Mayfly Molly. And Uncle Barry was dying. All my fault? he wondered. Some intestinal yen for self-immolation? His ancient sense of not having a home, not having a place except on a stinking trawler, of always being the one man alone, indifferent, disconnected, had come to this: Most of his windows were empty now, blasted, the stars peeking in, his stone floor littered with shards of hope, splinters of irresolution, as he crunched through his nave searching for some way out.

"This isn't good," he said, as he raised his eyes.

The Jig Is Up

Ozzie dropped the keys into his pocket and knocked on their door for the first time in his life. Elspeth answered, a blue floury apron with its ruffles over her shoulders: "Come in, dear. Someone finally met you coming the other way," she said, as she touched his face. He stood still while she peeled the gauze. "Oh, Oz—that should be looked at. It's deep."

He smoothed the tape on his cheek. "Is Lizbeth here?" he said, stepping into her kitchen.

"She's upstairs. Where have you been? I have looked everywhere for you."

Her solid pie-roller was white with flour on the counter. "Wash your hands," she said. "I've made turnovers."

Ozzie stood at the sink with her, the water rushing over his knuckles. Aunt Elspeth went back to rolling out dough. "I got these apples last week," she said. "They're older than I am."

"I need to talk to both of you," he said.

"Start with me, dear. You know your Aunt Lizbeth has a nap after work. That bank has become a torment for her. Something's terribly wrong there. And their computer is on the fritz—the girls had to post all their business by hand this afternoon. That Boynton man yelled at your Aunt Lizbeth." She handed him a warm raspberry turnover, its edges pinched with a fork, the jam baked crisp where it had leaked. "I'm worried about you, Ozzie. I went down to your boat. I went to Mildred's. Have you seen Louise?"

"I hope I never see Louise again."

"Don't be cruel, Ozzie."

"Uncle Barry's chickens in finger-lickin' pieces in the cellar freezer?" he said.

"I can't feed this house and those chickens at the same time. Lizbeth won't. It was shameful to have them out there without him. They're all at the meat locker now."

"Uncle Barry's very sick."

"We know he is." Aunt Elspeth rolled her dough with precise uniformity, the perfect thickness for brown chicken-pie crusts.

"They're killing him," he said.

"I can't take care of your uncle any longer. They're not killing him."

"Where's Bud?"

"Bud's not home yet."

"He living here?"

"Ozzie Barrett, you're being as nasty as you can be and you can be very nasty. Always could. Bud is a decent man."

"The medication is killing Uncle Barry."

"Get some milk from the refrigerator for your turnover. Ozzie, this last time has been the worst. I don't have to tell you how demanding your Uncle Barry has been over the years. But you took him out of the hospital into your home— and you didn't ask Louise. Now he's been arrested and he's back in the hospital. He's not coming home again. The sooner we all become accustomed to that fact, the better off we'll be. I'm very sorry. I am. But Lizbeth and Bud will be married in less than three weeks. The annual bank party at the country club this week will be somewhat in their honor. Lizbeth is very excited, and I am, too. These last few weeks have been a nightmare for us—Lizbeth was called into a private meeting with Mr. DeSilva during which he let her know in no uncertain terms that your behavior was directly influencing her prospects at the bank. Now, Ozzie, your Aunt Lizbeth has only a few years left there and she doesn't need her annuity torpedoed by you. She was very upset that Mr. DeSilva had to be so blunt about everything. Ozzie, he named you. Said you were directly linked to his difficulties— I find this hard to imagine, but he thought you knew something about that dreadful business at his home. Now, you'll yak away and say it ain't so, and god knows I love you, but you and your uncle have about ruined this family, and very nearly ruined the wedding for Lizbeth and Bud. I'm sorry your uncle is sick. I don't believe the police and that Mr. Tagliano—who, by the way, has been here three times asking questions about you two—I don't believe they'll allow your uncle to be tried, and he'll finish out his days with his friends and his violin at the hospital. Do I wish he were here now? No, Ozzie Barrett, I don't. I'm too old to chase the man. He's like a child—and you know that. I have done my best for him. But it's over. I want this wedding to be all that Lizbeth wishes. I want you to be there. I'll have the Harper woman in to do the flowers and that Manos woman and her girls are going to help with the food. The reception is here following the service. I have a new necktie for you that I want you to wear. The country-club get-together is not an evening I enjoy—too many of those fancy types from the bank—but it is Lizbeth's evening and I'll not spoil it for her. You may not like Bud—I'm sorry for that. But he's good to your Aunt Lizbeth—and he's good to me. We'll manage very nicely here in the foreseeable months. How's your turn-over?"

"Good," Ozzie said.

⚓ ⚓ ⚓

Ozzie kept to himself on Eldridge's stool while a kid mixed an ice-cream soda behind the counter, Ozzie on the last stool nearest the pharmacy wicket. He could hear Eldridge muttering to himself behind the stress tabs and medicinal notions. Tagliano sat down and ordered coffee from the kid, Tagliano in a leather coat reminiscent of Gestapo birthday presents in the Ninth Circle of Europe, 1943.

"You're a hard man to find," Tagliano said.

Ozzie wanted to finish his coffee and leave. "I've been away from my desk," Ozzie said.

Tagliano dumped sugar into his coffee. "Been in the bank lately?"

"They closed my account," Ozzie said.

"Tell me about the towel in the guest room."

"Came to me in a dream—the Shroud of Strike's Landing."

"Did it?" Tagliano said. "Well, dream this, asshole—you know too much. I think you're my guy."

"If you thought that, you wouldn't be talking to me in a drugstore. And DeSilva's wife wouldn't be charged with attempted murder."

"Never hurts a state's attorney's reputation for guts to arrest moderately well-to-do people, Barrett. And it quiets the town—gives them a shooter."

"Like my Uncle Barry?"

"Sure," Tagliano said. He slid his spoon onto his saucer. He hadn't once looked at Ozzie, nor Ozzie at him.

"DeSilva shot his wife's lover," Ozzie said. "He wasn't in Las Vegas at all."

"Oh, but he was, Barrett. He was. I called him myself—roused him out of a sound sleep in the Las Vegas Hilton. One of his annual bankers' meetings—he almost missed his flight out from Logan. Has a ticket from the Logan parking garage with the dates and times stamped on it. Nice try, Barrett."

"Why did *you* call him?"

"Why not?"

"Your people don't know how to use a telephone, yet?"

"I stay busy, Barrett," Tagliano said. "That way there's no room for error. You know, I don't connect these two incidents until I consider you."

"Babs killed the girlfriend—DeSilva tried to kill the boyfriend."

Tagliano said, "That how it looks to you, Barrett?"

"Or, DeSilva killed the girlfriend *and* shot the boyfriend."

"Why would he do that?"

"Cover his ass," Ozzie said. "Too much to lose."

"What would he lose?"

"His laundry."

"What laundry?"

"His bank, Mario."

"I talked to your wife, Barrett. She says you've got unresolved rage you need to deal with."

"Oh, brother," Ozzie said. Then he saw Sheldon Boynton clap the doors shut and stalk into an aisle near the phone booth. Ozzie used the mirror behind the counter to watch Boynton's hat arrive at Eldridge's brass wicket.

"Do you have unresolved rage, Barrett?"

"Only when I think about Louise," Ozzie said and drained his cup.

"You couldn't take the heat in the corporate kitchen— bought a trawler, can't make a go of that. You haven't been out fishing for days. Two payments late on your boat. Little envy, little jealousy, little rage—I can see how you might hate DeSilva. He's everything you're not."

"He is that," Ozzie said.

"You surprised the Hammond woman in her house. You wanted some of DeSilva's pussy. Veronica wasn't willing to share. You killed her. Your Uncle Barry was with you. Then you think you're killing DeSilva the next time, but it turns out you shoot some poor bastard in DeSilva's bed for the night."

"All chum—chum," Ozzie said. "If you believed in your black heart that I was the shooter, you'd arrest me."

"I think I will," Taliano said. "Not yet—but soon."

Boynton came around the shelves to pass the time while Eldridge made up his prescription, Boynton shuffling slowly along a shelf of men's cologne and talc.

Tagliano pushed his empty coffee cup away. "Stay around, Barrett," he said, getting up.

"It is Mario, isn't it?" Ozzie said.

"That's my name," Tagliano said.

Boynton had opened a box of after-shave.

"I was going through some old papers the other day," Ozzie said to Tagliano, who was belting his Gestapo coat. "I found the name Mario and a phone number. I don't know a Mario, so I called the number. No answer. But after seeing you, I think I remember who Mario is."

"Call the guy and tell him you're going to be busy for the next decade, Barrett."

"I don't have to," Ozzie said. "He knows all about me."

Tagliano left the drugstore, left Ozzie fascinated with the way Sheldon Boynton minced along the shelf, poking boxes. Eldridge rang his counter bell and Boynton carried a box of cologne back to the wicket. Boynton opened a white prescription bag on the counter while Eldridge made change. Boynton dumped a metal inhaler out of a box and took two wheezy breaths, sucking on the inhaler's plastic throat.

Ozzie watched. Boynton an asthmatic? he wondered. Some asthmatics can't wear cologne. Boynton does, Ozzie thought, watching Eldridge fold the bag again.

The kid poured more coffee for Ozzie.

Ozzie spun on the stool, his feet tangling into Boynton's legs as the man tried to pass him. Ozzie pulled the bag out of Boynton's hand as he crashed into the guy.

Boynton glared at Ozzie, his best banker's vipery disdain. Boynton grabbed for the bag.

"Sorry," Ozzie said. He spilled the bag's contents on the floor. "Sorry," he said again. Then: "What the hell do you wear rubber gloves for, Sheldon?"

Boynton had mud on his shoes; his pants were baggy, wrinkled. His hair looked as though he'd had it styled by a Lawn-Boy.

"Leave me alone," Boynton said to Ozzie as he snatched the box of gloves off the floor. "I handle pigeons. I'm allergic to mites."

Ozzie found the inhaler behind his stool pedestal. An asthmatic's delight. "I'm very sorry," he said when the disheveled Boynton grabbed the inhaler away.

And his cologne is a cheap purgative distilled from a mash of rotting lilacs, Ozzie thought. Something called Lilac Vegetal.

Uncle Barry said he'd smelled the Peeping Tom before he saw him crouched behind Veronica Hammond's shed. The Peeping Tom with a cold . . . Uncle Barry had been worried the grass was wet for the man. Not a cold, Ozzie thought, asthma. Boynton left Eldridge's.

I'll be damned, Ozzie thought. Boynton was at Veronica Hammond's wake with his wife. The man's wife again at the bank when Boynton knew exactly how much Ozzie owed on his closed account. "You little devil," Ozzie said. "Sheldon Boynton, you little devil."

Fannydancers

OZZIE got off to Boston early in the morning, Rocket excitedly sitting rigid and wearing four different plaids in the jeep's passenger seat. Rocket had shined his work boots and shaved, a major relapse into conformity for the old man.

Ozzie prodded the jeep down Route 1 toward the city. Rocket began to jabber when they found traffic, jabbered all the way into the Common, jabbered as Ozzie left the jeep on Beacon Hill behind the statehouse, and jabbered through the morning crowds along Tremont Street. Stricken momentarily silent by the quivering elevator, Rocket held Ozzie's arm as they ascended to the lawyers on the fourteenth floor of an office building behind Jordan Marsh, where an unsmiling young woman in a blue suit was doubtful at first, but had them sign in and clip visitor's badges to their clothes.

Ozzie wanted to stay in the curved reception area, a room with a pink rug, onyx shelves, and track-lighted pointillistic renderings of fish on the walls . . . Bauhaus called to the bar. Ozzie needed a few minutes alone to connect his own dots.

"You come in with me, boy," Rocket said to him.

"I'll wait," Ozzie said, sitting down.

"Up, boy! These guys are oily."

This morning is a mistake, Ozzie thought, as he joined

Rocket in the corridor, following the receptionist who motioned them into a room with a long table and Breuer chairs. Rocket thumped his fingers on the table as they waited, nodding to himself as though rehearsing lines.

Four lawyers in vests, two shirt-sleeved clerks, and a recording secretary swept into the room, took their seats. The four lawyers reached across the table to shake Rocket's hand. Rocket wanted them to meet Ozzie, Ozzie with the botched face and gauze patch, Ozzie in his jeans and jacket, his frayed green woolen tie open for air. Ozzie saw the secretary study his face while the men spread files and unrolled blueprints on the table.

"Where's your lawyer?" Ozzie whispered to Rocket.

"They're all my lawyers, boy. Slippery as hell."

Ozzie guessed the men were patronizing Rocket, being ever so squiffily polite as they uncovered sheet after sheet of red-bordered legal pages. And then Ozzie realized they were talking about land, about a twenty-one-acre parcel abutting the Strike's Landing mall, saying that Rocket had bought the land in 1947 to log off the best timber, and that now a consortium of New Jersey mall kings had made a good offer. These lawyers were not only serious, they were being exceedingly deferential to the old man next to Ozzie.

They took Rocket through the drawings, through the land-transfer papers, and then started on the money, the secretary snapping her foolscap pad, scribbling quickly. When Rocket asked a question, she listened to the old man and then seemed to transcribe what he said.

A woman glided in with coffee in a silver service. Ozzie liked the coffee, and said so. The woman gave him a gelid little grin, then left the room.

As the lawyers collected their wits, Rocket leaned over to Ozzie and said, "Think o' that—most of it swamp, the damn fools."

One of the lawyers said, "No incremental payment schedule—as you requested. Payment in full," he said, placing a check in the center of the table. "They aren't happy," he said.

"Fair enough," Rocket said. "I am."

"And if you'll sign now, Mr. Willey," said the stocky lawyer, his cuffs monogrammed with Hong Kong silk.

Rocket penned his scrawl many times, then gave them back their Mont Blanc and reached for the check. "How's that?" he said to Ozzie, handing Ozzie the check. "Ever see a check for nineteen point three million buckaroos?"

Ozzie grinned for many reasons, but most certainly because Richie DeSilva's mall deal had just crashed in flames: This was the land DeSilva wanted.

Rocket shook all their hands, Ozzie among them feeling like a gerbil in a mink cage. Ozzie offered the check to Rocket, who said, as they went out the door, "Keep it for me, boy. I'll lose the goddam thing 'fore I get home."

Back into the elevator, Rocket bowed to the clutch of lawyers in the reception area as the door shuddered and the car plunged for the lobby.

"You're a clever old goat," Ozzie said to him.

"I ain't stupid."

"I'm agog," Ozzie said to him when they were in the street.

"What the hell is a gog?"

"I'm amazed."

"You should be," Rocket said. "Now we get us some lunch and see about those women. Try to enjoy yourself, Ozzie."

And Ozzie did begin to lighten, the city rinsing bile off him for a while until he was waiting for Rocket in the dark, purple motel cocktail lounge near Fenway Park, the claustrophobic room round: round bar, round chairs, round women. He'd found Veronica Hammond's parking-ticket meter numbers near the Haymarket Hotel and had eaten an abominable broiled OrgasMcBurger in a strip joint off Washington Street while Rocket's fannydancers jiggled on the runway over his head.

Rocket was upstairs with a woman who said her name was

Penelope. Penelope's partner, a kid from New Hampshire who claimed she was a psychology major at Boston University, had sidled into Ozzie's round purple booth. Ozzie wished her well, asked her about classes, reassured her that, yes, she was beautiful, yes, she was luscious. She hauled one breast out of her dress, aiming its nipple at Ozzie.

"You're a handsome guy, you know," she said. "You look like my cousin Denny."

"Not now," he said. "But thanks."

When she left him, Ozzie heard another chunk of tracery crash onto his stone floor, the morning's enterprise and now this purple lounge gone rancid with discord. He went out to the jeep to wait in the sun for Rocket, who joined him shortly, carrying two Manhattans.

"Watch the bumps, Gog," Rocket said, as they headed up Boylston Street, Ozzie driving hard to beat the rush-a-thon over to the airport.

Ozzie asked the airport parking-garage attendant about DeSilva and the cream Cadillac.

"Can't say I seen it," the man said. "I get off at four most days."

"Wednesday night—a little guy late for his flight. Black hair."

"I get off at four."

"He came back the next day from Las Vegas."

Ozzie took out two twenties. He smoothed one of the bills on the man's window shelf in front of a miniature television.

"Why are the cops looking for him—say again?"

"Nothin' big," Ozzie said. "He owes them money. They've jacked his rent."

"Name's not DeSilva—tha's Snake Eyes, sure. He goes to Vegas all the time."

"If you see him," Ozzie said, "tell him to call me—Tagliano. Guy can be a twerp, but he don't deserve this shit."

"Ain't no twerp. I give him fifty—he plays the slots for me. Won me two hundred and thirty dollars in Atlantic City, sure. Tha's Snake Eyes."

"Wire wheels?"

"Tha's him—a code door-lock. His alarm system don't work, so I keep his car close, sure. Don't he know the police want him?"

"Not yet."

"Tha's a shame. Police never get enough, sure. If the police come here, I ain't seen shit."

Ozzie smoothed the other twenty. "I'll tell DeSilva you said that—when I find him."

The attendant wrote the name Tagliano on his office wall. "Wha's Snake Eyes do?" the man said.

"Runs a bank."

"Sure—no wonder they want 'im."

"No," Ozzie said. "A real bank."

"Sure," the man said, mystified.

Ozzie said, "I know he went out Wednesday night. You know he came back Thursday?"

"Anyone saw him Thursday, saw trouble, tha's for sure. Look to me like he lost big."

"Put this on the ponies," Ozzie said as he tapped the money.

"Your old guy's got himself a mess," the attendant said, pointing over Ozzie's shoulder to the shambling figure directing traffic in the midst of a herd of yellow cabs near the Swissair loading zone.

"That flight connected with the red-eye from O'Hare to Vegas . . ." the baggage clerk said as he stared at his monitor.

Rocket had gone in search of an airport bar.

". . . and you reported the bag missing when you got to Las Vegas, Mr. DeSilva?"

"I did," Ozzie said.

"You got the claim check?"

"No, I told you—you people said you'd deliver the bag to my house this afternoon. I called home—the bag isn't there. I thought I'd stop here while I was in the city—see if maybe you had it here. The claim check's at home with my wife for your driver."

"I'm sorry, but I can't find a record of any bag missing on that flight. You say someone here called your house?"

"Isn't my name on the manifest?"

"Ya, you're here, but there ain't no missing bag."

"What do I do?" Ozzie asked the man.

"Jus' a moment," the clerk said as he ducked around a screen. Ozzie heard the man talking to another voice in the back of the airport lost-baggage room.

The clerk eventually returned, a stumped individual, gave Ozzie a lost-bag form. "Fill it out now," the clerk said.

But Ozzie sensed that the wind had suddenly swung around out of the east. He'd overstayed his visit to airport-land. "I'll do it at home—I'll mail it in."

"Be easier if you did it here," the clerk said.

The state trooper stepped inside off the sidewalk and appeared to be checking the area for humidity, or possibly the ceiling needed new panels.

Ozzie went directly along the main concourse, found Rocket sloshing another Manhattan in vibrant conversation with a Norwegian couple who were much relieved when Ozzie tipped the old man off his stool and guided him out into the tense, late-afternoon faces peering up at the arrival and departure boards.

Ozzie spotted the same state trooper on the sidewalk outside, but told himself that all would be well as soon as he found the jeep and got into traffic. Ozzie knew he was not very good at detecting anything.

Rocket burbled for miles until Ozzie used rope to bind the old coot into his seat in Saugus. They stopped again in Swampscott for stuffed clams to go, and two more Manhattans, which Rocket dumped into a used paper cup on the restaurant counter, and then they headed home.

Rocket appeared deceased with his chin tagged on his chest, but he'd awaken when Ozzie batted across bridges. Rocket was flush with gratitude. "You're a good man, Gog!" Rocket kept shouting. And then he'd laugh himself into coughing frenzies and slump again.

Ozzie carried Rocket into the old man's bedroom, into his bed between cases of motor oil and batteries. He loosened the old man's clothing, kicked his shined boots under the bed, and shut out the light.

Ozzie fed the lugubrious Owl, who thought about getting up off the rug but canceled his plans for dinner.

Ozzie left Rocket's check in an empty pigeonhole marked DUDS and slid the desktop shut before he went out to the warm night, the harbor painted in midnight blue and silver . . . and yellow posters plastered on the *Lucia*. NO TRESPASSING. The county sheriff had impounded his trawler. The boat could not be moved, entered, boarded. TAKEN IN LIEN. The posters had all been signed by the sheriff's consent.

Ozzie thought he heard the last shards of irreplaceable blue glass bash onto his stone floor.

"It's late, Ozzie," she said.

"I don't want to lose you."

"You never had me."

"Yes, I did."

"I thought so, too. We were wrong."

"We weren't wrong on the boat."

"Louise wasn't on the boat, Ozzie. Your uncle wasn't on the boat."

"Neither was Richie DeSilva."

"I can't go around again tonight," she said.

"He's here, isn't he?"

"Oh, you have lost your mind! What do you do—sit out here in that old jeep and watch me?"

"Pizza boxes," he said. "He nodded toward the two red-and-green pizza boxes on the floor by her couch. He remembered Veronica Hammond's kitchen. "Same boxes," he said, "the night Veronica Hammond was killed. Same pizza. Same asshole."

"Oz, he's not what you say he is. He's arranging a small-business loan for me at very good rates. You can't think about anything else, can you?"

"He's rigged his accounts at the bank. He's laundering money," Ozzie said. "His softball bat and pistol were used to murder a woman and shoot a man."

"Ozzie, it's late." She lifted her hand toward his face, but stopped. "Did I do that to you?" she said softly.

"How else would Tagliano know I'm late on two boat payments? And now I find lien posters on the *Lucia*. I've lost my boat and my bed in one night. Why would a Boston bank impound my boat? They wouldn't—not for two late payments. That's DeSilva."

"No, Ozzie. That's you." She lowered her eyes and moved to shut her door.

"Those pizza boxes!" he yelled.

"I can't do this," she said. "My father is missing."

"Rocket's home in bed—we've been in Boston all day," he said.

She was startled.

"I just tucked him in," he said.

"Are you lying to me?"

"I never have," he said. "Talk to him in the morning. Tell him how grateful you are that your old sweetie has generously given of his time and pizza to rescue a half-crazed, addled old man who doesn't know his ass from his elbow. Tell him everything. DeSilva's here, isn't he?"

"If I called my father, he'd answer?" she said. Her hair had somehow gone to ringlets, like chrome springs.

"I doubt it," he said. "He's been to Manhattan all day."

"He's okay?"

"He's more okay than anyone else I know right now. Give my regards to Larry."

Fog had crept into Strike's Landing not on cat's feet but on polar-bear paws. There had been fog between them, a wet haze netting the air as they stood on her porch.

From the catwalk he said, "Why did you let me think you cared about me?"

She said, "I'm sorry I hurt your face."

"Nothing wrong with my face," he said. He walked back to her. "I don't need this," he said, handing her Rocket's signaling device. "You better keep track of Richie—he'll get more than your pants off."

Mildred's was fittingly vacant, the bar shiny and free of plates and glasses, the food packed away. Malone was reading at the bar with a fresh beer winking at him.

"Want to see my autopsy report?" Ozzie said to his ponderous friend, Malone appearing tonight as the natty evangelist of higher education he was, white shirt, his Oxford tie, and a stiff academic tweed jacket.

Malone paused, then raised his great trout eyes over his specs. "Love to," he said. "Preliminary, I hope."

"Not mine—Veronica Hammond's."

"Oh, that," Malone said. "No, I don't want to see it. Missed you, Oz. Where've you been?"

"Errands," Ozzie said, greeting Mildred, who had jostled out of her kitchen. "You're squeaking," he said to her.

"Little WD-40 when I get home," she said. "DeSilva finally catch up with your face?"

"Ruby," Ozzie said.

"If you're hungry, there's chowder and two blueberry muffins in there. Malone ate the entire last tray."

"Nietzsche says all the interesting people are missing in heaven," Malone whispered, going back to his reading.

Mildred hobbled away, a new bar rag and a bottle of Fantastik in her hip holster, heading for her tables. Ozzie hadn't seen the couple hiding against the fog-gray windows, holding hands, nuzzling each other.

"Veronica Hammond was wearing a diaphragm on the night she died. But there was no semen present at the autopsy, so the evening didn't go quite as she hoped," Ozzie said.

"Tex is in jail," Malone said, as he sipped his beer. "Bit the mayor. Bozo says Tex is dying of a broken heart. The damn dog has lost the will to carry on. Vicious bastard killed a Pomeranian Bozo had in for a nail clip and shampoo. Bozo found another but younger Pomeranian in Maine—hopes the Milligans won't notice their Flippy got a new personality with his trim."

"I think I'm lost, Wilson."

"You are lost. Have been for weeks."

"My boat's been impounded."

"Only a matter of time—you can bunk in with me."

Malone turned the page.

"I'm dead in the water, Wilson," Ozzie said. He lifted his briefcase to the bar. "The boxes are in the jeep outside—will you take everything to Magnuson for me?"

"You want me to deliver a briefcase filled with crazed shit to a federal judge?"

"What should I do with it?"

"Heave it off the wharf, Oz. Every bit of it. This business is doing very evil things to you."

"I'm not good at anything anymore," Ozzie said.

"You used to be fun, Oz. You did. But now—hell, you're morose."

"Will you take the briefcase?"

"I told you I would—yes, I will," Malone said. "Look at you—you're unkempt."

"I've never been kempt."

"Louise wasn't good for you, but at least you had a certain joy to your life in despising the woman. You miss her?"

"I miss despising her. Tagliano may be in this with Richie. What d'you think of that—a crooked state's attorney?"

"I think I'm not shocked, Oz. All those guys are clutching the last sapling on the cliff."

"But I found the name Mario in Richie's files. Tagliano's name is Mario. And Sheldon Boynton has asthma. Uncle Barry said the Peeping Tom was snuffing, maybe had a cold."

"I am surprised, Oz. A cold, my god!"

"What'd I say?"

"It's everything you say. You're trying to revive a dead horse. Nietzsche went nuts clinging to a dying horse's neck. Your Uncle Barry is the horse."

"And you?"

"I'm your pal."

"Not for long, though—right?"

"Go get some chowder—eat the woman's muffins. I'll wait here for you."

"You think I'm nuts?"

"You're like a haunted house, Oz. You've got things going on in your attic that are sort of creepy—ambivalent, yes?"

"I went to Boston today with Rocket."

Malone returned to his reading. "How'd you find Beantown?"

"Looks like Cleveland, but then Cleveland always looked like Omaha to me."

"We need a new Frank Lloyd Wright, Oz. An architect with balls."

"Bozo can't kill animals—how's he going to get rid of Tex?"

Malone said he didn't know. "Man's a saint, isn't he?" Malone said. "Saint Bozo the Sissy. Talk about a fatal flaw for a vet—if people ever figure out he only kills animals that are in pain, if they ever discover he drives all over creation in his Subaru, giving away their cats, doggies, and canaries they don't want to people who do, they'll euthanize Bozo."

"Must be against medical ethics," Ozzie said as he trooped off to the kitchen.

"Undoubtedly," Malone said, sipping.

You Can't Get
Anywhere from Here

Zalinsky said, "Out to my car, Richie!"

DeSilva saw him but continued talking on the telephone.

"Now!" Zalinsky bellowed. The foul dentist kicked DeSilva's desk, rattling the man's lamps.

DeSilva hung up and leaned forward, his best DeSilva smirk. "What are you doing?" he whispered.

"Outside—now!"

Zalinsky stomped out through the doors, DeSilva dashing after him. The bank had halted trading for an instant, but now went on cashing checks, jotting nasty notes to the financially overwhelmed. Boynton sat at his desk like a tumulus of fetid remains; he'd worn his pigeon outfit today, his ripped khakis and bird-bespattered running shoes. He hadn't done a thing for the first hour this morning but peruse his American Express travel catalogues. His calculator had clacked only when he tallied a first-class passage to Turkey on an Italian ship.

Zalinsky had his black Lincoln parked in front of the bagel

shop. "The IRS showed up in my office yesterday after-noon—don't you ever check your answering machine?"

"I've been at the Supreme Court—my tennis club," DeSilva said. "Look, I've got enough trouble."

"Well, you've got more, smartass—you stupid son of a bitch! How did the IRS get to me?" Zalinsky hammered on the Lincoln's roof.

"Why are you asking me?"

"Who should I ask?"

"I didn't do anything."

"The hell you didn't—the IRS says I called them with concerns about my bank. You're not my bank, you son of a bitch! But they had your name and the name of this fucking bank—wrong bank, I says. But Richie, they had copies of my returns! They want my records!"

"I didn't do anything," DeSilva said.

"You better! Or you're goin' down with me! So help me god, Richie, I'll strip you clean."

"You threatening me? Don't threaten me," DeSilva said, as he opened the Lincoln and got in. "And don't yell, dam-mit! Don't yell."

Zalinsky skittered around the car, his belly jiggling, and got in behind the wheel. "How did it happen?" he said. He slammed the door.

"Wait a minute! We don't know what happened. Maybe they're fishing. I'll call Hank in North Andover."

"Richie, they aren't fishing. These guys knew about you. Explain that!"

DeSilva shrugged, but his gut had already sounded the first note of taps. "No way. Hank told me we were clean. We've paid that son of a bitch eighty thousand bucks over three years."

"Your IRS inspector, Hank—it's a sting!"

"Could be—but our files are secure— Oh, jeezus," DeSilva said softly.

"Let's hear it!" Zalinsky said, ham-fisting the steering wheel. "You son of a bitch!"

"Get off my ass, doc. I didn't do it! We've had some shit happening in the computer."

"You told me those records were safe."

"They are—or were. Oh, jeezus, doc—they've been into the computer!" DeSilva screeched and punched the Lincoln's dashboard. "Shit! Some Federal Reserve dink in Philadelphia—a numbnuts who works for me gave him our computer access codes—and the fucking computer has six extra hours logged on it we didn't use."

"You son of a bitch!" Zalinsky grabbed for DeSilva, but the bank president flinched.

"We all go down," Richie said, "unless we cut our losses now—let go!"

Zalinsky sucked in rhino breaths, releasing DeSilva's suit.

"They're fishing. They've got to be," DeSilva said. "I'll dump the accounts now." He scrambled out of the car.

The Lincoln started. Zalinsky blew his car horn. DeSilva ran back, leaned against the roof. "I'm gone," Zalinsky said. "I'll let you know where I am when I get there. Or I'll call Randall in Key West and leave a message."

"That's exactly what the IRS wants you to do!"

"They got their wish," the dentist said. The Lincoln's tires cheeped as he hit reverse. "You better vanish!" Zalinsky yelled at DeSilva. "Smartass bastard—you had nothin' covered."

"Don't run."

"You want me to sit in my office and wait for them to make an appointment with Betty?" he yelled.

A woman and her three cherubs in a triple stroller were curious.

DeSilva said hello to her as Zalinsky blew out of the parking lot, pulling south toward the dentist's favorite back road to Lynn.

Ozzie took off his Parris Island cap as he crossed the porch into Darla's kitchen. She scooped a breast pump and two baby bottles of Grade A mother's milk off her table and vanished into a pantry. Ozzie heard the refrigerator close.

She had the baby on her hip.

Ozzie handed her the bag with the Lilac Vegetal inside. Darla opened the bag on the table. "Very nice of you to bring this by," she said. "But Sheldon came home with his."

"I found it on the drugstore floor after he left."

"Wait—I'll look." She hurtled into a bathroom. Ozzie heard her shoving bottles around in a medicine chest.

Her kitchen was yellow, all yellow . . . life inside a lemon. Floral decals gleamed on her cabinets, her sudsy sink was crammed with baby clothes, tacked to a cupboard door was a bank calendar with pediatrician appointments lined in red. When she came back, she carried Boynton's cologne bottle. "I knew he did," she said, but caught him reading her calendar. "Shellie's got an ear infection." And jabbing at her sink: "I had to get a substitute today. I knew this was here— Sheldon loves this scent."

Ozzie reached for the bag. "Must have fallen off the shelf when we bumped," he said.

"But thank you."

"Sorry to bother you. I'm very sorry to hear Sheldon is not our new First Seaman's vice-president."

Darla's face clouded instantly as though a Texas thunderstorm had just knocked out the sun.

Ozzie said, "He was next, wasn't he?"

Darla nodded, almost absently, as though her head were filled with lightning strokes. "He was," she said. But her eyes had already pooled with tears and Ozzie felt sorry for her.

He wagged the bag at her. "Sheldon's lucky he can wear any scent—many asthmatics can't."

Darla tossed her tight curls, speechless with grief.

Ozzie saw the rubbers on the porch behind a bicycle's wheel. Boynton's pigeon-care clothes hung on hooks above a mat. There must be many things this woman wouldn't have in her house; Ozzie thought he was probably one of them. "Thank you," he said, pushing open the porch door. Boynton's dovecote was built as an adjoining shed to their garage. "Sheldon still jog, does he?"

"Not so much," she said at the door. "I want him to exercise more. You've hurt yourself."

"Gash on the nose," he said. "Hard to get up and run early in the morning."

"He runs at night," she said. "Thank you. Sorry you had to come over. I'll tell Sheldon."

Ozzie threw the bag into the jeep and got in.

Darla returned to her kitchen, returned Boynton's Lilac Vegetal to its proper bathroom shelf; then Darla took the baby up for his morning lie-down, pampering his pudgy bottom with powder.

Some minutes had passed before she heard the jeep back out of the driveway, realizing as it did that the bad Barrett man must have had trouble starting the junk. He hadn't fooled her one bit. All sorts of people wanted to get close to her Sheldon . . . people depended on bankers, needed a friend at the bank. Well, this man is no friend, she thought, as she watched the jeep slowly disappear in the new spring leaves from Shellie's upstairs bedroom.

They were sitting in rocking chairs on the wharf. Ruby poured her father another whiskey. "Why didn't you tell me you went to Boston?" she said.

"What for?" Rocket said. He let his legs swing with the chair. "I left the navy because I thought you needed me."

"I do."

"So you go off to Boston without telling me?"

"You're my daughter, not my wife."

"Richie DeSilva is going to help us."

"He's a chowderhead." Rocket let his eyes close again, feeling his nap overtake him once more.

"Why did I come back?"

"You were ready," he said. "You needed a home of your own."

"I had a home of my own. You're up to your old games."

"I'm not," he said.

"And what do I do with this loan I've arranged with the bank?"

"Do whatever you want with it—I won't take DeSilva's money."

"You are stubborn."

"I'm not," he said.

"How are you going to pay your taxes?"

Rocket squinted at her. "What taxes?"

"The taxes you owe on half this harbor! Do you understand that the town is going to sell your land at auction? You still don't read your mail, do you?"

"Never," he said.

"You haven't opened the letter from that woman, have you?"

"I might have."

"She mailed it fourteen years ago, or whatever it is, and you still won't open it. Don't you want to know her answer?"

"Nope."

"You know about the taxes?"

" 'Course I know," he said. "This is a nap, not a coma."

"How are you going to pay the taxes?"

"They'll get paid," he said.

"Why haven't you paid them?"

Again, Rocket opened his eyes a slit . . . inhaled impatiently. "Forgot," he said. "I'm gettin' old."

"The loan will at least let us save this place and my place, if we're very lucky. I'm going to repay it out of my business."

"If DeSilva's filled your head with this bunk, then that bastard's got his own reasons for saying so. Whatever he told you, it ain't true."

"It is true!"

"Is not. He'd dump us into the street without a pot to piss in—wouldn't bat an eye."

"I don't want to talk about him."

" 'Course, you don't. DeSilva never was any damn good. Ozzie is worth having. But what do you do? You kick the bejeezus out of him. He's the best man this town's got—after me."

"God, I feel like I should suck my thumb!"

"Haven't changed a whit. You never did listen."

"What's wrong with wanting to be a good daughter?"

"I keep tellin' you that, too—I have loved you longer and harder than I've ever loved any person in my life. Did you hear that?"

"And now?" she said.

"Still do, dammit!"

She rubbed his arm.

"You always had you own ideas," he said. "Crazy, most of 'em. They weren't solid. They ain't now! That Ozzie Barrett is a love-struck mess because of you. And you beat on him!"

"I don't love him," she said.

"The hell you don't, girl. Love isn't all frilly sheets and punkin pie—love is down in the bilge with you at three in the morning. Love is when you know you're not going to be alone for a while. And being alone is the worst thing that happens to us. I know."

"So do I," she said.

"Then act right. I didn't raise you to be some pansy-ass princess. I'm not saying you have to have a man to live your life, or that you have to marry Ozzie, but I am tellin' you that if you ever find one person who loves you clean, and you feel the same, then you better take the son of a bitch by the neck and not let go."

"What about my loan?"

"The hell with the loan—we don't need it."

"How do we pay the bills? You always make me feel so foolish."

"I've sold some land I've had since the Battle of Bunky Hill—there'll be enough money to pay the bills."

"What land?"

"Swamp—out near that goddam mall. Give us another splash o' licky, there."

Grub Dominions

Oᴢᴢɪᴇ slept until dark as a dream-soaked hulk on the *Lucia*'s berth. He awoke cold, sweaty, and glum, his internal mechanism dull. He'd slept with his hat on. He wondered if he'd ever fish again. He couldn't think straight, couldn't bend all the springs into his clockworks, couldn't even give himself a reason for sleeping the day away on a boat that some bank wanted. Stinking cabin, he thought, as he raised himself out of his blanket. The harbor was black, as black as he was as he stumbled toward the dentist's chair. He gripped the dead wheel. Like touching a corpse, he thought.

A half hour later, he let the library bulkhead down quietly, twisting to see the cellar door with his light. Two bolts on the outside slid silently and Ozzie was in. A concrete floor, a boiler and water tank, boxes, stairs. Ozzie heard the floorboards crack as people above strolled through the stacks. He wondered what day this was, surprised that the library was open so late, then went through a board door into another room, this one subterranean and brick like a root cellar. A plank floor lifted easily to reveal a capped cistern that must have once delivered the library's water. And near the concrete cistern cap, Ozzie's light flashed on a board hatch in the foundation wall.

He jumped down. The hatch came out of its frame with

a yelp of old nails. Ozzie listened for a second, then poked his light into the tunnel. Stone steps, and then concave brick walls laid up carelessly with globs of mortar, the floor littered with rats' bones and muck, his steps uncertain as he bent low to walk toward the bank. The tunnel seemed to slope even deeper for twenty or thirty paces and then rise abruptly to stone footings. Another hatch, this one like wet bread as Ozzie pushed against its wood.

He wondered what it was that sucked his Uncle Barry into dark tunnel mouths while other people sat at home reciting wedding plans, watching National Geographic specials, the late news, shambling over hallway rugs, their last few strides a welcome conclusion to their day, never knowing where their kids were. But not that old man, Ozzie thought. He felt the hatch give. He pushed harder when it caught, and then felt something much heavier move . . . his light quickly in: the coalbin, it's long planks swinging on hinges mortised behind a corner post.

Ozzie climbed up and out of the bin, his boots scratching anthracite dust off crunchy coal pieces. He went through two unlocked fire doors, the second opening into a tiled furnace room with stairs.

Ozzie went up to open the coatroom door, listened, then moved out through the bookkeeping office to stand behind the bank's counter.

The police cruiser was parked in front of the bank's doors, a cop's cigarette an orange spark in the cruiser. Ozzie kept his light off and hurried to Boynton's desk. Locked, but not for long, as Ozzie ran his machete blade all the way inside the center drawer and shattered the drawer's wood face. Banal bank business, photographs of Boynton on a bicycle at a beach, pens, pencils, junk. Third drawer down and Ozzie found the travel catalogues, flipped through them quickly, dropped them to pick up a collection of new greeting cards. And then picked up the American Express Caribbean catalogue again. Light held close under Boynton's desk, Ozzie found tickets for a one-way August flight to Jamaica. He closed the tickets and then hesitated; he whispered, "Veronica?" One ticket was made out to Veronica Boynton.

"Good christ," he said.

He looked up for the front door; the cruiser was there. "Veronica and Sheldon Boynton have a reservation for three weeks at the Rastaman Resort in Ocho Rios, Jamaica," he said. "Won't Darla love this one." He slipped the tickets back into the catalogue, tried to shut the smashed middle drawer . . . lifted out envelopes, files. He read. Sheldon Boynton didn't know "their" from "they're" or "there." "You little devil," Ozzie muttered. "You illiterate little devil. You've been sitting right here," he said, as he looked across the bank. "And she sat over there."

Ozzie found the narrow manila envelope in an unused calculator wallet and tore it open. Two bright keys dropped onto Boynton's blotter. Ozzie put both keys into his pocket. The center drawer was beyond repair, but Ozzie tried to leave Boynton's desk as he'd found it, sliding the little devil's chair forward.

"I have got you now," Ozzie muttered as he crossed to DeSilva's desk and stamped the bank president's signature onto a clean blotter.

He stopped to examine a framed painting he hadn't seen before, admiring the lightness of the hand and watercolors, and then recognized the painting as an architect's rendering of *his* harbor . . . with a long boardwalk and restaurant, tables and cutesy Cinzano umbrellas where Rocket's dock was now. The entire harbor was a pristine revelation of excessive modishness and lots of cash. The concept, as Richie undoubtedly referred to this thing, was lavishly precise, as shops and wharfs and condos had been realized in Marina del Rey dynamism. "Yuppie heaven," Ozzie whispered.

Ozzie unhooked the painting and took it with him back into the coatroom, as silently as he could, thudding the frame on the stairway and again at the last fire door. He forced the painting into the tunnel, kicked it in with his boot and then went in after it, straining the rusted coalbin hinges as he snugged the planks back against the tunnel bricks. Ozzie replaced the hatch cover and nearly ran back to the library, clattering and whacking the painting's frame on mortar gouts.

The library was silent, the floorboards still, as Ozzie shut the door on the cistern room and went for his last door and the bulkhead.

Slowly, like a turtle's head out of mud, Ozzie got the bulkhead up and open. The library windows were black. The bank black. Nothing but silence as he scampered over the lawns toward the jeep he'd left at the park.

Ozzie strode up Veronica Hammond's driveway, her house thick with impenetrable gloom, as he realized he knew more about this house than he wanted to, that this house was where he began, where Uncle Barry had fetched an old man's last brave act out of the pool.

One of Boynton's keys slid softly into Veronica Hammond's French doors and unlocked them effortlessly.

Ozzie separated the keys in his pockets, then hurried past her pool and picnic table to lope down her driveway.

Ozzie let the jeep roll against the pilings, its engine idling, as he grabbed the painting out of the back and ran across Ruby's catwalk. He held the painting up, glass cracked, against her door—lights within—flicked open his knife, and buried the steel tip into the painting and the door, impaled the painting, its glass now webbed and tight about his blade. She screamed at him when he had the jeep ready for first gear in the road, screamed again running on her catwalk. "Wait!" But he was gone, the jeep's lights out. And Ruby stood there in the road, wrapped in a reek of hot motor oil, alone with her vision of the man wearing combat boots and fatigues, a flak vest, a holstered pistol on his chest, machete clapping when he'd leapt into the jeep. Ruby knew a marine when she saw one.

⚓ ⚓ ⚓

There were lights on at DeSilva's as Ozzie passed. He drove up the Stearns' driveway and then turned the jeep into a rhododendron clump near the road, in under the maples. He cut the engine and, gathering himself, got his bearings. Through the woods, he thought. DeSilva's side lawn . . . the back of DeSilva's house.

"Got it," he whispered as he dropped out of the jeep and crept through the bushes and over the driveway into the woods, where he immediately fell over boulders in a briar patch.

The DeSilva house beckoned like a bright ocean liner at the end of the lawn. Ozzie moved out quickly, not running, but firmly confident in his best Parris Island demeanor, until he got to Richie's flagstone patio, sliding-glass doors, massive fronds of shrub and cedar, ground-hugging yew soft under his boots. He got to the rear door near the garage. Nothing but silence.

He tried the locked door, then felt Boynton's second key slide easily, felt the tumblers click. Through the window Ozzie saw a shaft of light from another room into this, the laundry room where Babs had her aerobic togs washed by the Waters woman, who worked for her.

More carefully now, as stealthily as on any reconnaissance he'd ever enjoyed, Ozzie moved through the hedges on point, his light blinking as he stopped frequently and then went on.

When he found it in the cedar hedge near the trellis, DeSilva's den alight but unoccupied at his elbow, Ozzie dropped to his knees, his fatigue pants soaked in mud. He opened his shoulder bag, chose the left one, and lowered

Sheldon Boynton's left rubber into the treadmark in his beam. "You little devil, Sheldon. You've been a bad boy again," he whispered.

But how can that be? he wondered. Rain almost constantly since that night should have obliterated this footprint. And there were more of them, as Ozzie ran stooping around the house and then halted. "Sheldon, you came back—of course you did. But why did you come back? Because you shot the wrong man the first time, you dumb bastard?"

Ozzie saw the blue bubble through the trees. The police were here! He hadn't opened the door! How would the security system respond—unless there were motion detectors? Infrared? he wondered.

Policemen swept the front lawn with flashlights; another cop banged on the front door.

Ozzie ran into the woods and then out to the street, where he used his flashlight to find a bicycle's tireprint like serpents' tracks in the sandy verge. He looked up for the cops before he went back into the woods and found where Boynton had leaned the bicycle against a tree: more treadmarks left by the man's rubbers.

He ran quietly across the Stearns' driveway and into the rhododendrons for the jeep, cruiser lights flashing blue strokes on the trees near the road.

"Now or never," he said.

No lights, but with the engine in top form, Ozzie allowed the jeep to roll over the Stearns' lawn, through a gully; it bumped softly onto the road near their lamp post. He rounded the corner and dipped down into Weyland Terrace. He coasted on the dark street. "Run silent, run deep," he said as he bounced Rocket's jeep up over the berm, in among the bushes guarding the fourth green, and then skidded up out of the sand trap. Ozzie let the machine have its head as he spanked over the links on the golf-cart trails, heading for the clubhouse.

How the World Ends

THE country club was hushed and nearly abandoned as Ozzie walked up to the padded oak ledge and rested his arm. The bartender, Malone's boon companion in the arcane arts of Freemasonry, needed but seconds to know what was up and rang open his cash register, lifting its tray. "Take it," he said.

Ozzie saw a bald man and two women rise from their table near the dead fireplace.

"I don't want it," Ozzie said to the bartender. "Where's the bank party?"

"That's all the money I got," the bartender said. "These creeps never carry cash."

"Here—you!" the bald man shouted from the fireplace. One of the women was trying to escape out a locked French door.

Ozzie waved at the guy to relax.

But the bartender had dropped the tray on the bar near Ozzie and backed away. "Don't kill me," he said, his hands coming up.

"The bank party!" Ozzie yelled. "Where is it? Why aren't they here?"

"Bank party?" the bartender said. "Oh! The bank party! At Walden!" he shouted, then pointed madly.

"Here—you!" The bald man was on the march, white-fringed head red with fury, hurrying between tables, sweeping his linen coattails angrily. "You get out of here!"

"Thanks," Ozzie said to the bartender.

Ozzie stared at the bald man for a second, then bolted out the door and through the lobby.

Walden was a near-perfect replica of Marie Antoinette's Versailles cottage, replete with ducks and swans in its pond, all stonework, buttressed brick and corbels, green copper château roofs, a miniature tower, an oriel here and there, with an orangery in its hedged garden. Built to assuage the pique of a Victorian Maguire daughter whose ship-captain lover went missing in Amazonia, Walden had been used by various Maguires over the decades as a sanctuary for their momentarily obsessed family members and correspondents, unescortable maiden aunts, women and children wronged and sired by various Maguire men, and now by Strike's Landing as the town's formal setting for the best weddings and most audacious celebrations.

Walden, on this night, had its crushed-shell curved drive over the golf course dotted with carriage lamps, its leaded windows brightly warm and secure, its ivied entry arbor alive with tossing tiny lights like hired fireflies. The Manos woman and her catering staff pushed through the ornate rooms carrying trays of goodies to about three hundred notables gathered to celebrate the stolid success of the First Seaman's Bank, and on this night to officially signal the banns of betrothal between Lizbeth and Bud. They were all here, favored bank customers and shop owners, doctors concerned that someone might chip their Jaguars' paint jobs in the dark parking area, bank employees and their spouses, the women with corsages by Tish and poufed hair, the men in uncomfortable suits and new shoes. Tonight was an annual do as the Chrysler dealers and cosmetologists-turned-land-barons met to swap business notes and bad jokes with the yacht owners and garden club. The town's Portuguese were represented by the catering staff and bank tellers, and by Richie DeSilva, who stood amiably under the ivied orangery rafters, which had been garlanded with yet more firefly lights to allow the sullen pond nearby, where a woman had drowned both her daughters in 1913, to gain on this gala evening a ludicrous festive note.

Richie had the bank people around him, the flighty tellers who would dance later and flash their thighs. But Babs wasn't here tonight, her absence like a lead bell in a carillon, as Richie encouraged his employees to circulate and laugh.

Elspeth, Lizbeth, Bud, and Louise stood near the champagne table in the orangery, constantly pumping hands, Lizbeth with snow-white, full-length gloves to accent her yellow dress. Sheldon Boynton had Darla out for the evening, Darla not taking her shame in stride, still a loan officer's wife, but robustly chatty, her screech of a laugh like a macaw's scream punctuating the conversation of clinking punch cups. Darla wore black, a choice she knew would announce her dissatisfactions despite her good cheer.

The evening was a treat until Elspeth heard Ozzie shout. She reached for her sister's arm as a reflex, searching for him, then heard him shout once more and saw him, as did the entire garden, those in the orangery and cottage tipping out to see what was what.

"DeSilva!" Ozzie yelled. Ozzie was in an oriel high over the garden.

Richie DeSilva had to be physically spun around by Bud, as though Richie knew well what was about to happen to him. Richie looked up at the marine in combat gear, the soft Parris Island cap close over Ozzie's face. Ozzie had camouflaged his cheeks with green and black grease.

"DeSilva!" Ozzie yelled again. "It's over, you son of a bitch."

"Who is that?" Lizbeth said, even though she knew.

"Dear god," Elspeth whispered, clutching Bud.

"Who is that man?" a doctor's tight blond wife said to the gathering with distilled disdain.

"I'll get him!" Noel Flagler shouted to Richie, and he dashed toward the cottage doors.

"Richie, the party's over!" Ozzie cried. "You're a thief and a bum. He's been robbing you blind!" he shouted over their heads. "He's embezzled millions! He and a guy named Zalinsky! He's manipulated your land and mortgages, skimmed your trust funds—your money market accounts are drained! Bone dry!"

"Who is that person?" Boynton said to Richie, but Richie was too far gone, too steeped in unresolved rage to do anything but stand there and shake.

"Oh, dear god," Elspeth said as she collapsed into a garden seat. Louise bent to minister to the woman.

"Son of a bitch is drunk!" a radiologist yelled. "Somebody do something!"

Boynton had stumbled to stand with Darla behind a punch table, dipping his hand into the punch bowl for a strawberry because he was cupless.

"What a shame," the Stearns woman said to anyone who would hear her. "First his uncle—and now this."

"Boynton!" Ozzie yelled, gathering his strength. "You killed Veronica Hammond and you shot Babs DeSilva's lover!"

"Oh, really!" someone said.

"Please—somebody stop him!" Darla screamed.

Boynton was bobbing from cup to cup, searching for a clean one on the punch table.

"Somebody shut him up!" Darla screamed.

DeSilva shoved people aside, stalked toward the cottage doors, but there was a shout followed by a scream as Noel Flagler tumbled out the oriel, Ozzie gripping the man's coat, suspending Flagler against the ivied wall below him. A chorus of screams. DeSilva stopped.

"Stupid bastard!" Ozzie grunted. "What the hell's the matter with you? Here, catch him," Ozzie said to men below as he dropped Flagler headfirst into the hedges.

"Uncle Barry is coming home!" Ozzie shouted to his aunts. "He's coming home! Boynton's the one!" he pointed.

Ruby stepped into the lights, her sequined motorcycle jacket sparkling when she lifted the framed architect's rendition of a sleazy banker's dream over her head. She shouted to Ozzie. She pushed the framed beauty through the throng until she stood beside DeSilva.

"Look familiar?" she said to him.

DeSilva was having trouble taking everything in. He studied the painting. Ruby lowered the painting for him to see. He was confused.

"Show me my father's shop," she said to him, jamming the glass in his face. "Show me! Show me where my father lives in this fucking painting!"

"Where did you get that?" DeSilva said.

"You lying bastard!" Ruby shouted at him. She held the painting aloft for all to see. "This look like home to ya'll?" she said. "Here's what this bastard wants for us—and it's all going to be his!"

"Ruby?" Ozzie shouted.

She looked up at Ozzie, her face softening. She said: "They can't have everything, Ozzie."

"What are you doing here?" Ozzie said.

The crowd was silent.

"Looking for you," she said, softly.

Boynton had already thrown one crystal punch cup at Ozzie, and now he motioned for the pitch again, took the sign from the catcher, and leapt off his feet as he winged another cup, this one crashing in splinters on the stonework above Ozzie. Then another and another, as Boynton cleared the table, Darla grappling to hold him, Boynton shoving his wife into the shrubs. A rain of punch cups went up like a mob assault on Versailles.

The men around Noel Flagler yelled for someone to call an ambulance.

DeSilva lifted his arms in victory, the only gesture he truly understood, and the bank president howled. He started making ones with his index fingers, shaking his fists, bellowing, "We're number one! We're number one! We're number one!"

Ruby hit him with the painting.

Lizbeth and Elspeth had put themselves into the care of Louise and Bud, both women infirm and fragile as they were led into the cottage.

Ozzie stood above the crowd, listening to the glass smash into the stonework, suddenly feeling gaunt and broken.

⚓ ⚓ ⚓

When Ruby got inside to the stairway, the police had Ozzie in a choke hold, bumping him down the stairs.

"Out of my way, miss," Cabral said to her, as he slammed Ozzie against the wall. "He's under arrest," Cabral said, trying to control the struggling Ozzie. Four other cops had pieces of the marine, his combat boots flailing at them, his face bloodied, eyes wild.

"Leave him alone!" she yelled at them, but they pushed her into the retreating crowd and dragged Ozzie out of Walden.

Ruby went after them, saw DeSilva spit at Ozzie under the arbor. DeSilva reached for her arm, restraining her. "Let him go," he said. "He's nuts."

Ruby punched him square in the face. The other men took her arms.

DeSilva grinned foolishly. "I'm glad that's over," he said, as he pulled out a handkerchief. He dabbed at his eyes and sniggered at the men around him for confirmation. The cops pushed Ozzie into a cruiser with its lights flashing. "Why do you keep hitting me?" DeSilva said to her. "He's completely out of his head."

Ruby resisted the men. They leaned on her together, crushing her.

"Okay—okay," DeSilva said to them as the police cruiser sped away. "Let her go," he said. "It's okay, Ruby. It's not what you think it is."

Ruby shook herself loose, her hair in her eyes, jeans ripped, as people spewed out of Walden, hurrying to their cars.

"You've got it all wrong," DeSilva said to her as he touched her hair.

But Ruby was gone, off over the hedges and grass like a cheetah into the darkness.

⚓ ⚓ ⚓

They wouldn't let her see Ozzie at the police station. Ruby paced a hallway of padded metal chairs. She asked for him every time someone came through the solid door with its heavy brass lock. They shook their heads at her and went about their business.

Tagliano arrived in sneakers and sweats, his hair matted, face puffy with abused sleep. He ignored her as he waited for the buzzer after knocking on the dispatcher's window, and then went inside.

A man carrying a first-aid box told her to go home. Ruby had telephoned for Lily, but got no answer.

Ruby waited.

⚓ ⚓ ⚓

Ozzie sat alone in the cell, his hand throbbing, head bleeding from one of Boynton's punch cups. The gash on his nose had opened again. He wiped fresh blood from his face. His knees had been wrenched and his throat ached where Cabral's nightstick had bruised his windpipe. He took long, slow breaths.

Tagliano appeared in front of the cell, two policemen at

258

his side. "Barrett! I've had all I'm going to take from you. I warned you. Now you're going to be charged."

Ozzie turned his face away from Tagliano.

"First-degree murder, Barrett! And not only can I make it stick, you are going bye-bye for a long, long time. You pushed—now I'm pushing back."

Ozzie let them leave without so much as a groan.

Judge Mahoney arrived from some distant sleep and said nothing as a Legal Aid lawyer went through the motions with Ozzie. Lily was on vacation somewhere, just gone. And Ozzie listened to very little they said, as they arraigned him in the police chief's office for the murder of Veronica Hammond and the attempted murder of Babs's Argentine. Tagliano's girl Friday delivered the honors with crisp, delicate strokes. No makeup, dressed in the middle of the night in a woolen skirt with black sensible shoes. Ozzie, when asked, said, "Give me five minutes alone, Mahoney. I'll tell you everything I know."

The groggy judge motioned with his head, and Ozzie was escorted into a county jail cell in the courthouse cellar; however, he had been there but a moment when they came for him again and brought him out to a sheriff's car.

As the car moved along the harbor road, the *Lucia* dark and empty against her wharf, Ozzie glanced in time to see Ruby standing on the police-station stairs, watching him leave town, the sheriff's car quickly past the bank and over the salt-marsh bridge toward Medford.

Some Blessed Hope

Boynton sat down at his desk, greeting his colleagues in finance, pleased to see Richard DeSilva coming over to talk.

"Dr. Biggy says I shouldn't be here this morning," Boynton said. "He gave me something to calm my nerves. I've got work to do. My drawer's broken, Richie."

"Your doctor was right—you shouldn't be here," DeSilva said. He leaned over Darla's photograph, the one she'd had taken at a Penney's special: "You're fired!"

Boynton screamed with laughter. "Hap Gault is coming in—we sign his loan for his pizza barn."

"Get out," DeSilva said.

Boynton shrieked again, cackling at the customers and bank people, asking them to share in his horror. "I was so embarrassed last night," he said. "Weren't you? That man is crazy."

"You're fired, Sheldon! Get out!" DeSilva yelled, coming over the desk, gripping Boynton's pigeon jacket, pulling Boynton up to his feet, hustling him toward the door.

"I'm medicated!" Boynton yelled to everyone. "Dr. Biggy said I shouldn't work today!"

DeSilva slammed Boynton into one door after another, finally hurling the pigeon fancier onto the sidewalk.

Ozzie waited for breakfast until midday, then he waited for lunch and expected at least a bowl of gruel when his cell door clinked at last and swung open to admit Uncle Barry in a wicker wheelchair.

The old man whisked at his face as though pestered by tundral mosquitoes.

"What happened to you?" Ozzie said.

Uncle Barry pocketed a key ring. "I'm cured."

"How'd you get cured?"

Uncle Barry almost smiled. "I decided not to be sick."

"Needles?"

"No needles, Oz."

"Pills?"

"I give 'em to Jamie—he's a college kid, works at night here. Ezra inherited half a million dollars. He's cured, too. Love your uniform."

"Sixty days—just like you. Tagliano had me arrested."

"You won't like it here, Oz." Uncle Barry crossed his legs, his institutional gray cotton pants clean and pressed. "Try not to antagonize them."

"He's charged me with Veronica Hammond's murder."

"That's two of us, Oz."

"You should be out of here soon."

"Naw—I can't plant tomatoes on your boat. Elspeth and Lizbeth have the big Bud. Town's not safe for an old man anymore. We're thinking of going to Ezra's house on Cape Breton Island."

"All of you?"

"Why not?"

"You'll be here forever," Ozzie said.

"Forever isn't very long, Oz. Don't make fun of us. And don't get scared, no matter what they do to you. Once a man gets scared, he'll put up with anything. Even this."

"I'm going to be evaluated."

Uncle Barry backed the wheelchair into the corridor. "Already happened—that's why they put you in here. Next sixty days only convince them they're right."

"Where are you going?"

"We're having a charades tournament this afternoon. I'm a contestant. I'll come back later."

"Care to leave your keys?"

Uncle Barry tossed the keys onto Ozzie's mattress. "Lock yourself in," he said. "Be careful, Oz. Don't irritate them."

Ozzie was taken at midafternoon to a basement medical lab, where a Pakistani medico drew vials of Ozzie's blood, the dark fingers jabbing Ozzie's arm repeatedly, trying to hit a vein. The man gave Ozzie his business card when he finished jabbing: a Stoneham address. "I am beginning to practice privately," the medico said.

"Practice what?" Ozzie asked, rolling down his fatigue sleeves.

"Family counseling is my speciality. Do you have a family?"

"Never have."

"I am having great hopes for myself."

"Well founded, I'm sure," Ozzie said. "You'll be a hit."

"Unfortunately, yes," the doctor said. He wiped his forehead with a lab cloth. "Many families hit themselves unnecessarily. Very astute of you to share that—you've had counseling?"

"Years," Ozzie said.

"Ring my phone," the doctor said, ushering Ozzie into the waiting grip of the Department of Corrections guard. "You might get out someday—we can set goals for you, make plans."

"I'll call."

"Very kind of you," said the Pakistani, bustling off amid heating pipes and laundry hampers.

When Shaw saw Ozzie an hour later, the hospital administrator couldn't contain his joy. "Quite a turn of events," Shaw said.

Ozzie sat heavily onto one of Shaw's gray chairs, his gaze drawn to the rain-lashed trees outside, Shaw's windows wet even under the veranda's protective roof.

Shaw snapped on his desk light. The man had a cast replica of the Washington Monument on his desk. Its embedded thermometer bloodless like a white vein. Shaw said, "We're not surprised, are we?"

"One of us isn't."

"The apple doesn't fall far from the tree, does it, Barrett? You have our complete attention now."

The office was steamy and sour. Ozzie watched the trees bend outside.

"Sixty days," Shaw said. "Common protocols. My staff will make recommendations. You cooperate, Barrett, and it's a walk in the park. You give us any shit, and we'll order you a room on the moon. Attempted murder on top of the big one should be a clear sign to you that you've got some problems. Someone wants to see you." He scraped his chair getting up. "Wait here."

The door hissed as it shut behind Ozzie. The man's windows were sealed, his bookshelves cluttered with psychiatric extracts and monographs. Ozzie got up and went to run his fingers along the window casing. Screwed shut, he thought. He heard voices and took a book off the shelf.

Tagliano came into the office, went directly to Shaw's desk, where he sat down as though he were in a rush. He opened a folder. When he said, "This is a helluva list," he gestured for Shaw to leave them. "Find yourself in one of those case histories, Barrett?"

Ozzie left the book on a videotape machine and leaned against the shelves.

Tagliano said, "You've got to be in one of those books, somewhere. Start with the letter 'A,' for 'asshole.'"

"What do you want?" Ozzie was cold, his mind a clammy echo of smashed tracery and groins, his walls stonily inert.

"How did you get into the bank's computer?" Tagliano said, clicking a ballpoint pen.

"Easy," Ozzie said. "I started with your name and went from there. Under 'C' for 'co-conspirator.' "

"I talked to Boynton. He's under a doctor's care," Tagliano said. "His wife says it's all your fault. That true?"

The trees were being bashed by wind, but all in silence from in here as Ozzie watched. "Or 'F' for 'fraud,' " Ozzie said. "Or 'S' for 'skimming.' "

"Someone telephoned Boynton. Said he was the Federal Reserve Bank—that you?"

Ozzie watched the trees.

"Helluva list, Barrett. Attempted murder—murder. Assault. Breaking and entering so many times it doesn't matter—computer-security violations—obstructing justice—harassment—withholding evidence—I mean this list goes on and on. You've been busy, Barrett. What did Richard DeSilva ever do to you, besides screw the Willey woman while you waited in line?"

Ozzie turned to stare at the man.

"You didn't know when to leave well enough alone, did you, Barrett? Is it his money—he's got what you'll never have?" Tagliano's face was tanned, his haircut fresh enough to expose white skin on his neck. "Well, you'll have years to ponder this shit," Tagliano said. "You're gonna live in Walpole State Prison longer than you've ever lived anywhere. Spill your guts all you want, when you get around to it—nobody's listening, Barrett. And no one's gonna listen. You're a schmuck."

Ozzie was blitzed; roof tiles and stone chunks crashed onto his floor; ominous rending reports ripped high over his head in his gloomy transepts.

Tagliano closed the folder and stood up. "You're so fucked up you can't see what you've done to that Willey chick. A conspiracy charge against her will ruin her chances to save her father's business. That's a real shame. No bank in its right mind will loan her a stamp. Nice tits, though."

Ozzie's roof came down.

"You pissed on a grizzly, Barrett. Now the damn bear's gonna eat you for lunch. Too bad," he said, tapping his folder. He started to leave, then stepped toward Ozzie, Tagliano's eyes like black suns. "Try not to drool on the floors around here—they notice things like that."

Tagliano laughed, slapped his leg with the folder, then turned for the door when he heard the woodbine voice.

Ozzie knew the cathedral's ceiling was open to the sky, open to rain and pitch, the stars leaking through. He heard the distant voice as a resonant boom of judgment on a very foolish man.

"See ya, schmuck," Tagliano said.

"In here?" the voice boomed.

Ozzie looked up. Malone came through the door, Shaw doing a Texas two-step to get around Malone, heading off the rabid educationist.

"Hey, Oz!" Malone said.

Ozzie wanted to speak. But he couldn't move a muscle. Malone pushed Tagliano aside, and bent down to study Ozzie's face.

More men came into the office.

"What'd they do to you?" Malone said. He took Ozzie's shoulders in his hands and rattled his friend. "Oz, you in there?"

Ozzie's eyes filled with tears. "Hey, Wilson."

The other men were shouting, Tagliano abrasive, Shaw a spasm of ineptitude as he made for his desk chair and sat down. Tagliano had his wallet out, identifying himself to the two men in jeans and track shoes. When one of these men turned to see Tagliano's wallet, Ozzie read the yellow letters on the man's blue windbreaker: FBI.

"It's okay, Oz," Malone said, gripping his arm around Ozzie's back to stand Ozzie away from the bookshelves.

The third man with Malone had a mane like Christmas

angel-hair, ruddy skin, eyes like frozen methane. He had on creased khaki pants, an L. L. Bean mackinaw like Malone's, only red. He wore wellies. This man came directly to Ozzie and put out his hand. "Name is Magnuson," he said. "Rupert."

Ozzie felt the judge take his hand. Ozzie wiped his sleeve across his eyes. "Barrett," he said, "Ozzie."

Tagliano yelled, "I want you all out of this room—now!"

"I have an appointment," Shaw said to one of the FBI men. Shaw started to stand. The FBI guy motioned once. Shaw sat.

The judge only glanced at Tagliano before he said to Ozzie, "You haven't made many friends lately, have you?"

"Just Wilson," Ozzie said, nodding to Malone.

"Thanks, Oz," Malone said, hugging him.

"You're pretty goddam far out on this limb," the judge said. "You almost got lost forever."

Tagliano yelled, "I'm requesting an immediate confidential briefing!" He moved for the door.

"Kelley?" the judge said to the FBI guy who was just slightly smaller than Malone. "Quietly explain to the prosecutor that the great brass eagle is about to shit all over him."

"Kelley sells diamonds," Malone winked to Ozzie. He rolled his eyes. "Gets 'em wholesale. Sapphires, emeralds, rubies. Kelley can get you anything."

Kelley and his FBI partner suggested Tagliano have a seat.

"Where is she?" Ozzie said to Malone.

"She's waiting for you at her place."

"She safe?"

"I guess so—she's made a godawful stink today, Oz."

"It's all over for you," the judge said to Ozzie. "Go home with Wilson."

Malone boosted Ozzie into gear, squeezing him hard.

"Can you do that?" Ozzie said to the judge.

The judge studied Ozzie, then said, "I just did."

"You cannot release that man!" Tagliano yelled. His feet pattered, as though he might do a Fred Astaire off the chair.

"I have an appointment," Shaw said earnestly.

Ozzie hesitated, turned for Shaw, then smiled at the hospital administrator. "Don't miss Shorty here," he said to the judge.

Magnuson said, "We won't. All these guys are gonna be sucked through a knothole."

"DeSilva?" Ozzie asked him.

"We'll get him."

"Zalinsky?"

"Him, too," Magnuson said.

"Boynton?"

"Take him home, Wilson," the judge said.

Tagliano said, "You are violating every procedure there is!"

Ozzie asked about his Uncle Barry.

"Not tonight," the judge said. "But real soon—we need to get all this clear, first."

"Barrett can't leave!" Tagliano said.

Malone guided Ozzie past the men. Tagliano had the coarseness of an infuriated bull about him, as though he couldn't decide whether to gore one of them or knock himself out ramming a wall.

"Sonny," the judge said to Tagliano, "you're a real pain in the ass. Do it," he said to Kelley.

Ozzie heard the handcuffs sizzle and click as he left with Malone.

"Where'd they put all your stuff?" Malone said.

"I want to get Uncle Barry."

Another FBI man stood at the end of the corridor.

"Do as he says, Oz. Rupert's got an awful short fuse."

"Since when do judges make house calls?"

"Rupert's not like other judges. But don't say anything to him about it—he's kinda touchy."

The Local Hero

Richie DeSilva ran back up the old man's ramp and turned off the office light, swore at the barking dog in the back room, then hurried out and along the wharf to the *Showboat.*

He hustled down the ladders into the engine-room passageway and listened. Heard nothing.

DeSilva eased the engine-room door open and listened. Nothing.

He pulled the door closed, its watertight latch squealing shut, and ran up the ladders, through the galley and up onto the bridge, where he ignited his diesels and left them running.

He could hear that damn dog barking as he leapt for the wharf and walked to his car, his deck shoes mushy with rain.

"Get lost," she said to him.

DeSilva said, "Did you hear me?"

Ruby came out onto her porch, a small cigar between her lips.

"Look," he said, "I took my boat over to get fuel—he's drunk! I told him to stay away from me, but he wouldn't. He's cut his head. I want you to get your father off my boat now!"

"Why is he on your boat?" she said, as she dipped inside for her jacket.

"He's drunk—the bastard pushed me in the compressor room and fell over. I think he's unconscious."

Ruby ran for the road, for the jeep, but DeSilva yelled, "My car! My car!" and she got in with him.

Then got out.

DeSilva skidded on the wet road, pushed the Caddy toward Mildred's, then turned along the docks, past the bank, the jeep's headlights bouncing in his mirror.

The Caddy rocked in park when DeSilva got out. He locked the door and watched Ruby Willey slide into the junkyard, the jeep rolling into the fence after she jumped. She was ahead of him on the wharf, fast up the gangplank and into the salon. When DeSilva got below, he could smell her. The engine-room door was open. DeSilva stepped inside, between the beating diesels, the small space alive with rumbling. DeSilva got through the compressor-room door at the rear of the engine room and saw Ruby kneeling over her father, who did not move on the vibrating plates.

"Did you hit him?" she said as she twisted to see DeSilva.

"I came down to check my water tanks. He followed me."

"Why did you lock him in, Richie?"

"I thought he'd come after me with a hammer or something. Is he all right?"

Ruby sat her father up, blood on the old man's face, in his mustache. She spoke to him, then let him down again onto his back.

When she next looked, DeSilva had gone. The compressor-room door had been latched.

DeSilva hid the Caddy between two hulls in the junkyard.

The *Showboat* was all white and inviting as he ran down the wharf. He got the gangplank in and stowed. I have a full load of fuel, he thought, as he dashed up the ladders for the bridge. His running lights on, radar screen glowing green, his digital gauges winking all systems up. When the marine operator called him, the name *Showboat* jolted him. He didn't want to answer. DeSilva snatched the receiver and identified the *Showboat.*

Tagliano said, "Hello, Mr. DeSilva. This is Mario Tagliano."

"What the hell are you doing?" DeSilva said. He shut off his deck lights.

"I need to talk to you, Mr. DeSilva. Could we meet in my office in an hour?"

"Sure," DeSilva said. The satellite navigation system pinged his longitude and latitude. "What's this all about? Why are you calling me Mr. DeSilva, Mario?"

"My office," Tagliano said. "Bye."

"You're supposed to say *over,*" DeSilva said. "This is ship-to-shore. Say *over.*"

"Screw *over,*" Tagliano said. "An hour."

"I'll be there," DeSilva said. "Over."

Tagliano hung up. DeSilva cleared the channel and pegged the receiver in its cradle next to the radar screen.

"Bullshit," he said to himself as he studied the screen. He had no idea what the green blips meant.

He ran below, his feet sliding on the wet ladders where he and Ruby had tracked in rain.

He knocked on the engine-room door. "Can you hear me?" he yelled.

Nothing but the constant throb of his diesels.

"Ruby!"

Nothing.

DeSilva spun the latch, released the door carefully, and stood back a bit. But the woman and her father were secured in the compressor room; that door was thin, though, its lock more a nuisance than a surety. "Can you hear me?" he shouted. The engine room was well over a hundred degrees already. He'd have to find Captain Brownie's toggles on the bridge panel and ventilate this compartment or the old man wouldn't last long.

He shouted again at the compressor-room door. Thought he heard her voice. He yelled again: "I love you, Ruby! Do you hear me? I love you!"

Nothing.

DeSilva scurried back between the thundering engines and sealed the engine-room door after him. He got topside, along the rail, the harbor still, the *Lucia* a dead hull ahead of him alongside Rocket's wharf. The dog had stopped yapping.

DeSilva let go the lines, hurrying now that he knew what he had to do. Ruby's stupid parrot had perched on the *Showboat*'s mast. DeSilva threw a fender at the bird, but Larry was an old hand and knew very well what men might do to a perched parrot. "Tagliano's a chicken-shit," he said as he slammed the bridge door closed behind him, glad for the inner peace among his instruments.

He backed the boat down, cleared the *Lucia*'s stern with his bow, and cracked hard into the old man's wharf. "Fuck it," he said. He brought the wheel over, searching for the engine-room ventilators on the breaker panel.

DeSilva ran over a small sailboat, aware that an aluminum mast whacking his rail probably meant the worst for the sailboat. He hadn't seen the damn thing on its mooring, and now concentrated on weaving through the harbor, MacAvoy's lights astern, the channel buoys marking his escape ahead.

When the harbormaster called him on the radio, DeSilva ignored the man as any banker might; the deadbeat was threatening suit against the First Seaman's Bank because, he claimed, the bank had improperly lumped a disputed three hundred dollars into his home-improvement loan. "Damn fool," DeSilva said as he turned the radio's volume down.

The radar screen had totally changed, its bright revolving eye half black with the Atlantic dead ahead.

The Chase, of Course

"She's not here," Ozzie said as he got into Malone's station wagon. "Larry's gone."

Malone drove back past Mildred's, past the docks, the harbor dark with no moon, few lights. "She working?" he said.

The rain had stopped. The streets were wet. Malone swept onto the northern harbor road.

"Maybe," Ozzie said. "The dragger's gone, isn't it?"

Malone waited on the wharf while Ozzie zipped into Rocket's office. Ozzie went back into the old man's bedroom, found no one, but let Owl out of the bathroom.

"Not good," Ozzie muttered. Owl sniffed through the rooms. There was a bottle of whiskey on Rocket's desk, a Ronald McDonald glass with an inch of booze in it.

Malone stepped into the office, took off his porkpie hat. "Oz, DeSilva's boat is not in the harbor."

"It has to be here," Ozzie said, heading out the door to stand on the ramp. "How can it be gone if DeSilva is having tea with the FBI?"

"He might not be," Malone said. He gripped Ozzie's shoulder to survey the harbor once again. Mildred's lights blinked distantly, Ruby's windows, the *Lucia* black and empty below them.

"Wilson, this isn't right."

"I know that," Malone said.

A Boston Whaler growled out of the pilings across the harbor near Phil's boatyard. The Whaler carried no lights.

Ozzie said, "Owl was locked in the bathroom—Rocket wouldn't do that. Jeep's here—tow truck is here."

Ozzie walked down the wharf. "So where are they?" he said. He shouted back for Malone to call the harbormaster about DeSilva's boat.

Ozzie used Malone's MityLite when he opened Rocket's sheds, the machine shop with Rocket's chain falls and lathes, the wood in here damp with oil. Into the junkyard, over Rocket's steel scrap, the rusting deckhouses rank as Ozzie poked the flashlight through portholes. And then he found the cream Caddy.

He heard Malone shout. Ozzie ran through the yard to the fence.

"He's gone!" Malone yelled from the wharf. "Twenty minutes ago!"

Ozzie crashed over junk and ran down the wharf to Rocket's office. A half-dozen radios sat dead on a shelf over Rocket's desk, but the Philco whispered when its yellow dials brightened.

Malone was behind him. He kneeled to rub Owl's head. "Gomez said DeSilva's boat almost clipped a trawler when it left," Malone said. "When Gomez radioed DeSilva's boat, he didn't get an answer."

"DeSilva couldn't handle an inner tube," Ozzie said. He'd bent behind the desk and returned with an antenna.

"You gonna watch TV?" Malone said, as he pulled a swig from Rocket's bottle.

Ozzie untangled the cable, darted backward out the door and down the ramp, the antenna up over his head. "Hold this," he said to the sauntering Malone, who took another pull on the bottle. Malone held up the antenna.

"Rotate, Wilson—slowly." Ozzie ran back up the ramp.

"Oz—I think we should call somebody. Magnuson? The FBI? What am I doing?"

But Ozzie was inside, the radio's volume up loud.

Malone turned on the wharf like a lawn duck in the breeze.

"Stop!" Ozzie yelled.

"Stop what?"

"Turn back—turn back!"

"Ozzie, what the hell are we doing?" Malone pulled on the bottle twice more, turning as Ozzie told him to.

Ozzie looked off toward MacAvoy's and the black pile of St. Mary's. "Once more," he said. "I don't know what it sounds like." Ozzie stayed on the ramp to listen as the radio's roar remained constant, Malone turning slowly. "Now back," Ozzie said. "More."

Malone scrunched his hat down in the freshening breeze and turned.

"Stop!" Ozzie yelled. "That's got to be Ruby—but it's too weak. Rocket doesn't build weak shit," he said. He faced the harbor narrows. "Rocket has Ruby carry a signaling device, Wilson. You're holding his directional antenna. Can you hear it?"

"That peeping sound? Oz, that's nothing."

"Wanna bet?"

Ozzie took the antenna from Malone and got back up the ramp near the doorway to listen as he turned to locate the signal. "Ruby's at sea," he said softly.

"Where's Rocket?"

Ozzie shrugged. "And Larry? And why would she be signaling to Rocket if he's not here?"

"She's supposed to be at home," Malone said, lowering the empty bottle. "Call the Coast Guard."

Ozzie dropped the antenna and ran to the wharf and his lines. "Wilson, get the spring lines and the bow line."

"Are you actually going to chase the son of a bitch?"

Ozzie flew down the ladder and jumped.

"Get aboard!" Ozzie yelled as he tore the sheriff's yellow

seizure posters off the *Lucia*'s wheelhouse and got the blowers on.

Malone threw the bottle into the harbor and tossed lines down onto the trawler's deck. He heard Ozzie's diesel start with a bang. He waited before tugging the heavy bow line off the piling. Ozzie had the *Lucia* under way before Malone dropped off Rocket's ladder. "We should call someone, Oz," he said, as he tripped into the wheelhouse.

Ozzie got his running lights on, wheelhouse lights off, the radio on. "You do it," he said to Malone. "Go to Channel Sixteen—tell the Coast Guard what we're doing, where we are. Have them call the FBI."

Ozzie hooked the wheelhouse doors open. He hauled the trawler hard over through the moorings, snatched the toggles on to spray the harbor with his floodlights to miss the moored boats, hard over again to weave between these fiberglass tubs and then out into the channel, wheel coming amidships for the narrows.

Malone chatted pleasantly with the Coast Guard in Boston. They didn't understand, but would make calls and get back to him. "Nice guys, Oz."

"Tell them we're steering south-southeast when they come back. Now call Gomez and tell him to quit signaling us—tell him what we're doing. Don't worry about the Coast Guard— they'll ride right over Gomez. And load the Winchester."

Ozzie let Malone enjoy the radio. Malone's pipe investing the wheelhouse with a woody incense. The Coast Guard did come back to them, still puzzled, but with an acknowledgment from the FBI in Boston. "*Lucia*, be advised we will respond," the Coast Guard radio operator said.

"They did respond, Oz. He called us."

"He means they're on the way."

"Jeezus, Oz! No kidding?"

Ozzie had the diesel full out, the trawler vibrating but solid as she plunged out of the narrows and split the buoys at Three Sisters. Ozzie clicked off the floodlights and settled into his dentist's chair. "He's got miles on us," he said to Malone, who was swaying with the trawler's roll across the waves.

Malone said, "He's running, isn't he?"

"The Bahamas are out here, Wilson."

"Can we catch him?"

"He's faster than we are."

Ozzie heard the *Lucia* being called on the radio again. "You sick yet?" he said to Malone.

Malone turned away from the radio to face him. "Oz, do you mind—I'm very busy just now."

Sheldon Boynton saw the bright lights go out far behind him. He tucked his plastic K mart rainsuit close in under his chin to fend off the spray as his tiny Whaler, a frail coracle on the briny steep, beat against the waves. His nearly new Yamaha outboard had no more to give, but Boynton clung to his steering wheel and grimly searched the darkness ahead for DeSilva's lights.

Ruby wedged her fingers between the compressor-room door and its rubber seal. She braced her feet, her legs taking the strain. The door clamped her fingers. Ruby breathed once, then pushed with her legs, tearing the door off its hinges. The engine room was a welter of noise forward. She got Rocket up off the plates.

"Don't fuss with me, girl!" he shouted. They climbed into the engine room, Ruby holding her father between the roaring diesels. She tried the engine-room door.

"We're being kidnaped!" he shouted to her.

Ruby lifted the intercom phone off the panel and signaled the bridge.

Boynton crested one eight-foot wave, saw the glimmer, blew down into the next trough and climbed again to confirm his sighting.

Anyone near enough to the Whaler could easily have heard the man yowl and shriek as the Whaler skidded down into another trough.

There were lights dead ahead. He was gaining.

DeSilva had thought the *Showboat* serenely remote from the chaos of home, despite the fact that he carried dangerous cargo. He had the bridge lighting softly muted, romantically pinkish, the glossy brightwork in here redolent with affluent panache.

He was proud of himself: aside from the two scrapes in the harbor, he had this mighty raft bounding over the ocean, his radar a cyclopic green eye.

Then, the bridge telephone beeped.

DeSilva said, "Hello?"

Ruby held her hand over her exposed ear. "Richie— what's going on?"

"How did you get into the engine room?" But no sooner than he'd said it did he realize Ruby had always been trouble, would always be trouble.

"Richie, where are we going?"

"South," he said. "How did you get into the engine room?"

"Where south?"

DeSilva could hear his diesels rumble more insistently over the phone. "I'm going south."

"Stop the boat, Richie."

"I can't do that."

"Why are you taking us with you? This is kidnaping, you know."

"That's only one more charge," he said. He found that he

enjoyed this; Ruby had to listen to him. "Nobody sticks me. I'll let your father go when we get to the Bahamas."

"Bahamas? Richie, you've lost your mind."

"I love you, Ruby."

"What?"

"I said I love you. I always have. And you love me. Or will."

"Or won't, Richie."

"Ruby, you didn't have a life back there. We can get married in the Bahamas. I've got millions waiting for us. You'll see. This Portagee has done very well for himself. Ruby?"

No answer. The engines roared in his telephone. DeSilva scanned the darkness, eyed his radar, then said, "Ruby? Are you there?"

His engines quit . . . first one, then moments later the second engine died and the *Showboat* instantly lost way; the sea began to heave her bow to starboard, her wheel lifeless. The radar continued to sweep. Richie got out of his bridge chair and wondered what he should do. "Ruby, start the engines! Ruby! Are you there?"

"I'm here," she said tenderly.

"Start the engines."

DeSilva hit the ignition buttons, but almost all his gauges had pegged themselves. "Ruby! Start the engines!"

"No engines," she said.

"Ruby!" DeSilva screamed. "Start the engines! I'll kill you!"

"I thought you loved me," she said, ever the seductress in a Gold's Gym sweatshirt.

"Ruby, I can't play games."

DeSilva heard the old man say, "Hang up the phone, girl."

"Ruby!" DeSilva screamed. "Ruby!" But nothing. DeSilva snapped on his decklights. He threw the phone at the window, smashed the glass, then hurried into his chartroom. The radar would tell him where he was; the Cobalt runabout would get him safely away.

Boynton was glad he'd worn his rubbers, as he madly bailed the Whaler while he steered for the lights. Once more up toward the heavens, his trusty craft as agile as a killer whale tracking scent. DeSilva's great pig of a boat lay ahead of him, seemingly stationary, its companionways and decks sparkling with a come-hither-and-ravage-me virginity to the lone corsair pounding gleefully out of the dark. And ravage, he would. Boynton opened his K mart tackle box to get at his Very pistol.

Down into a trough, the Whaler skewed beam on, then dug into the wave's belly and leapt up again. Boynton loaded the flare and flicked the pistol shut as he crested the next wave.

He had no idea what range a Very pistol had, so he fired on the next crest, and knocked himself off his seat and back against the whining Yamaha. Boynton crawled forward over the thwart seats, lunging for his steering wheel as the Whaler lost its steerage and nearly broached.

Hard on again, coming around into the wind, Boynton made the next wave and saw no flare. The *Showboat*, yes. But no flare.

DeSilva thought the flare was lightning, or some other seafaring St. Elmo's apparition Captain Brownie always reported during the dog watch. He stepped out of the chartroom onto the bridge, paused long enough to wonder again at the light, then went to the radar screen to figure out his chart.

Ruby warned Rocket to stay back before she hefted the sledgehammer for the third time and bashed the steel latch-handle clean off the engine-room door.

"I told you you'd break that son of a bitch!" Rocket said. "We'll never open it now."

"What next?" she said.

"You're so handy with that thing—try the hull."

Ruby rang the bridge. Got nothing. Not a click.

Boynton had the Very pistol loaded once more, and this time clung to his throttle cable when he launched a sizzling green flare straight at the *Showboat,* a hundred yards off.

On the next crest, riding roughshod now, his clear plastic rainsuit worth every penny, Boynton rose and stood. And saw that he'd parked the green wonder on DeSilva's stern.

DeSilva didn't know how to work the davits, but had his owner's manual with him under the deck lights near the Cobalt when the green flare whooshed at him. The flare seemed to lose heart and crunched into his stern below.

DeSilva could smell the smoke before he saw it, saw the green glow before he knew what had happened. He stood at the top of his ladder, hands cupped over his eyes to block his deck lights. How the hell did she get flares? he wondered. Who was she signaling? Where is she?

He peered over the cowling, the flare blasting itself to phosphorescent bits in his stern. His carpet was on fire. "Flames!" he yelled. "Ruby, cut the shit! You've started a fire, for chrissakes!"

The next flare, a white one, whistled over his head as he descended the ladder. The flare smashed into something topside. He dropped off the ladder away from the flames, swinging a quilted chair pillow at the carpeting. But the plastic carpet was shredding, liquidy now, and attacked his pillow with white-hot ticks. DeSilva swung the pillow into the sea.

He dashed into the salon for the fire extinguisher under the bar. As he ducked to wrench the extinguisher loose, the next flare, another green one, smashed glass forward.

"Oh, god," he cried. "Oh, god!"

Richie emptied the extinguisher. A waste of time. This carpet was bred to burn hot.

He ran forward through the salon, along the passageway into his formal dining room, where he'd never eaten a meal, and grabbed two extinguishers from the butler's pantry. Up the interior crewmen's companionway, topside now, DeSilva said, "Oh, god no!" almost as a prayer of atonement. His Cobalt runabout was a bonfire.

"Oh, shit!" He looked for her. Called for her. Where was she?

A man in a clear plastic rainsuit, in a miniature boat not much larger than a dinghy, careened out of the darkness, bashed through the *Showboat*'s glare, the man's shrieks and cackles hideously deranged as he fired another flare, a white one, directly at DeSilva.

⚓ ⚓ ⚓

Ruby clanged the sledgehammer again, splitting the hatch hinge over her head.

"Once more, girl," Rocket said. "What the hell's going on up there?"

She missed the hinge on the next four tries, but smashed the thing open on the fifth.

"Three more hinges and she'll give," Rocket said, standing below her, his eyes plaintive as he watched his daughter.

Ruby got her balance on top of the engine, the boat's motion now lively with the sea. The engine hatch above her was concealed beneath the salon's carpeting, weighted with furniture.

But she braced herself, waited for the boat to roll back . . . then swung hard. She took the hinge off with one blow.

DeSilva knew all was lost, his eighty-foot Trumpy an insurance adjuster's banquet. "They'll never pay," he moaned as he bounced along the deck. There were flames on his bow sundeck as he dove into the safety of his abandoned bridge.

He went for the radio, gripped the handset and yelled, "Help! Help!" just as another flare blasted into the bridge to explode inside a flag cabinet.

DeSilva ran out to the rail. "Who are you?" he screamed.

Boynton had the Yamaha in neutral, loading his next flare. "None other!" he yelled. "I should have been the next veep, Richie!"

"Sheldon?" DeSilva murmured.

"Here—catch!" Boynton honked and fired a flare over DeSilva's head.

"How did you get out here?" DeSilva yelled.

"I drove, stupid. Let's see you humiliate me now, you bonehead."

"I've got people on board!" DeSilva yelled.

"Sure you do, Richie. Henry Kissinger, maybe?"

"I do. They're in the engine room! Why are you doing this to me?"

"Only you and me, Richie! Only you and me. Out here, we're even, you peckerhead."

"But why?"

"You made me kill the only woman I ever loved—whaddaya think?"

"Bring the boat up—take us off! What woman?"

"No chance, Richie."

"Again!" Rocket shouted.

Ruby swung hard; the overhead hatches rattled. The

sweetest odor of burning plastic infested the engine room.

"Again!"

The hammer flew out of her hands when it glanced off the hinge to clang onto the deck plates.

"What's holding them?" Rocket said.

"Do you smell that?" she said.

"I'm afraid so, girl. I been smellin' it for five minutes—we're on fire!"

"Don't do anything stupid," she said down to him.

"Stupid! We're trapped in the engine room of a burning boat at sea, and you think I'm going to do something stupid? I'm surprised at you."

Ruby pushed on the hatches with her hands high over her head. Then she climbed up onto piping and engine supports until her back was just beneath the hatches.

"Be careful, girl—you're a christly ways up there. You slip and you'll come down on all kinds of nasty things."

Ruby braced her knees, adjusted her feet for anything unyielding, then raised herself, raised her back to the hatches.

⚓ ⚓ ⚓

The *Lucia* rammed the Whaler broadside, Sheldon Boynton screaming in terror when he was thrown into the sea. DeSilva hadn't seen the trawler until it was only yards distant, lights out like a giant squid.

The *Lucia* ran over the Whaler to plow into the *Showboat*. DeSilva flipped onto his head, feet suddenly out over the rail, hands clinging to moistly wet steel bars.

"Sorry, Oz!" Malone yelled out of the wheelhouse. "I didn't see the little guy!"

But Ozzie was aboard the *Showboat,* hurtling over the rails onto the lower deck. He hauled up the leader line, hauled in the heavy hawser and cinched the *Lucia* to DeSilva's boat.

Malone was pushing the *Showboat* through the water.

"Neutral!" Ozzie yelled. "Neutral!"

Malone gave him thumbs up from the wheelhouse door. The swamped Whaler floated off into the night.

⚓ ⚓ ⚓

Ruby had flown into the air, falling past murderously sharp engine parts to land like a bag of cement near Rocket, the old man down himself.

"Holy shit," Rocket said. "You all right?"

Ruby was up again, pulling on his arms for him to stand.

"What the hell was that?" he said.

"Something hit us," Ruby said. She grabbed the engine to climb again, her arm gashed and bleeding.

She struggled to get her legs tight in the piping, inched her back against the steel hatches. She grinned at her father, chuckled, and then stood up, stood the hatches open with grinding metal and crashing glass as the salon coffee table smashed somewhere above them. Then she couldn't move: the carpet covered the hatches.

Rocket tossed her his knife; she slit the coarse mat between the hatch edges, holding the entire thing with one arm over her head.

The carpet gave, ripped, the smoke came at her. She pushed once more, and let the hatches fall away.

She reached down for Rocket's hand; the old man had climbed the engine after her. She got up into the salon. Flames bathed the windows, smoke like burning tires, and hot. She pulled her father up.

"Forward!" he yelled. "Jeezus, what the hell is going on?"

"Wait," she said when they got to the dining room. She could hear shouting, distant screams. Then what sounded like a shot.

"Out here," Rocket said, yanking her through a door onto the empty starboard deck.

The boat was burning at both ends and topside. Smoke curls dipped to lick their faces.

284

"I can't see land!" Rocket said.

"Don't jump!" she shouted to him. "Stay with me—we'll find life jackets—anything."

They started foward. Stopped.

Larry was perched on the rail, that malignant eye more or less pensively upbraiding.

"That damn bird rode out on this barge!" Rocket shouted. "Ruby, don't mess with him! He can fly home."

"He won't," she said. "I know he won't."

She reached for the bird, but the wily parrot dodged along the rail.

"Ozzie's here!" Larry said.

Ruby brought her hands to her face. "He can talk!"

"Ozzie's here!"

"Forget the bird," Rocket said. "He'll get home." He pulled his daughter forward.

"Ozzie's here!" Larry said, fluttering after them.

And Ozzie Barrett kicked open a door, burst out onto the deck in front of them, wrapped in smoke, wearing his fireman's helmet.

"Ozzie's here!" the parrot screeched.

Ruby jumped into Ozzie's arms.

"Don't let him come near me," DeSilva said to Ozzie. "He shot at me!"

"Wilson won't hurt you," Ozzie said.

Ozzie had the *Lucia* backed off far enough so that explosions from the *Showboat* barely ruffled the air in his cabin.

"I'll hurt him!" Boynton said, leaping out of the berth to tackle DeSilva.

DeSilva and Boynton rolled on the cabin deck.

"What?" Malone said, poking his head in from the wheelhouse.

"Richie's afraid you're going to shoot him."

"I might," Malone grinned. "Although the first shot kinda put him on his knees, Oz. They fighting?"

Ozzie slowly closed the cabin door, easing Malone back into the wheelhouse, gently pressing the Winchester's muzzle toward the deck. "Wilson you gotta keep that thing down. Did you take the round out of the chamber?"

"You told me to—I did."

Ruby was at the rail with the Coast Guardsmen, their heavy helmets and life jackets making them look like mushrooms. The *Lucia* bobbed nicely in tandem with the cutter, the cutter's white flank near enough to touch as Ozzie left the wheelhouse and looked up for Larry, who was clinging to a net boom, his green feathers aglow with reflected flame.

All Is Revealed

Strike's Landing lay prone and exhausted in the spring sunshine, the fishermen getting away early to the Banks before the fog, the bagel shop and Eldridge's heady with rumor, the First Seaman's Bank lobby muted with culpability. Impatient FBI agents, wearing their badges outside their gray suit jackets, scoured the town for the guilty, the near-guilty, and the outraged. Richie DeSilva had been removed to Boston's Suffolk County Jail; Sheldon Boynton had been remanded into custody and shipped to the Walpole State Prison because the feds trusted no local jail. Zalinsky had flown himself to Florida and then on to Haiti, where he'd taxied his Piper Comanche into a sensible platoon of veteran Tontons Macoutes waiting for their prey at a Cyclone fence.

Ozzie had seen Tagliano in the police station, the state's attorney agreeably locked alone in a glass office while FBI guys brought new questions to Mario. Lawyers materialized like fiddleheads in a ditch. The Securities and Exchange Commission's men wanted every dime tracked, repeatedly ticked off account after account, page after page out of Ozzie's cardboard box. The State of Massachusetts bank examiners closed the First Seamen's Bank at 11:03. The

Strike's Landing constabulary was relieved by the Massachusetts State Police just before noon, Cabral and his confused cohorts herded into an empty courtroom for
processing and questions. The FDIC and treasury people
arrived in a yellow Ryder van from Logan Airport.

Ozzie skipped across the street to the docks, his bomber
jacket lacerated and singed, his Parris Island cap soft over
his eyes, combat boots as light as ballet slippers on the docks
as he bounced along past the art galleries and shops, where
tourists now appeared tentative, haggling in their realization
that carved sea gulls and worm-shell necklaces might be
overpriced in this very fishy town where every third car
parked on the main street seemed to have a short whip
antenna on its trunk.

He hopped from float to float under Mildred's windows
and climbed the ladder that brought him up onto Ruby's
wharf. Ozzie stopped for a moment. The valiant *Lucia* was
tight against Rocket's dock across the harbor. All the glass,
all the tracery and lead, every ounce of mortar and tile had
collapsed into his cathedral's sandy nave, as it should have
long ago, he now thought. He let his hands relax on the
weathered railing, the peacefulness welling up inside him.
He was experiencing the first moment of freedom in his
life; the stony ruin he'd been so afraid would shatter had
revealed itself as only another pile of inspired madness, a
cold cavern buttressed with rocklike resolution and a painful
yearning for any afterlife. This life, this morning, this sun
and water, was not only here but good, he thought. As it
should be. The harbor smelled salty, oily with diesel exhaust,
and had not a thing to do with having faith in anything but
being alive.

Ruby had come out to drink her coffee on her rail, her
face gradually registering pride as she smiled when she saw
the man walking along the wharf. She carried her navy mug,
the breeze riffling her white gown in the sun, her hair in

moist silver ringlets, as she came to meet him. Her arm was bandaged.

Ruby left her mug on the rail to hold this warrior, his face patched and taped. "I stayed with him until he fell asleep this morning," she said. "I'll go over later and see how he is. He had an awful scare last night."

They walked to her doors, Ozzie quietly at rest in the sun with her. "Are you okay?"

"Better than ever," she said.

Ozzie went inside for coffee, stepped like a new man into her home, over her floors to the stove. Larry was asleep in his cage, a corner of his cloth lifted by Ruby earlier to suggest a new day. But the exhausted Larry hadn't moved.

"I have to go to Boston with the FBI," he said.

"When?"

"Tomorrow—the next few days. They'll be months at this. Boynton is telling his tales to anyone who'll listen to him. He thought he was shooting Richie when he shot the Argentine. Babs has moved Kurt into her house. Boynton knows Richie's laundering schemes inside and out—millions!"

"I feel very sorry for that little Boynton man," she said. "Prison will finish him."

"He's been in prison all his life—after Darla and DeSilva, prison will be a refuge for him. He'll be the Birdman of Walpole. He loved Veronica. She led him on for months—she and Richie got a kick out of Sheldon's crush. Sheldon asked her to run away with him. She laughed in his face. If he couldn't have her, he wasn't going to let Richie have her. And he *was* in her house when Uncle Barry was there. He stashed his bike in her bushes. Tex chased him down the street, knocked Boynton on his ass. Boynton wanted to make it look like Veronica and DeSilva were having a dip and a fight."

"Poor man."

"I'm going out to get my Uncle Barry this afternoon. Wilson's home asleep—he'll go with me."

They went back out to the sun, to the rail.

"I'd like to go with you," Ruby said.

Ozzie touched her cheek with his hand, her skin like nothing he'd ever known. "I'd like that," he said.

"Would you?"

"You love me, right?"

"I think I do," she said. "And you?"

"More than I know."

Larry flapped out of the door, winging a wide circle around the harbor and glided back to the rail. Ozzie spoke to him. Larry strutted nearer. Ozzie spoke again. The bird hesitated, then pattered down the rail to stand next to Ozzie's arm. And watched him with that inscrutable eye.

"You should have told me about my father," she said.

"Not for me to tell."

"But you knew he had millions—and you let me go on and on with Richie. My father told you not to tell me, didn't he?"

"He did." Ozzie scratched Larry's head.

"You're an honest son of a bitch."

"It's not honesty," Ozzie said. He looked into her eyes and whispered, "Semper Fi."

Ozzie ran Rocket's jeep up his aunts' driveway and charged up the back stairs. Knocked. Elspeth in her apron: "Oh, Ozzie! Isn't this horrid?"

"I'm going out to the hospital for Uncle Barry this afternoon," he said, letting the screen door smack his back as he stood just inside their kitchen.

"Ozzie, Louise is here. She's upstairs."

"Why?"

"She's selling your house and needs a place until things get settled for her."

"Here?"

"Why not? I don't get into these things. She asked and your Aunt Lizbeth and Bud agreed. You can't bring him home, Ozzie."

"I'll find a place for him—and for me."

"No, Ozzie," she said. She wound a dishtowel through her fingers. "Your Uncle Barry can't come home. There's a committal hearing in three weeks. We all think it's best for him. He's not well, Ozzie."

"Wait a minute!" he said. "All the charges against him have been dropped—I saw his release papers this morning."

"It's not that awful business. It's him. He can't live here."

"He can live with me!"

"Again? No, Ozzie. He's going to be committed. We all knew it would happen. We haven't seen you in so long." Elspeth was going to cry.

"You can't commit him," Ozzie said. "He's not sick."

"I know you love him, but you've got to face facts. The doctors will present their evidence at the hearing. There's no question. Nothing can be done."

"Committed?"

Elspeth nodded.

"For how long?"

Elspeth shrugged helplessly.

"And the wedding?" Ozzie said.

"Will proceed as planned. We all need something fruitful after this parade of ghastly experiences. What a terrible spring we've had. I want you to be there."

"With Louise?"

"However you can. Your Aunt Lizbeth has died a thousand deaths, what with your uncle, and then your performance—all that terrible business at the bank. She feels like no one wants her to be happy, Ozzie. That DeSilva woman had the nerve to return her RSVP in this morning's mail—can you imagine? She's bringing that Armenian man to the wedding."

"Argentine," Ozzie said. "He's from Argentina! For crying out loud, Uncle Barry cannot be committed!"

"Ozzie, stop! Think! It's for the best. We're eating his chickens. The lord works in mysterious ways, Ozzie."

"He's a vicious bastard," Ozzie said.

"He is not."

"Not Uncle Barry—your lord."

"Ozzie—bite your tongue!"

Nietzsche Nuts

"MALONE, your fish is getting cold," Mildred said.

"Oz, I'm tutoring tonight," Malone said, watching Mildred bustle away with dinners for her customers, her bar a commotion of plates and silverware, laughter and strange loud voices as legions of suits with Maryland accents had doubled her business in a single day. Malone whispered, "She's a cum laude from Northwestern."

"You don't have to go," Ozzie said. He knifed into his halibut. "You've done enough as it is."

"The dean didn't care for the FBI in his office—gave me hell. He's had a breach of security in his computer lab. Can you imagine? You gonna have pie? Mildred's got chocolate pie tonight."

"Some of Zalinsky's cash came from Boston's North End— drug money, Wilson. DeSilva tried to make Boynton the fall guy in the bank scams. And Boynton tried to make DeSilva look like Veronica's murderer—how'd you like his rubbers last night?"

Malone had spread a lake of tartar sauce over his fish. "We're all victims of seemingly random events," he said. "My tutorial tonight came East looking for a lost boyfriend—had a cat given to her, the cat had kitties, she couldn't move the kitties, the college asked her to teach. If the damn cat hadn't

293

got pregnant, I wouldn't be tutoring. Winona was on her way back to Chicago, all packed. Winona ferments her own wine, Oz."

Ozzie sipped his beer and nodded to some of the federal faces at the window tables.

"Somethin', wasn't it? Boat blowing up like that—Richie like a flea on a burning mattress. I think you're a hero, Oz."

"I didn't have any choice—you did. You're the hero, if there is one," Ozzie said.

"Al Wasserman doesn't think we're heroes. They shut down his computer lab. Probably one of these guys," Malone said, turning in his chair to grin at Mildred's supper crowd.

Her favored customers were tightly gathered at the bar like refugees, anxiously eager to appear civil, nervously passing cornbread to the gathering of hidden badges in the room.

"They'll have your ass for this one," Malone said.

"Which one?"

"Let the dust settle, Oz. I'll call the judge."

Ozzie said, "I can't wait."

"What'd Ruby say?"

"She's going with me."

Malone said, "That's peachy! Oz, everything I do with you has bars written all over it."

Mildred was back, leaning to take Ozzie's hands. "Sleep on it," she said to him.

Malone stabbed another blueberry muffin from the basket, then skidded the butter bowl down the bar with his knife.

"I can't sleep on it," Ozzie said.

Mildred sighed and clattered into her kitchen.

"Have another muffin, Oz," Malone said. "Damn fine fish, isn't it?"

The Mobley woman was suddenly between them, buried in a crush of gray suits who were leaving. She said, "Is he here?"

"Who?" Ozzie said, chewing.

"My husband!" the Mobley woman said.

"You'll have to look, Margaret," Malone said. Then he sneezed and muttered, "What're you doing here—you're the realtor on duty?"

Her husband had been acting as Mildred's headwaiter, delivering beers on trays to the melee.

"I know he's here," she said. "His raincoat is by the door."

"I don't think so," Ozzie said. "His coat's been here for over a year."

"He's not here," Malone said. "Mildred, love!" he yelled. "I'll take the pie!"

"How you gonna tutor carrying that load?" Mildred said as she passed them, five dinners in her arms, her gaze instantly sinister as she studied the Mobley woman.

"I'm just looking," the Mobley woman whined.

Mildred said, hesitating for a moment, "Not here."

"How's Vassar?" Ozzie asked the woman.

"I think you're cruel—all of you," the Mobley woman said. "Jenny is getting out of the hospital tomorrow—nerves. Vassar is not good. Not fair."

Malone put his arms around the Mobley woman. "Buck up, Margaret. Jenny has her father's brains."

"That's what I'm afraid of," the woman said, as she spun out of Malone's grasp. "You're both such jerks!"

As the woman barreled off toward the door, whipping her husband's raincoat off its hook and drop-kicking the thing into the rafters, Peter Mobley came around the bar with a heaping tray of dirty dishes.

"Your wife was just here," Ozzie said to him.

Peter Mobley froze. "And?" he said.

"Gone."

"You sure?"

"Gone!" Malone yelled. "As gone as gone gets—thanks, Mildred," he said, taking his pie from her. "Sustenance—

295

Ozzie's gonna break his Uncle Barry out of the cooler to-night."

Mildred shook her head and walked away.

⚓ ⚓ ⚓

Malone shut off his station wagon headlights before seven o'clock. His wiper made one more pass over the windshield, then stopped. "In and out?" he whispered.

"Won't take a minute," Ozzie said.

"Big place, isn't it?" Malone said. "Do you know where he is?"

"Wait for me," Ozzie said. He cracked the door.

"Be careful," Ruby said, obviously mesmerized by the ranks of state-hospital windows, those white squares all in perfect rows.

Malone fluttered his fingers on the wheel, then patted Ruby's knee beside him and said to Ozzie, "We'll be right here."

Ozzie went in through the side door, in and up the concrete stairs to the top floor and its filthy walls, open doors, and shuttered minds. He replaced Uncle Barry's keys in his jacket pocket and strode down the corridor to the solarium where some of the men were watching television. He found Uncle Barry in Ezra's room.

"Hi, Oz!" Uncle Barry came off Ezra's bed, holding out his arms.

"Let's go," Ozzie said.

"Go where?"

"You're leaving." Ozzie took the man's arm and pulled him into the corridor.

Ezra looked up from his book.

"I can't, Oz! They won't let me. I asked!" Uncle Barry said, trying to grip the door jamb. "Ozzie, I can't!"

"Do you know that you're a free man? No charges?"

"They told me." Uncle Barry was frightened.

"And do you know that you're about to be committed to this place?"

"They told me that, too. Ozzie, I can't leave."

"Why not?"

"Because I can't."

"Don't want to?"

"I can't."

"You gonna die in here? Behind bars and locked doors?"

"I'm going to die somewhere. Please don't."

"Do you remember when I was a kid, you told me about France? You told me that after France, nothing much mattered to you?"

"I remember, Oz."

"Do you remember telling me that when governments go to war, governments never get hurt—only men get shot?"

"I remember better than you do! I was there!"

"Do you remember how you used to hear the guns late at night when the house was quiet?"

"Of course, I do."

"Well, I can hear my guns—my war."

"Oh, Oz, that's unhappy."

"And do you remember when you used to say, 'What if someone screamed for help and all the good people came running?' "

"Yup."

"You're one of the good people."

Uncle Barry lowered his eyes, his huge hands coming together, fingers clasped. "Where are we going?" he said, as he looked up at Ozzie. "I am a good person."

"Best I've ever known," Ozzie said.

"I think you're wonderful, Oz."

"Get your things." Ozzie turned his Uncle Barry down the corridor. Ezra glowered at Ozzie from his door.

⚓ ⚓ ⚓

297

"Where is he?" Ruby whispered.

Malone was smoking one of her cigars, flicking the ash out of his window. "He'll be along," he said.

"I'm scared," she said.

"I'm always scared when I'm with Ozzie," Malone said softly. "If you're gonna drive around with this guy, you better get used to scared. Nothin' wrong with being scared— lets you know you're alive."

A blue hospital dump truck came out from behind a hospital wing, its lights off. The truck slowed, stopped, jerked backward over the curbing and reversed across the grass to stop beneath screened porches. A man got out and ran into the side entrance.

"Maybe he can't find his uncle."

"Maybe not," said Malone.

"Maybe they've caught Ozzie?"

"I doubt it—he looks like one of them."

A white bag flew out of the porch and landed in the dump truck. Another bag.

"What are those people doing?" Ruby whispered.

"Oh, no," Malone said. He spun the cigar out the window.

White bags came out of the screened porch, dozens of them all into the dump truck, one after the other, like floating marshmallows in the lamplight.

Malone started his Mercedes, let the thing creep forward along the hospital drive. Stopped. There were no more bags.

"Wilson, I don't like this," she whispered.

"Are you thinking what I'm thinking?" Malone said.

"I think so," she said.

The hospital door opened slowly; men scampered over the grass toward the dump truck. They climbed up the tires, up the sides, and into the truck bed, in where all the bags had been loaded.

"How many?" she whispered.

"Too many," Malone said.

"They're breaking out," she said. "My god."

One man gestured for the others to duck down, and then he leapt to the ground and got into the cab. The truck started, came quickly over the grass, and lurched into the drive. Ozzie stopped the truck to speak to Malone. "We're set!" Ozzie said as he crunched the truck into gear and drove away.

Malone got the station wagon turned around. The dump truck waited at the hospital gate, its lights on now, blinker signaling left.

Ozzie drove very fast up Route 128, got off at the mall exit near Strike's Landing, and powered into the mall parking lot to stop near the front entrance where shoppers always waited for husbands named Buck to bring the Buicks around in the rain.

When Malone got out of his car, he looked up and was greeted by seven shining faces all in a row like eggs, peering at the mall.

Ruby had Ozzie by the arm.

"Okay, guys," Ozzie shouted. "All out. Wilson, I need to borrow your gold Visa in here."

"Sure, Oz."

"Where are you taking them?" Ruby said, trying to hold Ozzie back.

Ozzie helped the men off the tires, some of them clinging like fruit to the steel box and afraid, their hospital slippers sliding on ribs. "We're going to Cape Breton Island," Ozzie said to her.

A one-eyed man fell off the tire, but got up quickly to grin at Ruby. He was every eight-year-old's version of what lives under the bed.

"You're what?" she said to Ozzie, riveted to this creature before her.

"Everyone inside," Ozzie said, tugging the one-eyed man, herding them all toward the entrance. "Uncle Barry? Do you remember the army-navy store in here?"

"I'm not feeble, Oz," Uncle Barry giggled, leading this merry band.

The men ran for the entrance, Ozzie shouting, "Walk! Walk! Dammit!" Their hospital clothes were nothing but bags, their arms flapping rags as they went in under the lights, the mall doors sliding open to welcome them.

"Ozzie!" Ruby stopped him. "You can't do this."

Ozzie looked at Malone, then to her. "I can't not do it, either."

"All of them?" she said.

"Why not? Even if they get sent back, they'll have a night they won't forget."

"We all will," Malone said.

"Ozzie, slow down, please," she said.

"I think it'll work," Ozzie said. "Ezra—he's the guy with the electric hair—Ezra has a house at Marble Mountain, Nova Scotia. Or at least he says he does. We'll see. He also has money waiting for him there—he's all alone, Ruby. He's got this grubby calendar on his wall with a photograph of some Nova Scotia bog. They're all single, nobody wants 'em, and they love being together. Uncle Barry wouldn't leave without them. Why not?"

"It's against the law," she said.

"Is it?" Ozzie waited for her.

"Must be," she said.

Ozzie waited, his hands in his jacket. As still as a rock.

"They'll have all our asses," she said as she kissed him.

"See what I mean about being scared?" Malone said, as they skipped into the mall after the men.

The army-navy store hadn't actually seen anything quite like this tribe. The men went for shirts and pants, all combat gear because Ozzie was their model mercenary in camo.

Each man built a pile on a table near the back wall, while the clerks toted up the damage on calculators. Ozzie made them all go into the dressing rooms—Evelyn Cameroon had stripped down near a display campfire and tent—where they got on their outfits, lop-eared hat flaps, shiny belt buckles, and paratrooper boots, field jackets and canteens, web belts, and compasses. Malone passed out MityLites.

Ozzie had them chuck their hospital clothes into a hamper and asked one of the clerks to find a dumpster. "Their big night out," Ozzie winked to the clerk, who was dialing Visa with a $2,200 bill. "Special Olympics," Ozzie said to the other clerk.

Malone's card came up all cherries and Ozzie assembled his squad of surreal survivalists near the door. "You might frighten women and children when you walk out of here," he said to them.

Francis Sparkman raised his hand. Sparkman wore his new Australian bush hat squashed down over his eyes.

"But don't stop until you get to the truck," Ozzie said. "Don't run, and stay together. We're almost there. You guys okay?"

Every man in the outfit jabbered.

"You look good, guys," Ozzie said. "What?" he barked to Sparkman.

"What if it rains?"

"Don't raise your hand again," Ozzie said. "Real people don't raise their hands. They speak up."

Sparkman lowered his hand.

"You've got ponchos in your duffel bags," Ozzie said.

"We can't ride all the way to Marble Mountain in that truck, Oz." Sparkman said. "There's garbage in there. We have to take a train."

"There are no trains," Ozzie said. "We're going by boat. But we've got one more stop, haven't we?" Ozzie said to Uncle Barry.

Uncle Barry said, "One more stop, Oz."

The squad was shattered with joy. They hit each other. Ezra rolled under a table, laughing.

Malone folded his receipt into his pocket. "They look like senile terrorists, Oz. We've got to get that guy an eye at Lenscrafters or something."

"We will," Ozzie said. He thanked the clerks, took Ruby's arm, and led the men through the mall, his adrenaline firing only when they passed four security guards who were standing in front of an arcade where kids in Guns n' Roses shirts kicked machines because closing time was nigh upon them.

⚓ ⚓ ⚓

"I won't even ask why we're here," Ruby said to Malone.

"Patience," Malone said.

The guys in the truck lined the box rail, waiting quietly, as Ozzie had instructed them.

"Thanks for riding with me," Malone said. "I thought you'd ride with Oz."

"I never liked you much," she said. Ruby reached a silver flask from her jacket. "That's only because I didn't know what a sweetheart you are. I couldn't let you ride alone, could I?" She handed Malone the flask.

"Ozzie kinda jumps into things, doesn't he?" Malone whispered.

Bozo's fence clanged open. Uncle Barry ran across the vet's driveway carrying a Doberman in his arms, the dog so insanely happy he couldn't keep his tongue off Uncle Barry's face.

Ozzie got the old man and dog in over the tailgate, then climbed up to chain the gate tight.

"Someone we know?" Ruby asked softly.

"That's Tex," Malone said, as he started the Mercedes. "He's been incarcerated. He's vicious."

The harbor was dark, the few lights misty weak, the Baptist church spire a vision with its white shaft and gold cross like a Mexican spray painting on velvet. Nearly midnight, most of the town paralyzed with uncertainty over recent events, most houses dark, their beds within cradling phantoms, the ghastly time when all that's held dear removes its mask to grin at the sleepers. When a bank goes belly-up, that's one thing; but when a bank president goes belly-up with golf-crony money, that's quite another. Add a dash of sleaze, a couple of foul dentists, guardians of the law who couldn't guard a hydrant, snip a few of the tethers that bind a town like this one to its pillows, add a pinch of greed and lust and insolence in equal measure, and the sky that isn't any limit becomes as dark and pitiless as the night sky over this town.

But apart from Rocket Willey, no man was outside to see. Not on this night. Rocket sat on his wharf, rocking, watching for Ruby's lights to send him to bed.

There was a gray escarpment of fog visible beyond the harbor narrows, waiting to smother Strike's Landing.

And moving along the harbor road, headlights.

Ozzie asked Rocket if he wanted the dump truck.

"I might," Rocket said, counting the men in combat gear as they lined his wharf, their MityLites like glowworms.

Most of the guys were suspended in the hushed thrall of the night's magic, shoulder to shoulder, gazing out over the wonder of being alive once more, Uncle Barry and the wagging Tex acting as guides.

Rocket said, "I'll have to paint it quick like, though. State will probably miss it, doncha think? You're loaded with fuel and water."

Ozzie hugged the old man. "She'll be all right," Ozzie said to him.

"You say, you damn fool. It'll take you at least two days to get there."

Ruby was back, quickly out of the jeep, walking down the wharf now, swinging a navy seabag.

"I know you're crazier than most," Rocket said to Ozzie. "But you can't ever hurt her."

"I won't," Ozzie said, watching her toss her bag down to Malone on the *Lucia*'s deck.

"Good night for mischief," Rocket said. He kissed Ruby, who, when she realized what he'd done, grabbed her father and kissed his bandaged head.

Ozzie got the men down the ladder. "Inside," he said. But they couldn't help themselves and went as a group to the bow where they stood like the campaigners they were, leaving the war for home.

Larry flew into the rigging, beating along a cable, looking for Ruby.

Ozzie fired up his diesel, hit the running lights on. Malone held the remaining line on the wharf.

Rocket banged down the ladder, Ruby passing down gear to him. The old man turned for the wheelhouse, saw that Ozzie wanted an answer, and said, "You're not goin' without me." Rocket had a bulky blanket in his arms.

"Who's gonna take care of Owl?" Ozzie said.

"I am," Mildred said from high over their heads. She handed down wicker baskets, cases of beer, and cardboard boxes. "How many you got?" she shouted down.

Ozzie looked around him. "Eleven, counting Tex," he said over the diesel's throaty rumble.

The cripple stood up there, hands on her hips, her fur coat like a gorilla suit on her. She handed more boxes down to Ruby and Ozzie.

"Make that an even dozen," Malone said, as he lowered himself down the ladder.

"What about your classes?" Ozzie said to him.

"The dean can teach them," Malone said, his trout eyes huge in his specs. "I'm not staying here without you, Oz."

Rocket handed Malone a full bottle of whiskey.

"Mildred?" Ozzie shouted up to the woman in mink.

"Not on your life," she said, giggling. "There's enough in each box for three days, I hope. Each of your nuts gets a box, except for Malone—he'll need the extra box. Ruby, honey, you watch yourself."

Rocket and Malone stowed the food in the cabin, the *Lucia* drifting on the tide beside the wharf, lines hauled in.

"Send me a postcard?" Mildred yelled to them.

Ozzie blew Mildred a kiss, then came to sit in his dentist's chair, his legs on either side of Ruby as she stood at the wheel in front of him.

The one-eyed man fell into the wheelhouse, then chuckled as he got up. "I never been on a boat," he said. He brushed off his new camo coat. He held out his left hand to Ruby and Ozzie, that empty eye socket like an open grave.

Ozzie shook the man's hand after Ruby.

"My name's Perry," the man said.

"Glad you're with us, Perry," Ozzie said.

Rocket stowed the lines. Malone had stepped through the cabin from the aft door.

Perry looked like he was about to cry. "I want to say—no one's ever done—" Perry swallowed.

"Just don't kill anyone, Perry," Ozzie said. "And keep one hand on the boat."

Perry gripped the wheelhouse bulkhead.

"That's right," Ozzie said. "One hand on the boat until you get your legs."

"I have my legs," Perry said.

"That you do, my lad," Malone said. Malone helped Perry turn around, Perry gripping every edge he could find, and led him back to the guys at the bow.

305

"Ready?" Ozzie said to Ruby, leaning to kiss her.

"I thought you'd never ask," she said, as she kissed him back and threw the trawler into gear, reversing against the rudder. She spun the wheel hard over and shoved the lever forward to dance them out into the harbor.

Ozzie took a long last look at Strike's Landing, knowing he'd not be back for a week or so, and at that he'd come back a better man for having left.

"I'm going to miss the wedding," he said to her, as Ruby doused the wheelhouse lights and clicked on the radio.

"Louise will never forgive you," she laughed.

"Where's Larry?"

"Still up there," she said.

Ruby signaled the harbormaster as they entered the narrows, the men as solemn as monks on the bow, stricken with images, gentle with each other, Ozzie's loony terrorists.

Rocket came back into the wheelhouse. "We'll be goddam lucky the Coast Guard doesn't get us." His bandage was hanging loose.

"We're fishing," Ozzie said. He took the wheel while Ruby snuggled her father. She took the old man into the cabin.

When the *Lucia* slid into the fog, the men became instantly frightened, hurrying into the dimly lighted cabin, huddling in there.

Ozzie heard Francis Sparkman shout, "That's a moose!"

"What's the matter with them?" Malone said, hopping in off the deck, motioning to the cabin. He handed Ozzie the whiskey.

"They're agog," Rocket said from the cabin door, patting his head. "Absolutely agog."

"It's all right, guys," Ozzie shouted to them. He gave the bottle to Rocket. "Come up here and watch."

One by one, clutching each other, the men squeezed into the wheelhouse.

"It's just fog," Ozzie said, backing off the throttle. "It can't hurt you."

Ozzie let the trawler ease over the sea, its running lights glowing red and green in the dense fog.

"Nothing to worry about," Ozzie said. "Relax."

The minutes passed until Malone said, "I don't know, Oz. This is fog!"

Ruby watched from behind Ozzie, nipping at a nail, silently aware that all sorts of things lived in fog. Big things with big hulls.

"We don't want to lose them now," Malone said.

"Still a helluva night, though, isn't it?" Ozzie said.

Rocket had left the wheelhouse to go forward.

Uncle Barry came to stand next to Ozzie.

"How's Tex?" Ozzie said.

"He's skinny."

"Your fiddle okay?"

"Fiddle's fine, Oz."

"And you?"

"Scared," Uncle Barry said.

"You like fog," Ozzie said.

"Not the fog," Uncle Barry said. "I'm going to miss you."

"Not for long, you won't," Ozzie said. He brought the throttle down more. "I'll get to Marble Mountain as often as I can."

"I know you will," Uncle Barry said, "It's just that you're my boy and I don't want to leave you."

"I've always been your boy," Ozzie said.

"No. I mean you *are* my son."

Ozzie couldn't take his eyes off the old man.

"You are, Oz. They made me promise never to tell you. They said they'd lock me away. Your mother was married to your Uncle Robert. But when he went off to the war, your mother and I decided to love each other. When I went to France, she stayed at home with Elspeth and Lizbeth and had you. I was missing for a long time—Robert died."

Ruby looked at Malone, who slowly raised his hands in disbelief.

307

"They hated her, Oz. She came looking for me—she never found me. But I found her marker in France—a dinky slab of white marble with her name on it. That was all that was left of her. I couldn't even bring her home dead."

"She's buried in the Pacific—near him."

"Nope. France."

Ozzie pulled his helmet down over his eyes. "You're not my uncle?" he said, turning to see where Ruby was.

"Nope," Uncle Barry said.

"My father?"

"Are you ashamed?"

"Why would I be ashamed?"

"Lizbeth said our shame was our curse. But I'm not ashamed, Oz."

"Neither am I," Ozzie said.

"Isn't this a kick in the ass," Malone said.

Ozzie kept the old man near him at the wheel, the windows greasy with fog for a long time, until the *Lucia* broke out onto a clear sea under silver stars.

The men rushed out on deck to see it all, the mountain of fog behind them, Barry with them at the rail with Tex. Ozzie buried the throttle and brought the trawler around on course for Nova Scotia.

Malone had the old charts unrolled, seeking Marble Mountain with his MityLite, nibbling a corned-beef sandwich. Ozzie punched the CD player for *Norma* and held Ruby tight to his side.

"Quite a night," he said.

"Keep your arm right there," she said.

There was the faintest blush of orange forward on the bow, just a spark. Then a blast. The men looked up. Ozzie heard the lightning crack and echo, waited, then saw the fear drain from their faces in a radiant burst of pink.

How could they not cheer?